To danny —

I hope y- enjoy!
Thanks for all
 your support

love

Gary
x

Hugo & Josef

BY
GN HETHERINGTON

First Published in 2021 by GNH Publishing.

The right of Gary Hetherington to be identified as the author of this work has been asserted by him in accordance with the Copyright, Designs and Patents Act 1988.

Copyright © Gary Hetherington

All rights reserved. No part of this book may be reproduced, stored in a retrieval system or transmitted in any form or by any means, electronic, mechanical, photocopying, recording or otherwise, without the prior permission of the publisher.

www.gnhbooks.co.uk

grâce à

Thank you very much to all the lovely people who support Hugo and his adventures. For the longest time, I've wanted to explore the origins of the character. He is complicated; he is fun, and if you've read his many investigations, you'll probably know he has a chequered past. That chequered past is what I've always wanted to dip into. When did he first fall in love with a person? When did he first fall in love with the career he would finally choose? It's taken me a while, but here we are. I hope you'll think I've done it justice, but more importantly, I hope those of you who love the later Hugo books don't mind too much about the Hugo minus Ben story. My darling friend Dawn always forbade me from writing an origin story, such was her love for Ben. In the end, I did it as much for her as I did for myself. There would be no Hugo and Ben, if it wasn't for Josef… Let's just hope future Hugo never has to choose between his first and last love…. I desperately hope Dawn is looking down on me and shrugging, 'd'accord, you got away with it… *just*!'

Big shout out to my lovely girls June Russell and Jackie Waite who keep my days full of love and light and to my beaux parents, Bill and Chris and my dear friends Joy Edwards, Jennifer Trieb, Suse Telford, Sandra Scott and Pam Pletts. Huge applause to my French teacher Bastien Greve for his never-ending patience and not minding too much when I ask for clarification on very strange French phrases…

My inspirations as always keep me motivated - Sheena Easton, Julien Doré and any French TV I can find.

Special nod to Nitzer Ebb, the band which lead me to my very own Josef.

There would be no books without my family - Dan, Hugo, Noah and Charlie & Seth. And Dawn.

Notes:

The story, the places and characters are a work of fiction.

For further information, exclusive content and to join the mailing list, head over to:

www.gnhbooks.co.uk

We are also on Facebook, Twitter and Instagram. Join us there!

The artwork on the cover, the website and social media accounts were created in conjunction with two incredible talents: Maria Almeida and Deborah Dalcin and I'm indebted to them for bringing my characters to life. Thanks also to Mai Cadiz for her help with the manuscript.

For Charlie, Seth and Dawn. Tu me manques.

Also available:

Hugo Duchamp Investigates:

Un Homme Qui Attend (2015)
Les Fantômes du Chateau (2016)
Les Noms Sur Les Tombes (2016)
L'ombre de l'île (2017)
L'assassiner de Sebastian Dubois (2017)
L'impondérable (2018)
Le Cri du Cœur (2019)
La Famille Lacroix (2019)
Les Mauvais Garçons (2020)
Prisonnier Dix (2021)
Le Bateau au fond de l'océan (2022)
Chemin de Compostelle (2022)

The Coco Brunhild Mysteries:

Sept Jours (2021)
Métro Boulot Dodo (2022)
Cercueils en spirale (2022)
Quatre Semaines (2022)

Also available:

Hugo & Josef (2021)
Club Vidéo (2022)
Hugo & Madeline (2023)
Josef (2023)

ROSH HASHANAH

PARIS, FRANCE
SEPTEMBRE 1995

I

Hugo Duchamp lifted his hands to shield his face. The blows had begun in his stomach but were moving upwards and coming in rapid succession, like clenched fists smashing against a punching ball.

'Fight back, you sissy,' the boy hissed, covering the backs of Hugo's hands in his spit. Hugo was sure he did not even know the boy's name, not that it mattered. Random bully numero un was as good a name as any. They all looked the same, spouted the same sort of violence, eyes dark and pinpointed, flecked with the red of rage.

'Fight back, you sissy,' the boy repeated, filling his throat with phlegm and launching it onto Hugo's forehead and hair. 'Make this fun for me, or I swear I'll only make it worse for you.'

Fight back. The words bounced around Hugo's skull as he pulled his knees upwards. *Fight back.* The words were not his, and the voice he heard was not his own. It belonged to his father, Pierre Duchamp. *You won't embarrass me, boy.* It was because the words were not Hugo's own, he found himself unable to act upon them. *The problem isn't mine,* he thought to himself, *and you won't make it mine, none of you will.* The pain was coursing through his body now, which he knew was a good thing. It meant the attack would end soon. The bully would either get bored, or a teacher would appear, yelling at the other boy and scrambling to pull him off Hugo's rigid body.

'Alain, get your damn hands off him.'

The voice was soft, but it had a force to it, Hugo realised. But it was not a teacher. The blows stopped and Hugo could hear the scraping of feet, and the angry voice of his attacker, who he now knew to be called Alain, shouting his protests. 'Get your hands off me, Josef, or so help me Dieu, I'll give you a bit of what the sissy's getting.'

Josef. Josef Levy. Hugo did not need to open his eyes to see him. The golden-brown curls falling over his ears, eyes the same colour, wide and keen, watching the world in front with burning interest and curiosity. The long, gangly limbs, not yet quite grown into the shape of approaching adulthood. And the heart-shaped birthmark on a smooth neck. Hugo suddenly yearned for the blows to begin again, to smash the sissiness out of him. He did not want to feel like he did. He wanted to be free of it.

'Give me your hand,' Josef commanded.

Hugo tried to open his eyes, but only one would. The lid of the right eye seemed to be stuck, telling Hugo he was most likely going to have to go to the school nurse. It would almost certainly mean Pierre would have to be called, no matter how much Hugo protested. It always ended the same way, Pierre would say he was away on business and Hugo was currently, *temporarily*, staying with his Grand Mère, Madeline Duchamp. Hugo was not sure how it could be temporary because he had been staying in Madeline Duchamp's townhouse for several years already. Ever since… ever since…

Hugo felt his body being pulled upwards, the tensing of Josef Levy's hand showing a strength unusual in a fifteen-year-old boy.

'You're going to need to see the nurse,' Josef said.

Hugo tried to focus on him through his bloodied eyes. He shook his head, wincing with the pain. 'I'm fine,', he said, spitting blood through a loose tooth. He did not care about the pain, he just could not face the disappointed, heavy silence which would pass between him and his father on the telephone. *Fight back.*

Josef snorted. There was no malice in it. Hugo was not sure his voice lent itself to malice or anger. 'Sure you are, come on, I'll go with you. Any excuse to get out of English class, non?'

Josef began leading Hugo through the schoolyard, his hand holding tightly onto Hugo's forearm as he guided him. Hugo knew he should open his eyes and guide himself, but for once he did not want to. Behind them, Hugo could hear his attacker getting his second wind after being pulled off by the stronger Josef.

'Look at the sissy, he'll be holding hands next and,' he stopped and began making loud, vulgar kissing and sucking noises.

Josef leaned in and whispered in Hugo's ear. 'Don't listen to him, he's only jealous.'

Hugo said nothing because he could not imagine a single reason why someone might be jealous of him.

They walked along the boulevard leading to Faubourg Saint-Germain, where Madeline Duchamp's mansion was situated. Hugo had grown used to living in the central Paris apartment he had shared with his parents, with its sweeping views of the Paris skyline. But when he had been moved to Madeline's vast home in the 7e arrondissement, it had come as a shock. The house was cavernous and filled with antiques, the names of which Hugo did not know, but he knew to avoid at all costs. Madeline had reluctantly turned over the seventh bedroom at the top of the house, for his exclusive use. Hugo had taken some comfort in the fact the most likely reason she had chosen to give him that room was because it was tucked away from the rest of the house and could only be entered by a narrow staircase behind an unobtrusive door. Out of sight, out of mind. Madeline had filled the room with the sort of furniture she would not allow in the main part of the house, but was perfectly suited for a teenage boy. The room had become Hugo's solace in the dark days which followed when his father had sent him there to live.

They continued walking in silence. Hugo found himself unable to think of a single thing to say to the taller boy. It was true he had watched him discreetly in the classes they shared, where Hugo had imagined several different subjects he could begin a conversation about, but in that moment, in that instance, he could think of nothing. For his part, Josef also seemed unable, or perhaps unwilling, Hugo considered, to also begin a conversation.

'So, you 're the kid whose mother died?' Josef finally spoke, before immediately biting his lip as if he was mortified by what he had said.

Hugo hid a smile. There was something endearing about his schoolmate's awkwardness. He had thought it was only himself who was awkward in a world full of dynamic and exciting people.

Hugo shook his dead. 'Non, Maman isn't dead,' he answered before frowning. 'At least I don't think she is,' he added softly, wondering whether anybody would actually tell him if she were. The name Daisy Duchamp was certainly never spoken by Madeline or her son.

'I don't know why I said that,' Josef said. 'It's just I overheard my parents talking about her. She said your Grand Mère told them she was dead, and that's why you came to live with her and that your father is an important avocat and doesn't have time to raise a kid on his own. Maman told me I should befriend you.'

A thousand thoughts fought against Hugo's consciousness, but he could not articulate a single one of them. Instead, he laughed. 'I imagine Madeline wishes my mother was dead, but non, I think she's still alive.'

'Madeline?'

'Ma Grand Mère,' Hugo replied. 'However, she only answers to Madeline. She says Grand Mère's are old and matronly, two things she has no intention of ever becoming.' He paused. 'My mother is an actress, I think.'

'I heard some kids at school saying she was a prostitute,' Josef said, biting his lip again. 'Désolé, I have a big mouth. My mother says it all the time, I speak without thinking. She says I should be more like my older brother, Joann, and I have to bite my tongue every time. He's the perfect son, you see, in their eyes at least. They imagine he's going to end up being a Rabbi like my Papa,' he stopped, throwing his head back and laughing, 'but they do not know the kind of things he gets up to behind their back! He has at least four girlfriends that I know of and not a one of them is Kosher, or even Jewish! I would tell Maman that her perfect son isn't so perfect after all, but she has to have at least some hope that one of her kids is going to grow up perfect, so I don't want to take that away from her.' He snorted. 'Joann is the go-to guy if you want anything illegal in Faubourg Saint-Germain.' He shrugged. 'But yeah, sure, he's the "perfect son."'

Hugo had to fight the urge to say, *she has a perfect son, you*. Hugo chastised himself. It bothered him he felt that way. He did not want to feel that way about another… about anyone. He could remember the first time he had seen Josef and the bolt of electricity which coursed through his body. He did not understand what it meant, and he was not sure he wanted to. He stared at Josef. 'Mother isn't a prostitute either,' he said, 'although she's an actress, which in my father's book, is pretty much the same thing.' He was not sure why he did not want Josef to think his mother was a prostitute, because he was fairly sure it would make absolutely no difference to him.

Josef laughed but did not comment, and they continued their slow walk along the boulevard. Hugo was not even sure why Josef had agreed to make sure he got home, other than the school nurse had suggested calling Madeline's driver to come and collect him, and Josef had said there was no need, he would make sure Hugo got home safely. It came as a surprise to Hugo, because they had sat in the nurse's office in silence. He had imagined Josef was embarrassed and thinking of a way to politely extract himself. Hugo stopped walking.

'Is something wrong?' Josef asked, concern clear in his tone.

Hugo smiled. It was the first time in a long time he had heard anyone show concern for him. He shook his head, thumbing behind him. 'This is me.'

Josef blew an impressed whistle, pushing his nose through the iron railings. He lifted his head slowly as he took in Madeline Duchamp's mansion. 'I've got a crick in my neck just from trying to take it all in,' he laughed. 'Jeez, what's it like living in a place like that? Our place is pretty big, but it's really old and Papa refuses to do anything about it. He says it would be disrespectful to waste money on such vanity when so many people are starving.' He laughed. 'You can just imagine how much my mother agrees with that!' He whistled again. 'But this is a pretty cool place to live.'

Hugo turned, facing the four-storey mansion. He supposed it was impressive, although he had never really thought of it that way. It had always terrified him. He closed his eyes for a moment, and he saw it instantly. A young boy, dressed in a light blue woollen suit, blond hair smoothed neatly under a cap to match the outfit. White socks pulled up to his knees, with patent leather shoes polished to an intense shine. A hand in the crook of his back, pushing him through the iron gates. A man with a face as grey as his complexion whispering in his ear, 'you're going to be staying here for a while. Make sure you behave.' The words had stuck with Hugo. He may have been a child, but he already understood the importance and significance of behaviour, and he had told himself over and over, maybe if you behave she'll come back. She never had and now he was almost fifteen-years-old, something told him she never would, or if she did, it would not mean as much as it would back then.

'I don't really live here,' he said, finally answering Josef's question.

Josef frowned. 'You don't?'

Hugo smiled, pointing to a small window on the roof of the mansion. 'I live in the attic.'

'You live in the attic?' Josef laughed.

Hugo nodded. 'Yeah. I find I make less mess up there.' He shrugged. 'Madeline doesn't like mess, and apparently I have very messy hands and surprisingly greasy fingerprints.'

Josef grabbed Hugo's left hand, his eyes scanning it as he turned back and forth. 'It doesn't look greasy or messy to me.'

Hugo snatched it back, wiping it on the back of his chinos. Josef watched the action with something Hugo could only imagine was amusement.

'You look good,' Josef said.

Hugo coughed. 'I-look-what?'

Josef laughed again, pointing at Hugo's face. 'The nurse did a good job. You'll be bruised and cut for a week, but you won't lose your looks,' he laughed.

Hugo gulped. He looked towards Madeline's mansion. 'Do you want to come in?' he blurted, not at all sure how it would be possible to have a guest in the mansion. He had never thought of it before, primarily because he had no one to invite. Often on weekends, he would press his nose against the railing of the staircase leading down from the attic, watching the comings and goings of life downstairs. The rich and beautiful and powerful, dressed in jewels and finery and were so incomprehensible to Hugo they might as well be aliens. He watched with no understanding of the ease in which they spoke, laughed, danced, found a way to be together. He knew it should make him sad that the only person he spoke to on a daily basis was Elise, the maid whose job, so far as he could tell, was to feed and cater to him and to keep him away from the rest of the house. She was a kindly, elderly woman who appeared interested in little more than watching her "programs" on the tiny television in the kitchen. She was, however, seemingly fond of her teenage charge. She would, occasionally, pull Hugo into a tight embrace, run her fingers through his hair and stare into his eyes and tell him he had the most beautiful eyes she had ever seen -

as green as the emerald sea she had once seen on a trip to visit the place of her ancestor's birth.

Josef lifted his wrist and stared at his Casio watch. 'I have to get home,' he turned away, 'but peut être, as they say in the American movies, a rain check?'

Hugo smiled. He did not know what he meant. 'A rain check,', he repeated with a click of fingers.

Josef disappeared down the boulevard. 'You're funny, H, you're funny.'

II

Hugo closed the front door behind him, dropping his book bag onto the parquet floor. As always, there was nothing but silence in Madeline Duchamp's mansion. A clock ticked somewhere, probably in a room Hugo had never been in.

'Hugo.'

He stopped dead in his tracks. Madeline had that sort of voice. The sort of voice which said nothing, but said everything. She had the ability to convey an entire sentence in the way she expressed one word. He always assumed he was in trouble no matter how she sounded. Despite everything that had happened to him, and realising he had nothing to base it on, he felt his Grand Mère had something bordering on fondness for him. Fondness, but fondness from a distance.

'Madeline,' he said, not turning. He did not want her to see his face.

'Turn around,' she said, tapping an ornate silver cane against the highly polished floor.

Hugo turned, his head dropping, and he noticed instantly one of his shoes was badly scuffed. He hoped she would not notice. He would leave it outside the door to the attic and it would mysteriously reappear the next day - immaculate and gleaming. He was never sure whether Elise cleaned them, or simply brought him a fresh pair.

'Your father called,' Madeline said. 'He was very disappointed.'

Before he could stop himself, Hugo snorted.

Madeline moved her head to the side. 'I agree, it is his default setting.' She moved towards Hugo and stopped just in front of him. She raised a hand. It hovered around Hugo's face but did not touch it. 'Just because your father tells you to hit back, you shouldn't refuse just because it was he who told you to, non?'

She moved away, leaving Hugo to bask in the Chanel No.5 she seemingly bathed in. He glanced down at his dishevelled, bloody clothes and he realised, even if they were freshly pressed and laundered, he would likely feel no different. It also constantly amazed him that whatever time of day he saw her, Madeline Duchamp looked no different. The colour of the Chanel suits changed, but they always seemed new and fresh and her grey hair was always swept up into a perfect bouffant, her make-up seemingly applied professionally. It had occurred to him, more than once, he was not even sure who else lived in the mansion. His tray was delivered every night and collected from outside his door. He fell asleep each night in front of the television, or listening to a CD, but he heard nothing else from the house. On occasions he imagined he should feel lonely, but he did not.

'Maybe we should talk,' Madeline said.

Hugo's eyes widened.

Madeline smiled, her perfectly smooth face crinkling. She stopped smiling, face immediately re-tightening. 'At some point,' she said finally. 'Mais… mais, are you comfortable?'

Hugo frowned. 'Comfortable?' He glanced upwards. 'Oui, my room is very comfortable.'

She shook her head dismissively. 'I didn't mean that. I meant…' she trailed off, searching for the words, 'in general,' she added finally, as if she was unsure what it meant. She studied his face. 'Elise mentioned your clothes are often bloody.'

He shrugged, but said nothing.

'You're a delicate boy, and you have your mother's eyes,' his grandmother said finally. 'It's unfortunate, but not such a bad thing in the grand scheme of things. We must work with what we have. Mais, you shouldn't get used to it.'

'Get used to it?' he countered in surprise.

She shrugged, striding across the entrance hallway. She stopped in front of an ornate sideboard and began rearranging the ornaments on it, tutting as if she was annoyed by the way in which they had been placed. Hugo noted someone would most likely be in trouble for it later.

'There are bullies in all walks of life,' she said without looking at him. 'They thrive on making other's feel inferior. It's happened to me occasionally.'

Hugo's eyes widened. 'I find that hard to believe,' he said with conviction.

She smiled at him. 'Well, I never said they tried twice. They weren't so foolish.' She moved back toward him, her heels clicking against the highly polished floors. 'You've had a few missteps in your life so far, cher,' she said, extending her hand but again, not quite touching his face. 'And I'm sorry to say, you'll probably have more to come in the future. Mais, for now, you have to find a way to get out of this pattern you've found yourself in.'

'Pattern?' Hugo asked, his voice rising sharply.

Madeline picked up some letters, flicking through them. She placed them back down. 'I do not know who the boy is who did this to you today,' she snipped, 'and nor do I care. I imagine him to be a pimply faced plebeian, with a father who most likely is of new money. I imagine the child has a small penis, like his father, and also like his father, probably does not know what to do with it.' She smiled at Hugo. 'You're a threat to boys, to men such as them. You can't see it, but they can. That's why they hate you. It isn't because you're...' she trailed off, meeting Hugo's gaze. 'Different to them,' she added. She shrugged. 'Different is all we have in life. We should strive for it.'

Hugo looked at her in surprise.

Madeline watched him. 'I can assure you, whatever you think of me, my interest is not in being a Grand Dame, rather to be THE

Grand Dame. I see the way people look at me sometimes with contempt and I tell you this, I like it. Because as much as they hate me, I know it comes from a place within them. A place where they hate themselves more. And it is the same with these boys who torment you. They are jealous, nothing more.'

'Jealous? Of me? Why on earth would they be jealous of me?'

'Because you're not dull. You're not ordinary. You're not boring.' She counted them off on her fingers before taking a deep breath. 'You may be different from them, but that's because you will never be them. You will be better. You *are* better.'

Hugo frowned again. 'Then you're saying I should fight back?'

She nodded. 'Most certainly. Mais, not with your fists. With your mind, child, with your mind. You'll beat them every time if you do. As for the school. I have placed a call with Directeur Adnet.'

'Madeline…' Hugo pleaded.

She raised her hands. 'No names will be mentioned,' she said. 'But I have known Gilles Adnet for a very long time. In fact, I am in no small part accountable for the very position he holds now. Fortunately, he knows it too, and therefore when I tell him this sort of behaviour in a school such as École privées de Faubourg Saint-Germain is not only unacceptable, it is embarrassing. For a moment he tried the "boys will be boys" ridiculousness,' she guffawed. 'I quickly disabused him of that. I think you will find things will be better from now on, Hugo,' she added, a softness appearing in her tone.

'They'll know it was me who told,' Hugo whispered. 'And it'll only get worse.'

Madeline waved her hand angrily. 'Non, it won't. Gilles knows how to deal with such matters and he will do so discreetly.' She folded her hands together. 'This will not come back to you, but more importantly, this isn't about you.'

Hugo's eyebrows raised. 'It isn't?'

'Non, it isn't,' she replied. 'This is about the Duchamp name. We cannot, we WILL not tolerate such attacks on our family. Directeur Adnet understands that, and so should you.' She sighed. 'Now, go and rest your head. Elise will be up soon, no doubt. She ignores me these days in favour of you,' she added, her lips twisting into a smile.

Hugo moved towards the door.

'It will get better,' she called after him. 'Eventually. However, in the meantime, use the side entrance if you insist on dripping blood everywhere. Blood is incredibly difficult to remove from these floors.'

'D'accord, Grand Mère,' he called over his shoulder, smiling at her reverting to form.

Madeline Duchamp shook her head, her jaw tightening. 'Now, there was no need for that, child.'

III

Hugo placed the headphones over his head and pressed play on the Walkman, music instantly filling his head. He closed his eyes momentarily, stuffing his hands into the pockets of his weekend jeans, and made his way down the boulevard. He was not sure why his Sunday evening walks meant so much to him, but they did. He loved walking through Paris alone, his head covered by a hat and headphones, his eyes lowered just in front of him. He did not need to see the world around him for him to feel that he was a part of it. After a weekend alone in the attic, it was something he looked forward to, a way to move into the week ahead. He did not need to speak to anyone, and he did not seek out company. All he needed to do was walk to feel free. It was something he needed in ways he could not yet express.

Hugo moved into the park, stepping quickly between the trees. He followed the same route every Sunday. It was dusk, and he knew he would be alone, for a short while at least. The park changed when darkness descended and he knew it was no place for him to be. He stepped into the clearing and glanced around, relieved that he was alone. Then he reached to his Walkman and turned up the volume, threw back his head and at the top of his lungs, screamed along to the music:

Don't want no… Don't want no… Don't want no… Don't want nobody!

He stopped. He only ever sang for a moment, afraid of someone hearing him and spotting him. His self-consciousness had to be contained, and he could not bear the thought of anyone taking away his moment. He sank to his knees and sang to himself.

He stood, a smile covering his face. He could go to his attic now and ready himself for the week ahead. The path in front of him was uneven and filled with moss from heavy rain. It caused him to sidestep and move in a different direction towards the pathway which lead out of the park. The night was descending quickly, and he knew he had little time, so he hurried, his feet slapping against the moss and sliding beneath him. He slipped, his hand jerking in front of him to steady himself against a tree, knocking off his headphones.

'How much?'

Hugo stopped again, suddenly aware he was not alone. He narrowed his eyes, trying to see through the fading light. He had been noticing lately that his eyes were not as strong as they should be. He pressed the stop button on the Walkman.

'How much?' the voice repeated.

Hugo frowned. He thought he recognised the voice, but he could not be sure. It sounded familiar, so he wondered whether it was someone from his school, but he realised that was futile. Other than speaking to Josef on Friday, he was not sure he had ever really had a conversation with anyone in his class and therefore the voices all sounded the same - young boys on the verge of adulthood.

'Why has the price gone up so fucking much?' another similar voice asked.

A man laughed. His laugh was cold and harsh with a cruelness Hugo had only ever heard before in his own father's voice.

'Because it fucking has,' the cruel voice spoke. *'And if you don't like it, why don't you go and tell "daddy?"'*

It was suddenly silent, and Hugo was frightened to breathe in case they heard him.

'You have no idea what you're dealing with,' the first boy answered.

The man with the harsh voice laughed again. *'Oh, I know exactly what I'm dealing with, and the sort of people. You want your drugs for your stupid party, then you're going to have to start paying more. You're rich and you think you get to pay cheap rates? If that's what you think, find yourself some brothel in Paris and they'll sell you whatever shit you want, but it won't be good, and it won't be the class product I get you.'*

The second boy sighed. *'We don't have a choice,'* he said.

'Hey! Who is that in there!' A loud voice boomed from a different direction. 'This is the police! Stay where you are!'

Hugo gasped, breaking into a run in the opposite direction. As he did, he glanced over his shoulder and saw the retreating figures of the three people he had just overheard. His eyes locked on the last figure - a tall, thin man with a shaved head. He turned away, running as fast as he could. He wanted to be in the attic. He wanted to be safe.

He stepped out of the park, his feet grinding to a halt. Josef was standing at the end of the boulevard, staring straight at Hugo. Hugo took a tentative step forward, as did Josef.

'What are you doing here?' Hugo whispered.

'I was looking out of my window,' Josef said with a nonchalant shrug. 'I saw you going into the park.'

Hugo turned his head to the side, staring at the park. He wondered if Josef had been watching something else.

Josef took another step forward. 'I wanted to make sure you were safe.'

Hugo stood rigid. There was something puzzling about the way Josef was approaching him. Slow and poised, like a lion sizing up its prey.

'And are you safe?' Josef asked, his tongue darting across his lips.

At that moment, Hugo was unsure if he was safe. Josef stopped in front of him, his warm breath dissipating into the night air. He was staring at Hugo in a way that scared Hugo. 'Do you want me to do this?' Josef asked.

'I don't know what you mean,' Hugo replied. 'Do what?'

'You know what I mean,' Josef replied inching forward. 'You know what I mean,' he repeated. His chin was almost pressing against Hugo's. 'You know what I mean,' he said again. 'You know what...' He extended his hands and pulled Hugo by the forearms, slamming their lips together. Hugo's body went rigid. Every urge he had was to pull away. To run. To hide. But he could not. The lips felt cold against his, but there was a sweetness to them which had already begun spreading through his body like wildfire. His tongue pressed against the roof of his mouth and Hugo had to stop himself from moving it, but finally, he could not stop it. It pressed itself against Josef's lips and slowly they parted. Josef's tongue moved into Hugo's mouth. Hugo opened his eyes at the same time as Josef and they stared at each other. All Hugo saw was light. The light of possibility. The light of a future. However, before he knew what was happening, Josef pulled himself away, dragging some spittle from Hugo. He wiped it away with the back of his hand.

'I can't do this,' he exhaled, glancing anxiously behind and around them.

'Can't do what?' Hugo cried desperately, his eyes filling with tears.

'This.' He pointed at Hugo's lips, touching them with his fingers. 'That. It's wrong and I have to go.'

Hugo watched helplessly as Josef ran away, knowing nothing would ever be the same for him again. A door had been opened, but it had closed quickly.

IV

Catherine Krief wiped her hand across the steamed-up bathroom mirror, squinting as she stared at her reflection. She knew she should probably wear glasses, but since turning forty the previous spring she had decided it was probably best not to look too closely at what time and gravity was doing to her. She supposed it was probably not as bad as she imagined. Her short black hair was natural, cut into a chic pixie style. Her face was smooth, with only the irritating lines which had formed around her mouth and eyes, showing her true age.

Since her divorce, she had been left reasonably comfortable. But like her marriage, she knew how fleeting money could be. If she was to live a long life in her modest, but well-located apartment, she knew it was no longer in her best interest to rely on, or assume, that a man would come to her rescue. There was a man, but she had vowed not to be become too involved, to get too attached, just in case he, like her husband before him, sought to seek comfort in younger flesh. She pressed against the lines, her mouth twisting into a grimace. She could afford a little work, and were it not for the exorbitant school fees she was forced to pay for her son to go to the exclusive prep school his father insisted on, then she would have already gone under the surgeon's knife. She tutted, pulling her attention away from the mirror.

Catherine padded along the hallway, suddenly aware of how quiet it was. Her son, Gad, was usually anything but quiet. The music and the television at unreasonably excessive volumes was one thing, but it appeared to her Gad could do nothing without the resulting din being offensive to her ears. Her hand reached for the handle to his bedroom and she moved it downwards, quickly stopping herself as she recalled what had happened the last time she entered Gad's room unannounced. She had seen more of her son than she wanted to. She knocked on the door, the satisfying sound of her diamond ring reminding her that despite his many shortcomings, her former husband had never scrimped on jewellery.

'Gad,' she called out. 'Come on, get up! It's past 08H00. You'll be late for school and your know how the headmaster gets when you're late. We're already on a warning, and if you get expelled, your father is going to kill you.' She stopped, listening for the tell-tale grunt of a fifteen-year-old boy been forced to get out of bed when he did not want to. There was no sound. She knocked again. 'Gad, I'm coming in so you'd better not be...' she shuddered, 'better not be doing *anything*,' she added with a grimace. She pushed open the door and entered the teenage boy's bedroom, the smell instantly making her gag. She was never sure how he managed it. The maid did her best, deep cleaning the room at least once a week, but it was as if the combination of hormones and testosterone coursing through his body saw it as a challenge to create as much smell and havoc as it could.

Catherine's brow crumbled with confusion. The room was as messy as usual, but the bed was completely made. And properly made, as if done by a professional, as if... as if it had not been slept in, she mused. She looked at her watch again, making sure that it really was 08H00. The maid was not due for two hours, so whoever had made the bed, it was not her. Catherine shook her head, flabbergasted by the possibility her son could have done it himself, after getting himself up and off to school with no fuss. If he had done that, it could only mean one thing. He had done something wrong and was worried about the trouble which was about to come his way. Catherine studied the bed once again. It really did appear to have not been slept in. She tried to remember when she had seen him last. She had been out the previous evening and returned home late, and had therefore decided not to look in on him, as was their usual routine. She shrugged, turning away. 'Time to get on with your own day,' she announced, 'the brat can look after himself.'

V

Directeur Gilles Adnet stepped across the veranda, wrapping his hands around the ledge. He leaned forward, pressing small feet into the asphalt, pushing his body upwards in an attempt to see the entire schoolyard. It always bothered him he had never grown as tall as his father and brother, nor shared their own thick head of hair, but he had taken a small amount of solace because whatever he lacked, he had certainly been given the brains in the family. His father had died on the factory line, a position Gilles' brother had taken over and would no doubt meet a similar fate, eventually. Gilles had always been different. He had made something of himself.

Headmaster of École privées de Faubourg Saint-Germain, one of the foremost private boys' schools in the whole of France. For almost thirty years, Gilles had guided some of the young visionaries of modern France. Boys who had grown into important men. Men who had become part of institutions Gilles could only dream of. He knew his contribution was invaluable, and it was all that mattered to him. He wanted more, but what he had was enough, because it was more than the cards he had been dealt.

The Directeur glanced at the pile of notes on his desk. *Please call Madame Duchamp.* He shuddered. The thought of another conversation with Madeline Duchamp was more than he could bear. All conversations with parents always amounted to the same sort of thing. *My child is in danger.* Or, as the responses usually came - *how dare you call my child a bully?* Adnet always thought he was walking a tightrope, trying to keep everyone happy but never completely achieving anything. It was exhausting and impossible, and for every child such as Hugo Duchamp, who did not know his position or the power he held, there was the counter - a child whose position had been ingrained in him from the second he could walk and talk. The only thing Adnet knew for sure was that the child whose parents shouted the loudest was the one most likely to win, and there was very little he could do about it.

'Directeur Adnet?'

Gilles turned on his heels to face Anna Moire, his assistant. She was a tall woman with a frame bordering on being painfully thin. Her face was gaunt and pale, and her red hair short and thinning. He liked her because she did not make him feel inferior in the way some of the teachers under his command did. They were attractive and vivacious, and it bore into him every time he saw them. Anna made him feel comfortable because he knew she was like him. They understood each other: *we have little in life, but we will make the most of the chances which come our way.*

'Oui, Anna?' he asked. He noticed the clock over her right shoulder. It was barely 10H00, and he hoped whatever she wanted, it was not a problem which would command his attention and change the course of his day. He had reports to file with the school authorities and it was something which needed his total concentration.

'We have two students missing,' Anna answered.

He frowned. Under normal circumstances, in normal schools, students missing would not necessarily be cause for concern, but in École privées de Faubourg Saint-Germain it was. His charges were not the sort of boys expected to skip school. For one thing, most of them were transported in private limousines directly from their mansions.

'Which students?' he snapped. His voice was loud and nasal, with a volume tending to increase exponentially when he was stressed.

'Gad Krief and Henri Dukas,' she responded.

Gilles smacked his head. 'Not those two again,' he cried in

despair. Henri Dukas was the grandson of Andre Dukas, the current Finance Minister, a man prominent in the French government, and a man not frightened to make his feelings very clear. *My grandson must have a first-class education and graduate with honours.* He had said this to Gilles in such a way that he did not need to add any caveat. *If you want to keep your job and ever work in France again,* was what he meant. The trouble was, not only was Henri Dukas one of the most academically challenged students Gilles had probably ever seen, he also had no interest in changing that. He was a bright enough boy, Gilles reasoned. He could be warm and charming when it suited him, but he was, as was very often the case, a child who had been raised to know whatever he did with his life, he would never have to worry about a thing, because his family would always bail him out. Henri and his partner in crime, Gad, had made skipping school an art form.

Gilles sighed. 'Get me Madame Krief on the telephone,' he instructed Anna, deciding it was best to deal firstly with Gad's mother. Then he would call Henri's father, a weak, lazy and vain man whose only response to his son being absent from school would be. *So? It's school hours, he's your problem.*

'Bien sûr, Directeur Adnet,' Anna replied, leaning over him and filling the air with her sickly-sweet perfume.

Gilles sighed, hoping his day would not turn out as he feared.

VI

Captain Bertram Hervé twisted his legs, pushing his body into a standing position. He steadied himself on the door and sighed as he took a series of deep breaths. *Twenty-eight years down, two to go, and then you can retire and sit in your chair and watch old American Westerns and do nothing else but drink brandy,* he told himself as he sucked in as much air as his nicotine-stained lungs could manage. His wife, Ada, had moved him onto chewing tobacco because she read somewhere it was better for him than smoking cigarettes, but Bertram suspected her motives had more to do with twenty-five years of marriage being about as many as she could stomach. He grabbed his coat from the car and pulled it around his body. It barely fit him any longer, but like most aspects of his life, he had decided with retirement approaching, there was little point in wasting money on pointless things.

'You're looking...' a tall thin man said, appearing by Hervé's side. His voice was deep with the hint of an accent which appeared non-descript, but of decidedly foreign descent. He continued to search for words. 'Ready for business,' he added finally with a flourish.

Hervé moved next to the tall man, wishing he could pull himself upwards. It had always pleased Hervé the height requirement for joining the Police Nationale had become less stringent than when he had been a cadet. He sighed. 'We should always be ready for business, you and I,' he grumbled.

The tall man, Dr. Jaques Oppert, a pathologist who had been assigned to the Commissariat de Police du 7e arrondissement, alongside Bertram for more years than either of them cared to count, shrugged rounded, bony shoulders. 'These days, the only thing I am truly ready for is death.'

Bertram threw back his head and laughed. He and Jaques could hardly be considered friends. Neither was he the sort of man who needed or sought male companionship, but they had, at the very least, formed a begrudgingly amiable partnership. Bertram tipped his head in the direction of the tent, which had been erected a few hundred metres away from where they stood. There was something about the area which seemed vaguely familiar to the weary Captain, but he could not immediately recall what it might be.

'I've been here before,' Oppert said out loud. 'As have you.'

Bertram's thick eyebrows knotted. He smoothed them out, irked as usual that the hair on his face seemed to bloom, leaving the wisps on the top of his head to duke it out in an ever-failing attempt to cover his egg-shaped head. 'It means absolutely nothing to me,' he said with a shrug. He pointed into the densely covered park area behind them. 'What are we looking at?'

Dr. Oppert cleared his throat. 'About two hours ago, a dog walker on his usual route came through the clearing here.' He stopped, pointing to a well-worn walkway which moved between two ancient trees, disappearing into a dark, overgrown park. 'There's a trail. It's overgrown and not really used these days,' Oppert continued. 'We only really know about this…'

Bertram smiled, 'because the dog ran off.'

Oppert nodded. 'And there he was. Our victim.'

Bertram trudged in silence, flat feet slipping against the dewy grass. He had long since stopped wearing leather shoes because he did not like the way they felt on his tired feet. 'Why do I know this place?' he muttered irritably to himself, though pleased he did not remember. He had almost thirty years of memories from his time as a police officer, and he knew he needed to erase those dark remembrances if he was ever to enjoy his forthcoming retirement.

Bertram stopped dead in his tracks. They had placed the

forensic tent in front of a tree, but it was a feeble attempt to shield the crime scene from prying eyes. He steadied himself, and it took him only a moment to remember why the area seemed familiar. 'Mon Dieu,' he cried.

Oppert took a long, deep breath. 'Twenty years ago - more or less, give or take,' he added with an awkward shrug.

Bertram sucked his teeth irritably, more so because he too could not remember the specifics. He inched forward, his feet slipping against the uneven grass verge. He narrowed his eyes. A man was bound to a tree, ropes binding his feet and arms to the trunk. He was naked, his head twisted onto his left shoulder, revealing the tell-tale signs of a slit throat. The blood had run down his arm and his side, congealing in a pool next to his feet. Bertram had been a flic long enough to spot the thickness and colour of the blood showed the man had been there for some time. The Captain glanced at his watch. It was 10H00, by his estimate the man had died sometime in the early hours of the morning.

As if sensing his colleagues' train of thought, Dr. Oppert said. 'I can't really be one hundred percent sure until I get him into the morgue, but we're probably looking at murder by the severing of his carotid artery, probably around midnight.' He stepped forward, extracting a pen from his pocket and moving it around. He began at the bound hands. 'There is clear evidence of struggling.' He then pointed at the man's feet. 'He tried to wriggle free. You can see where the rope has cut the skin as he tried to do so. Mais…' he trailed off, 'the rope was knotted too tightly. Alors, the more he struggled…'

'The tighter they became,' Bertram concluded.

Oppert continued, pointing at the slit throat. 'The throat was cut from left to right, which suggests his attacker was right-handed, and the wound appears to be deep and uneven, jagged even,' he added as he squinted near the body. 'Certainly it wasn't clean, like you would expect with something like a scalpel. I'd say our murderer was hesitant, however, more than that is going to be difficult to say. Some kind of sharp-bladed knife is about as much as I can say right now, but peut être if I had something to compare it to, I may be able to narrow it down a little.'

Bertram tutted. 'Useless,' he groaned as he scanned the surrounding area. There were no obvious signs of movement or activity, or how the deceased came to be placed naked in the middle of the park. He turned back to face the road.

'You can't see this area from the entrance to the park,' Oppert stated. 'Especially when it's dark. There are no lights in this area. Our man would have had privacy.'

Bertram nodded. 'Peut être,' he said, not sounding entirely convinced. 'But he took an enormous risk.' He pointed at the deceased. 'You said it yourself. He struggled a hell of a lot. It wouldn't have been quiet and all it would have taken was for someone to come into the park at the wrong time and he'd have been rumbled.'

The doctor moved back to the tree, cocking his head to the side, his eyes narrowing as he examined the face. He lifted the glasses which hung around his neck and placed them over his eyes. He moved his head, turning it slowly. 'Ah-ha,' he cried aloud after a moment.

'What is it, Jacques?' Bertram asked.

He pointed at the dead man's mouth. 'I see the fair appearance of what looks like the remains of an adhesive, and several small hairs removed in a line.'

'His mouth was taped shut,' Bertram concluded.

Oppert rose to his feet. 'It could explain how the murderer kept his victim quiet.' He faced the Captain. 'Are we going to continue to ignore the similarities?'

Bertram did not answer immediately. 'I've been trying to ignore it for a long time, *period*,' he grumbled. He turned back, his eyes flicking carefully over the deceased. 'This victim is older,' he said.

'And he's alone,' Oppert added.

Bertram agreed. 'Then it could just be a coincidence, or some depraved idiot who read about what happened here before.'

Oppert gave him a doubtful look. 'Our man is naked, just as the boys were. As far as I can tell, they were tied to the tree, the SAME tree, unless I'm very much mistaken. The investigation concluded the young men had their throats cut and there was evidence they were drugged and additionally, their mouths had been taped shut.'

Captain Bertram Hervé had to fight the urge to place his hands over his ears and scream, *no more!* Instead, he cleared his throat. 'They were boys.'

'Fifteen, as I recall,' Oppert confirmed, his mouth twisting into an angry grimace. 'One of the worst days of my life,' he hissed. 'And one of the worst mistakes I've ever made.'

Bertram reached over and touched Oppert's shoulder before removing it quickly. It was not the sort of working relationship they had. He knew nothing about Oppert's personal life and the doctor knew nothing about his, and it seemed to suit them both fine. 'I was there too, Jacques,' Bertram said softly, 'and I missed it, as well.'

Oppert shook his head. 'Oui, but it was my job not to miss it, especially something as important as that.'

They lapsed into silence. 'He didn't die,' Bertram said finally.

'With no thanks to me,' Oppert shot back.

Bertram closed his eyes for a moment, and he was instantly transported back twenty years to 1975. He was a young beat cop but already weary, and it was the first call of the day. He could smell the rain. It was thick and heavy, and his boss had sent Bertram out to report on the crime scene. He had been dispatched from the 7e Arrondissement station without even being told what the crime was. When he arrived, it was clearly one of the worst things the young flic would ever see. Two boys, teenagers barely out of puberty, were tied to the tree, their heads resting on one another, blood from their gaping throats mingling and being washed away by the torrential rain. Bertram had kept his distance, watching the newly appointed pathologist, Dr. Oppert, as he slipped and slid his way around the crime scene, at one point even steadying himself on the thigh of one of the boys. It was then Bertram saw it. He thought it was his imagination, but it seemed to him the boy had flinched when Oppert slapped his hand on him. It only lasted a second, a jerk in the boy's hand, an involuntary twitch, but as far as Bertram knew, dead people do not twitch. He ploughed through the rain, pulling the collar of his raincoat uselessly over his neck. He was already drenched and could feel the chilly dampness already taking root in his bones.

'Doctor! Doctor!' he yelled at Oppert.

'What the hell is it?' the doctor hissed.

Bertram pointed at the boy. 'His hand moved,' he yelled, struggling to make himself heard above the relentless rain.

Oppert's face creased in confusion. 'What are you talking about, you stupid man?'

Bertram stabbed his finger angrily. 'His damn hand moved!' he yelled again. 'Check, for Dieu's sake, check!'

Oppert glared at him, pressing his fingers against the boy's wrist, while holding his contemptuous look on Bertram. After a moment, his eyes widened in horror. 'Get a medic over here, now!' he yelled towards the Pompiers. 'This kid's alive!'

Bertram took a tentative step forward. There was no sign of life. 'How can this be?' he asked Oppert.

Oppert moved his hands quickly around the body. 'He should be dead, but the cut mustn't have quite severed the artery. His pulse is thready though, he's barely here.' He lowered his voice. 'The chances are he will not make it.'

'He has to,' Bertram said, clearing a path for the fast approaching medic. 'He knows who did this.'

'Bertram? Bertram?'

Bertram's eyes snapped open. 'Désolé, I was... I was...'

'Remembering,' Oppert finished for him. He shook his head. 'He should have died. It was a miracle he didn't. All that blood loss.' He smiled at Bertram. 'If you hadn't spotted his hand jerking, he would certainly have died.'

Bertram vaguely remembered the aftermath. The naked boy being cut from the tree and moved swiftly to the ambulance. Bertram recalled watching it disappear into the darkness, the lights blurred by the rain. 'I don't even remember his name,' he said finally.

'Nor do I,' Oppert agreed. He looked over Bertram's shoulder. 'Where the hell's the forensic team? I can't be standing here in this damp weather all day waiting for them.'

'There's an accident on the ring road,' Bertram shrugged. 'They'll be here soon enough.' He scratched his head, pulling one of the few strands of hair he had left across his shiny scalp. 'Why can't I remember his name?'

'Because we had a hundred and one cases on our desk at the time, most likely,' Oppert retorted. 'And a million more since then.'

'We never solved it.'

Oppert nodded.

'We <u>should</u> have solved it.'

Oppert stared at him. 'It was impossible. We were dealt an awful card. The boys were drugged. The kid who survived remembered nothing because of it.'

Bertram continued. 'I saw him once, and all he remembered was a man in a van who knocked him unconscious, and the next thing he remembered was when he woke up in hospital. I've always felt like I let him down.'

'Any evidence was washed away - no fibres or clues left by the attacker. There was no sexual assault, no DNA back then. There was nothing to go on,' Oppert reasoned. He continued.

'And…'

'A hundred and one other cases to move on to,' Bertram sighed. 'It doesn't excuse the fact I don't recall his name.'

'I understand,' Oppert replied. 'Mais, we can't think about these things too much. We have to move forward. For every case which falls by the wayside, we make sure the next one doesn't. Listen, two kids were abducted, they weren't abused sexually, or physically even. It never happened again, and I'm sure you checked. There were no similar crimes in the past. It was a one off.'

Bertram stared at the naked man tied to a tree. 'I didn't believe that at the time, and I still don't believe it now. The kind of depraved mind who would do something like that to young kids doesn't just stop.'

Oppert frowned. 'Well, he seemed to have stopped.' He stared at the dead man. 'They were kids and this victim, well, he's at least thirty years old, I would imagine.'

Bertram raised an eyebrow in the pathologist's direction. 'Either way, are you seriously suggesting there is no similarity between the two murders?'

Oppert did not answer. He stepped away, clapping his hands at the arrival of the forensic team. 'Finally, we can get out of here.'

Bertram stepped away. 'Bon. Call me as soon as you have something, like an ID, par example?'

Oppert laughed. 'He doesn't exactly have a wallet tucked away, mais I'll try my best. Let's hope he has a criminal record, non?' He paused. 'Where will you be?'

Bertram continued down the track. 'I need to see Madeline Duchamp.'

Oppert snorted. 'Are you sure that's a good idea?'

Bertram did not turn back. 'I think it's a crazy idea, but I have to do it. Find me this poor man's name, and pronto, d'accord?'

Dr. Oppert smiled. 'Bien sûr. Give my love to Madeline, why don't you.'

This time, Captain Bertram Hervé stopped and turned around. 'I don't think that's a good idea. I remember what she said about you the last time I mentioned you.' He smiled and continued walking towards the road. 'I had no idea she knew such foul language.'

VII

Hugo pulled at his blond hair, wishing for the fortieth time that day it was longer and darker so that he could let it drop over his face and cover his eyes. He imagined it would be comforting to have something to hide behind. To peer inconspicuously into the world. As it happened, his attention was focused on only one thing. Not the other hundred students in the assembly hall, or the teachers lined against the wall. It was honed-in on the one boy who had walked into his life a day earlier and disappeared as quickly.

Josef Levy had not even acknowledged Hugo in the hallway, despite the fact Hugo had lifted his hand halfway into an awkward wave. It was clear that whatever Hugo imagined had happened between them was just that - his imagination. Instead, Josef had turned his head, laughing at a joke told by the student next to him. It had crushed Hugo in ways he did not understand. He was used to being ignored, so he was sure it was not that. But it had seemed different with Josef. It was almost as if… almost as if he did not see the need to ignore Hugo. And then he had, and it had reaffirmed everything Hugo had come to believe about himself. Everything his father had said was confirmed. He was worthless. He was pointless and as boring as paint drying on a vast wall.

'I have called this assembly for a very important reason,' Directeur Gilles Adnet addressed the students.

Hugo turned his head in the directeur's direction, ready to give him his full attention. It was certainly unusual for an assembly to be called mid-afternoon. A thought occurred to Hugo, and it made his blood run cold. He hoped this was not a meeting regarding bullying, or fights because Hugo knew it would instantly mean every person in the room would turn in his direction, noting the cut lips and cheeks and bruised eyes and know it was all about him. It had happened once before, and Hugo had received a worse beating the next day for his supposed 'grassing' to the Directeur.

'Two of your fellow students have not turned up for school today,' the Directeur continued.

Hugo exhaled, breathing a sigh of relief at the realisation it was not about him. Missing students, though? It seemed an odd reason for an assembly, particularly since he was sure a lot of his fellow students played truant most days.

Adnet pressed on. 'Under normal circumstances, I would not be unduly concerned.' He paused, shooting an angry look at the students in the auditorium. 'I would be extremely irritated, but not entirely surprised. However, it seems as if both of the boys in question have likely been missing since yesterday evening.'

'Ha! I bet they're queers and they've run off together!' a student called out. A student whose fist Hugo was almost certain had left an imprint on his face.

The Directeur glared at the vocal student. 'See me after this assembly, Baxter, and then we'll discuss your comments further, d'accord?' He turned back to face the students. 'Gad Krief and Henri Dukas are missing. I realise it may be a ruse. They were bored, wanted to kick back and have some fun, but the fact remains - they are minors. They are not adults, and because of that, we do not have the luxury of allowing them the freedom to disappear as they see fit. They are missing, and soon the police will have to become involved, and as I'm sure you can understand I would rather that did not happen. Therefore, it is imperative if any of you know of their whereabouts that you tell me without haste, or,' he paused, 'if you do not feel compelled to do that, then contact them yourself and inform them their presence is required here within the hour.' He paused again, the muscles in his neck flexing as he added, 'no questions asked.' He tapped his fingers on the lectern. 'Tres bien. You are dismissed and may return to your classes. Mais, I counsel you all. If you know where Gad and Henri are, I ask you to make sure for all of our sakes that they are aware of the trouble they will be in if they do not return to school or to their homes immediately. Dismissed.'

Hugo rose slowly to his feet, the scraping of the metal feet of his chair against the parquet floor made him wince. He had taken a blow to his ear, and it was still ringing. He turned and before he realised what was happening; he stumbled into the arms of Josef. Instinctively, he threw up his hands, grabbing onto Josef's biceps. He tried to extract himself, but it seemed as if his hands had locked into place.

Josef stepped backwards, a wry smile on his face. 'Sorry to creep up on you, H,' he said. 'I didn't mean to scare you.'

H. There was something about the way in which he said it which troubled Hugo. He was not sure why, but it did. 'You didn't,' he spluttered.

Josef pointed at Hugo's face. 'I haven't seen you today. I just wanted to check you were okay. It doesn't look too bad.'

'I saw you earlier in the hallway,' Hugo retorted, immediately biting his lip, realising he had just acknowledged he had been watching Josef and had seen him ignore him.

Josef's pupils dilated. 'Ah, yeah, I thought that was you,' he retorted quickly. 'I wasn't sure though.'

Hugo's own eyes widened. He wished he could lie, but he knew he could not and that his expression would tell Josef he knew he was lying.

Josef's cheeks filled with blood, but he said nothing.

'It's okay,' Hugo said, moving to the side of Josef in order to pass him.

Josef touched his arm. 'It isn't, but it will be.'

Hugo frowned, unsure what he meant. 'I have to go,' he muttered.

'I'll see you later?' Josef asked as a question, not a statement.

Hugo stared at Josef's hand, still on his arm. 'I doubt it. Salut, Josef, take care.' He hurried away in the direction of the exit without looking back, but he could feel the burning intensity of Josef's stare on him.

VIII

'Monsieur Duchamp?' Do you have a moment?

Hugo stopped suddenly, afraid to look behind him. As usual, he had been moving quickly along the corridor to his next class, his head down as he concentrated only on getting safely from one room to another. He turned around slowly to be greeted by a warm smile from Anna Moire, Directeur Adnet's assistant. She was almost as tall as Hugo, but much thinner, with a gaunt face.

'Do you have a moment?' she asked. Her voice was soft with the trace of an accent Hugo could not pinpoint.

Hugo looked around, wondering if she was talking to someone else. 'Moi?'

Anna laughed. 'Oui, you.' She pointed towards a door which lead into the schoolyard. 'We can talk outside.'

Hugo glanced fearfully at the door. He could not imagine what the Directeur's assistant would want with him. 'I have a class to get to,' he blurted.

She shook her head. 'I'll give you a note to give to your teacher to explain why you were late.'

Hugo felt his spirits sink. Walking late into a classroom was one of the worst imaginable things. It felt like a walk of shame, walking through the rows of desks where invariably more than one of his fellow students would try to trip him or dig him in his sides.

As if sensing his reticence, Anna approached him and touched his arm. 'It'll be okay,' she said reassuringly.

Hugo nodded, but he was not at all sure she was correct. He moved slowly behind her as they left the school building. He shielded his eyes from the sun and for a moment imagined he was walking into a life far removed from his own. It was a fantasy he lived in more often than he should, a fantasy where he walked from one room to another and in the second room he was fully grown and successful and loved. It was a room he could only imagine walking into.

'You're looking better,' Anna said, pointing at his face. They had stopped in a corner of the building, a corner which Hugo was relieved to note was secluded. He was relieved he was at least out of sight of prying eyes. 'Do you feel alright?' she continued.

Hugo shrugged. 'Sure,' he answered softly.

'Things are going to get better, Hugo.'

'Sure,' he repeated.

She took a step closer to him. 'They will. You're a smart kid, one of the smartest. I see you standing in the corner, hoping no one sees you, but you know what's special about you? You see everything. That's such an unusual trait for a kid, for anyone really.' She paused, glancing over her shoulder. 'I shouldn't really say this, I mean, I'm supposed to be impartial, but some of the kids in this school are so far up their own asses it's crazy. They somehow think that being rich gives them a free ride in life. I should know. I was one of those kids too - once. But I know the reality of life is very, very different. It's supposed to be my job to teach that to them, but it's hard to convince someone when they're told from an early age how their lives are going to be.'

'Have I done something wrong, Mademoiselle Moire?' Hugo interjected.

Anna laughed. 'I don't know, have you?'

Hugo frowned, unsure how to respond.

'Listen, I just wanted to talk to you in private,' Anna said. 'Directeur Adnet's hands are tied, and that makes it difficult. We're not going to do anything formal about what's been going on, which is actually a good thing, because I know if we did, it would only make things worse for you.'

Hugo gave her a grateful smile.

'But I also wanted to make it clear to you that things can't, WON'T, carry on as they are for you right now,' she continued. 'Bullying is difficult to stop, especially in a school such as this, for several reasons, but particularly because the cause of bullying is much more complicated than one person exerting dominance over another.'

'That's how it feels to me.'

'I used to feel that way, too,' she answered.

Hugo raised his head. 'You were bullied?'

'I was taken from Paris when I was a kid, younger than you are now. We moved to a different country, so you can just imagine how cruel the kids were to me. This awkward, spotty kid, always with a snotty nose and,' she ran her fingers through her fine red hair. 'I was so anxious I used to pull chunks of my own hair out. The kids in my school thought it was funny, so they joined in.'

Hugo took in a sharp breath. 'I'm so sorry,' he said.

She shrugged. 'Believe it or not, it helped.'

'It helped?' he asked, confused.

'Oui,' Anna replied. 'I know that sounds crazy, and it probably is. But in a weird sort of way, it helped distract me. It made me stop focusing on what was really bothering me and focus on what was currently happening to me, and you know what? It worked for me. By the time I got better, my past was behind me. I'd healed.'

Hugo scratched his head. 'So, you think I should be happy about getting bullied?'

She laughed. 'Not at all. What I suppose I'm saying in my own roundabout way, is that this period of your life will pass. It will be hard but you will survive and more importantly, you will thrive.' She smiled. 'I just know it.'

He gave her a doubtful look.

'But in the meantime,' Anna continued, 'know this. Things are going to change in this school.'

'How?' Hugo asked. 'You said yourself, there's not a lot you can do.'

She smiled. 'There's not a lot Directeur Adnet can do,' she paused, 'but there is a lot I can do,' she added with a wink.

Hugo smiled back at her. He was grateful for her words, but he knew what it meant. Any intervention would only make the situation worse.

'This doesn't need to be a bad thing, Hugo,' she said. 'I'm not saying that I'm going to follow you around like some weird bodyguard. Nor am I saying I am going to lambast the rotten boys who see singling you out as a sport.'

'Then what can you do?' he asked.

She smiled again. 'Boys tend to be frightened of me,' she said. 'I know that should bother me, but it doesn't. I will be watching you Hugo Duchamp, and I will be watching them. That should be enough, but if it isn't,' she took her bag from her shoulder and opened it, rooting through the contents. She pulled out her purse and opened it, removing a small white card. She handed it to Hugo. 'This is my home phone number. Call me if you need to talk, or anything. D'accord?'

Hugo reluctantly took the card, unsure of what he would do with it.

'You can go back to your class now, Hugo,' she said.

Hugo nodded and began trudging towards the door.

'Hey, tell me about Josef Levy,' Anna called after him.

Hugo's eyes widened. 'What about him?' he asked quickly.

Anna smiled. 'I've seen the way he looks at you,' she laughed. 'He looks at you as if he wants to eat you.' She stopped, raising her hands and laughing. 'I don't mean that in a creepy, Hannibal Lector kind of way.' She sighed wistfully. 'Enjoy it. Men don't look that way very often, and we think they're always going to, but they don't.'

Hugo's face froze. 'I don't know what you mean.'

She nodded. 'Bien sûr, but you will. All I'm saying is, be ready and be open. Not everything should be the way people tell you it should. If you want my advice…' she stopped.

Hugo shrugged.

'Take your time,' she added. 'You're still a kid, so is he. You have options and time and a whole life, all I'm saying is this. Enjoy the moment, if it's the moment you want to enjoy. As for the rest - leave it up to the adults, won't you?'

Hugo smiled. 'I'll try. Merci Mademoiselle.'

IX

Catherine Krief stole a look at Willum Dukas. He was seated on an antique Louis IX chair, one leg crossed casually over a knee as he studied his manicured fingernails. His head was lolling to the side, his lips parted in the way he indicated he was bored or that something was beneath him. It was the only way to tell, she reasoned, since his face-lift surgery and numerous subsequent procedures it was practically impossible to register any kind of reaction from him. She noted that there were also a few dots of blood on his forehead, which, she realised now, was most likely why he had been difficult to reach all day and why he was presumably so irritated. Willum never liked to be interrupted whilst at his dermatologist, and particularly over something she was sure he would consider mundane.

'They've been missing a long time,' she spoke finally, piercing the stuffy air of the Dukas living room.

Willum turned his head with such abject, deliberate slowness it appeared in slow-motion. When he finally locked eyes with her, she saw nothing but coldness. It bothered her that it affected her. She had known for a long time she meant nothing to him. Nothing but a distraction when he was bored.

'They haven't even been gone twenty-four hours yet,' he snapped.

'They're just fifteen-years-old,' Catherine cried desperately, suddenly aware she had never been apart from Gad for an entire night in his entire life.

Willum threw his hands in the air. 'Exactement!' he cried. 'Which means they snuck out to a party last night, got wasted and are most likely still sleeping off whatever it was they drank.' He lifted his arm, staring at the solid gold Rolex on his wrist. 'It is almost 16H00, which means school will be finished soon. They are probably well aware of that and will sneak in as if nothing happened.'

'They had to have known the school would have noticed their absence.'

He shook his head. 'Why would they? It's only because YOUR son has a predisposition for testing boundaries,' he narrowed his eyes, 'because he has none, and now he's dragged my son into it.'

Catherine sighed. 'I don't think it's fair to blame this all on Gad,' she said with little conviction.

'Speaking of no boundaries, what does Raul have to say about this?' Willum questioned.

She did not answer immediately. She had been unable to locate Gad's father, Raul, at any of his numbers and, as he owned his own company, it was not unusual for him to be absent for extended periods of time. She knew she should not be surprised. He had never been the sort of man who could be relied upon. He had always been moody and contrite and prone to mood swings. He had never been violent to her or their son, but he was often surly and withdrawn. In the end, it had come as a relief to all of them when he had left. She was not even sure his interest in the young woman was anything other than an excuse to extract himself from marriage and fatherhood.

'I haven't been able to contact him,' she answered.

Willum managed to slightly raise an eyebrow. 'You haven't?'

'Non,' she replied with an irritated shrug. 'Mais, that's not unusual. He doesn't exactly keep in touch or show a great deal of interest in my life or his son.'

Willum sighed. 'What are we supposed to do? Sit around here and wait?'

Catherine looked at the antique clock in the corner of the

room. 'As you said, school is finishing soon, they'll be home then.'

Willum nodded. 'And then you need to have a serious talk with your son,' he snapped.

'And you? You aren't going to talk to Henri?'

Willum stood up and moved towards the doorway. 'Henri is not the problem. My family is never the problem.'

X

Madeline Duchamp pivoted her body around. She had positioned herself in the corner of her living room, where she knew the sun was kind to her complexion, basking her in the late afternoon sun. She was dressed elegantly. Chanel suit and pearls, gray hair set into a firm bouffant. She watched with keen, cat gray eyes as the doors opened and Captain Bertram Hervé was led in by a maid. The maid pointed to a chair which had been positioned in front of Madeline. The maid clicked her heels, looking at Madeline. Madeline gave a curt nod, and the maid moved swiftly and silently backwards from the room, gently closing the doors behind her. Madeline did not take her eyes off Bertram, watching him shuffling uncomfortably on the chair. He pulled off his hat, placing it on his lap, fiddling with the corners with an obvious anxiety.

'When my majordomo informed me you had requested a meeting with me, I was, I will admit, slightly taken aback,' Madeline began. Her voice was slow and deliberate, each word poised and perfectly pronounced.

'You haven't changed, Madeline,' Bertram said.

She smiled, as if acknowledging how correct he was. 'You have,' she retorted.

He laughed, looking down at his battered hat and the raincoat splattered with mud. 'I won't ask if it's for the better.'

Madeline nodded. 'Merci. It is never good to force a lady to lie in circumstances such as these.'

He laughed again.

She cleared her throat. 'How is Madame Hervé?'

'Fiesty,' Bertram retorted.

Madeline snorted. 'I bet she is after decades of being married to you.'

He continued staring at her. 'She still hates you.'

Madeline's nose twitched. 'Now, that is impressive after all this time.' She picked a piece of fluff from her Chanel coat. 'Although, they do say focusing on something such as hatred keeps a person young.'

They stopped speaking, but did not move their eyes away from one another.

'It has certainly been a long time,' Madeline said.

Bertram nodded. 'I was sorry to read about Daisy.'

Her eyes widened. 'My son's wife isn't dead,' she snapped, before adding, '*unfortunately*. However, it was for the best she left. She was not suited for…' she searched for the correct word, but it seemed as she could not find one, 'anything.'

'Wasn't there a child from the… union?' Bertram asked.

Madeline lifted her face towards the ceiling before turning her attention back to Hervé. 'You have kept up to date, I see.'

He shrugged nonchalantly.

'He lives with me.' Madeline said, her voice suddenly softer. 'His name is Hugo.'

'He lives with you?' Bertram asked with apparent surprise.

Madeline's mouth twisted. 'His father is very busy. It seemed prudent for him to remain here with me, under the circumstances. Boarding schools are adequate, but not for a Duchamp, and certainly not for a child such as Hugo.'

'Hugo? There is a problem with the child?'

She pulled back her head. 'There is no problem with the child,' she snapped. She exhaled. 'Why are you here, Bertram?'

Bertram folded his hands in front of him. 'Earlier today we found the body of a man in the park. *Your* park.'

Madeline sucked in air angrily. 'The park was named after my husband, because of his benevolence. Mais I have no involvement in the trust.' She paused. 'Therefore, I cannot imagine for a second why you would think it would be of any concern, or interest to me.'

'Because of what happened twenty years ago.'

Madeline raised her hands. 'I will not have you speak of that in this house.'

Bertram leaned forward in the chair. 'We have to, Madeline.'

She shook her head with sheer determination. 'We have to do no such thing, you old fool.' She turned her head. 'You said you found a body?'

He nodded.

'Who?'

He shrugged. 'He had no identification. When I leave here, I will go to his autopsy. I can only hope to have more answers then.'

Madeline nodded. 'Was he…?'

He nodded. 'Oui. He was naked.'

'Was he a child?'

'Non,' Bertram responded. 'He was an adult, thirty or so, I believe.'

She twisted her head to face him. 'Then there is no connection.'

Bertram's eyes widened. 'The poor man was naked with his throat cut. We can't ignore that.'

'I most certainly can,' Madeline gasped. 'And so must you.'

'I can't, cherie,' Bertram said. 'We ignored it once before. We must not do it again. Two boys were left for dead twenty years ago. I can't be sure, but I believe it was almost to the day. We cannot ignore the similarity to what has happened today.'

Madeline slammed her fist onto the table next to her chair with such force, a china cup bounced, crashing onto the floor and smashing into pieces. 'I will not allow this to be dragged up. The boy's death was nothing to do with any of us, and if you drag this up again, you have to know what I will do to protect my name.' She paused, her attention suddenly diverted to the doorway. She had not noticed the doors to the living room had been opened. Hugo was standing, his mouth twisted into a nervous decision. *Should I stay or should I go?* 'What are you doing, lurking there, child?' Madeline snapped.

'Désolé, Grand Mère,' Hugo whispered. 'I know I shouldn't trouble you,' he said, his fragile voice breaking. 'It's just that when we left school, they told us we had to tell our parents or guardians we made it home. The school said they would check. Alors, I thought I'd better tell you before I went to my room.'

Madeline stared at him, wondering how long he had been in the doorway. She frowned. 'Why on earth would the school check if you made it home? It is a ten-minute walk. I believe even at your advanced age, you should be able to manage that, non?'

'Two students have gone missing,' Hugo answered. 'I suppose they're just being cautious.'

Madeline turned her head sharply towards Bertram, her eyes widening in surprise. She then moved her attention back to Hugo. 'Did you say two students?'

Hugo nodded. 'Oui, Gad Krief and Henri Dukas.' He shrugged. 'Everyone seems to say they must have gone to a party last night and they're just scared to come home, mais…'

Bertram rose to his feet and turned to face Hugo. 'Et mais, quoi, Enfant?'

Hugo stared at the strange-looking man, waiting for an introduction.

Bertram tipped his head. 'Captain Bertram Hervé, Commissariat de Police du 7e arrondissement. It is a pleasure to make your acquaintance.'

Hugo looked to Madeline, but she had turned and was staring out of the window.

'You said, "mais,"' Bertram continued, 'as if you were suggesting there was no party.'

Hugo shrugged. 'I couldn't say. It's not like I would have been invited in the first place. Everyone is talking about it at school and they all seem to be saying there was no party last night, so…' he trailed off.

Bertram shook his head slowly. 'Gad Krief.'

'Raul Krief,' Madeline whispered.

'Who is Raul Krief?' Hugo asked with a confused frown.

'I have to go,' Bertram said, hurrying towards the door, brushing past Hugo. Hugo took a tentative step into the room. 'Madeline?'

She did not turn her head. 'Leave me alone and go to your room, Hugo,' she replied, her voice as cold as ice.

XI

Lieutenant Suzette Carman pushed open the door to École privées de Faubourg Saint-Germain, the scent of boys instantly filled her lungs. *Dirty boys, ripening boys, annoying boys.* It took her back, and she found the smell had not changed, nor how it made her feel. She strode with determination along the hallway, her feet clicking as if she was trying to force herself to move more quickly, just by the sheer force of her nature. She had spent most of her childhood in such a school. She knew the halls, the polished trophies lining the wall, none of which ever held her name, and she hated every inch of the polished floor, the clean walls, because she knew they meant only one thing. *You are better than anyone else outside these walls, now go prove it.* She had known only one fact in her life. Her family had paid for her education, but her own mind had freed her from the shackles it had imposed on her.

'Are you the police?'

She turned sharply, her fingers instantly wrapping around the gun on her right hip. It annoyed her that people assumed because she was short with a paunch; she was not an obvious police officer. It annoyed her more that men assumed because her dirty blonde hair was short and spiked, that she was a lesbian. She hated the fact her looks proved them right.

'Yeah, c'est moi,' she replied with a flick of her wrists. 'Lieutenant Suzette Carman. And you are?'

Directeur Gilles Adnet held out his hand. She did not take it. He took it back, glancing at it self-consciously. 'Er... I am Directeur Adnet.'

Suzette nodded. 'Ah, oui, we spoke on the phone.'

Adnet's eyes widened. 'That was you?' He paused. 'Well,

what do you have?'

She regarded him with surprise. 'I have nothing. What were you expecting? The kids aren't exactly missing. When I was their age, I met this guy, a Brit - all sniffy and stuck-up, but he had a kind of way about him, and he asked me to go to a party with him. I said sure, why not? I got in his car and promptly fell asleep and when I finally woke up, we'd driven all night and were almost in Spain. I thought, well, we've come this far, we might as well go to the party, so we did.'

The Directeur nodded. 'As interesting as that is, I fail to see what it might have to do with my two missing students.'

Suzette's nose twitched with irritation. 'My point is, I was a kid who didn't give a shit about the worry I left behind. All I could think about was partying with the snotty Brit.'

'Are you suggesting that is what my students are doing?'

Suzette laughed. 'Partying with the snotty Brit? Well, that would be a little weird, he's probably an old man by now, mais,' she paused, 'my point is, they are two kids. They're just off somewhere having fun. Hell, if it wasn't for the fact one of them was the grandson of some government big wig, I wouldn't even be here. You know that.'

Adnet shrugged. 'It's the price we pay in our professions. Our patrons demand our complete attention at all times.'

'I should talk to their friends,' Suzette added, with obvious reluctance.

Adnet shook his head. 'The students have all gone home for the evening I'm afraid,' he said. 'We were expecting you earlier.'

'I have a desk full of <u>actual</u> crimes to take care of,' she said huffily.

'Would you like to examine their lockers?' Adnet offered.

'Sure,' she retorted irritably, 'just how I want to spend my day, I…' before she could finish, her radio crackled. She pulled it from her pocket. 'Yeah?'

'Lieutenant Carman? This is dispatch. Captain Hervé left a message for you. He wants you to meet him right away at the morgue.'

Suzette tutted. 'I've just got to the damn school. I haven't had a chance to talk to anyone yet,' she responded. The last thing she wanted to do was spend her evening with Captain Hervé and Dr. Oppert. They were called the dinosaurs of the 7e arrondissement for good reason. They were old, crusty, and set in the ways of decades past.

Dispatch crackled. 'He said to come right away,' the bored voice answered.

Suzette nodded. 'D'accord, I'm on my way.' She placed the radio back in her pocket. 'Désolé, I'll have to come back and search through the porno mags and cigarettes in the lockers tomorrow. Bonne soiree, Directeur.'

Gilles Adnet nodded. 'À demain, Lieutenant Carman.'

Suzette retreated wearily back in the direction from which she had come.

XII

Suzette pushed open the doors to the morgue and immediately fought the urge to retch. It was not so much the aura of death, nor the rising mist of formaldehyde, rather the combined stench of two middle-aged men with remnants of whisky and garlic chicken lunches stagnating about their person. She stopped dead in her tracks. Captain Bertram Hervé and Dr. Jaques Oppert had both stopped what they were doing, turned to face her and Oppert was using the sleeve of his shirt to push the papers they had been looking at to one side. Suzette looked to her Captain, and it told her all she needed to know. He was too lazy to lie, and his face told her he was making his best effort to do exactly that. She steadied herself on her feet. She had thought she was about to walk into something routine, but now she knew, as if by some acute sense, she was walking into something altogether different.

'You took your time, Lieutenant Carman,' Bertram grumbled.

Suzette nodded. It was too late for him to pretend to be irritated. She could smell the fakeness. She had walked in on something, but what the hell was it? She shrugged as nonchalantly as she could. 'I was told to go to École privées de Faubourg Saint-Germain, and then,' she paused as if for drastic effect, 'I wasn't.'

Bertram flashed a concerted look in the doctor's direction. 'We have somewhat of a situation.'

She took a tentative step forward. 'A situation?' She knew Bertram Hervé and had been working under his command for almost two years. She had always suspected he had been a good cop once, but was now just coasting towards retirement. She had never suspected him to be corrupt - rather just lazy and uninterested, and she had realised early in her career it was not the sort of terrible combination she had thought it would be. It meant he did his job, exerting no more effort than he needed, but it also meant it worked both ways. He had told her once police officers who are lazy often make the best law enforcers because they have no desire to please anyone, rather their ambition is to clear their desk and be done with whatever presents itself to them. 'A situation?' she repeated after no response was forthcoming.

Finally, Bertram nodded. He pointed at the corpse on the gurney, covered by a white sheet. 'Earlier today this man was discovered in a park in the 7e arrondissement, not far from here.'

Suzette nodded. 'Sure. I heard about it. I hadn't started my shift yet, so I wasn't called out.'

'I was,' Bertram interrupted. 'Which was good. We have a problem, Lieutenant.'

She frowned. 'And I have two missing kids. Kids who are probably off partying somewhere, but because one of them has a grandfather high up in the government, it apparently means I have to spend the rest of my day searching out every place where there may have been a teenage party in the last twenty-four hours.' She paused. 'I can't tell you how thrilled I am about that,' she added with a bite.

'Twenty years ago, to the day, as it happens,' Bertram said with a deep breath. 'Two young boys were found tied to a tree. They were naked and left for dead. As it turned out, only one of them actually died, the other, was somewhat of a miracle. He survived having his throat cut.'

'Yeah,' Suzette said, vaguely recalling the case. 'What about it?'

Bertram pointed at the gurney. 'Guess where this man was found.'

Suzette turned her head slowly. 'The same park?' she offered.

Bertram nodded. 'Not only the same park. I checked the photographs. He was tied to the same tree.'

Suzette twisted her shoulders. 'Well, that's... that's...' she continued a shrug, 'weird, I suppose,' she added with little conviction.

Bertram pointed to Dr. Oppert. 'Jaques here has run the victim's prints through the database and the result is, well, a cause for concern.'

'In what way?'

'The deceased is a man called Raul Krief,' Bertram announced.

She frowned. 'Krief?'

He nodded. 'He also happens to be the father of one of the missing boys. Gad Krief.'

Suzette moved towards the gurney, her finger trailing across the covering sheet without actually touching it. 'Well, that's weird, I suppose, mais...'

'It's not the only thing which is odd about this whole situation,' Bertram interrupted. He took a deep breath. 'Twenty years ago, the boy we saved, the boy who was left for dead - can' you imagine who he might have been?'

Suzette did not move her eyes from the outline of Raul Krief's face, hidden by a sheet. 'Raul Krief,' she whispered.

Bertram nodded. 'Raul Krief survived a massacre twenty years ago, but today, today, it came back for him.'

Dr. Oppert cleared his throat. 'Peut être it is time we looked at Monsieur Krief and try to understand exactly what happened to him.'

Bertram nodded and gestured for Suzette to step back. She did, her eyes wide with concern and confusion.

'I'll send the samples to the lab, but there is such a backlog, I wouldn't expect an answer for a week or two,' Dr. Oppert announced.

'I'll kick them up the ass, if I have to,' Suzette offered.

Bertram snorted. 'And they'll tell you to get lost, and drag their heels even longer for you having annoyed them,' he grumbled. He looked to Jaques. 'What CAN you tell us?'

Oppert shrugged. 'There is no obvious sign of trauma. I didn't find any bruises or cuts. Death was quick and simple. His throat was cut, and he bled out.'

'Was he… was he…?' Bertram interrupted.

Oppert smiled at the Captain's apparent embarrassment. 'There was no evidence of any sexual abuse,' he said, before adding, 'just like the last time.'

Suzette turned her head. 'Are you telling me two fifteen-year-old boys were tied NAKED to a tree and they weren't fuc… abused?'

'That's exactly what I'm telling you,' Oppert replied, before adding, 'murder isn't always about sex. It's often about control and power.' He shrugged. 'In my humble opinion, évidemment.'

Suzette stood up. 'D'accord.' She lifted the sheet covering Raul Krief. 'Alors, he wasn't raped either time?' she asked.

'Not according to the evidence,' Bertram responded. 'It appears this wasn't about sex.'

Suzette shuddered. 'It's always about sex, in one way or another,' she replied. 'You men always think sex is about penetration, but it isn't always. It's more often men trying to pretend they are "real" men,' she grimaced. 'Often they need to strip their victims of their clothes, because apparently it diminishes their so-called masculinity.'

Bertram covered his mouth with clear boredom. 'Just because you've taken a "class" hardly makes you an expert.' He said the word *class* as if was a curse word.

'And just because you *haven't* taken a class, doesn't make you an expert either,' she retorted.

He pulled back his head, taken aback by her response.

'Désolé, Captain,' she whispered, lowering her head.

Bertram smiled. 'Don't be. You are right. Taking classes was never part of the job when I was your age,' he said. 'We learnt our craft on the streets not having some fancy doctor lecturing us about stuff he read in books.'

Suzette nodded. 'That's not such a bad thing.' She shrugged. 'I'm just saying, sometimes having both sets of knowledge isn't such a bad thing. As I see it, there can be three reasons for the victims to be rendered naked - sex, power, and,' she counted them off on her fingers, 'to leave no evidence of their attacker.'

'Or a fourth,' Dr. Oppert added, 'none of the above.'

Suzette frowned. 'What do you mean?'

He smiled. 'Maniacs read books, too. The removal of clothes could be simply because they WANT us to look at it being a sexual crime, when in reality it is anything but.'

'Murderers are often very methodical,' Bertram said, 'and as Jacques says, it could be a simple case of misdirection.'

Suzette stared at Raul Krief. 'This is different. It has to be. You said it happened twenty years ago, who was the other victim?'

'His name was Gerrard Le Mache,' Bertram answered. 'He was Raul's neighbour and best friend. They went to the same school.'

'École privées de Faubourg Saint-Germain?' Suzette questioned.

He nodded.

Suzette tapped her skin as she contemplated. 'And now, twenty years later, Raul's son goes missing with his best friend. How old was Raul when this happened to him?'

'Fifteen.'

She grimaced. 'The same age as his son. What happened after he was rescued?'

Bertram considered. 'I couldn't say. He was in hospital for a long time, and his statements were vague at best. He knew nothing, he saw nothing, that sort of thing. There was nothing to go on. And there was no evidence on either boy to suggest who had abducted them.'

'Did you speak to Raul?' she asked.

The Captain shook his head. 'Non, I saw him in the hospital, but that was about it. I moved on to different cases. There are always different cases to move on to, as well you know.'

'I think I read he went back to Spain,' Dr. Oppert offered. 'If I recall correctly, his family was from there originally. I suppose they felt it was a better place for him to recuperate and start over.'

'Then why did he come back, and more importantly, when did he come back?' Suzette asked.

'I couldn't say,' Oppert replied.

She turned to her Captain. 'Don't you think it's odd he came back here after everything that happened and decided to start a family?'

'People are strange,' Bertram said, 'and they're often creatures of habit. This was his home. Maybe he didn't like the thought of being pushed out of it by what happened to him. And also, maybe he just got over it.'

'All the same, in the light of what happened, we should look into it,' she responded. 'In the meantime, what do we do about the missing boys?'

'I've called the Commander, and he's authorised a search,' Bertram replied. 'We're waiting on extra cops from other arrondissements to help with that. Mais, the truth is, we don't have a lot to go on. Can you go and speak to his ex-wife? We'll need her to make a formal identification and she might be able to shine more light on what he was up to, the sort of man he was, that sort of thing.'

Suzette nodded. She looked again at the remains of Raul Krief. 'And there's nothing you can tell us about him? What about time of death?'

The doctor tapped his chin. 'Cases like this are notoriously hard to understand. But he had not been attacked by wildlife nor was rigour very far advanced. So I'd say he would have been tied to the tree no less than six hours, probably not more than ten before we discovered him.'

'Hmm,' Suzette considered. 'Then it was sometime during the night.'

'It makes sense,' Oppert agreed. 'There wouldn't have been many people around. The murderer could take his time.'

She nodded. 'I'll check for cameras in the area. We may at least be able to spot him coming into the park.'

Bertram shook his head. 'I looked before I left. There don't appear to be any cameras in the vicinity. There may be some in the approaching streets, but I can't see them being much help in this instance.'

'And they'd probably not be working anyway,' Suzette grumbled. 'What else, Dr. Oppert?'

He shrugged. 'As you saw, I extracted some dirt from underneath two of his fingernails, but that could have come from anywhere. The lab might give us more of an idea. The same goes for the remnants of adhesive tape around his mouth. However, I wouldn't get too excited or expect too much from them.' He moved in front of Raul. 'All in all, he was a perfectly normal, average thirty-five-year old man. Reasonably fit and healthy. His blood results will tell us more hopefully.'

'We can't ignore the connection,' Bertram said.

Suzette's lips twisted. 'And yet someone waited twenty years to do what, finish the job?' She shook her head. 'I don't see it.'

'All I'm saying is, the connection is there,' Bertram answered.

'Peut être,' she replied, 'but that doesn't explain what has happened to his son and Henri Dukas.'

'Speak to the mother, and I'll meet you back at the Commissariat,' Bertram said. He paused. 'We'll need her to make a formal identification of her ex-husband's body, but don't tell her right away. Question her about her son and his friend. Get as much as you can out of her before you tell her about Raul. They may have been divorced, but she might still have feelings for him and could just go to pieces, and then she'll be useless to us.'

'D'accord,' Suzette replied, nodding at Bertram and Jaques. 'Au revoir, Captain, Dr. Oppert.'

The two men watched her leave.

'She's a good flic,' Oppert stated.

Bertram nodded. 'She is. They say she'll go far.'

'Then she's good?'

Bertram shrugged. 'Not for me to say, nobody would listen anyway. I've heard she's tipped for my job when I go. The first woman Captain in this arrondissement.'

Oppert coughed. 'She could cause trouble.'

Bertram spun on his heels. 'I did nothing wrong twenty years ago, Jaques, and you know it. I made a mistake, that's all. A stupid, irresponsible mistake.'

'Bien sûr,' Oppert retorted. 'It's just it would be an awful shame for it all to come out, especially when you're so close to getting your pension.'

Bertram turned back to face the door. 'Then we'll just have to make sure that doesn't happen.'

XIII

'Psst... Psst!' the voice grew louder and more insistent. Hugo tried to ignore it. 'For Dieu's sake, what the hell do you think PSST means?' Hugo stopped dead in his tracks, unsure whether he could turn around, even if he wanted to. It annoyed him he knew exactly whose voice it was. He turned around slowly. Josef was standing in a tunnel behind a pillar. He was not alone. Next to him was a boy Hugo vaguely recognised as Maxim Spire. He had seen the two of them together frequently, their heads almost touching in the way two friends who are perfectly comfortable around each other have no trouble sharing personal space.

Hugo was not sure, but he had heard Maxim's mother was a famous singer, or actress. He was not familiar with that sort of world, although his own mother seemed to be part of it too. It was not something which Hugo felt connected to. Maxim bothered him in other ways as well. There was a confidence to him which Hugo could barely aspire to. He was handsome, tall and lithe, with a smooth buzz cut and square jaw and the blackest eyes Hugo had ever seen. Hugo had only heard him talk once and his voice was already deep and manly, filled with authority Hugo imagined was out of his own reach. Maxim stepped out of the shadow of the pillar. He walked towards Hugo with a slight limp. Hugo recalled overhearing a conversation once which suggested Maxim had broken his leg following a spectacular skateboarding accident.

'I need to talk to you,' Maxim mumbled, tugging at the sleeve of Hugo's jacket and pulling him into the shadows, 'and Josef said I could trust you.'

Trust me? Hugo could not imagine a single scenario where his name might come up in a conversation between the two boys.

'Trust me with what?' he mumbled.

Maxim looked around. 'Not here. Let's go to the skateboard park.'

Hugo nodded, unsure if there was such a thing as a skateboard park. Josef stepped from the shadows, immediately placing his hand on Hugo's arm and pulling him in the direction of the exit.

Hugo watched Maxim sucking on a cigarette. It appeared he was draining it, as if his very existence depended upon it. He was sitting, his legs slightly ajar, swaying gently back and forth. Hugo had noticed it in other boys, as if their reactions were normal and without consideration. It troubled Hugo because it had always felt as if he had to think about every movement he made and how it would be perceived. *Don't move your hands that way. Don't cross your legs. Don't purse your lips. Don't… Don't… Don't…*

'Want a cigarette, Hugo?' Maxim asked.

Hugo moved his shoulders in the most nonchalant way he could. 'Sure,' he said, extending his hand and pulling the cigarette from Maxim's hand. He placed it in his mouth and sucked and sucked and sucked. Suddenly his lungs felt like they were exploding, and they sent plumes of smoke into the cool afternoon air. It hurt his body in ways he was sure he had not felt before. But then a second wave came. He felt calm. He felt relaxed. He placed the cigarette back in his lips and took a second, shorter drag. He exhaled and did not cough. He took a third, longer drag. He exhaled, narrowing his eyes toward Maxim. He smiled. He understood something he had not understood earlier. Something he could not articulate, but knew he did not need to. All he knew was that he was going to buy a packet of cigarettes on his way home, and be damned the consequences.

Josef pulled the cigarette from Hugo's hand and placed it in his own mouth, his eyes creasing as the smoke drifted across his eyes. 'You're a bad influence on me, Duchamp,' he laughed. 'But you make it look so good.'

Hugo looked at him in surprise. He had never imagined he would be a bad influence on anyone. He also knew he should be appalled by the action of such intimacy of Josef taking the cigarette from him, but he knew he would take it back from him and place it again in his own mouth. 'What is this all about?' Hugo asked Maxim.

Maxim pulled his skateboard between his legs, twisting a baseball cap around his head. He sucked on his cigarette. 'I know what happened to Gad and Henri,' he said finally.

Hugo's eyes widened. He was not sure what he had been expecting to hear from Josef's friend, but it had not been that. 'What do you mean? What happened to them? Do the police know?'

Maxim exchanged a look with Josef who tipped his shoulders in a way which seemed to say, *tell him*.

Maxim sighed. 'They hooked up with a dude.'

Hugo could not lift his head. He did not want to look in Josef's direction.

Maxim smiled. 'Not like that, you idiot. A dude who has the best stuff,' he said.

'The best stuff?' Hugo asked in clear confusion.

'He sells drugs, Hugo,' Josef clarified.

Hugo frowned. 'Then this is about drugs?'

Josef nodded. 'Yeah. They had the best contact. Some pretty special stuff, not your usual run-of-the-mill blow.'

Hugo took the last drag of the cigarette and wished he had another. 'What do you mean by "special"?'

Maxim shrugged. 'We normally have weed, a bit of E, but this was some pretty special stuff.'

'Heroin? Cocaine?' Hugo questioned. He stopped having

exhausted his not exactly extensive knowledge of hard drugs.

He shook his head. 'Nope, they were pills. No idea what they were, but some pretty weird, and actually pretty amazing stuff,' he added with a smile.

Hugo resisted the urge to say, *you took drugs when you did not know what they were?* Instead, he stared at Josef, wondering if he also was so foolish. Josef smiled at Hugo. *No, I'm not,* the smile clearly said. Hugo covered his mouth, hoping to bury the smile he could not force away every time he was near him.

Hugo turned back to Maxim, wondering what on earth any of this could have to do with him. 'Are you saying that's where Gad and Henri were going when they disappeared? They were on their way to get drugs?' he asked.

'Yeah,' Maxim responded. 'There's a party at my place at the weekend. It was for that. Henri rang me and I placed an order. He said fine, no problem, I'll see you later, and that was that.' He shook his head. 'This wasn't the first time. There was no reason to think there was anything weird going on.'

'Why are you telling me this?' Hugo asked.

Maxim tipped his head in Josef's direction. 'Our boy here said you would know what to do.'

Hugo raised an eyebrow. 'He did?' He looked at Josef. 'And why would you say that?'

'Because we can't go to the police,' Josef answered. 'We'd all get in trouble, and to be honest, we don't know it has anything to do with what might have happened to Gad and Henri.'

Hugo nodded. 'I agree, but again, what do you think I can do?' He paused. 'I wasn't even going to the party.' He bit his lip, wishing he had not said it because he knew it sounded as if he was bothered. Which he was not. Or was he? He hated the fact he was standing with two boys, more or less the same age as him, but he felt as if he was so far removed from them he might as well be from another planet. He stole a sly look at them. Josef was dressed in jeans, torn at the knee and the upper thigh, a tight t-shirt emblazoned with the words, *"Nitzer Ebb,"* which meant nothing to Hugo. Maxim was dressed similarly, his t-shirt most likely announcing another band or movie Hugo knew nothing about. He looked down at his own outfit. Beige chino and a white buttoned shirt, both of which had been pressed so fiercely, they still looked fresh despite the fact he had been wearing them all day. He suddenly felt even more self-conscious than he normally did, and that filled him with a sadness he had not imagined. *I can't be like these boys. I will never be like these boys.*

Josef lifted his head, opening his mouth to speak, but he closed it as quickly.

'We thought you could help,' Maxim said, nudging Josef before adding, '*Josef* thought you could help.'

Hugo shook his head. It made no sense to him. There was nothing he could do, nothing he could think of doing. Why on earth would Josef want his help? A thought occurred to him. 'My Grand Mère knows a police Captain,' he said finally, 'and I think he's involved in the investigation somehow.' He paused. 'I guess I could say I've heard rumours around school, rumours about some drug dealer or something. As I have no connection to any of it, or had any involvement in the drugs or the parties, I could legitimately say I had no idea who was involved.' He shrugged. 'It's not a lot, but it might give the police somewhere to start, somewhere to look for Gad and Henri.'

Josef nudged Maxim. 'See, I told you he'd come up with something.'

Hugo hid another smile. 'It's going to draw attention to your party, Maxim,' he said. 'They'll ask questions.'

He shrugged. 'Let them. I know nothing. I don't know any names, or where Gad or Henri went. That's the whole point. We can't tell what we don't know.'

Josef moved closer to Hugo. 'He's right. We won't be lying

because we don't know anything.' He sighed. 'But if there is a chance it has something to do with Gad and Henri's disappearance, then we have to tell, non?'

Hugo nodded, unsure whether he was being used, or just that they needed his help. He supposed it did not matter. Gad and Henri were missing, and if he could do something to help with the search, he knew he should. 'D'accord,' he said. 'I'll see what I can do.'

Josef touched his arm again in a way which bothered Hugo. It was not so much the physical intimacy of it which bothered him, rather as he had suspected, it was a clear statement. *I know you like this.*

Maxim tugged at Josef's sleeve. 'C'mon, Jo, we've gotta go.'

Hugo watched them disappear across the tarmac. His eyes locked on Josef, whose head was turned, staring at him as he was dragged away.

XIV

Lieutenant Suzette Carman stepped into the living room, taking a quick glance around. There appeared to be nothing out of place, nothing out of the ordinary, nothing to suggest… something. Her eyes widened before she had a chance to hide her surprise. She had met Willum Dukas before, so she recognised him instantly. She hoped this meeting would be better than the last.

'I came to be with Madame Krief,' Willum said, as if sensing Suzette's confusion as to his presence. 'She was very upset,' he said before quickly adding, 'we both are.'

'Do you have news? Have you found them?' Catherine Krief called out from the corner of the room. She was standing next to a curtain, her hand resting on it, pulling it back so she could stare out of the window. Suzette wondered how long she had been standing there, staring at an empty path leading to the house.

'We are mobilising a search team,' Suzette answered.

Willum tutted. '*Mobilising*? Why is it taking so damn long?'

'Paris is a big city,' Suzette replied, 'and we don't have a lot to go on. But we do know what we are doing, and once we have a team in place, we will begin a thorough search. That is why it is so important we have received all the information we can get. For example, we need to determine exactly when the boys were last seen.'

Catherine and Willum exchanged a look, which Suzette could only describe as one of guilt. She supposed it was perfectly normal to feel guilty when your child has gone missing, but the look which passed between the two parents seemed to be a different kind of guilt to Suzette. Neither Catherine nor Willum spoke.

Suzette cleared her throat and pulled out her notepad,

flicking it open. 'We know your sons both left school as usual yesterday afternoon, but what we don't know is what happened to them after. What can you tell me about that?'

Another guilty look was exchanged, and it lasted long enough this time for Suzette to understand what it meant. *They are having an affair.*

'I was at the office,' Willum said, 'until late, and then I had dinner in town with a friend. I didn't see Henri.'

Catherine lowered her head. 'I was out, too. It was late when I got home, so I didn't want to disturb Gad, and then this morning, well, I assumed he had gone to school.'

Suzette nodded. 'And is that normal? I mean, for your sons to be home alone?'

'They are fifteen, Lieutenant Carman, not five,' Willum snapped. He gesticulated around the room. 'And they hardly live in a dingy home in a rough neighbourhood. They are not children.'

She nodded again. 'And how have they been lately?'

'What do you mean?' he shot back.

Suzette shrugged. 'Oh, I don't know. Teenage boys aren't always the easiest to live with, are they?'

'Gad is a good boy,' Catherine interrupted. 'He never gives me any trouble.'

Willum smirked. 'Henri adheres to every stereotype of a spoiled teenage boy. He's rude, surly, antagonistic, lazy, and selfish. I tried taking him to task for it once and he said, *I learnt from the best, Papa.*' He smiled. 'And he was right. I'm afraid I haven't set the best example for my son, Lieutenant. If his mother had stuck around, things might have been different, but she didn't. I'm afraid I rather fell into the same pattern as my own father. Let a nanny deal with the child until they're old enough to do it themselves.'

His honesty surprised Suzette. She turned to Catherine. The fear and worry had already spread into lines across her face. 'What I suppose I'm asking, is if there is anything, anything at all, no matter how small it might seem, which has happened recently and may suggest why your sons would go missing.'

'There's been nothing, nothing,' Catherine replied, shaking her head vigorously.

Suzette said nothing. She did not imagine there was anything else she would get out of either of them. 'What about Henri's mother?' she asked Willum.

He snorted. 'The bitch lives in L.A with her lazy-assed so-called actor boyfriend, who surprisingly seems happier lying around a pool in the mansion I paid for, than getting an actual job and supporting himself. And before you ask, non, she has no contact with Henri. She'll send a birthday card, or a Christmas card, if she can be bothered to remember. A phone call sometimes, but that's usually because she wants to whine to me and knows she can't do that without at least speaking to her son first.'

Suzette made a note. 'I'll need her details, just in case. Did Henri try to keep in touch with her?'

Willum shook his head. 'He hates her. I mean, why wouldn't he?'

'Then there's not a chance he would go to see her?' Suzette posed.

He laughed. 'I doubt it. He doesn't even know her address, as far as I'm aware.' He paused. 'I'll have my secretary send you her address and phone number, but I beg of you, don't insist she comes back to France. That's all any of us need!'

Suzette turned her head slowly towards Catherine. She took a deep breath. 'And Gad's father?'

Catherine's fingers twirled gently around the curtain she had been holding. 'Gad and Raul are usually very close.'

Suzette leaned forward. *Usually?*

Catherine nodded. 'Raul is... Raul is...' she trailed off, seemingly unable to complete her thought.

'A waste of space,' Willum hissed, 'is what he is.'

'Willum,' Catherine pleaded. She faced Suzette. 'Raul has problems, he's always had problems,' she said.

Suzette waited for her to elaborate, but she did not. 'Problems?'

'From his childhood,' Catherine answered finally.

'Something he's been using to excuse his destructive behaviour ever since,' Willum retorted. 'He's always been the same. He finally found an excuse to continuously mess up and not bother himself. He was the same at school.'

'He was not!' Catherine exclaimed. 'He was kind and gentle, and you know it. He only changed… later.'

Suzette continued writing in her notebook. She was surprised Raul, Catherine and Willum had known each other since childhood, but she supposed it was not so surprising after all. 'Did something change lately?' she asked.

Catherine frowned. 'Raul has moods, dark moods. They sometimes last for weeks, months even. We always knew when they were coming and what we had to do, which basically was to avoid him. As he's gotten older, Raul has controlled it better, I think, but it has always been tough on Gad. He can go from seeing his father three, four times a week, to not seeing him for six months, even a year. Raul has been missing for a while, a few months, peut être. I've tried contacting him, just in case Gad got in touch, but he's not answering his phone, but that's no surprise, he rarely answers his phone to me these days.' She paused. 'Do you think that's where the boys are? With Raul?' she asked, almost as if she dared not to hope for it to be true.

Suzette exhaled. 'I'm afraid I have some news which is going to come as a terrible shock to you, Madame Krief,' she whispered.

'Gad!' Catherine screamed.

Suzette hurried to the other woman, touching her arm. 'Non, je suis désolé, I have no news regarding your son, but I am afraid there is something I need to tell you.'

'He's dead, isn't he?' Willum interrupted. 'The bastard finally did it.'

Suzette fought the urge to reprimand him, instead concentrating on Catherine. 'Earlier today, we discovered a body in a park near here. A body we believe is your ex-husband, Raul Krief.'

'Are you sure?' Catherine asked desperately, her eyes filling with tears.

'We have fingerprint evidence,' Suzette answered, 'but we will need you to make a formal identification when you are ready. As far as we can tell, he has no other living relatives.'

'His parents are dead, and he was an only child, but he had a cousin, though I don't think they're close,' Catherine whispered. 'We are… *were*, all he had.' She looked to Willum. 'I should have gone to him. I knew he was in the dark place again, but you told me to ignore him, to let him sort it out for himself finally. Well, he has, he's FINALLY sorted himself out, so we can all be happy, non?' she added with clear sarcasm and bite.

'I'm afraid, it isn't that simple,' Suzette spoke. 'We have opened a murder investigation into Raul's death.'

'A murder investigation?' Catherine gasped.

Willum stood. 'You said they
nd him in a park.' He moved to the window. 'Do you mean the Faubourg Saint-Germain park?'

Suzette nodded.

Willum turned sharply to Catherine, but he said nothing. Her eyes widened as the shared realisation hit her.

'How did he die?' Willum asked.

'Obviously, I can't go into too many details at this stage,' Suzette reasoned. 'Mais, we are looking at similarities with what happened to Raul twenty years ago.'

'Mon Dieu!' Catherine cried, making the sign of the cross across her chest. 'Raul always said he would come back for him.'

'He?' Suzette spoke quickly.

'The monster who broke him,' Catherine retorted. 'Raul was the happiest boy you could have ever hoped to meet before it happened, but afterwards, well, his physical scars healed, but the rest of him didn't.'

'Catherine, s'il te plaît. Let's not drag this all up again. It's so long ago,' Willum pleaded.

'For you, peut être,' she snapped. 'Mais, for the rest of us, it never went away. Raul was destroyed by what happened, as sure as if he had died like Gerrard. He never got over the guilt that he had survived and Gerrard had not.'

'Ridiculous,' Willum snipped.

'They were your best friends, too,' Catherine pleaded. 'None of us came out of it unscathed.'

He snorted. 'Non, mais some of us, like Raul, used it as an excuse to live life as if there were bogey men around every corner. The rest of us had to just get on with life, didn't we? You had to become both a mother and a father to Gad, because Raul found it "too much" to be a full-time husband and father. He was weak then, and he just used what happened to become even weaker, to stop even trying.'

Suzette continued scribbling in her notebook.

'You said there were similarities?' Catherine asked Suzette.

She nodded.

'Was he tied to a tree again? His throat cut?'

Suzette was unsure how to respond, but after a moment nodded once again.

Catherine sobbed, glaring at Willum. 'Raul always said he would come back. He always said it!' She stopped, her hand flying to her head. 'I feel... I feel...' she stopped, her body crumpling to the ground.

Willum ran towards her, dragging her body upwards. 'Quick! Call for help!' he yelled to Suzette.

XV

Madeline Duchamp pulled back her head, turning it very slowly to the side. She moved it back, gray eyes staring intently at her petit-fils squirming in the antique chair his ever-expanding frame had no business trying to fit into.

'You asked to speak with me, Hugo,' she said with faint amusement. 'Although, I'm not sure you need my approval to take up smoking as a pastime.'

Hugo's nostrils flexed. *How can she smell it from so far away?* Her living room was vast, and she had not moved from her chair when he had been shown into the room.

'My father smoked, as did my mother,' she said. 'And they did it with style, I thought. Unfortunately, my lungs forbid me from joining them, and your father, well, your father is your father. He is vain and more concerned with how he appears in public and apparently that does not come with the smell of tobacco attached to his lapels.' She smiled. 'You, however, it suits.'

'Grand Mère,' Hugo began before giving up.

She smiled. 'Bon. Do not bore Madeline with pointless protests. Instead, tell her why you have asked for this meeting. It is nice to see you, obviously, but it is... *unusual*.'

Hugo smiled. 'Pour moi, aussi.'

'Then tell me, what is this about?' she asked.

'The boys who went missing from my school,' he said.

Madeline pulled her head back in surprise. 'They were your friends?'

Hugo laughed. 'Bien sûr, non,' he retorted.

Madeline's pale lips twisted into a smile. 'Bon. Dreadful families, all of them.' She leaned forward. 'You do have friends though, don't you?' She asked the question forcefully. 'The whole point of sending you at such ridiculous expense to École privées de Faubourg Saint-Germain is to try and forge some kind of successful relationships which will help you in the future. Alors, tell me you at least have made some friends.'

Hugo tried his best to keep eye contact with Madeline. 'Bien sûr, I have friends,' he gushed. He did not want to disappoint her any more than he was sure he already managed to do daily. He took a breath. They were not his friends, but he could think of nothing else to say. 'My friends are Josef Levy and Maxim Spire.' He said the names quickly, hoping she would pay little attention.

'Josef Levy?' Madeline questioned. 'You mean Rabbi Levy's son?'

Hugo shrugged. 'I believe so,' he answered.

Madeline clenched her fists, but said nothing.

'You know Rabbi Levy?'

Madeline moved her shoulders slowly and deliberately. 'I know Serge and Anouk Levy, very well,' she answered in a way which confused Hugo. He could not be sure, but it appeared she was being polite in the same way she talked with her favourite maid about her family, when she had no real interest in them.

She frowned. 'Maxim Spire?' she continued.

Hugo nodded and slowly raised himself from the chair.

'Son père est un cochon,' Madeline muttered under her breath. 'Ideas above his station and all because he comes from new wealth.' She visibly shuddered. 'Import and export.' She mouthed the words as if it was painful for her.

Hugo suppressed a smile. It always amazed him how little patience Madeline had for those who orbited in the same social circle as she. He was not sure where the Duchamp wealth had come from, but he had enough snippets over the years to suggest it was from Madeline's family, not the Duchamp's.

'Well, at least you have friends,' she said with an exasperated wave of her hands. 'It is better than nothing, I suppose. Your father chose friends based upon their parentage, which was fine, and in comparison, unless your career aspirations extend to becoming a Jew or a,' she paused, shuddering, 'a haulage magnate, then I hope you have chosen your friends on the assumption they interest you in one way or another,' she paused again, staring intently at Hugo, before adding, 'for a small period of time until you become an adult, that is.' She tapped her cane on the floor. 'I find it prudent to ensure we cultivate contacts, not friends, as we move through life.' She banged the stick onto the highly polished floor. 'Now, what is this about? Why are you concerned with the boys who went missing?'

'Because there was a party,' Hugo answered, 'this weekend. It seems Gad and Henri used to bring… used to bring *things* to the parties.'

Madeline's nostrils flared. 'It does not surprise me. It is no secret what sort of things Willum Dukas gets up to. It is no wonder he has influenced his son in such an abhorrent way.' She narrowed her eyes. 'And what is this to you?' She slammed her stick again. 'Smoking is one thing, child, drugs are quite another. I will not have a Duchamp known to be a common drug user. I will not tolerate it.' She slammed her cane against the floor. 'Do you understand?'

'I have never taken any drugs, Madeline,' he reassured. 'I have enough trouble keeping my mind focused as it is, without using something to alter it.'

She turned her head, but it was not quick enough for Hugo to see she was smiling. She turned back; her face composed again. 'I asked why you were concerned about the missing boys?'

'Josef and Maxim didn't know what to do. They came to me. They don't want to get in trouble, but I suppose they also thought somebody should know about the drug connection.'

Madeline frowned. 'But why did they come to you?'

'Josef thought…'

'Josef?' Madeline interrupted. She tipped her head, studying Hugo with an interest which made him uncomfortable. It was as if she had caught him out on a secret. A secret he was not sure he was part of.

'Oui,' he responded as clearly as he could. 'They don't want to get into trouble.'

'But they don't mind if you do?'

He shrugged. 'I wasn't even invited to the party. I suppose they figured I was squeaky clean enough to help.' He paused. 'Your friend who came the other day, the police Captain. Perhaps you could speak to him?'

She slammed her cane again with such force, Hugo could see the dent on the parquet floor. 'Bertram Hervé is no friend of mine,' she hissed.

Hugo's eyes widened in surprise. It was not the impression he had imagined when he had seen the two of them together. He watched Madeline. Her face told him she was not in the mood to be questioned, but it made him want to question her all the more. 'Two boys are missing, Madeline,' he whispered.

'It wouldn't be the first time,' she muttered.

'Quoi?' he questioned.

Madeline shrugged. 'You haven't heard?' she asked. 'It was all over the news.'

Hugo shrugged. He pointed at the headphones around his neck. He had picked up a new cassette on his way home and he was desperate to get to his room so he could listen to it on his Walkman. *Nitzer Ebb - Big Hit.* He wondered whether Josef would be listening to it at the same time, and instantly hated himself for thinking about it. He had also picked up a packet of cigarettes and had felt like a criminal when buying it from the amused kiosk seller.

'Hugo?'

'Désolé,' Hugo gasped, pulling himself back to reality.

'You were a million miles away,' she said with a slither of a smile. 'Who was occupying your time?'

'Nitzer Ebb,' he mumbled.

'Is he one of the Berlin Ebb's?' Madeline snapped. 'Dreadful people. They like to ignore the fact grandpapa Ebb was a Nazi. Mind you, he was a delightful man, until he met Adolf,' she added.

Hugo frowned. He did not know what his grandmother was talking about, and upon reflection, he realised it was probably best he did not. He knew little of her past, and he knew she would most likely not tell him anything should he ask. 'What did you mean about something being all over the news?'

'Raul Krief was found dead,' she said simply.

'Raul Krief?' he repeated.

She nodded. 'He was Gad's father.'

Hugo sank into one of the chairs which lined the wall. He was never sure whether they were there for seating or for display purposes only. Either way, at that moment, he did not care. His eyes crinkled. 'Gad's father,' he repeated.

Madeline sighed. 'Something happened a long time ago.' She stood, steading herself on the lip of the chair. She ambled towards the bay window. Hugo noticed she was walking slower than he remembered, and he thought he detected a tremor in her steps. At that moment, she appeared old to him and it struck him as odd. He had never thought of Madeline Duchamp as anything other than a resilient, towering force of nature, but then, as the afternoon sun sliced through the curtains, he saw something he had never imagined he would see in her. Fragility.

'I was walking my dog, Fou,' she said. 'He was a beautiful boy, but he was…' she paused and smiled, 'a little intolerant. My staff refused to walk him because,' her face tightened, 'they claimed he nipped them. Nipped them!' she exclaimed. 'Bien sûr, he nipped them,' she added. 'Fou did not tolerate weakness,' she said proudly.

'You said you were walking, Fou?' Hugo interrupted, keen for Madeline to continue her story. 'What happened?'

Madeline traced her finger across the glass pane. She shook her head. 'I don't want to talk about this, Hugo,' she sighed. 'It was so long ago.'

'Is it relevant?' he asked.

She shrugged. 'How am I supposed to know?'

He stood, moving slowly across the room. 'Two fifteen-year-old boys are missing, Madeline,' he said. 'They may not be my friends, but I know them, at least, I know what they look like. Par example. I know Henri hates his family. He wants to do whatever he can to be different from his father and his grandfather.' He paused. 'And I certainly understand that.'

'Your grandfather was a good man,' she snapped. 'Just because you didn't know him, doesn't mean you can make assumptions, particularly if you are basing it on your own father.'

Hugo ignored her and continued. 'Gad just wants an easy life,' he said. 'Like most boys my age.' He took another step. 'They are my age,' he said. 'If there's something going on here, Madeline. You should tell me.'

She turned away. 'They were fifteen, too. Gerrard and Raul.' Her hand moved to the pearls around her neck. She turned her head back towards the window, cloudy eyes gazing in the direction of the park. 'They were just boys. Babies, even,' she whispered. 'Twenty years ago. And what happened to them was nothing short of monstrous. Strung up like slaughtered animals.' She shook her head. 'On that very day, I broke my own rule about respectable women not having a glass of champagne before midday.' She paused. 'In fact, I had whisky. I had only done that on my wedding day.' She paused again. 'And the day after,' she added with a sly smile.

Hugo frowned. He did not recall ever hearing anything about two young boys being murdered. He scratched his head. He was fairly sure it would have been mentioned in his school.

'Raul Krief was Gad's father,' Madeline said.

Hugo pursed his lips. 'I thought you said he was murdered when he was fifteen.'

She coughed. 'Well, whoever strung him up, certainly believed so.'

'Are you saying Raul Krief didn't die twenty years ago, but instead he died today?' Hugo posed. 'At the same time his son went missing?' She did not respond to him. 'Madeline?' he continued. 'Is that what you're telling me?'

She sucked her teeth. 'I am telling you nothing, Hugo, but more importantly, I am telling you this has nothing to do with us.' She stared at him. 'And I will not tolerate you interfering.'

Hugo studied his grandmother's face. He was used to her words and the way in which she always made clear her intentions and her requirements. But it was always tempered and regimented. It was always thought out. She was not the sort of woman afraid of making her intentions crystal clear. This was different. She was warning him about something he did not understand, something which had nothing to do with him. Josef had asked for his help, and all Hugo knew was he did not want to disappoint his new friend.

'I am almost fifteen years old,' Hugo began. 'And the only thing I know how to do, is to not interfere.' He took a deep breath. 'And frankly, I'm sick of it. I live in an attic. The only person I talk to regularly is your maid. I have no idea where my mother lives. I have no idea where my father lives. I have no idea about anything, as it happens. All I know is you are here, watching me, pushing me, not pushing me, whatever you want to call it. I'm sure you, like both my parents, don't really want me around either. I do not know where I am going, or how I am going to get there. And the only thing I know for sure is I am lonely. So lonely it hurts, some days more than others, but it hurts. I can't ask for anything because I have everything, and I have nothing, and there's no one to ask even if there was. I'm an embarrassment, and I guess I'm only here because I share your name, and to send me elsewhere would be more of an embarrassment.'

Madeline tilted her head to the side, fixing him with a look he was not sure he had seen before. It was as if she was looking at him for the first time. She moved slowly across the room. As usual, she wore a black Chanel suit, and it appeared to Hugo as if she glided across the highly polished floor, such was the lack of movement in her legs. She stopped a short distance from him, steadying herself on an ornate mantlepiece. Near enough to him, yet far enough away to dismiss any suggestion of intimacy.

'Is that what you really think?' she asked. Her voice was softer than he was used to hearing.

'Bien sûr,' he answered, confused as to why she might think otherwise.

She snorted. 'If you were an embarrassment, I would have sent you off to a Swiss boarding school like I did your father,' she said with a slow shrug of wide, boney shoulders.

Hugo frowned. 'I don't understand.'

'Your father went to the same school as you,' she replied. 'The only difference was he was too busy social climbing at the expense of his education. I was advised if he was to make anything of himself, I should enrol him in a highly disciplined school out of the country. Your grandfather wouldn't have heard of such a thing. Fortunately, he was dead by that point, so his input was not needed.' She ran a finger across the mantel, tutting when she found a few specks of dust. 'Being in different countries saved my relationship with your father,' she added. 'Or rather, it allowed us to learn to tolerate one another.'

'Then why am I here with you now?' Hugo asked. 'Is it all about pity?'

'Pity?' she scoffed. 'Pity? What a ridiculous thing to say. What do I care about pity?' She moved away again, back towards the window. 'I admit, I did what I had to do to encourage your mother and father to part. They were not a suitable match for each other, but more importantly, they were not a suitable match for *you*. If they had stayed together, it would likely have destroyed you, and them too. But I care nothing for either of them.' She turned to face him again. Her head movement was slow and considered. 'I am sorry you feel lonely,' she mouthed. 'I had considered you would have made friends and have had no need for me, but I suppose, in the end, it is the Duchamp way. We are solitary people. But I don't want you to be unhappy. What can I do to change your situation, petit-fils?'

Hugo studied her face. It was stoic, as was to be expected, but the tone of her voice told him she was being genuine. The question, however, was not one he could answer, at least not out loud. Instead, he shrugged. 'I suppose I am used to my situation. I won't be this age forever, and perhaps when I'm older things will change for me.'

Madeline nodded. 'But in the meantime, it would be nice if it wasn't quite so dull, non?'

Hugo smiled. He shrugged again.

'This boy. Josef. You like him, non?'

Hugo coughed, knowing instantly his cheeks had turned the colour of the plush red velvet drapes which lined the windows. 'I hardly know him,' he said.

Madeline smiled. It seemed to Hugo as if the smile was one born of knowledge. As if his grandmother was in on a secret only she knew. 'But you *want* to know him, non?'

Hugo shrugged with as much nonchalance as he could muster. 'I like his taste in music,' was all he could think of to say.

'Great partnerships have been born from less,' she quipped. 'Did I ever tell you how I met your grandfather?'

Hugo shook his head, unsure of the relevance.

'He was brought into this very room,' Madeline replied. 'He was added to a line of similar young men and I was asked to choose.'

'To choose?' Hugo asked, his voice rising sharply.

She nodded. 'It was a serious line-up. Starched cummerbunds and name drops as far as you could see. I chose your grandfather out of the ten boys who had been brought here for my auction for one reason, and for one reason only.' She paused. 'He was a homosexual.'

Hugo gasped. 'My grandfather was gay?'

'Well, he wasn't very happy,' Madeline retorted. 'But he was a good man. And he made a dutiful husband.' A cloud descended over her face. 'I was sorry I wasn't the wife he needed me to be.'

Hugo frowned. 'You said he was gay. I don't think the problem was yours.'

She laughed. 'Times were different. They're not so different now, but back then…' she trailed off. 'They were worse. Ecouté. I needed a husband to satisfy my parents. What I didn't need was a man who would bother me and get in my way. Hubert was perfect in that role. I assumed, wrongly, as it turned out, that we could go about our lives in simultaneous and yet different ways. I suppose he thought being married would change him and it came as a tremendous surprise to him that I did not want to change him.' She smiled. 'He was a good man, though. He didn't deserve the son he got.' She stared at Hugo. 'He would have loved you, jeune homme. He would have loved you. You look like your mother, but there is everything about Hubert in you.'

'Madeline,' Hugo pleaded, 'I'm not…'

She raised her hand. 'You are our petit-fils and you are exactly as you were meant to be. Like Hubert. Like me. Even your own parents,' she added with distaste. 'Sometimes we all need to come together to create something very special.' She pointed at Hugo. 'You are the result of much wrong. But you are a result. It breaks my heart Hubert had to live a life in the shadows.' She stepped back to the mantelpiece and picked up a framed photograph. Hugo looked at it and it was as if it was the first time he had ever noticed it, and it surprised him. All the other photographs were encased in solid silver frames, but this particular one was old and battered and seemingly inexpensive.

'Hubert's mother was Jewish. She died in Auschwitz. This rotten frame belonged to her. It was the only thing he wanted in this house, and I wouldn't allow it. *It matches nothing,* I said. I made him put it in his room.' She pressed it against her chest. 'I brought it here the night he died. And I was reminded again of the sort of woman I was. The sort of woman I am. This was the only thing in this entire house which belonged to him.' She pointed at the mantelpiece. 'But it has sat there for the last two decades. Out of place and out of time.'

Hugo stared at the photograph in the frame. It looked like him, only with dark hair and eyes. Eyes as cold as Hugo felt most of the time. Eyes which said only one thing. *I have a secret.* 'Did my father like him?' he asked.

'Your father hated him,' Madeline said with a smile. 'And your grandfather hated Pierre right back. He once said to me. *How on earth did we produce such a thing?* I said I imagined they had swapped him at birth.' She shook her head. 'I'm talking out of turn, child. We loved your father. We just didn't make the right choices, that's all. Your grandfather had his life, and I had mine, and we left it to everyone else. My parents wanted me to climb the Parisian social circles. Finally, they understood it would not happen with my husband, so they put all of their efforts into ensuring our child was the one who would carry the flame. I admit I couldn't have cared less. With hindsight, I would say I'm not proud of it, but it is what it is. Nobody is perfect and the sooner you realise that for yourself, the better.'

'That's sad,' Hugo mumbled.

She shrugged. 'It is what it is. We had our lives. We had our lives together, and we had them apart,' she added with a sly smile.

Hugo felt himself blushing again. Madeline cackled. 'I've shocked you, child. Bon. A child should be shocked from time to time. Your grandfather had his "life" and I had mine.' She emphasised the word *life* with a great flourish.

'You're talking about the police Captain, aren't you?' Hugo asked.

She studied his face. 'This really is none of your business, Hugo,' she grumbled with little conviction. 'Mais, I want you to understand it is possible to live two lives. Separate and yet the same.' She moved her head. 'You understand what I'm saying to you?'

'I… I'm not sure,' Hugo stammered.

She tutted. 'Your grandfather understood and you will too,' she paused, 'when you're ready to. My point is, it is possible to be who you are in private, and who you are expected to be in public life.'

Hugo nodded. 'And that's where the police officer comes into it?'

Madeline smiled. 'Bertram's not much to look at these days.' She stopped, pushing her hand over her lined face. 'Mais, who is? Time ravages us all in one way or another. It is the price we pay for serving and making it to the next part of our journey.'

Hugo tried to recall what the police Captain looked like. As far as he could remember, he was small and rotund with thin wisps of hair and a pencil-thin moustache which clashed with thick, bushy eyebrows. He was not the sort of man Hugo imagined his grandmother would be attracted to. Then again, he had trouble imagining Madeline Duchamp being in any sort of relationship.

'Back then, when we first met,' Madeline continued. 'He had a certain charm, you might say. He was most certainly one of the most interesting men I had ever met. Ridiculously opinionated and incorrect mostly. His politics were diabolical, still are most probably. But he was firm in his convictions, I'll give him that. And that means something. Remember that, Hugo. You can be unpopular by your beliefs, but only if you do not believe them yourself. Never be cruel. But be true to yourself. Bertram Hervé was certainly true to himself. It was a revelation when we met. He didn't give a damn about who I was, or how much money my family had. He was interested in who I could be.' She snorted. 'Typical of the bourgeoisie. He didn't understand that I could never be like that, or like him. You see, I'd grown up expected to be one way, to act one way, and to never, NEVER, step out of line.' She stared at Hugo. 'You think you have it hard. Go back in time to when Hubert and I were your age. Our choices were never ours and there was no escape.' She smiled. 'You only have to put up with it until you're eighteen, or when I die, whichever comes first. You'll be taken care of, either way.'

'Taken care of?' Hugo questioned.

She tapped her fingers on the window ledge. 'You don't need your father. And you don't need your mother. For anything. You will be able to leave Paris, should you choose to do so. And if you do, you will be able to do it under your own terms and without having to look back over your shoulder.'

'I'm not sure what to say,' Hugo said.

Madeline shrugged. 'Then say nothing until you are sure. The world is already full of pointless men saying pointless things just because they feel as if they should. I refuse to accept my grandson following in such a pointless tradition.' She raised her hands. 'Don't get too excited. We're old money, which basically means we have a name and a few assets, but that's enough for you. You will do whatever it is you are destined to do, and you will do it with honour to the Duchamp name.'

'That's rather a lot of pressure, Madeline,' Hugo said.

She shrugged again. 'Not my problem. I'll be dead, but don't think I won't haunt you if you disappoint me.'

Hugo smiled. He was sure of only one thing and that was

that if anyone could come back from the dead due to the sheer force of their character; it was most likely Madeline Duchamp.

'But you won't disappoint me,' she continued. 'And not just because you wouldn't dare.'

Hugo stared at her, realising it was as close to a compliment as he was ever likely to see from a member of his family. He cleared his throat. 'About Raul Krief,' he said.

Madeline frowned, evidently unsure of what he was talking about.

'Gad's father,' Hugo pressed.

'Oh, we're still talking about that,' she replied, waving her hand dismissively.

'Oui, we are.'

She sighed. 'Tres bien.' She drifted across the room and took her place in her usual upright chair. She folded her hands in front of her. 'I will tell you what I know about what happened, but I will also tell you this. We will not get involved. Not again. Not this time. Those are my conditions. Do you understand?'

Hugo frowned. 'I don't,' he answered honestly. 'I don't know what I'm even supposed to understand.' He clasped his hands. 'All I know is two boys I go to school with are missing, and you tell me something similar happened to one of their father's twenty years ago. At the very least, we need to tell the police that, non?'

Madeline snorted. 'Bertram is only too aware of the connection, believe me.' She shook her head with irritation. 'We can't get involved in this, Hugo. Not again,' she cried.

'We're not involved in anything,' Hugo replied. 'Mais, if there is anything we can do to help, then we have to, don't we? We'd just be passing on information which might help the police as they search for Gad and Henri. Isn't that what we should be doing? Because unless I'm very much mistaken, that's what you've just spent the last ten minutes telling me. You want me to be my own person.' He paused. 'I don't know what that means right now, other than I know I am the sort of person who needs to help other people when I can.'

She sighed. She stood, moving to a sofa in the corner of the room, slowly lowering herself into it. She tapped the seat beside her. 'Come join me,' she said.

Hugo rose to his feet slowly and moved across the room, each step feeling slow and laboured. He sat down with a thump next to Madeline. She waved her fingers. 'Not so close, Hugo,' she quipped. 'We're not Swedish.'

Hugo suppressed a smile. 'What happened twenty years ago, Madeline?' he asked.

XVI

'As I said, I went out to walk my dog,' Madeline began.

Hugo resisted the urge to speak, finding it difficult to imagine his grandmother not delegating such a task to one of her staff.

'I had heard talk of the two boys being reported missing,' she continued. 'It had been a week, longer even. I confess I didn't give it too much thought. I was not associated with the families in any meaningful way. Pierre was in Switzerland by then, and Hubert's health had taken a turn for the worst the previous winter. He rarely left the house that summer and,' she paused, indicating the reason for her keenness to leave the house, 'he was an awful patient,' she added. 'And for some reason he seemed to expect that *I,* tend to him.' She laughed as if she thought it had been a ridiculous assumption.

'And then what happened?' Hugo asked.

'I went into the park and ran into Serge Levy.'

'Josef's father?' Hugo interrupted.

She nodded. 'He said he'd been jogging,' she added, the emphasis making it clear she did not believe him. 'Although his choice of outfit betrayed him,' she concluded.

'Didn't you say he was a Rabbi?'

'Not then,' his grandmother replied. 'Back then he was just another pious, sanctimonious religious zealot who belonged to a family who imagined being a Jew meant you were closer to Dieu than a family of Roman Catholics, such as ours. Non, back then Serge worked in the family business. The Levy family run a chain of kosher supermarkets and he was the CEO before he gave it up all up to become a Rabbi. Quite the career change,' she added with a flourish.

'What made you think he was lying about where he'd been? Was it just his clothes?' Hugo questioned.

Madeline smiled. 'Ah, you haven't heard about the park at night then?'

Hugo shook his head quickly.

Madeline threw her head back and laughed. 'Bien sûr, you have. After dark, the park which our family name sponsors, attracts different kinds of people with different moral values.'

'Are you saying Serge Levy had been visiting a prostitute?'

She shrugged. 'It's not for me to say, other than it seems to be those who are the most pious often are projecting their own guilt onto others.' She extended her hands. 'Either way, it was no concern of mine. He was more worried about being caught than anything else,' she said.

'And then what happened?'

'I went into the park to allow Fou to do… what he needed to do. I released her lead and then he was off, like a rat into the darkness,' Madeline huffed. 'He refused to answer my call, and I had no intention of scrabbling about in the undergrowth to find him. *Fine,* I told him, *stay there if that's what you'd prefer, but don't think you're getting into my bed tonight if you roll in anything.* I turned to leave, and that's when he started barking. I knew his bark. This wasn't playful, or excited. This was the sort of bark reserved for men who came too close to me,' she added with a proud smile. 'Anyway, despite my reservations, I went after him.' She shuddered. 'I wish I hadn't. I have never been able to get that image out of mind since then.'

Hugo scratched his head. As he lifted his arm, he caught the scent of cigarette smoke and it reminded him of Josef. The craving was growing in his chest. He could feel it. He wanted to hide in his room and listen to his new cassette and light a cigarette. It felt grown-up and exciting, and he knew it was something he could not quit. He was not sure what had changed in his life in the last few days, but he was sure of one thing. There was no going back from it. His eyes snapped wide open, and he was irritated with himself for delving into something so trivial and selfish.

'What did you find?' he blurted out.

Madeline crossed her legs, kicking off a high-heeled shoe. She did not reach forward to pick it up, instead placed her stockinged foot onto the floor.

'Raul Krief and Gerrard Le Mache,' she whispered. 'Tied to a tree, naked as the day they were born. It was dark, but the moon showed me enough of their blood to know they were gone.'

'Except they weren't,' Hugo interjected, 'or at least one of them wasn't.'

She twisted her head in his direction, fixing him with the same look which he knew terrified every maid she had ever had working for her. 'And how was I supposed to know that? They were tied to a tree. What would you have had me do? Run over and check for a pulse? I can assure you, I had no intention of doing such a thing. Especially when I did not know what was happening.'

'Then, what did you do?'

'I retrieved Fou and went home. I had the maid call the police. It was some hours before they came to take my report,' she added.

'Bertram Hervé,' Hugo concluded.

Madeline turned her head, suppressing a smile. 'He told me I had been very brave. *Very brave*, I laughed. It's not like I gave them the kiss of life, or anything. Bertram informed me they were indeed the boys who had been missing for ten days. To my surprise, Raul was still alive, though at that stage they weren't sure he would last the night. I told Bertram there was nothing I could tell him.'

Hugo stared at her. 'What about seeing Serge Levy coming out of the park?'

'Why would I have told him about that?' she countered.

Hugo's eyes widened. 'Because at the very least, he may have seen something, or he may have been a witness, or he may have…' he trailed off, leaving the silence to finish his thought.

'I may not like the Levy family, Hugo,' Madeline shot back, 'but I understand scandal. And I won't tolerate it. I didn't tolerate it when your mother left, or when your father decided being a father was not something he was "cut out for."' She stared at her grandson. 'You can be whoever you choose to be. You can love whoever you choose to love, but par Dieu, I will never forgive you if you scandalise my name.'

'I would never,' Hugo managed to say.

'Don't be so quick to assure me,' she retorted. 'Why are you so concerned about all of this? And give me an answer I will believe, child.'

'Josef seems to like me,' Hugo said, turning his head. 'And I don't know why.' He took a deep breath. 'And the truth is, I'm not used to it. It puzzles me.'

Madeline sighed. 'Oh, dear boy,' she said finally. 'Dear, dear boy.' She stood, grabbing her cane and moved again towards the mantelpiece. She picked up the photograph of her husband, staring at it. She placed it back, her finger trailing slowly across the frame. She mouthed something which Hugo could not hear, but it appeared tender. She turned back. 'I'll call Bertram and tell him to expect you. I will ask him to assist you.'

Hugo's eyes widened. 'I can't go and see him,' he stuttered. 'I just thought you would mention to him about the drugs.'

She shook her head. 'It's out of the question,' she said with determination. 'He cannot come back to this house. I will not tolerate…'

'Scandal,' Hugo muttered at the same time as Madeline.

She smiled. 'He shouldn't have come in the first place, dragging up the past. Mais,' she extended her hands. 'The dirt has been kicked up into the air and it appears that it has disturbed something.'

'What happened afterwards?' Hugo asked. 'There must have been talk, speculation?'

'Are you suggesting I'm a woman prone to listening to gossip?'

Hugo laughed. 'I wouldn't dare. But there must have been some talk.'

'I think everyone just put it down to some pervert,' Madeline replied. 'It didn't help that Raul could not, or would not, talk about what had happened to him and Gerrard.'

Hugo raised an eyebrow. There was something about the way his grandmother said *would not*, which caught his attention.

She continued. 'And he was gone so quickly afterwards, the investigation never really went anywhere.'

Hugo leaned forward. 'Who thought he was holding something back?'

'I never said that,' she retorted quickly.

'Captain Hervé?'

She sighed. 'Bertram always believed Raul remembered more than he was saying. The doctors believed it too, but what could they do? He maintained he did not remember who abducted them.'

'Did he mention where they had been for ten days?'

Madeline sighed. 'I really don't recall. You'll have to ask Bertram about all of that,' she stated. 'It appeared the young boy had very little knowledge of his time in captivity, and therefore there was very little to go on to enable the investigation to progress.'

Hugo considered. It seemed strange to him. Why would Raul Krief not divulge everything he knew or remembered about his attacker and the captivity? There was only one reason Hugo could think of and that was he did it because he was hiding something or protecting someone. He shook the thought from his head. Raul was likely traumatised by the events. He had been around fifteen-years-old, after all. The same age as Hugo was now. Still, Hugo reasoned, if he was in a similar circumstance, he was sure he would remember every little detail.

As if sensing his thoughts, Madeline pointed a finger at him. 'It's easy to walk in someone else's shoes, Hugo, when you don't have to,' she said.

Hugo nodded. 'Bien sûr,' he replied sheepishly.

'But you weren't the only one to come to such a conclusion,' she added. 'And that's probably why they left soon afterwards. To make a new start and forget what had happened, but also to get away from the gossip.'

'Did you ever seen Raul again?'

'Oui,' she replied. 'Twice. Once twenty years ago, soon before he left. He came here with his mother. He thanked me for what I had done. I told him it was nothing, but I told him I was pleased he looked so well.'

'And did he? Look well, that is?' Hugo questioned.

'He looked exactly as you would imagine a fifteen-year-old who had just been through a terrible experience to look,' Madeline snorted. 'He was wearing a suit which didn't fit him, and his hair had been slathered with oil. I remember thinking how sweet he looked as he kept trying to brush down a clump which would not stay in place. His mother did not find it quite so sweet, it seemed, because she slapped his hand away every time he did it.'

Hugo's lips twisted. 'She was angry?'

'Peut être,' she added. 'Or just anxious.' She smiled. 'I don't know if you're aware of this, Hugo, but some people find me a little foreboding,' she added, picking at a stray thread on her jacket.

Hugo suppressed a smile. Still, it confused him. Anxious or not, he found it difficult to conceive why a mother who had just been granted a second chance with her child would be angry over something so petty. He stopped himself from thinking further, realising his own experience with parents rendered his thoughts somewhat redundant.

'You said you'd seen him twice?'

Madeline nodded. 'Oui. A year or so ago at a charity function.'

'And you spoke?'

'Oui. He was perfectly pleasant. Asked how I was, said he had been sorry to hear of Hubert's death and that was that. Neither of us made any reference to the past.'

'And how did he seem?'

She shrugged. 'Old.' She paused, then smiled. 'But now I think about it, he still had the same annoying clump of hair.' She took a breath. 'If only he'd stayed away, he might still be alive.' She looked at Hugo. 'Do you think it could all be connected?'

'Well, I'm not a police officer…'

'Thank goodness,' she interjected, 'terrible profession, and they have the cheek to pay you a pittance for it!'

'Mais, we can't ignore the connection,' he continued. 'Not just the manner of death, but also the fact Raul was involved twice.'

'I never liked the family,' Madeline said. 'Common and "Spanish." No doubt they belonged to some cartel, and it was all drug-related.' She sighed. 'I remember when Paris was a dignified, world-renowned city, not the one which appears besieged by gang-bangers these days.'

Hugo smiled, surprised his grandmother knew such words. Twenty years was a long time between murders, he supposed, especially as it appeared Raul Krief had been back in Paris for some time before his murder. He wondered why he was feeling so involved in the whole affair. Was it just because Josef had asked him to be? Or was it something else? All he knew was his interest had been piqued, and it felt as if he was interested in and involved in something for the first time. Another thought occurred to him. Did Josef know about his father being seen by Madeline twenty years earlier and that was why he was being friendly to Hugo.

'You've drifted away again, boy,' Madeline said wearily. 'You really have to curb your daydreaming. It's very off-putting. How is a person to know if you are using your intelligence, or that you're just bored by their company?' She raised her stick towards the door. 'Go and see Bertram now.'

'What about Serge Levy?' Hugo asked.

'What about him?' she snapped back.

'The fact he was at the scene of the last murder,' Hugo replied. 'You said you never told Captain Hervé about it, but did anyone else?'

She shook her head. 'I don't believe so. He certainly never mentioned it, and I saw him frequently over the coming months,' she added distantly.

Hugo gave her a surprised look. He found it hard to believe or imagine that his grandmother may have had a relationship with the police officer. He cleared his throat. 'Don't you think you should have told him about seeing Serge Levy running from the scene?' She did not answer. 'Well, I'm going to tell him,' he said with determination.

Madeline moved her shoulders in a slow shrug. 'If you think that is the best course of action, then who am I to stop you?'

Hugo waited for her to finish, knowing she still had plenty to say.

'If you are willing to drag a seemingly well respected Rabbi into this sordid mess,' she continued, 'then that is entirely up to you. But no one will thank you for it, least of all your new friend.'

Hugo took a sharp breath. She was right. He did not want to implicate Josef's father in something which he may have nothing to do with. Worst of all, was if he did and he was proven wrong, Josef would likely bear the same stigma Hugo was forced to endure at the school. He closed his eyes. The thought of having someone to share his loneliness and ostracised life was enticing to Hugo, but he knew instantly he could never do it to Josef.

Madeline smiled at him. 'There is an alternative to ease your conscience,' she said. 'Go see Rabbi Levy and tell him what I have told you about that night twenty-years ago and see what he says.'

Hugo frowned. 'What can he say? And why would he speak to me?'

She shrugged again. 'Who knows? All I know is that I cannot get involved any more than I am. My name must be kept out of this. I will not allow the Duchamp name to be dragged into a mess not of our creation.'

'Mais, you did nothing wrong,' Hugo reasoned.

Madeline shook her head. 'People won't see it that way. They'll see that I lied to protect the Levy family.'

'And didn't you?'

Her mouth twitched. 'I did what people of our class do. We close ranks when necessary.'

Hugo shook his head. 'I can't just go up to the Rabbi, and ask him questions,' he said. 'However, I do it he's going to think I'm accusing him of something.'

'That is his problem,' Madeline replied coolly. 'But whatever it is, you'll know if he's lying. You're an observer, Hugo. And you have the eye for detail most people would die for. Bertram had it once, he may still have, though from what I saw recently, it's buried somewhere deep in the weariness of life he carries with him.' She paused. 'Speak to Josef first.' She frowned. 'Because you are correct about one thing - the timing of him befriending you strikes me as odd.'

'Odd? In what way?' Hugo asked.

She shrugged. 'I can't be sure. Ask him. You may be right. I probably shouldn't have remained quiet twenty years ago, but on the off-chance Serge Levy saw something, it appears as if we must intervene before it blows up in our faces.'

'Won't you get into trouble for withholding evidence, if it comes out?'

She cackled. 'From Bertram Hervé? I'd like to see him try!'

She sat next to Hugo again. 'Go see your friend and if necessary, Serge Levy himself.' She smiled. 'Your friend will appreciate you coming to them first. And when you're done, go and see Bertram.'

'And tell him what you saw that night?'

'If the Rabbi gives you his consent, which he will if he has nothing to hide,' Madeline answered. 'Unless, of course, he is foolish enough not to have an alibi for that night.'

Hugo stood and moved towards the door. He stopped and looked back. 'Did you ever talk to Serge Levy about that night?'

'Non,' she answered. 'Our paths crossed from time to time. His father died soon after all of this happened, and he took his place. I was busy with your grandfather, so our paths didn't really cross until some time later.' She paused. 'When we did, we were cordial, obviously.'

'What about his wife?'

Madeline sniffed. 'Anouk Levy is a social climber - nothing more, nothing less. Her breeding is less than satisfactory. Mais, the fact remains, the Levy family have money, social ties and history, and obviously the religious aspect added to it, makes them practically untouchable. Anouk and I serve on the board of directors for several charities, and we have been known to lock horns from time to time. The fact she isn't scared of me would impress me if it were anyone else. But she irritates me and I don't have the patience to be irritated by people, especially when I have to pretend to tolerate them.'

Hugo pulled open the door, still unsure what he was going to do.

'Be careful of Anouk, Hugo,' Madeline warned. 'She has high plans for both of her sons. Plans of her choosing, and she will not tolerate deviating from them.'

'I have no intention of…' Hugo stammered, 'deviating her plans,' he added weakly.

Madeline smiled as she reached for the telephone. 'I will call

Bertram now.'

XVII

'Hugo!' Josef Levy gasped. He had pulled open the front door with such force it bounced against the wall. 'You're… you're… *you*.'

Hugo frowned. 'I guess so,' he answered.

'W…w…what…?'

Hugo smiled. 'What am I doing here?' He stopped, the frown expanded across his face. 'I don't know what I'm doing here, other than I've spoken to my grandmother and…'

Before he had a chance to say anything else, Josef glanced over his shoulder and with a swift movement, grabbed Hugo by the arm and pulled him into the house. He dragged him up a large central staircase with such force and speed Hugo stumbled, trying desperately not to trip over his own feet. They were moving so fast, and Hugo had to concentrate so much on staying vertical, he did not have a chance to take in his surroundings. Josef pushed open a door at the end of a long hallway and shoved Hugo inside a dark room, slamming the door behind them. Hugo narrowed his eyes, trying to acclimate to the sudden lack of light. Josef flicked on a light switch, illuminating the room with a dull light. Hugo took a moment to take in his new surroundings, and he understand instantly where they were. It was Josef's bedroom. Hugo stepped further into the room, stumbling over something on the floor. He looked down and realised he had just stepped on a balled up pair of boxer shorts.

'Oops, sorry about that,' Josef said, grabbing them and throwing them into the corner of the room. 'The maid has started refusing to come into this room,' he laughed nervously, 'finally!'

Hugo threw back his head and laughed, immediately

regretting it, because he was sure it sounded forced and fake, and worse, high-pitched and girly.

'Grab a seat,' Josef said, pointing at something.

Hugo looked around, realising Josef was pointing at a large round bed. Hugo lingered over it and perched himself on the edge. He twisted his legs to steady himself because he was so near the edge.

Josef watched him with interest. 'You want a drink?' he asked. 'I got beers, whisky, vodka, gin, the usual…'

'Non, I'm fine…'

Josef did not listen, instead reached under a table and flicked open the door to a mini-fridge. He extracted two cans of beer and threw one at Hugo. He caught it awkwardly. He stared helplessly at it. Josef laughed again and moved next to him on the bed. He took the can from Hugo and flipped the lid open, spraying them both with beer.

He laughed again and reached to Hugo's chin and wiped the beer away from it. 'Désolé,' he said. He opened his own beer and took a healthy gulp of it.

Hugo looked at his own can and lifted it to his mouth. He took a tentative sip, surprised at the cool amber liquid touching his tongue. It felt strange to him, but as it moved down his throat, it filled him with a warmth he had not felt before. He took a second, longer drink.

'Your first beer?' Josef asked.

'Absolutely not,' Hugo answered.

Josef looked at him doubtfully.

'Well, my first today, at least,' Hugo added.

'Want to listen to some music?'

Hugo shrugged. 'Sure, why not,' he answered like he imagined a cool kid would respond. 'Got any Nitzer Ebb? They're the bomb.'

Josef stood and moved to the stereo in the corner of the

room. 'Yeah, they're "da bomb,"' he replied.

Hugo stared. It seemed as if Josef was mocking him, but he could not detect any malice in his tone. A moment later the music filled the room, and Hugo felt grateful for the pulsating noise coming from the speakers.

Josef sat next to him. He was so close to Hugo their thighs touched. It was all Hugo could do to stop himself from running from the room. He wanted to be back in his own room at Madeline's house, where he would be safe and alone.

'Why are you here?' Josef asked.

'I'm sorry. I shouldn't have come.'

Josef shook his head. 'I didn't mean it like that. I'm glad you're here.'

I'm glad you're here.

'It's just unexpected,' he added.

'I'm on my way to see the police,' Hugo said finally.

Josef's eyes widened, and he spat out his beer. 'Well, I don't know what I was expecting you to say, but it wasn't that!' he laughed.

Hugo laughed loudly again, this time finishing it with a snort. *Stop doing that!* He chastised himself.

'Is this about Gad and Henri?'

Hugo nodded. 'My grandmother has telephoned the officer in charge. I'm not sure what good it'll do, but I can tell him about the drug connection,' he added with a shrug. 'It's worth a try, I suppose.'

'It's worth a try,' Josef repeated slowly. 'Then why are you here?'

'I'm not sure,' Hugo answered, because he was still unsure of it himself. They stopped talking.

Josef's foot moved awkwardly in time with the music. 'It's about Papa, isn't it?'

Hugo turned his head sharply. 'I… I don't know,' he

answered softly.

Josef sipped his beer. 'I heard my parents arguing about it,' he said finally. 'They're always arguing.'

Hugo nodded. 'I know how that feels.'

Josef touched Hugo's arm. 'Yeah, of course you do. Sorry.'

Hugo shrugged. 'Don't be. I'm not.'

'If they're not screaming at each other, they're silent,' Josef continued. 'Sometimes I think the silence is worse than the screaming. I hate a silent house. That's why my music is on all the time, and as loud as it can be. Deafening silences drive me crazy.'

'It depends on the silence,' Hugo whispered, sipping his beer. He stood and moved away. He stopped, realising he did not know where he was going, as it was not his home. He sank back onto the bed, ensuring he left a gap between him and Josef. 'Most of the arguments were about me,' he exhaled. 'And that gets old very quickly,' he added. 'Especially when no one is interested in your opinion, or,' he trailed off, 'you, even.'

'Your Grand Mère loves you, though, doesn't she?'

Hugo laughed. 'Madeline gives me a different kind of silence,' he gave by way of an answer.

'And that's good?' Josef pushed.

Hugo met his gaze. There was something about Josef's golden-brown eyes which rendered him unable and afraid to turn away from. 'It's a riot,' he managed.

It was Josef's turn to cackle. 'You're the weirdest kid, Hugo,' he said, reaching over and touching Hugo's leg again. Hugo recoiled and pulled back. Josef stared at him with evident confusion. 'I didn't mean that as an insult, kid,' he said.

'I'm not a kid,' Hugo snapped in a harsher tone than he meant. 'I'm not much younger than you.'

'Désolé,' Josef retorted. 'I didn't mean to insult you. It was meant as a… as a… nice thing to say. It's just I hate boring and by Dieu, you're anything but boring.'

'You don't even know me.'

Josef touched him again. 'I know you,' he mouthed.

Hugo slapped his hand away. 'You don't know me,' he hissed.

Josef gulped the remainder of his beer, crunching the tin when he finished. He stood and moved to the minibar and pulled out two more cans. He opened them and handed one of them to Hugo.

Hugo took it with obvious reluctance. 'Can we smoke?' he asked.

Josef grinned and ran across the room. He pulled a chair and pushed it across the door. He moved to the window and pushed it open. 'You're a bad influence on me, Hugo.'

Hugo shook his head. 'Non. You're the bad influence on me, *kid*,' he said.

Josef snorted. He lit two cigarettes and handed one of them to Hugo. He sat next to him again. Hugo did not move.

'Does she love you?' Josef asked. 'Madeline, I mean.'

Hugo shrugged. 'I don't know if there are words which exist that could describe Madeline and her emotions,' he answered. 'But it's as close to love as I've ever felt,' he said. 'Apart from Elise, our maid,' he added after a moment. 'She knows I don't like meat, so she does her very best to make sure my meals don't contain any.'

'That's love,' Josef laughed. 'What do you know about my family?'

Hugo shrugged again. 'Not a lot. Only what Madeline told me. Your family own a chain of kosher supermarkets or something?'

Josef nodded. 'Or something. My grandfather wanted some kind of legitimacy brought into the family. He hated the thought of us "just" being rich Jews, especially after what happened to him and his family in the forties. Trouble was, he only had one kid, my Papa - a good businessman, but a lousy religious one.'

'Mais, isn't your father a Rabbi?'

'Oui,' Josef answered. 'Mais, not by choice. He did it because his father forced him to do it. Papa is lazy and boring, and he and Mama have no interest in being poor. So, they had one choice - do what is required of you and you can keep your lifestyle.' He laughed. 'I can't say for sure, but I'm fairly sure my grandfather had it written in his will. There will always be a Rabbi in the Levy family, or else the money will be donated to charity.'

'Madeline said your father was the CEO of your company,' Hugo said.

'He was. Now it's my mother. And then it'll be my brother.'

Hugo sipped his drink. 'What about you?'

'There will always be a Rabbi in the Levy family,' Josef stated monosyllabically.

'Quoi?'

There will always be a Rabbi in the Levy family,' Josef repeated.

'What about your brother?'

'Joann is the golden kid,' Josef spat. 'Or so they seem to believe. In reality, he's a coked-up asshole. My parents know it really, but they've done fuck all to stop it. When it suits him, he can pull himself together and look respectable, so they can wheel him out as the future of the Levy empire. My parents know all they really have to do is appoint someone to oversee the company to satisfy the shareholders.

'And why couldn't that be you?' Hugo countered.

'Because I'm not so good a liar,' he replied.

Hugo scratched his head. 'But a good enough liar to become a Rabbi?'

Josef sighed. 'I'm fifteen. I have time, or not. In the end, it doesn't really matter.'

Hugo stared at him, unsure what he meant. He took a deep drag on the cigarette. He was sorry he had started it, because he was sure he could never stop. He watched Josef smoking, and it bothered him he looked so much cooler. He was dressed in a pair of jeans, holes ripped into the knees and thighs, and a black t-shirt, which also had a hole stretching from his armpit across his chest. Hugo could see his skin was pale and that there was a faint mark of a scar which had already healed.

'So, you're going to see the flics?' Josef asked after a minute had passed.

'You kind of asked me to,' Hugo replied. 'Which makes me wonder…'

'Makes you wonder what?'

'Why you did?' Hugo asked. 'Was it because of something you heard during one of your parent's arguments?'

Josef did not answer.

'Was it?' Hugo pressed.

'She told you, didn't she?' Josef replied. 'That she saw him.'

Hugo nodded. 'Oui.'

'And that's why you came?'

Hugo shrugged. 'I don't know why I came, exactly. But when Madeline told me about your father, what she'd seen, it made me wonder whether that had something to do with why you asked me to get involved. I don't understand why, but that's what I thought.'

'My parents are terrified it's going to come out,' Josef said. 'They don't deal with scandals well.'

'It appears nobody does,' Hugo said, recalling his own experience. 'But what scandal are you talking about?'

'I think you know. I think your grandmother knows. My mother *certainly* knows.'

At that moment, Hugo wished he could be anywhere else. Away from the complexity of family dynamics. He had lived through his own. He did not care to live through another.

'They're worried,' Josef continued, 'that your grandmother will talk.'

Hugo shook his head. 'She didn't then, and she's not about to start now,' he answered.

'Et toi?'

'I do not know what happened twenty years ago,' Hugo said. 'I had thought it would help find Gad and Henri, mais if there is no connection…'

'Bien sûr, there's no connection, Hugo,' Josef hissed. 'Your grandmother caught my father coming out of the park after having a little bit of nighttime… *excitement*.'

Hugo nodded. 'I see.'

'And for what it's worth, I can't say I blame him.'

'He never came forward,' Hugo continued.

'Because he saw nothing,' Josef retorted with an exaggerated shrug. 'He had his fun, and he ran home with his tail between his legs. There was nothing to say, there was nothing to tell. His father would have gone crazy if he'd known. It was for the best.'

'Are those your words?' Hugo asked. Josef did not answer. 'So, why the concern now?' Hugo continued. 'Why are you all so worried Madeline might suddenly tell what she saw twenty years ago?'

'We're not,' Josef answered defiantly. 'My father has always said he won't talk about this again. My mother insists he doesn't. And as far as they're concerned, if anybody accuses my father of anything, he'll just deny it.' He stopped for a moment. 'And then it will just be their word against his.' He smiled. 'My father may not be much of a fighter, but mon Dieu, my mother is. She'll annihilate anyone who threatens her cosy little life.'

Hugo took a breath. "That seems a little extreme. Why would she be so concerned?'

'Because things are different for my family,' Josef said. 'We have more to lose.'

Hugo nodded. 'More to lose,' he repeated. 'Like Gad and Henri, peut être?' He took a deep breath and finished his cigarette, stubbing it out in the overflowing ashtray. 'Or what about Raul

Krief?'

'My father has nothing to do with that,' Josef cried. 'He was here. All evening.'

'With you?'

'With me,' Josef replied, a second too late for Hugo to believe him. 'You can't tell the police about what happened twenty-years ago. You can't. I'm begging you.'

'If your father has nothing to hide, what difference would it make?'

Josef reached over and touched his leg again. 'It would make a difference to me. I thought you were my friend.'

Hugo shook his head. 'You've never spoken a word to me before this week.'

'Because I was afraid.'

'Afraid of what?'

'Just afraid,' came the reply. Josef's fingers trailed across Hugo's leg. 'In the end, I suppose I knew you would like this, and if I did it, then you'd see things my way and you'd understand why I need your help…'

Hugo slapped Josef's hand away with a ferocity which surprised him. Josef pulled his head back in surprise. 'What did I do?'

'What did you do?' Hugo cried. He rubbed his hands across his jeans as if trying to wipe away any lingering presence of Josef. 'You thought… you thought…' he trailed off, unable to finish the sentence. A myriad of thoughts crashed against his skull, and he came to only one instant conclusion. Josef had seen a weakness in Hugo, and he sought to exploit it. A secret Hugo was not even sure he knew.

He stood, knocking the ashtray from the bed, scattering cigarette butts in every direction. 'Putain!' Hugo cried. He dropped to his knees and began scooping them back into the ashtray.

Josef slid to his knees and grabbed Hugo's arm again. 'Leave it. I'll get a dustpan from the kitchen.'

Hugo slapped his hand away. 'Stop touching me!' he hissed.

'What did I do?' Josef wailed. 'I thought things were going well.'

'Going well?' Hugo barked with incredulity. 'You just admitted you thought I wanted you to touch me, so you did it to try to get me on your side and keep your family secret, even though you insist it's not really a secret at all.'

Josef shook his head. 'Shit. That's not what I meant. I didn't mean it that way. I swear, Hugo. I'm not good at saying what I mean. I…'

Hugo jumped to his feet and sprinted towards the door. 'It seems to me you said exactly what you meant to say to get what you want. So, well done. You can tell your father I won't tell the police what Madeline told me. Congratulations, your little plan worked. I hope it was worth it, because you won't get a chance to use me again.'

'Hugo! S'il te plaît!'

Hugo yanked open the door. He turned his head back towards Josef. 'Do me a favour. When we see each other at school, just go back to ignoring me. I much preferred it that way. I don't need you touching me just because you think I'm… because you think I want you to, because dammit, I don't!' He ran towards the staircase, desperate to hold on to the tears until he was far away from the Levy house.

XVIII

'So, we have nothing. *Absolutely* nothing.' Captain Bertram Hervé said, throwing the forensic file onto his desk. 'How on earth is that possible?'

Lieutenant Suzette Carman shrugged. 'Forensics have gone through the park with a fine-tooth comb. The fingertip search found nothing but empty condom wrappers and used needles. There are no witnesses. None at least who are willing or able to talk. There are no working cameras to indicate how or when Raul Krief was brought into the park, and…' she trailed off. 'I can't find anyone who saw Raul Krief in over a week, probably longer. His secretary thought he was abroad, so did his family.'

'And they didn't question not hearing from him?'

'Not really,' Suzette replied. 'Apparently they're used to him disappearing for extended periods of time.'

'But did they know he was going?' Bertram pressed.

Suzette frowned. 'What do you mean?'

'Did he tell them he was going away, or did he just disappear?' he replied. 'Because it could be important.'

'I'll check,' she said. She paused, staring at him. 'Can we talk about what happened twenty years ago?'

Bertram whistled irritably. 'It's obviously a copycat, that's all,' he answered. 'Someone wanted Raul Krief dead, and they thought it would be fun to get rid of him that way because they knew we'd eat it up.'

'We can't just ignore the fact Raul was almost killed the same way twenty years ago,' the Lieutenant interjected.

'We most certainly can,' Bertram shot back. 'If someone wanted him dead, why did they wait so long?'

'Any number of reasons,' she retorted. 'We know Raul has been in and out of the country. The opportunity just may never have presented itself before now. And then there's the possibility the perp has been away, or in prison for some other crime. We can't just ignore the similarities.'

'That's what everyone says,' he grumbled. 'But if you ask me, we're wasting our time.'

'Maybe so,' Suzette replied. 'But it's only a matter of time before the press are going to find the link, and they'll certainly put two and two together and taint the investigation. Especially with the two kids missing, one of which is his son.'

'Parasites,' the Captain muttered. 'Tres bien, Lieutenant. Get me a timeline. Find exactly when and where Raul Krief was last seen, and where he was supposed to be, and maybe then we can try to figure out where he has been before he ended up in the park.'

Suzette rose to her feet. 'And what will you be doing?'

Bertram glanced at the telephone. 'Putting out fires from the past,' he said.

Suzette gave him a quizzical look. 'D'accord. I'll be back soon.' She opened the door to be greeted by Hugo standing in the shadows. 'Are you waiting to speak to Captain Hervé?'

Hugo looked down at his shoes and mumbled. 'Oui.'

Suzette gestured for him to enter, rolled her eyes and moved quickly out of the office.

Bertram stared at Hugo

'Have you been crying, kid?'

Hugo sniffed. 'Non,' he blurted. 'It's cold outside, that's all.'

Bertram wiped a layer of sweat from his forehead. 'It's summer.'

'I meant I have allergies,' Hugo retorted. He shuffled uncomfortably to the busted leather seat opposite Captain Hervé's desk. He had spent almost an hour outside the Commissariat de Police du 7e arrondissement trying to build up the courage to go inside. He still did not understand why he was there, and what Madeleine and Josef wanted of him.

Josef. Even thinking about him made Hugo feel as if he was being stabbed in the guts. The journey to the Commissariat should have taken little more than ten minutes, but each step felt like he was lifting lead boots. He did not know why he felt so desperately sad. Was it because for a moment, he had foolishly imagined his life could be something different? Days filled with laughter, friendship, and companionship? Hugo had concluded that he was used to the feeling of abandonment. It had consumed him for a long time, but he had already made peace with it. Josef had made him feel used, and it bothered him because he had allowed it. He had allowed it to happen. He had allowed himself to dream for a moment.

'Say, you okay, kid?' Captain Hervé asked, his face locked in a helpless frown. 'You need some water or something?'

Hugo shook his head. 'Non, merci. I'm fine.'

Bertram glanced at the telephone. 'I'll admit it was quite the surprise when your grandmother rang. Nothing for twenty years and then suddenly twice in a matter of days.'

'Merci for agreeing to see me,' Hugo said.

'Madeline said you had something to tell me. Something about the missing boys. You go to school with them, I understand?'

Hugo nodded. He cleared his throat. 'I don't know if this has anything to do with their disappearance, but you see, there's a party this coming Saturday. I heard that Gad and Henri, well, they often get "things" for these parties.'

'You mean alcohol?'

Hugo shook his head again.

'You're talking about drugs?' Bertram leaned forward.

'I believe so,' Hugo answered. 'But I can't be sure exactly.'

Bertram nodded. 'Well, that might explain something, but I'm not sure what.' He stared at Hugo. 'You said you heard they got things for these parties. Who exactly did you hear this from?'

Hugo did not want to lie, but he also did not want to talk about Josef, or Maxim even. 'I just overheard some students talking about it at school. I don't know who. I don't really have friends there, but I heard enough to know that they were worried. For obvious reasons, they don't want to come to you, but I thought you should know, and that's why I asked Madeline to get in touch with you.'

Bertram scribbled something on a pad on his desk. Hugo watched him intently, turning his head slightly to try and read it. However, it appeared the Captain's writing was indecipherable. 'Well, this is very helpful, Hugo,' Bertram said, carefully placing his pen on top of the pad. 'And we'll certainly investigate the drug connection. Now, is there anything else?'

Hugo took a breath. 'Madeline told me what happened twenty years ago,' he said.

Bertram sighed.

Hugo studied the Captain. There was something about how he stroked his pencil-thin moustache slowly and deliberately, which confused him. It appeared he was considering how to respond. 'It must have been awful for Madeline, that night,' Hugo said.

Bertram laughed. 'She'd certainly never admit that, mais oui, she was upset.' He stopped, turning his head to the side.

Hugo was surprised. There seemed to be a tenderness to the Captain's tone. A tenderness which he was not used to hearing in discussions which concerned Madeline.

'I know she didn't tell me the whole truth,' Bertram said suddenly. 'Madeline is many things. An expert liar even, but I knew she wasn't being completely honest with me.' He turned to Hugo. 'And that's why you're here, non? To see if what she said, or rather didn't say, was relevant, or could be relevant to the missing boys.'

Hugo continued staring at him, but did not respond.

Bertram laughed. 'I knew from the moment I met Madeline that night that she had seen something else in the park that night, something she felt unable, or unwilling to share with me. It puzzled me because I was not sure whether she was remaining silent to protect someone she knew. In the end, I surmised she was just typical of the sort of people who live in that area. They close ranks to protect one another. I knew she would not tell me what she had seen, but the fact she wouldn't was irrelevant. Her silence told me to look further.'

Hugo nodded. 'And you did?'

'It didn't take me long to work out the person she had seen that night was Serge Levy.'

'How?' Hugo asked.

Bertram winked. 'I'm a detective, Hugo,' he answered. 'I detected.'

Hugo smiled. 'You interviewed the prostitutes who work in the park.'

'Oui,' Bertram replied.

'Mais, not Serge Levy?' Hugo questioned. 'You didn't speak to him?'

'There was no need.'

'There was no need?' Hugo repeated.

Bertram leaned forward. 'You're a kid, Hugo, and you've got a way to go before you have to deal with people. Whatever job you choose, whatever career calls you, it's all the same. You'll deal every day with people in power. People who are paid a lot more than you to do a lot less, and because of that they feel as if it's their right to tell you exactly what you should and should not be doing. I had two in my life back then - my Commander and the Minister of Justice. My Commander was a drunk who wanted a simple life, and the Minister of Justice was a jumped-up man who thought he had to shout louder than anyone else to be heard. I pray you never have to deal with such imbeciles.'

'Me too,' Hugo replied. 'But what does that have to do with what happened twenty years ago?'

'I'm sure I don't need to explain this to you, boy,' Bertram replied. 'Mais rich people attract a certain amount of protection that mere mortals like me don't. When I realised Madeline was keeping something, I also realised she wasn't about to tell me what it is, no matter how much pressure I might put on her. In fact,' he paused, 'I would imagine she'd actually consider it a challenge to see how far I would go just to get her to say absolutely nothing.'

Hugo smiled. He agreed. Madeline Duchamp would see such a challenge as nothing but an amusing waste of her time.

'It didn't take me long,' Bertram continued. He snorted. 'I've been working this beat for a long time, kid, and back then I was a rookie, which meant no one wanted my job. I knew all the hookers who worked the area.' He noticed Hugo was shuffling. 'Don't be embarrassed, kid. It's a fact of life. A business like any other. You'll get used to it.'

'I doubt it,' Hugo grumbled.

Bertram laughed. 'You look exactly like Madeline when you groan,' he said. 'Thank Dieu you don't look like that schmutz of a father of yours, but I'm sure you know that already.'

Hugo met the old Captain's gaze, sharing a conspired look which made him feel grown-up and part of something. He nodded. 'I do.'

'Anyway,' Bertram continued. 'As I said, it didn't take me long to find "Candy."'

'Candy?' Hugo repeated.

'Candy,' Bertram repeated. 'Taller than you. Dark as night, a blonde wig down to her ass and breasts as big as bowling bowls…' he laughed at seeing Hugo's blushing face. 'I'm only glad Madeline hadn't run into her that night. I can barely imagine the exchange which would have followed! But Candy confirmed she had spent a… a "delightful" ten minutes or so in the undergrowth with jeune Monsieur Serge Levy.'

Hugo raised his hands to his cheeks as if he was trying to

push the blush away from them. 'And Candy didn't see anything?'

Bertram shook his head. 'She claimed she was too busy,' he answered. 'But she confirmed she opened the gate at the other side of the park and let in Serge Levy. They went for a "walk" and after they'd finished their "walk," she watched him leave. She hid in the trees because she saw Madeline. Apparently they had encountered each other once before, and Candy had no interest in repeating that experience.' He paused. 'Which surprised me because I once saw the result of Candy beating the shit out of two johns who got fresh with her. It is no understatement to say that both men suffered life changing injuries because of that particular interaction.'

Hugo smiled. 'Then you're saying Serge Levy could not have been involved with what happened to Raul Krief and Gerrard Le Mache?'

The Captain shrugged. 'It certainly appears that way,' he answered. 'Candy certainly gave him something of an alibi, and I accepted it. Mais, it didn't mean he wasn't involved. I would have liked to talk to him, but it wasn't going to happen.'

Hugo nodded. 'You were told not to speak to him.'

'Oui. The Levy family had a lot of clout then. My Commander and the Minister of Justice both told me in no uncertain terms to move on. Levy had an alibi, an alibi no one could know about, but an alibi none the less.'

'And you were satisfied with that?' Hugo asked.

Bertram shrugged. 'I would have been happier to speak to Serge Levy myself. Mais, it was out of my hands.'

'And you've never spoken to him? Not even afterwards?'

Bertram snorted. 'We hardly travel in the same social circles, boy. Et non, I've never seen him since. But to answer your real question. I wasn't scared off by my superiors as much as I was scared of Candy, but I suppose I believed her. And to be honest, there was no real reason to suspect Serge Levy had anything to do with it.' He paused. 'Does that answer all your questions, boy?'

'I guess,' Hugo answered. He took a deep breath, realising he desperately wanted a cigarette. 'I'm not trying to get involved in something, but I just can't shake the feeling there is something wrong.'

'I don't disagree,' Bertram affirmed. 'Twenty years ago, I wasn't allowed to interview Serge Levy. If Madeline had come forward with all her influence, then maybe it could have been different, but she didn't, and it wasn't. And every time I tried, I was ordered not to bother the Levy family.'

'So you spoke to Candy and her friends?'

'Bien sûr. We talked to every pro and every john we could track down. They all claimed they saw nothing. I believed them a little, probably a lot. The truth was, there was nothing to go on. I moved on from Serge Levy because I suppose I didn't want to rock the boat and damage my career before it had started. It was foolish of me, but I was sure enough to be able to sleep at night.'

'And now?' Hugo interjected. 'Do you still believe it was the right decision?'

Bertram sighed. 'There's a lot going on, kid. I have no idea what connection there might be to what happened decades ago. And I can't afford to get bogged down in that. I have a murder investigation and two missing kids to find. I have no time and no staff for two such huge investigations.' He pushed himself back and rose to his feet. 'Merci for the info about the drugs. Let's hope it's all that is going on and that Gad and Henri will turn up soon with their tail between their legs.'

Hugo stood. 'I hope so, too.' He turned away.

Bertram smiled. 'Take care, and say bonjour to Madeline for me.' He paused. 'And remind her of the time in Venice.'

'Venice?' Hugo responded.

He nodded again. 'Venice.'

Hugo moved to the door.

'Keep your ears to the ground, kid,' Bertram called after him.

Hugo shrugged. 'I don't think there's anything I can do,' he said.

'That's what everyone says,' Bertram snapped. 'But it's usually because we've got a lot to lose. You're fifteen, kid. What do you have to lose?'

Hugo zipped up his hoodie. 'Nothing,' he answered, 'as usual.'

XIX

Catherine Krief awoke with a start, her eyes straining to see through the darkness. A slice of daylight peeked through the heavy drapes which covered the windows of her bedroom and told her it was not yet dark. She shook her head irritably, trying to remove the cloud of fogginess which pressed against her skull. She moved her hand awkwardly around the bedside table, searching for a glass of water. She grabbed it, draining it in one long gulp.

She pulled herself up on the bed. Her doctor had given her a sedative after she collapsed, saying she needed to rest. She had protested, but he had insisted. Since then she had been in and out of fitful sleeps - one nightmare after another. The final one, the one which brought her back to consciousness was the nightmare she had hoped would not be true, but it was. Raul was still dead, and Gad was still missing. And she did not know what any of it meant.

She had met Raul when he was still a teenager, and she was six years older. They had grown up only streets apart, but she was not sure she had ever seen him in person. But then, she, like everyone else in Paris, had become fascinated by his story. The sudden disappearance of two fifteen-year-old boys and then the discovery of their bodies - one still alive, but barely. Each evening Catherine and her family watched the news, desperate for an update.

And then he was gone as quickly as he arrived. She remembered seeing the television news reports as they followed him and his family as they left Paris for a new life in Spain. He had only been on camera briefly, but it was all she needed. His face was pale, and he appeared gaunt. His clothes hung limply on his body as if he had recently lost a lot of weight. Catherine had freeze-framed the video on the one shot of his face, the static of the VHS flickering as his eyes seemed to stare right at her. And they said one thing. *Help me.* Her girlfriends had all felt the same. There was something exotic and interesting about the kid who had narrowly escaped a vicious murderer. How had he done it? What had he done to survive? As she watched the plane leave, it saddened her to think she would never get a chance to ask him.

After a while, she had almost forgotten about him. And then one day she had picked up *Le Monde,* and the headline startled her - *teenage survivor of massacre to return to Paris for the funeral of his Grand Mère.* He had only been gone four years, but he had changed immeasurably. She watched him being interviewed. He was shy, but it seemed he had healed in his time in Spain. His skin was darker and his French accent was now tinged with a Spanish lilt. She did not know how, but she knew she had to see the boy who had looked directly at her and asked for her help. In the end, it was not as difficult as she had imagined. She had purposefully been walking back and forth past the house he once lived in, and then it happened. She bumped into him, dropping her shopping onto the ground and falling to her knees. It was that easy. He was extremely apologetic and insisted on taking her home. She had played it cool and when he told her his name; she had acted nonchalantly, as if it meant nothing to her. The surprise and relief was clear on his face and he was obviously delighted she did not appear to know what happened to him.

He asked her out for a pizza to apologise. She had said there was no need, but that she would like to go out with him anyway. In the intervening years she wondered time after time how different all of their lives would have been if it were not for her foolish and selfish behaviour. Raul would have returned to Spain and she would have lived a different life.

But he had not returned. The first date had gone well, the second even better, and without planning, they conceived Gad. She had not intended for it to happen, and the truth be told, she did not even want to marry him, but the decision was out of their hands. Both of their families insisted they be married.

At first it went well. Raul's family was wealthy and provided them with a beautiful home and enough money to start a life together. Catherine was not sure exactly when it all went wrong. Her pregnancy was difficult, and she spent most of it feeling sick and helpless. So, she did not notice that Raul was not coping well with being back in Paris, near the scene of the horrific crime he had barely survived. It had started with night terrors, and then eventually his drinking had become extreme, and he spent more and more time away from her and their home.

She gave birth alone and later discovered at the time he was with one of his many girlfriends. She soon discovered the extent of his bad behaviour, and it had devastated her. She knew he was not a dangerous man, but she also knew he was damaged. Far more damaged than she could have imagined when first seeing him on the television news. They had tried to save their marriage for the sake of Gad, but it was not meant to be. He had left her because he said he had to - informing her he did not know how to be a husband, a father, or a person even. He believed he should have died like his friend and could not forget what happened, or accept that he had been given a second chance.

The door to her bedroom opened and Willum Dukas entered, two drinks in his hand. He handed one to her. She sipped it, the sting of the whiskey warming the back of her throat.

'Did you sleep?' he asked.

'Not really,' she replied. 'Too many thoughts going around my brain.' She finished her drink. 'They are going to find Gad and Henri, aren't they?'

Willum took a drink. 'Bien sûr they are. I spoke to my father, and he's making sure they have all the resources they need and that finding our sons is their ONLY priority.'

Catherine nodded. 'I was thinking. We should tell the police what we know.'

Willum moved quickly to her, grabbing her arm with such force she screamed in pain.

'You're hurting me!' she cried.

He shook her. 'Now, you listen to me, Catherine, and you listen good. You will not under any circumstances speak to the police. You would ruin our sons if you did. Is that what you want?'

She pulled away from him. 'But what if it could make a difference? What if it could help find our boys?'

Willum shook his head dismissively. 'It has nothing to do with their disappearance.'

'How can you say that?' she asked with incredulity. 'It could have *everything* to do with their disappearance.'

Willum moved next to her, his face almost touching hers. Suddenly he reached back, grabbing her by the throat and yanking her upright. He threw her against the wall with such force, it winded her.

'You will not embarrass me or my father,' he hissed through gritted teeth.

'Mais, it could save our sons…' she wailed feebly.

'You will not embarrass me or my father,' he repeated. 'He won't tolerate it, and neither will I.'

'I just want my son back,' she cried.

Willum let go of her and finished his whiskey. 'Be careful what you wish for, Catherine,' he snapped. 'Haven't you already caused enough trouble? This is, after all, all your fault. If Gad and Henri die, it will be down to you, don't forget that. Dragging our names through the dirt to make yourself feel better will not happen. I'll kill you myself, if I have to.'

He moved towards the door. Catherine pulled herself up. 'Willum, don't go. I beg you.'

He turned his head back towards her. 'You really are pathetic, aren't you? Go and get drunk, because it's all you 're good for.'

'Where are you going?'

'I have to find a way to clean up this mess before it gets out of hand,' he shot back.

'Just bring back my son, that's all I ask,' she called after him, 'and you can tell your father, I'll keep my mouth shut.'

XX

Suzette closed the door behind her and stepped into Bertram's office. She threw a folder on his desk. He lifted his head, tired eyes fixing on her with an irritated glare. 'What do the Duchamp's have to do with this investigation?'

Bertram frowned. 'What do you mean?'

Suzette tapped the folder. 'I was going through the original reports from 1975 when Raul Krief and Gerrard Le Mache were kidnapped, and I found some statements. One in particular caught my attention - a hooker called Candy.'

'What are you doing going through old files?' Bertram grumbled.

'My job,' she snapped back.

He pulled the folders away from her. 'Which is, as far I'm aware, what I tell you to do. And I thought I had done that already.'

Suzette nodded. 'Yeah, you did. But I have this insane ability to multitask, especially when I'm investigating two things which are likely connected.'

'*Allegedly* connected,' Bertram corrected.

She pulled her head back as if she was trying to understand what was wrong with him.

He sighed. 'I knew Candy. You didn't. Her word isn't exactly something to be relied upon.'

'I get that,' Suzette replied. 'And her statement doesn't really tell us anything about what happened to those poor kids. But she said something which caught my attention.'

'Et?'

Suzette reached for the files and had to grapple them from him. She extracted one and opened it, extracting two statements.

She placed the first on the desk. 'The last sentence caught my attention.' She pointed. 'Candy stated she had just "finished" with a john and was walking him out of the park when she had to step away because they were about to run into,' she paused, 'and I quote, "an old dame with a yapping little dog." She then states that she went back into the park, leaving her customer chatting to the old dame.'

Bertram shrugged. 'Et?' he repeated.

Suzette frowned and placed the second statement. 'Here is the official statement from Madeline Duchamp. She mentions the fact she was in the park because she was walking her dog.'

'I am well aware of her statement, Lieutenant Carman,' the Captain answered. 'And I cannot see the significance.'

'An old dame walking a dog…' Suzette retorted.

'It's a park,' he shot back. 'I imagine there were many people walking their dog.'

'Really?' she replied. 'At that exact moment? An old dame with a dog?'

Bertram shrugged. 'I don't know what it is you're suggesting, Lieutenant.'

'Then I'm obviously not speaking French,' she snipped. She sighed. 'Cut the crap, Captain. Who did Madeline Duchamp see and why did she keep quiet about it?' She paused. 'And more importantly. Why did you let her?'

'Because it wasn't important,' he answered.

'It wasn't important? Who did she talk to?' Suzette asked with apparent confusion.

'That's irrelevant, Lieutenant.'

'The hell it is,' she cried. 'What are you hiding, Captain Hervé?'

He pushed himself back in his chair. 'I'd be very careful with what you accuse me of, Lieutenant Carman.'

'I'm not accusing you of anything. I'm just merely saying I

don't understand the discrepancy between the statements,' she said. 'At the very least, I believe it should have been explored.'

Bertram sighed. 'Leave this alone, Lieutenant.'

Her eyes widened. 'Is that an order, Captain?'

He did not answer.

'Is that an order, Captain?' she repeated, her voice rising.

'Do you want to rise above the rank of Lieutenant, Suzette?'

'Obviously,' she snapped. 'Is that relevant?'

'Bien sûr, it's relevant,' he retorted. 'Haven't you worked it out yet? Policing is as much about politics as it is using your brain. You need both.'

Suzette shrugged her shoulders dismissively. 'I know that; I'm not stupid.'

Bertram smiled. 'Je sais, mais…' he spread his fingers in front of him.

'Mais, quoi?' she shot back.

'Sometimes we have to know when to step back. Sometimes we have to know which arguments to pick and which to lose. Sometimes we have…'

'Sometimes we have to do our fucking jobs!' she hissed.

He laughed. 'I agree. Tell me, do you trust me, Lieutenant?'

She stared at him hard. 'I don't even know if I like you.'

Bertram threw back his head and laughed. 'I like you, young lady. I like you a lot. And you will go far. If only…' he paused. 'If only you understand the game.'

'The game?' Suzette questioned.

He nodded. 'It's a game we can never win, because the cards are always stacked against us. But we must learn to play it, if we are to survive.'

Suzette ran her hand across her spiky hair. 'I'm a short, dumpy dyke, Captain Bertram. I'd say the cards are already well and truly stacked against me!'

Bertram's eyes widened in surprise, but he did not respond.

After a few moments, he smiled. 'Who knows, those things could actually help you in the long run.' He pushed himself back in his chair and sighed. 'My point is, there are times when things are out of our hands. When investigations are derailed through no fault of our own. To play the game, you have to know when to concede and when not to.'

She frowned. 'I don't understand.'

'The day is coming when I will have to hand in my badge, so I'll give you a little piece of advice. When someone knocks on your door, or rings you on the telephone and tells you to back away from a particular line in your investigation, ask yourself and them two questions. Why and what will happen to me if I don't? Their answer is irrelevant, but it will lead you in one direction. Find out what it is you're supposed to be ignoring and eliminate it from your investigation.'

Suzette frowned. 'What does that even mean?'

Bertram sighed again. 'When they warn you off, don't fight it. Accept it and learn from it. Twenty years ago I was told to ignore a certain field of enquiry.'

'The man who was with Candy?'

He nodded.

'And did you?'

'Bien sûr,' he answered as if was the most obvious thing in the world.

Suzette shook her head. 'You're telling me you deliberately ignored a lead?'

'A dead end, is what I ignored,' he replied. 'Candy was with a client who would rather not be named. A client who had nothing to do with the crime, but someone whose presence would cause problems for everyone involved.'

'You didn't even ask who it was?' she asked with evident incredulity.

Bertram cracked his knuckles. 'I'm not new to this,

Lieutenant. I satisfied myself the Monsieur in question was there only in an *entirely* different capacity.'

'Mais…'

'Mais, rien,' he interrupted. 'This is what I am trying to make you understand. Choose your battles, Carman, or they will choose you, and if that is the case, you might as well quit now.' He took a deep breath. 'All you need to know is that a person of means and influence was in the park the night Gerrard Le Mache and Raul Krief were left to die. But they had been elsewhere for ten days. He was in the wrong place at the wrong time, nothing more.'

'This stinks. He could have seen something,' Suzette reasoned. 'At the very least there should be a statement from him.'

'A statement was taken from someone above our pay grade - way above our pay grade. And that statement is what we have to believe.' He leaned forward. 'Does that make sense to you?'

'It makes no sense to me,' she retorted.

'Then you may wish to consider another occupation, Lieutenant Carman, because this is the way of the world. Now move on, d'accord?'

Suzette did not answer.

'Tell me what you have on Raul Krief,' he said after a time had elapsed.

Suzette opened her mouth to say something, but thought better of it. Instead, she reached inside her jacket and pulled out a notepad. She cleared her throat. 'Raul Krief was born in Paris in 1960. His mother was Spanish, the daughter of a shipping magnate. His father was French, the son of an industrialist. Both families were incredibly wealthy. On September 5th 1975, Raul and his schoolfriend Gerrard Le Mache left school as usual, but they did not return home.'

Bertram closed his eyes. He was immediately transported back. He could see it in his mind's eye, as clear as anything. The sights. The smells. The intrigue. He was young and desperate to secure a career in the police department, and he had seen it as little more than a stepping stone. Had he known this particular steppingstone was going to derail his entire career and personal life, he might well have called in sick that day.

'Despite an extensive search,' Suzette continued. 'There was no trace of Raul and Gerrard.' She paused, steeling a look at the Captain. 'I suspect the case then was much as it is now. Two missing adolescent boys garner much less attention and concern than two girls. It was assumed the boys had merely run off somewhere, or were partying etc. etc. They were found in the Faubourg Saint-Germain park on the 15th September. Discovered by Madame Madeline Duchamp, or rather, her little dog,' she added with a smirk. 'Then she had her maid call the police and…'

Bertram waved his hand angrily. 'I know the rest, you damn fool. I was there!' he hissed. He gestured for her to continue.

Suzette's leg began twitching as she continued. She pressed her elbow on her knee to try to stop it. 'Raul Krief was taken to the local hospital where he was given immediate medical intervention and then eventually rehabilitation, which took some time. Once he recovered, he left for Spain. He was never able to fully cooperate with the police or provide any detailed information regarding his kidnapper, or his ten-day incarceration. The doctors believed he was suffering from a nervous breakdown and was likely never to retrieve the information he had suppressed without intense psychoanalysis which the family refused. They removed him from the hospital and took him to his mother's home in Spain. He returned three years later for a funeral and it was around this time he met and later married Catherine Krief, born Alles and it was shortly afterwards, in 1980 their only child, Gad, was born.'

Her eyes scanned the pages of her notebook. 'The marriage fell apart soon after, but it was on and off for a long time, and they finally divorced last year. And as far as I can tell, Raul has been in and out of one rehab or another for the last decade - drugs, alcohol, gambling, sex addiction, just about anything it seems.' She exhaled. 'He was one messed up kid who was never fixed and became a messed-up adult.'

'Some things cannot be fixed, young femme, no matter how hard we want them to be,' Bertram reasoned. 'What do we know about his last few years?'

'He was the figurehead of the family company,' Suzette replied. 'But no one could actually tell me what he did on a day-to-day basis. He had a young lover, but again she didn't really seem to have any idea of his movements.' She pointed at the notepad. 'All I can tell you with any degree of certainty is that he attended a board meeting on the 22nd of September. He told his secretary he was going away for a few days. She didn't question him because she said it was quite usual and he wouldn't have told her, anyway.'

'And nobody missed him?'

She shook her head. 'He wasn't due to attend a meeting until 10th October, so, non.'

Bertram tapped his chin. 'Then we know he went missing sometime after the 22nd September until he was discovered in Faubourg Saint-Germain park on the 3rd October.' He glanced at the calendar on the wall. 'Which suggests he was missing for at least ten or eleven days before he was discovered.'

Suzette nodded. 'As was the case in 1975. Raul and his friend were missing for ten days.'

Bertram waved his hand dismissively. 'That was a long time ago. Where was Raul for the last ten days? That is the question we need answering.'

'I spoke to his bank,' Suzette answered. 'And there were no withdrawals, or cheques cashed. That's not to say he didn't have some other means. You know what rich folks are like. He could have been off somewhere, but at this stage, we don't have any proof or evidence of where he might have been or how he paid for it. His secretary didn't seem to think he was the sort of man who had friends or acquaintances even, and she couldn't give me any names.'

The Captain nodded. 'And what about his ex-wife?'

'Catherine Krief said she barely spoke to him these days,' Suzette replied. 'And it was hit and miss as to whether he contacted or spent any time with Gad.'

'What about a lawyer?'

'I've put in a call to the firm who represent the family, but they haven't responded yet.'

'And what about his family?'

She shook her head again. 'Both parents dead, and he was an only child. The company is really run by his cousin, Hakim Krief, and as far as I can tell there is no love lost between them. Hakim wants the company, but it was left to Raul. According to the gossip, that gets right up Hakim's ass because he's the one who does all the work, while Raul lives the playboy lifestyle.'

'Ah,' Bertram said. 'I'd hardly say Raul lived his best life from what I've seen, but all the same, the cousin angle sounds like a lead to me.'

Suzette gave him a doubtful look. 'Peut être.'

'Well, it's better than nothing,' Bertram shot back. 'Interview the cousin and anyone else who may have known Raul Krief. There has to be something.' He stopped. 'You said he was rich. Who inherits?'

Suzette shrugged. 'I couldn't say. Until his avocat gets back to me, I won't be sure. But I would imagine whatever he had would pass to his only heir, his son.'

Bertram cocked his head. 'His petit fils, who is also now conveniently missing.' He tapped his chin. 'And then there is Gerrard Le Mache.'

Suzette frowned. 'Gerrard Le Mache. Ah, the other boy who was murdered. What about him?'

'I seem to recall his family was less than happy with Raul,' he replied.

'What on earth for?' Suzette cried. 'For surviving?' she added with incredulity.

Bertram sighed 'Not so much that. It had more to do with the fact he had no recollection of where he and Gerrard had been or what happened to them.'

'The poor kid was traumatised. He almost died,' Suzette reasoned.

The Captain shrugged. 'His family suggested that he was lying, that he may have done it himself.'

She shook her head. 'That's crazy!' She stared at him. 'Isn't it?'

'Dr. Oppert examined him. The pathologists examined him. No one suggested anything untoward to me,' Bertram answered. 'One quack even hypnotised him, but nothing helped. Whatever happened to Raul, it was long gone - buried in some part of his brain he didn't, or couldn't get to again. I saw him. And if you ask me, he was on the level, mais,' he sighed, 'I've been fooled before.'

'Are you suggesting Gerrard Le Mache's family could somehow be involved in what happened yesterday?'

'Je sais pas,' he stated. 'Mais, it's a possibility, non?'

'We keep coming back to the same scenario. Why now, after all this time?' she reasoned.

He pointed to the door. 'All the same, rule out the cousin angle, and see what you can find on the Le Mache family - where they are, what they've been up to, that sort of thing.' He rose to his feet. 'I'm going to École privées de Faubourg Saint-Germain. It seems they may have a drug problem there.'

'You think it's connected?' Suzette asked.

'Everything's always connected in one way or another, Suzette. Au revoir. We'll talk later.'

XXI

Captain Bertram Hervé stopped in front of the huge wrought-iron fence which wrapped around École privées de Faubourg Saint-Germain, and it filled him with the same sense of distaste he always felt when he was there. It was not so much the result of jealousy. He had, after all, grown up in one of the roughest arrondissements in Paris, to a mother of questionable morals and a father who had never found his way to the bottom of a bottle of whisky. Bertram had always believed it was because of the sense of entitlement, which so often came with the privilege of such an upbringing. He would have loved to have had the opportunities such a school might have afforded him. He also knew one thing for certain - he would not have ruined it by imagining for a second he was better than anyone else. He had been a police officer long enough to know wealth and power were nothing when it came down to it. At the end of the day - everyone was the same, driven by the same primitive instincts and desires. Men were brought down by sex or money, or both, no matter who they were, what their name was or how much wealth they had. Bertram also knew, without a doubt, money was no guarantee of happiness.

As was usual, when his mind turned to such matters, he saw her - a beautiful woman, trapped in a loveless, sexless marriage. A woman of means and power in her own right, but born into a time when it meant little. She could be the strength behind a man, so long as it was not seen. It had been the most defining six months in Bertram's life. A mere sprinkle of sand in the timer of his life, but it was enough to define what had come before and what had come after. It was a glimpse into the infinite possibilities which followed when he considered how his life could have been different if only he was born elsewhere and to different, *better* parents.

Those bittersweet six months, twenty years earlier, Bertram had caught a glimpse of what his life could have been, and it had been a brutal and quick education. It ended as quickly as it begun. Whatever his life could have been, it could not suddenly transform into a different sort of life. Madeline Duchamp had known that. She had told him from the beginning. *You cannot be my destiny, any more than I could be yours. We can be ships who traverse in a violent sea, and at the moment they pass, they are in the eye of the storm, in a sea of tranquility. But tranquility is fleeting and passes before you know it. We can be calm, but just for a while, and then we must go back into the storm.* The words had crushed him, but he had never doubted their authenticity. He had glimpsed another life, and it had been enough to sustain him. He hated himself for thinking that way. He had lived a happy enough life, but he was wise enough to know that "happy enough" was not necessarily sufficient to sustain a person.

Bertram's eyes widened. Something had caught his attention in the far west corner behind the gates. A boy appeared to be slumped against the wall, his body contorted, his school jacket twisted around his midriff, his legs flayed around him. Bertram pushed open the gates and hurried into the courtyard, his eyes trained on the student. He could not detect any sign of trauma, and as far as he could tell, the boy was staring into space. He was sure the boy's eye twitched, but Bertram was not sure if it was just wishful thinking. He did not recognise the boy, and it annoyed him, because at that moment he could not even remember what Gad Krief or Henri Dukas looked like, so he had no way of discerning whether this boy could be one of them. *These kids all look the same,* he had muttered to himself while he stared at the photographs on his desk.

Bertram reached the alcove where the student was slumped, and he sunk to his knees, wincing with pain as they cracked against the cobbled stones. He placed two fingers against the boy's neck and took a deep breath. It was there. The pulse was there. It was thready, but it was there. Bertram scrambled to his feet, turning his head back and forth. 'Aide-moi! Aide-moi!' he cried.

Bertram watched as the ambulance sped away. He shook his head. He had held the boy for fifteen minutes, feeling his life force seeping from him. However, the pulse remained, most likely because of his tender age. The pompier had declared his pupils showed it was most likely a drugs overdose. Bertram had let the boy go, leaving him to the experts. And now he was gone, being whisked across the streets of Paris to a hospital, hopefully to save his life.

'Captain Hervé?'

Bertram turned. Directeur Gilles Adnet was standing behind him, his assistant Anna Moire a step behind him.

'Who was the boy?' Bertram asked.

'His name is Maxim Spire,' Anna answered.

Bertram nodded. He turned to the directeur. 'And what can you tell me about him?'

Gilles Adnet's nostrils flared. 'He is a student here,' he sniffed.

The Captain snorted. 'Really? Here was me thinking he was a homeless man who snuck in and stole a student uniform....' He pointed to the road. 'What happened to him?'

The directeur shrugged and said nothing.

'He was a problem kid,' Anna said.

'Mademoiselle Moire!' he hissed. 'Show some decorum, s'il vous plaît.'

'The Mademoiselle has the right idea,' Bertram interjected. 'I'm a police officer and I shouldn't be lied to.'

'Nobody is lying to you, Captain Hervé,' Adnet shot back. 'Merely our clients insist we act professionally and discreetly at all times.'

'Does that include when crimes have been committed?' Bertram replied.

'What crimes?' Adnet asked, his voice rising sharply.

'You tell me.'

Gilles Adnet shrugged his shoulders nonchalantly, but said nothing.

Bertram sighed. 'Tres bien. I have it on very good authority, there is a drug problem here in your school.'

'On good authority?' Adnet snapped. 'On *whose* good authority?'

'That is irrelevant,' Bertram retorted, 'and none of your concern in an ongoing investigation.'

The directeur stared at Bertram. 'Do you know the sort of people you are dealing with, Captain?'

'I am well aware,' Bertram nodded. 'And I could not care less. Two boys are missing. One of their fathers was brutally murdered, and I believe there is a drug connection.'

'And you're basing that on, what? Some gossip and a troubled child?' Gilles Adnet sniffed. 'I hope you know what you are doing, Captain Hervé. The parents of the children who come to this school do not take false accusations well.'

Bertram turned to Anna Moire. 'Mademoiselle Moire. A moment ago you indicated Maxim Spire was a troubled child. What exactly did you mean by that?'

Anna turned her head towards Directeur Adnet. Her cheeks flushed deep red. Bertram thought he had never seen such a pale, thin woman before. Anna tugged anxiously on a wiry strand of ginger hair. She said nothing. Bertram stepped in between her and the directeur. 'I asked you a question, Mademoiselle, and I expect an answer.'

Gilles moved across the pavement, stopping next to the area where Maxim Spire had been discovered. 'École privées de

Faubourg Saint-Germain isn't for everyone, Captain Hervé, especially when their journey here has not been straightforward.'

'What do you mean?' Bertram asked.

'It's not for me to say, or to speak out of turn,' Gilles answered, lowering his voice conspiratorially. 'Mais, the Spire family have only recently gained their wealth.'

'In what way?'

'Import and export,' he replied. 'I believe Monsieur Spire gained some valuable government contracts which turned his company from a small enterprise into a very large one. It is my experience that in such cases, one of the first things parents do is to ensure their social status improves, and that usually involves sending their children to schools such as mine,' he added with pride in his voice.

Anna continued. 'Maxim isn't a bad kid, by all accounts,' she said. 'It's just taking him a little while to acclimate himself to the way we do things here.'

Gilles nodded. 'Our curriculum can be punishing. We are creating the next generation of world leaders, after all, so it has to be. If a student isn't used to it, it can be hard to get a grip of, especially when they come from an overcrowded public school and are academically challenged to begin with…'

Bertram fought the urge to slap the smugness from the directeur's face. He had gone to an overcrowded public school, and as far as he was concerned, it had done him little harm. He stepped past the directeur and stooped, his eyes focusing on something glinting in the sunlight. He reached in his pocket to retrieve a handkerchief and picked it up. Raising it to his nose, he sniffed before wrapping the handkerchief around the foil and placing it back into his coat pocket. 'Drugs,' he said simply. 'Drugs.'

'You don't know that,' Gilles replied rapidly.

Bertram tapped the side of his nose. 'Oh, I most certainly do, Directeur Adnet. I most certainly do.' He shrugged. 'But when I leave here, I will do two things. Un, I will drop it off at the lab and wait for them to confirm it is cocaine and then deux, I will head straight over to the court and get a mandate and then my team and I will turn this school upside-down looking for drugs.' He stopped, staring at the directeur, waiting for his response.

'What do you want?' Gilles asked finally.

'The truth.'

'The truth is, we don't really know,' Anna answered. 'We believe there is a slight drug problem in the school and we also believe Maxim Spire is connected to it…'

'And you base this on what?' Bertram demanded.

Anna turned away from Gilles and faced Bertram. 'I have been here a long time. It would surprise me if there wasn't, mais what I can tell you is that there are several problem students who think they are above the law.'

'Nobody is above the law,' Bertram retorted. 'At least not in my department.'

'Ah-ha! That's what you think' Gilles shot back, wagging a small, fat finger at Bertram. 'You have no proof of anything as far as I am concerned, and certainly so far as the parents of my pupils will be concerned. And as most of them are avocats, they take libel incredibly seriously. If you want to keep your job, I suggest you remember that.'

Bertram moved his shoulders quickly. 'Regardless of my opinion, the fact remains a young man has taken a drug overdose. I'm not suggesting at this point he is selling them, that is a question for when he awakes. In addition, I have it on good authority, Gad Krief and Henri Dukas are also involved with drugs.'

Anna shook her head. 'I just can't see it. They're good boys.'

'Good boys still take drugs,' Bertram replied. 'Or if they're really smart, they sell them.'

'I'm sorry,' she continued. 'I don't believe it. Gad is one of our best students.'

'And Henri?'

'Also one of our best students,' Gilles spoke before Anna had a chance to respond.

Bertram watched her face, and it told him all he needed to know. Henri Dukas was a problem student, it seemed. It did not surprise him. Bertram had met both his father and his grandfather, and he disliked them both immensely. Privileged and spoiled, they made no secret of the fact they thought they were better than anyone else. It was not too much of a stretch to imagine Henri Dukas would have inherited that particular trait. But why then would he risk it all and become involved with drugs? Because he feared nothing, Bertram realised. He knew if he ever got in trouble, his family would swoop around him to protect him. Yet they had not been able to. Whatever had happened to Gad and Henri, their wealth and privilege had not stopped them from being kidnapped, or worse.

'I've met his father and grandfather,' Bertram said. 'And if he's anything like them, I can't imagine him being a talented student.'

Gilles' eyes widened. 'His grandfather is a very important man, as well, you know. You don't rise to the ranks he has without being a good student,' he reasoned.

'Or without a lot of help,' Bertram replied. The rich help the rich. Henri Dukas' grandfather most likely had been bequeathed his position in a deal created before his own birth.

'Henri just lacks focus, that's all,' Anna added. 'Like a lot of boys his age. But he is a good boy, Captain. They both are, really.'

'Then where are they?' Bertram countered.

She shrugged.

'Did they run away? Did they go to buy drugs and something went wrong? Were they lovers?' Bertram pressed. 'There are so many questions we just don't have answers for.'

'Hush your mouth!' Gilles hissed. 'Nothing like that goes on in my school, I can assure you.'

Bertram's fingers covered his mouth, hiding the smile. 'Bien sûr, it doesn't,' he mouthed.

'They have obviously been taken by some madman, or… or….' Anna stopped, seemingly unable to finish the sentence.

'They have now been missing for three days,' Bertram stated. 'And we cannot ignore the fact three days ago, Gad's father was also found murdered.'

'Are you suggesting they're related?' Gilles asked with incredulity.

'Non, évidemment, non,' he replied. 'Mais, there is obviously a connection.'

The directeur shrugged but did not respond.

'Tell me about the drugs,' Bertram pressed. 'Or I will keep my promise and we'll tear the school apart looking for them. We will also interview each and every student. I can't guarantee the press won't catch wind of it and camp outside your rather wonderful gates, and then I'm sure the parents will catch wind of it, and the scandal will no doubt…'

'Directeur Adnet,' Anna interrupted, pressing her hand on Adnet's forearm. 'We don't want that to happen, do we?'

Bertram watched the exchange between the directeur and his secretary with interest. It seemed strange to him, almost bordering on intimate. He supposed that was not so unusual. He knew for certain the Commander at Commissariat de Police du 7e arrondissement was engaged in an affair with his secretary. Bertram lowered his head, realising he himself should be the last person to judge because he had done the exact same thing - once, but once had been enough. And he had vowed never to do it again, not just because of the betrayal of his wife, but because he had allowed himself to believe that for one moment, he could have a different kind of life. The realisation that he could not had troubled him for twenty years.

Gilles stared at Anna before turning to Bertram. 'We routinely search the student lockers.'

Bertram nodded. 'And you found drugs. Where?'

'In several of them,' Anna answered. 'Including Maxim Spire's.'

'And Gad Krief and Henri Dukas?'

She shook her head. 'Non.'

Bertram shrugged. 'Well, if they were dealing, I suppose they wouldn't be so stupid as to leave them in their own lockers.'

Gilles tutted. 'Captain Hervé! I have asked you to stop with this approach of yours. It is unhelpful, and it is most likely slanderous.'

Bertram waved his hand dismissively. 'Tell the bastards to sue me then. Non, I have a murder and two disappearances to investigate. There is no room for pleasantries.' He turned back to Anna. 'You said several of the lockers contained drugs. I'll need names so we can interview the students concerned.' He glanced at Gilles. 'With the utmost of discretion, of course. Tell me, Directeur Adnet, what did you do after you discovered these drugs?'

'We took it very seriously, évidemment. We held a school assembly and hammered home that such behaviour would not be tolerated, and anyone concerned would be expelled immediately from the school.'

Bertram scratched his head. 'But didn't you just say Maxim Spire was one of the boys found to have had drugs in his locker? How come he wasn't expelled?'

'Because, as I said, it was a warning to ALL students,' Gilles answered. 'I didn't see the need to take such extreme steps when reading the students the riot act would suffice…'

Bertram stabbed his finger towards the ground where Maxim Spire had been lying.

The directeur sighed. 'Being the directeur of a school such as this is very rewarding, Captain Hervé, but it also has its own set of unique and very different problems. It's not just a matter of expelling a student. We have to be very sure of what we are doing. One wrong step could be disastrous for me and the school.'

Bertram snorted. 'I'm sure Maxim's parents will take great comfort in that when they see their child in hospital.'

Gilles smiled. 'I may not have expelled Maxim and the other students, but I most certainly spoke to their parents.' He paused. 'They were very grateful for my discretion and assured me that not only would such an event never occur again, they would make sure their child received professional help and counselling.'

'Thus covering your back.'

Gilles shrugged again. 'I did my due diligence, nothing more. It is what is expected of me.'

Bertram stared at the ground. 'And yet here we are and Maxim Spire is now in hospital after a drug overdose, and two of your other students have disappeared after skipping school to buy drugs.' He moved closer to Gilles. 'The pattern is clear, and the danger is evident. If anything has happened, or will happen to those missing boys and we discover there was something you could have done to prevent it, the reputation of your precious school will be the least of your problems. I will personally make sure you are arrested and stand trial. Do I make myself clear?'

Gilles pointed towards the gates. 'I think you'd better go, Captain Hervé. I have nothing more to say to you until I have had the chance to speak to our legal counsel.'

Bertram nodded. 'Tres bien.' He nodded towards Anna Moire and noticed her hand was still on the directeur's arm.

XXII

Lieutenant Suzette Carman moved her head and stepped backwards in order to take in the full proportions of the KRIEF INDUSTRIES building. It was certainly one of the tallest, most impressive skyscrapers she had ever seen. She tried to imagine Raul Krief walking the same steps each day, and she found she could not. She had only seen him in the morgue, and he had seemed so small. So different. She could not explain why, but the building did not appear to match him. She shook the thought from her head and made her way into the building.

'I'm here to see Hakim Krief,' she said to a stern-looking receptionist.

The receptionist stared down her nose at the small, odd looking Lieutenant, the hint of a smug smile appearing on her face. Suzette was used to it. It was the same look every attractive woman gave her.

'Obviously, Monsieur is very busy,' the receptionist said, her voice hard and cold, although she was petite and pretty. 'If you'd like to leave your details, I can have his secretary make an appointment for you, but I would imagine it wouldn't be for some weeks.' Her eyes flicked over Suzette's short, spiked blonde hair, before adding. 'If at all.'

Suzette slapped her ID card on the reception desk with enough force to make the receptionist jump. 'I'm a cop, doll, so be a good girl and call upstairs and tell the boss I want to see him right now, d'accord?'

The receptionist bit her lip as she stared at the card as if she was contemplating what to do. Finally, she picked up the telephone.

'Can I get you un café or un thé?'

Suzette took a moment to study Hakim Krief. As far as she could tell, he shared no similarities with his now deceased cousin. He was much smaller with a dark seemingly Mediterranean skin, jet black hair scraped into a small ponytail. 'Non, merci,' she answered.

Hakim sunk into his chair. 'This is about Raul, right?'

Suzette nodded.

'Awful. Just awful,' he said, clasping his fingers together. He flexed his jaw as if he was unsure what else he could add. 'Awful. Just awful,' he repeated.

'Bien sûr,' Suzette replied. 'The two of you were close?' she asked.

Hakim smiled. It was a practiced smile, one Suzette imagined he used to pacify clients and board members. 'We were cousins, but really, we were more like brothers.'

Before she had a chance to hide it, Hakim witness the surprised look on her face. 'Ah, you've heard different?' he stated, before shrugging. 'It happens. We were rivals, it's fair to say. And we fought, that's also fair to say, but I only ever had his best interests at heart.'

She nodded. 'And what were they?'

'This company takes a lot to run. A lot of time. A lot of patience and a lot of energy,' he replied. 'Raul had none of those things in abundance. I'm sure you know… I'm sure you know what happened to him twenty years ago.'

Suzette nodded.

'It was an awful time for the entire family. I don't think I slept the entire time he was missing. I just kept looking at his bed and when I finally fell asleep each night, I was sure I'd wake up the next morning and he'd be there.'

'You shared a room?' Suzette asked.

'Oui,' he replied. 'My own parents died in a car crash. My aunt and uncle took me in. That's what I meant about Raul and I being more like brothers than cousins. We shared a room for most of our lives, and we were very close.'

'And yet you didn't know where he might have gone?'

Hakim shrugged. 'We were close, but I was two years younger than him. It made a difference when we were younger, because I suppose a fifteen-year-old wants to spend his time with other fifteen-year-olds, not his annoying orphaned cousin.' He added, the bite appearing in his voice. 'But I looked up to him all the same. When he disappeared my heart broke.'

'But he came back.'

'But he came back,' Hakim replied with a tone which suggested he was not necessarily sure it had been a good thing. He stared at Suzette. 'Don't get me wrong, we were all so happy he survived. We really were. But the boy who came back wasn't really Raul.'

'What do you mean?' she questioned.

He considered his response. 'At first he was quiet, and we thought that was bad. But then he was angry, and that was worse. And then he was quiet again. It was an endless cycle of arguments, doctors, shrinks. In the end his parents decided the only chance he had was to get him away from Paris, for a while at least, so they took him to Spain, where my aunt was born.'

Suzette nodded. 'But you stayed in Paris?'

'Oui,' he replied. 'With my grandparents. There were only the two of us, you see. Raul and I. The next generation of Krief's. I think they wanted to make sure that if anything happened to Raul… if he could not take over the reins, that I would be able to instead. Raul came back when our grandmother died, and it was my grandfather's wish that both of us work together to run the company. He died soon afterwards too, and I suppose Raul wanted to honour his wishes.'

'And did you? Work together, that is?'

Hakim's lips pulled into an irritated smile. 'Well, we tried.'

'But it didn't work?'

He clenched his fists. 'I don't want to speak ill of him, truly I don't,' he answered. 'But he was a pain. It was like when he came back the first time - he was up, he was down. He was angry one day, happy the next. Shrinks tried to help him and he stuck with them for a while and then convinced them and himself he was better, but he never was.' He stood and moved to the window. 'Raul was still fifteen. He was always fifteen. He never grew up, or out of it, I think. It was awful to see. And oui, we fought. I said things I shouldn't have, and he certainly did too. He didn't want to be here, but he felt as if he had no choice because he had promised our grandparents and his parents that he would.'

He moved back across the room, pressing his body against the desk. He was so close to Suzette she could smell his cologne. She did not know what it was, other than it smelled expensive. She had to fight the urge to move away, or say something about how she was always surprised by the fact men seemed to have no boundaries.

'So,' he continued, 'I'm guessing you've heard talk about the two of us, haven't you?' he asked. 'The fights, the punch-ups?' He paused. 'Well, that's only half the story. There were just as many make ups as there were break ups. I loved my cousin, and I hated him too.'

'And Raul?'

He gave her a sad smile. 'He didn't love anyone. Not me. Not himself. Not his wife, not even his kid. It was as if that part of him had been cut out of him that night he was tied to the tree. He was always at war, but it was usually with himself.'

Suzette took a moment to appraise Hakim. He certainly seemed to be on the level, but there was something about him - something which she could not quite explain. And in the end, it had been her experience when it came down to it, money was the biggest motivation for anyone. 'Who actually owns the company?' she asked.

Hakim moved back around his desk and sat down. 'We are a public company,' he replied. 'But the Krief family has the majority of shares. We own sixty percent.'

'We?' she questioned. 'Who is the we?'

'Raul and I.'

Suzette pursed her lips. 'I imagine that's a whole lot of something.'

He shrugged. 'The company does very well, oui.'

'And who gets Raul's share now he's dead? His son?'

Hakim stared at her. 'Let me tell you about Raul. He came into the office when he feels like it. Sometimes when he was sober, most often when he wasn't. He'd attend the board meetings when he could be bothered, most often he couldn't. Even when he did, he was disruptive and unhelpful. My grandfather wanted Raul to run the company, but he wasn't stupid. He didn't trust Raul to have our best interests at heart. It was written into his will that Raul and I would run the company together. I would be joint CEO, so ultimately I would be in charge. It was also stipulated that in the event of the death of one of us, the shares would revert to the other.'

Suzette's eyes widened. 'So, as of this week, you own sixty percent of this whole shebang?'

He nodded.

'And not his son?'

Hakim grimaced. 'Raul never mentioned his son, or expressed any interest in bringing him into the company.' He raised his hand. 'I know what your police detective brain must be thinking, but let me disabuse you of it right away. I am very close to my nephew, and it has been my intention to bring him into the company - to teach him so that one day he can take over from me.'

'I see,' Suzette replied. 'And about your nephew. What do you think has happened to him?'

'Nothing, I hope,' he retorted. 'I hope he and his buddy are crashed out at a party somewhere and that they'll sober up soon and realise what a mess they've made.'

Suzette frowned. 'And you don't see any connection between your cousin's death and the manner of the boys' disappearance?'

'Not really,' he answered. 'Raul was obsessed with that sort of thing, not me.'

She leaned forward in her chair. 'What do you mean, he was obsessed with that sort of thing?'

Hakim sighed. 'He was convinced the same thing that happened to him, would one day happen to Gad. He said it was his fault, because he had escaped. He said the devil would come back for a second try.'

'The devil?'

He nodded. 'My cousin was fucked up, Lieutenant. A lot of what he said made no sense.'

Suzette tilted her head. 'If Raul was so worried about his son, why didn't he do anything to protect him? Like move him out of Paris, for a start.'

'I can't answer that. All I can tell you is, he didn't really know how to be a father, because I guess he was still a kid himself. He left Gad to Catherine, and that was that. He said she should never have gotten pregnant.' He paused. 'I'm pretty sure he said that to Gad too.' He stared at Suzette. 'Ecouté. I know I must be your primary suspect. I also know you must have heard some horror stories about me and my relationship with my cousin. You'll probably hear a lot more if you keep digging. There's only one thing I can tell you for certain, and you can choose to believe it or not, but if I wanted my cousin dead just so I could have a company I'd probably end up with anyway, I wouldn't have done it this way.'

She stared at him. 'And how would you have done it?'

He leaned forward. 'In a way I'd never get caught.'

Suzette nodded. She felt the hairs on the back of her neck stand on end, but she did not want to let him see she was rattled. 'Is there anything else you can tell me about your cousin?'

Hakim shook his head. 'I'm sorry he's dead, but really, he always has been.'

She looked at him in surprise.

'I'm sorry to sound harsh,' Hakim said. 'Especially now he's dead, but I have to be honest, it's a bit of a relief. No more constant fights. I told him time after time he didn't need to be at *Krief Industries* if he didn't want to. He was never happy here, but he felt as if he should be. It was a difficult situation for us all. I feel sorry for Gad, but I'll do what I can for him. Raul was never much of a father to him, but I will try to be something close.'

'With your cousin out of the way, I'm guessing that it will make your life a bit easier, non?' Suzette posed.

Hakim smiled. 'Yeah, you're right. Having to run things past him was a bore. Not because he wasn't interested, but because he just enjoyed rattling my cage. If he'd been interested in what we do here, then I wouldn't have minded so much, because at least it would be productive. He argued for arguing sake, that's all. I offered to buy him out once and he just said, *what else would I do? Sometimes coming here is all I have to do.*' He paused. 'So, if you're asking in your roundabout way, did I have a motive to get rid of my cousin, then the answer is oui. Did I do it?' He shook his head. 'I had about sixty million reasons to kill my cousin, but I didn't.'

Suzette studied his face, and she realised she could not tell if he was telling the truth. His dark face was smooth and impassive.

Hakim rose to his feet once more. 'Now, if that's all, I have a lot to do today. As I'm sure you can understand, Raul's death has thrown rather a big spanner into *Krief Industries*. Au revoir, Lieutenant.'

Suzette rose and placed her card on the desk. 'If you think of anything else, about your cousin, or where his son might be, call me.'

Hakim picked up the card, his eyes narrowing as he scanned it. 'Sure,' he agreed nonchalantly.

XXIII

Hugo pressed his hands against both sides of the headphones, as if he was trying to push the sound into his brain. He realised he was in danger of wearing the Nitzer Ebb tape out because he had been listening to it non-stop since he bought it. He had fallen asleep listening to it and woken when the tape ended. He had simply turned it over and started again. It was not his usual type of music, but the range from hard rock, to angry pop, to simple, almost tender songs had spoken to him. It was not just because he imagined Josef would be listening to it too, rather the songs made him feel less alone, less of an outsider.

He had decided against going to school, and it was the first time he had missed a day in a long time. He was not even sure why he could not face going, though he had his suspicions. The prospect of facing Josef Levy was too much for him. It was not just because he felt used, but more because he had allowed Josef to use him. No, he would face the world tomorrow. Today he would stay in the darkness of his bedroom and listen to his music. He closed his eyes and allowed himself to drift away.

Hugo did not know how long he had been sleeping, other than the tape had stopped playing again. His eyes snapped open, widening in horror as he saw Josef's face leaning over, inches away from his own. Hugo shook his head and closed his eyes, trying to rid himself of the dream. He opened his eyes again, but Josef was still there, golden brown eyes twinkling mischievously at him, full lips pulled into a grin. Hugo's eyes locked onto the birthmark on his neck, and it was all he could do to stop himself from reaching out and touching it. He pulled himself up in the bed, slapping the headphones from his head. The Walkman clattered to the floor, hitting the play button. Seconds later the sounds of Nitzer Ebb reverberating around the room.

'You really like the Ebb, too, don't you?' Josef asked.

'What are you doing here?' Hugo asked breathlessly. Josef was so close to him he could smell the soap on his skin.

'Elise let me in,' Josef answered, dropping onto the bed next to Hugo. 'She thinks the world of you, too, by the way,' he added. 'We're both *quite* the fan.'

She thinks the world of you, TOO. The words were not lost on Hugo and he was again reminded that he was a big fat loser who was ridiculous.

Josef moved closer to Hugo. 'Listen, I don't like how things ended the other day between us, and I just wanted you to know, I forgive you.'

'You…forgive…me?' Hugo responded with biting incredulity.

'Sure,' Josef retorted. 'You didn't mean to hurt my feelings, I get that. So, we'll say no more about it, okay?'

'Say…no…more…' Hugo spluttered.

Josef laughed. 'You gotta take a breath, Hugo,' he said, touching his leg.

Hugo slapped away his hand.

'Now what do you want to go and do that for?' Josef asked. 'I just said, I'd forgiven you.'

Hugo extracted himself from the bed and made his way across the room. He stopped at the far wall, wishing he could push through to escape the confines of his attic room. He wanted to be anywhere but where he was right now. 'What are you doing here?' he managed to ask.

'You weren't at school,' Josef answered matter-of-factly.

'Et?' Hugo snapped. 'I thought we'd agreed we were never

friends, so we just go back to ignoring each other. Me not being at school is none of your business.'

'Hugo,' Josef sighed. He began making his way towards him again, but upon seeing the horror on Hugo's face, changed his mind. He held his hands up. 'D'accord, I'll keep my distance.' He paused before adding with a wink. 'For now.' He sank back onto Hugo's bed, picking up Hugo's pillow and holding it to his chest. Hugo watched him and knew he would throw the pillow away once Josef left and then most likely retrieve it from the bin ten minutes later.

'I never agreed to anything,' Josef said. 'You dumped me, that's what happened.'

'I didn't…' Hugo found himself unable to finish the sentence. 'We're not friends, Josef,' he said desperately.

Josef smiled.

Hugo noticed his smile was perfect. He covered his own mouth.

'You're right, we're not friends,' Josef confirmed. 'We are more,' he added, speaking the words slowly.

'Will you just stop,' Hugo whispered.

Josef laughed. 'Jamais.'

'Why are you here?' Hugo cried desperately. What he wanted to say was: *Please leave. We can't be in the same room.*

'Why are any of us really here, H?' Josef countered. 'Isn't that the question we really oughta be asking?'

Hugo rolled his eyes.

'You have beautiful eyes, H,' Josef said. 'They're like so green, it's weird, but weird in a good way. A sexy way,' he added.

'Josef, arrêt!' Hugo cried.

Josef stared at him. 'Jamais.'

They both fell silent. Hugo was sure he could hear someone moving around outside the door and it terrified him. It was almost as if someone was listening in, ready to judge and comment.

'School was weird today,' Josef said finally. The tone of his voice was contrite.

'In what way?' Hugo asked, happy to have a change of topic.

'Maxim got bored, it seems,' Josef stated, before flashing Hugo a sad smile. 'More bored than usual, anyway.'

Hugo frowned. 'What are you saying?'

'He took too many drugs.'

Hugo gasped. 'He's dead?'

Josef shrugged. 'Dunno. I thought you'd come with me to the hospital to see.'

Hugo's frown deepened. 'Why would you think that?'

'Cos.'

'Cos?' Hugo shook his head, realising Josef was not about to become any more forthcoming. He studied Josef's face and at that moment he appeared to Hugo to be very young and fragile. It reminded him of his own reflection every time he looked in the mirror.

'Well, will you come with me?' Josef questioned.

Hugo shrugged. 'Why?'

'Because he has no one. He has a family who care fuck all about him.' He pointed at Hugo. 'I know how that feels, and I figured you would, too. I care about him. I care about you. Do *you* care about *us*?'

Hugo found himself unable to look at Josef.

'Come with me to the hospital,' Josef said finally.

Hugo did not respond because he could not.

'He has no one and he could die,' Josef said.

'I'll get my coat.'

Josef smiled. 'I bet you will.'

Hugo's eyebrows knotted. 'What does that even mean?'

Josef shrugged. 'It means whatever you want it to mean.'

Hugo grabbed his coat. He shook his head. 'And I thought *I* was weird,' he mouthed to himself.

Hugo stared at Maxim in the hospital bed. Pale and thin, with a gruesome-looking tube stuck in his mouth. His eyes were closed and the way in which his chest rose and fell appeared forced to Hugo. He had seen no one he knew in a hospital bed before. He wondered if it was just like sleeping, or whether Maxim was aware of his surroundings but just too weak to do anything about it. Josef was standing next to Hugo, both of their hands by their sides, close enough that Hugo could feel the warmth of Josef's skin. It felt as if there was an electric charge between them. Hugo was scared and despite himself, when Josef's little finger touched his, he did not pull away.

'What a waste,' Josef whispered.

'He's not dead,' Hugo responded.

'But he might die. He *could* have died,' Josef replied. 'What a stupid, fucking waste.'

Hugo frowned. 'Do you think it was deliberate?'

Josef twisted his head. 'You mean he tried to kill himself?'

Hugo shrugged. 'I don't know him, you do.'

'I don't know him, not really, we just mes…' he stopped. 'We just hung out sometimes.'

Hugo stared at Josef, wondering what he had been about to say, and more importantly, why it bothered him so much. 'Did he say anything to you?'

Josef shook his head. 'Not really. He was pretty freaked out about Gad and Henri going missing, but we all are really.'

'Was he close to them?'

'Dunno,' Josef replied. 'We all hang out together sometimes. Gad and Henri are a little extreme for me, but I think Maxim liked that.'

'Extreme?'

'Yeah. They don't take life too seriously, because they have no one to answer to,' Josef added with a trace of bitterness to his tone. 'It's alright for some, but you know all about that. It must be great not to have someone watching your every move.'

Hugo did not answer immediately. 'At least if someone is watching you, it shows they care.'

'Non, it doesn't,' Josef snapped. 'It means they're watching you because they're convinced you're gonna screw up. You get to live your life your own way, don't you? You deserve it, but I'm so jealous.'

Hugo did not say what he felt. *I live my life my own way because I have no choice. No one wants me.* He could not imagine for a second why anyone would feel jealous about that.

'It must be cool to be you,' Josef added.

Hugo snorted. 'Well, that's certainly the first time anyone said that.'

Josef moved back to where Hugo was standing, dropping his hand again. This time there was no gap between them, and the back of their hands touched.

'What about Maxim's family?'

Josef shrugged. 'Same old story - too rich and too busy to care.'

Hugo glanced around, noticing they were the only ones in the corridor and that there was no one in the room with Maxim. 'Where do you think he got the drugs from?'

'I don't know,' Josef answered. 'Like we said, Gad and Henri took care of that. Maxim probably had some left and just didn't realise he'd taken too much.'

Hugo gave him a doubtful look. 'You said earlier you and Maxim are close.'

'Hugo…' Josef cried wearily. 'That has nothing to do with this.'

Hugo shook his head. 'It might… it might if he thought there was… more to it.'

Josef threw back his head and laughed. 'Trust me. Whatever's going on with Maxim, that's *definitely* not it.' He turned to Hugo, lowering his voice. 'Listen, we fooled around a little. That's it. I'm not his type, and he's most certainly not mine.'

'Who is?'

Josef's eyes widened. 'How can you be so perfect, and yet so slow to take a hint?'

Hugo turned his head, hoping Josef would not see him blush. 'I meant Maxim,' he spluttered.

Josef laughed again. 'Sure you did.' He turned back, pressing his nose against the window into Maxim's room. 'For Maxim I was nothing but something to do, to relieve the boredom. And that's okay, because that's all he was to me. This was no love story, believe me.'

'Was there anyone else?' Hugo asked. 'For Maxim?' he clarified.

Josef shrugged. 'There were a couple of girls he hooked up with sometimes, but again, I don't think it was anything serious. He just isn't the type. I can't say I was his best friend, or that we shared any "secrets" but I think I hung around him enough to know that he wasn't the sort of dude who got bogged down by things. Not love affairs, not life, not school.'

'Then it's just a simple drug overdose?'

'There's nothing simple about a drug overdose, Hugo,' Josef responded.

'But it wasn't his first time taking drugs?'

Josef snorted. 'Not by a long way. Listen, don't get me wrong, Maxim isn't a junkie, but he is a user.'

'Is he addicted?'

'What does that even mean?' Josef retorted. 'If you're asking, does he shoot up? Then, non, I don't think so. Does he smoke a lot of weed? Yeah, probably a few times a day. Harder stuff? A bit of coke, a bit of E, the usual. Is that what you want to know?' he snapped.

'Why are you angry at me?' Hugo asked, bewildered.

Josef stared at him. 'I don't know. Damn you, I don't know.'

Hugo's eyebrows knotted. He pushed his hand through his long blond hair; it fell straight back across his face.

'Stop doing that,' Josef said desperately.

'Pourquoi?' Hugo asked.

'You know why.'

'Obviously, I don't, or I wouldn't have asked.'

Josef pulled back, touching Hugo's arm. 'You really are that perfect, aren't you? You do not know what you do to people.'

'Will you stop saying things like that? It's weird and I don't know how to respond,' Hugo said.

'Pourquoi?' It was Josef's turn to ask.

'Because it's not true, and it's just…'

'Perfect?' Josef asked.

'I… can't be who you want me to be,' Hugo stated. 'I'm not who you want me to be.'

Josef smiled. 'You're you. That's all I want you to be. I knew from the second I saw you, exactly one year ago. You walked past me in the corridor - backpack casually thrown across your shoulder, your hands stuffed in the pockets of your trousers. Blond hair falling over your face. You tucked it behind your ears, it fell again and you gave up. I saw your eyes, the greenest I'd ever seen, but this time they looked irritated, like you were hoping no one had noticed you. I think you wear green because you think it makes you blend into the background, but it doesn't help. Nothing helps. You can't be in the background, as much as you might want to be. You are the foreground. You will *always* be the foreground.'

Hugo gulped, swallowing whatever feeling was spreading through his body.

'Et moi?' Josef asked. 'When did you first notice me? Because I'm pretty sure you <u>never</u> noticed me.'

Hugo turned his head. 'Do you know the last time I spoke to my mother or my father?'

Josef shook his head.

'Me neither,' Hugo answered. 'And because of that, I tend not to notice anyone. People leave. My grandmother took me in because it was the best thing for the Duchamp name. But she will leave me, one way or another, and then I'll be alone again. I like my maid, Elise. She's kind to me. But she has the hots for the chauffeur. One day they'll drive off together and she'll leave.' He stared at Josef. 'I don't pay attention to people because I know they're going to leave sooner or later.'

Josef shrugged. 'So what?'

'What do you mean?'

'Don't use it as an excuse to live a lonely life, that's what I mean,' Josef responded. 'What does it matter if everyone leaves? That's life. People live. People die. What are we supposed to do? Not love each other because *eventually* we'll break each other's hearts in one way or another?' He paused. 'Listen, I get it. People keep breaking your heart. As I said, so what? Enjoy the time before they do.' He pointed at Maxim in the bed. 'He may never wake up and imagine if that's his life. Is that what you want for you? A life missed?'

Hugo too stared at Maxim. 'It seems as if he's already lived much more of a life than I have.'

Josef sighed. He took Hugo's hand in his. 'D'accord. I get it. I have to be direct with you. I thought we could be discreet, for both of our sakes, but I see that will not happen anytime soon.' He moved his head around the corridor to satisfy himself they were still alone. 'I kissed Maxim at parties when we were both wasted. I held him in my hands, because we were both wasted. But every time I did, I imagined it was you. I *desperately* wanted it to be you. Maxim didn't care either way. It could have been anyone. Most nights, it WAS anyone.' He squeezed Hugo's hand. 'I don't want this life. I really don't. Not because of my feelings, but because of what those feelings will mean for me. But I have to know. Do you know what I am talking about?'

Hugo trailed his finger across Josef's hand. 'Let's go for a cigarette,' he said.

'That's all you have to say?' Josef asked with incredulity.

Hugo shrugged. 'It's enough, non?'

Josef smiled. 'You have no idea of your power, do you?'

Hugo pressed his hands around his biceps, his fingers perfectly wrapping around them.

Josef laughed. 'D'accord. Let's smoke. We'll have to find a shop because I don't have any.'

'I bought my own,' said Hugo.

'Oh, you rebel,' Josef countered. 'Did you buy them at the same time as the *Nitzer Ebb* cassette?'

'Maybe a lover gave them to me,' Hugo said, with as much conviction as he could manage.

Josef snorted. 'Words I never thought I would hear coming from you, Hugo Duchamp!'

Hugo lowered his head. 'You're a bad influence on me.'

Josef grabbed his hand. 'Oh, I don't think so. You're the one who is the bad influence on me.' He pulled Hugo towards the exit. 'I can't begin to imagine the sort of trouble you're going to get me into, but I can't wait to find out.'

XXIV

Dr. Jaques Oppert threw a dossier onto Bertram Hervé's desk. Bertram was pleased to note the pathologist was not wearing his usual bloody apron, rather an equally stained suit. He assumed the stains were food, not some biological matter. 'What's this?' he asked.

'I was passing the lab and picked up the results from the blood I extracted from Raul Krief,' the doctor replied.

Bertram nodded. 'Bon. Et?'

'He had drugs in his system.'

'I would assume so,' Bertram sniffed, 'in one way or another.'

'Peut être,' Oppert replied. 'But that's not what makes it interesting.'

'Then what does?' Bertram sighed.

'The hospital noticed a similarity in the toxicity with another blood sample they examined at the same time.'

Bertram raised an eyebrow. 'Vraiment?'

'Oui,' he responded.

Bertram sighed. 'Jaques. We're old. Don't keep me in suspense. Neither of us can cope with such a luxury. What's the scoop?'

Oppert laughed. 'I have no idea what you're saying, but what I can tell you is, the same drug compound was found in two cases they were working on.'

Bertram nodded. 'Sounds promising,' he said.

'What kind of drug?' Suzette asked from the corner of the room.

Oppert turned around. 'Oh, I didn't see you there, Lieutenant,' he said.

She pursed her lips. 'You never do, I'm a woman.'

Oppert ignored her, instead turning back to Bertram. 'It was diazepam, or Valium as it's more commonly known.'

'The stress reliever?' Bertram questioned.

'It's more than that,' Suzette said. She stood and walked across the office. 'It was designed for stress relief, oui, but also for treating anxiety, seizures, those sorts of things. It's also highly addictive and in high enough doses gives the taker a sense of euphoria.'

Bertram looked at Oppert. 'Isn't it prescription only?'

Oppert nodded. 'Oui. Not that it really matters. There's quite a black market for it.'

Bertram scratched his head. 'So why was Raul taking diazepam?'

'I checked his medical records, he was prescribed it,' Oppert answered, 'but according to his doctor he was only to use it in extreme circumstances. Seems he had a bit of a problem with it at one point. He hadn't filled a prescription in some time, so his doctor wasn't unduly worried.'

'Hmm,' Bertram pondered. 'Then peut être he got his fix elsewhere.'

'Or the perp could have given it to him,' Suzette reasoned. 'If he knew what he was doing, diazepam would make Raul pliable, docile, and easy to control. He may not even have been aware of his surroundings.'

Bertram lifted his head. 'Jaques, you said they found the drug with the same chemical compound in another sample they were testing.'

'That's correct,' Oppert replied. 'A student from École privées de Faubourg Saint-Germain.'

Bertram's eyes widened. 'You're talking about Maxim Spire?'

'How the hell did you know that?'

'Because I'm the one who found him, that's how.' He stood,

pacing across his office. 'What does this mean?'

'It means the tip-off about Gad Krief and Henri Dukas going off somewhere to buy drugs isn't so far-fetched,' Suzette stated.

Bertram looked at her. 'Do you think Gad could have been getting drugs for his father?'

She nodded. 'It seems possible.'

'None of this really helps with finding those kids, or how Raul Krief ended up tied to a tree.'

'I've put some feelers out with the drug squad,' Suzette said. 'Now we have the diazepam angle, it might help narrow down dealers who specialise in it.'

'Is that likely?' Oppert asked.

'Sure,' Suzette responded. 'Most dealers specialise in what they can get easily. Diazepam is unusual and I would imagine hard to get, unless you have a source, a contact who can get them.'

'These drugs are highly regulated,' Oppert said dismissively.

'That's never stopped scum from getting them onto the streets before,' Bertram shot back. He sat back down. 'Still, we have a link. It might be tenuous, but it's a link nonetheless. It gives us somewhere to start, because I'm getting it from all angles - the boss, the press, the goddamn government,' he added with disdain. 'And all I can tell them, all I can keep telling them, is that we have nothing. We have nothing. How is that even possible?' he shouted.

Suzette shrugged. 'Paris is a big place and we have absolutely nothing to go on. We don't even know for certain when Gad and Henri disappeared. If there'd been a ransom, we'd at least know what we're dealing with.'

'There was never a ransom in the original abduction,' Oppert interjected.

Bertram snorted. 'And look how that ended up.' He pointed at them both. 'This can't end the same way.'

'Bien sûr,' Suzette agreed. 'But as you said, we don't have a lot to go on.'

'How's the kid?' Bertram asked Oppert.

Oppert shrugged. 'He had a lot of drugs in his system, so it's hard to say. He's young, so that's in his favour. But he took a lot of drugs, deliberately or otherwise isn't really important at the moment.'

'The hell it is,' Bertram hissed. 'I want him to wake up so he can tell me where the hell he got them from. That stupid kid lying in the hospital could be the link to solving both of our cases.'

Oppert extended his hands. 'Don't hold your breath, old friend,' he said. 'It'll likely be days, weeks before you get a chance to ask le pauvre garçon where he purchased his drug of choice.'

Suzette interrupted. 'What if someone else gave him the drugs?'

'What do you mean?' Bertram shot back.

She shrugged. 'Je ne sais pas, mais…' she paused. 'Let's try to imagine a scenario. Maxim Spire knew where Gad and Henri got their drugs. The same drugs they'd been giving to Gad's father. The dealer got spooked, and decided to get rid of the witnesses. If he's touting hard drugs that are hard to get, he's probably got a lot to lose.' She paused. 'I don't understand how that fits in with Gad and Henri being missing, nor Raul's murder, but you're right, there's probably a connection.'

'A rather fanciful connection, Lieutenant,' Oppert said.

Bertram laughed. 'Fanciful I can deal with, as long as I can sell it.' He smiled at Suzette. 'And maybe we can sell it.' He nodded. 'Oui. Drug dealer kidnaps the kids, kills the father, and tries killing the students. Neat and tidy and he gets to go off and peddle his wares elsewhere.' He picked up the telephone. 'I'll call the Commander of the drug squad. We need a name for a local dealer and we need it fast.'

Suzette frowned. 'What about Raul Krief? What about what happened to him twenty years ago? What's the connection?'

Bertram shrugged his shoulders. 'As far as I can tell, that's irrelevant. Our drug dealer saw a way to rid himself of a problem and he took it. The two matters probably aren't connected, but the current drug connection most certainly is.' He clapped his hands. 'Bon, we're getting somewhere! What about the cousin angle?'

'Ah, well, that's interesting in itself,' Suzette replied.

'Is he involved?'

She shrugged. 'Well, he certainly has a few million incentives.' She paused as she considered. 'He's arrogant, he's confident. I don't like him much and he probably likes the police less. He's not scared of us, and he's not afraid to come under suspicion.'

'Is that because he's innocent or untouchable?'

Suzette did not answer. A minute passed. She ignored Oppert's tuts. Finally she spoke. 'There was certainly no love lost between Hakim and Raul Krief, but I got the impression there was genuine affection, at least there used to be, on Hakim's side at least. I can't really say much about Raul, other than what I've been told, and that mainly is that he was troubled and argumentative and could be highly disruptive.'

'Probably something to do with a long term opioid addiction,' Oppert interjected.

'And what happened to him twenty years ago,' Suzette added.

Bertram sighed. 'Is the cousin a suspect, or not?'

'I checked with his secretary,' she continued. 'At the time Raul's body was discovered, he was out of Paris at a conference. There are probably a few hundred witnesses. Not that it matters, really. Hakim could have paid someone to dump the body, because we don't even know how long Raul was actually missing.'

Before Bertram could speak, his telephone rang. He snatched the receiver. 'Allô, Hervé ici.' He listened to the person on the other end. 'Quoi? Vous êtes vous sûr? D'accord. Merci.' He replaced the receiver, shaking his head.

'What is it, Captain?' Suzette asked.

'We have a witness.'

'A witness to what?' she pressed.

Bertram turned away, staring at the wall. His eyes locked on a mould stain.

Suzette moved forward. 'Captain?'

He shook his head. 'We have to be careful.'

'About what?'

'The witness said they had seen Raul Krief several times over the last few months causing a disturbance.'

Suzette frowned. 'A disturbance. Where?'

Bertram looked outside his office. 'Faubourg Saint-Germain Synagogue,' he said, lowering his voice.

'Synagogue?' she questioned. 'What on earth for? I didn't know the Krief's were Jewish.'

Bertram shrugged. 'I don't know if they are, but that's not the issue. Apparently Raul Krief has been making a nuisance of himself for a long time, according to the witness.'

'And who is this witness?' Oppert asked.

'I don't know. It came as an anonymous tip. They claimed Raul often argued with a certain Rabbi.'

Suzette gasped. 'Rabbi? As in…'

Bertram nodded. 'And apparently the last occasion, a week or so ago, it became violent.'

'How do they even know each other?'

Bertram and Suzette exchanged a look.

'It get's worse,' Bertram added. 'According to the witness, Rabbi Serge Levy told Raul Krief that if he didn't… if he didn't stop bothering him,' he paused as if he could not finish what he was saying. He took a deep breath. 'He said if he didn't leave him alone, he'd kill him.'

XXV

'Elise, I've told you, I cannot, I WILL not receive visitors before midday,' Madeline Duchamp hissed.

'Je suis désolé,' the maid replied, fear clear in her voice. 'Mais, she insisted.'

'She?' Madeline responded, her voice rising to a shrill. She pushed past the terrified maid, stepping into the long hallway, her walking stick stabbing against the ground as if she intended to do it some damage. 'Who is it? Who is at my door without an invitation or an appointment?'

'It is only I, Madeline,' the soft voice of a woman called out from the shadow at the end of the hall.

Madeline stopped dead in her tracks. She turned around and waved her stick towards the maid. 'Elise, show our guest into the sunroom and bring us thé immediately.' She waved the stick behind her. 'Follow the maid.' She lowered her voice in Elise's direction. 'Make sure she doesn't steal anything,' she instructed the maid.

Anouk Levy folded one hand in front of her, and with the other, smoothed the mousey brown shoulder-length wig she was wearing. She was a small woman, with a pinched face made up with too much powder. She smiled at Madeline, a polite and warm smile, the sort Madeline immediately recognised as one she used herself for congratulating a member of her staff when they had done something well, something they were paid to do.

'It's been a very long time, Madeline,' Anouk said.

Madeline shrugged. She winced. The arthritis in her shoulder was giving her trouble.

'You're in pain?' Anouk asked.

Madeline smiled. 'Non. I'm just old.'

Anouk laughed. 'Oh, Madeline, you'll outlive us all, I'm sure,' she said, before lowering her voice and adding, 'in one way or another.'

Madeline leaned forward. Her hearing was not what it once was, but she did not wish to show it to Anouk. It was too late. Anouk leaned forward in her chair. 'Should I come closer to you?'

Madeline pointed her stick, waving it at Anouk. 'Non, you are perfectly fine where you are. I find it wise to keep a safe distance away from uninvited guests.'

Anouk nodded slowly. 'Bien sûr,' she replied, 'it's just, under the circumstances, I thought it prudent to come and talk with you.'

'Under the circumstances?' Madeline bounced back, her voice sharp.

Anouk nodded again. 'It is my understanding our sons,' she paused, 'désolé, my son and your petit-fils, have become *close*.' She heavily emphasised the word before continuing. 'It is my experience that friendships, particularly those between fine families such as ours, should be encouraged. Mais…' she trailed off. 'Like any sort of relationships, they need to be moulded, controlled for want of a better word, or else they can turn into something… else.' She narrowed her eyes. 'Do you know what I mean, cheri?'

Madeline clenched her fists. 'Tell me Anouk. How is your other son, Joann? I hear such,' she stopped for an extended pause, 'exciting things about him. It must be wonderful to have such an *exciting* child.'

Anouk's mouth twisted into a grimace. She rearranged it as quickly. 'Having children can be a challenge, as I'm sure you know. Speaking of that, how is Pierre? We see very little of him these days. And whatever became of that delightful wife of his, the nightclub singer? It must be hard on poor Hugo being apart from them.'

Madeline nodded. 'It is hard on us all when families are separated by circumstance.' She took another deep breath. 'Tell me, how is Rabbi Levy these days?' She paused, her eyes narrowing. 'I so miss seeing him in the park at night.'

Anouk narrowed her eyes. 'Mon mari is fine. He is just very busy.' She rose to her feet. 'As are we all, therefore, I won't take up any more of your time. I am here to invite you and your petit-fils to my home tomorrow for supper.'

Madeline snorted. 'That's out of the question, I'm dining with the…'

Anouk nodded, turning her head dismissively. 'That's good. We'll expect you at seven for cocktails, d'accord?'

Madeline's mouth opened, her nostrils twitching. She covered her mouth with her hand as she appraised Anouk with interest. 'Isn't it your holy night, or some such thing?'

Anouk bowed her head, smoothing her hand across her nylon wig. 'Oui. It is Shabbat, and that makes it even more special to share it with dear old friends.'

Madeline continued studying her as if she was trying to understand Anouk's reasoning. 'As I said, I am having supper with the Arnastes, and they are not the sort of people who like being stood up at the last moment.'

Anouk moved towards the door. 'I am close friends with Allena. I'll call her myself, and I can assure you there won't be a problem.' She paused, her fingers tapping on the door. 'And don't forget to bring your petit-fils. I'm so looking forward to finally meeting him.'

Madeline shook her head vigorously. 'It's out of the question, he does not attend such events.'

Anouk smiled. 'I understand Hugo is a lovely boy. A boy you can be proud of,' she paused, her eyes fixed firmly on Madeline. 'Just like my Josef.'

Madeline nodded.

Anouk smiled. 'Then let us make sure we are *always* proud of them. Our families are connected, aren't they? And therefore we must stick together, non? Just as we have always done. Scandal serves no purpose, does it?' She laughed. 'What am I saying? You know better than any of us the stigma of scandal.' She gave a saccharine sweet smile. 'You're so brave, Madeline. I've always admired your resilience, your ability to rise above what life has thrown at you. Lesser women would have crumbled under similar circumstances.'

'C'est possible,' Madeline replied, 'but I have never thought of myself as a lesser woman.' She stared at Anouk. 'Mais, you are correct. We all have our paths to walk, our crosses to bear. Some of us,' she waved her stick in Anouk's direction, 'have more to bear, it seems.'

Anouk nodded her agreement. 'Families such as ours have to look out for one another. '

'So it seems,' Madeline replied.

'I knew you'd understand,' Anouk retorted. 'The *older* generation often have the unique ability to see the ENTIRE picture. Bon. I'll see you and Hugo both at seven. Bonne journee.'

Madeline watched her leave. She slammed her stick onto the ground. 'Bitch,' she mouthed.

XXVI

Hugo tried for what felt like the twentieth time to smooth down his hair. As always, it bounced back defiantly, throwing blond locks across his face. Madeline sighed, making sure her irritation and discontent were clear. She was dressed in a full length Chanel dress with a Hermès scarf wrapped around her shoulders. Hugo was wearing the only thing he had in his wardrobe - beige chinos, crisp white shirt, and a fitted dark-blue blazer wrapped around his chest. It made him feel stiff and uncomfortable, and he knew he would spend most of the night with his fingers on his collar, trying to move some air into his torso so he could breathe. He still did not understand why he was being forced to go to dinner. He was NEVER invited to any party Madeline was attending, and the fact this particular evening was being held at the Levy house, *Josef's* house, filled him with an anxiety he was having trouble containing. He watched the streets of Paris whizz past them as they sped towards the Levy mansion in Madeline's limousine. He pulled at his collar again.

'Will you stop fiddling!' Madeline hissed. 'You're worse than your grandfather. He too seemed to take wearing suits as an affront to his civil liberties.'

'Why do I have to go?' Hugo whined.

She spun her head in his direction. 'Really, Hugo. Whining? How old are you, five? You are going because you were invited. To refuse to do so would be rude and impolite. And the Duchamp's are neither, no matter how much we are provoked.'

Hugo fought the urge to repeat his question. Instead, he asked. 'I take it you and Madame Levy don't get on?'

Madeline glared at him. 'Anouk Levy was born with ideas

above her station. Just because she married into a rich family does not give her the class she needs to sustain her position in society.'

Despite himself, Hugo found himself curious to meet the parents of Josef.

'And her children…' Madeline stole him a sly look. 'Josef seems to have turned out well by all accounts, but the other boy, Joann, certainly seems to have inherited his mother's genes. Anouk would never admit it, but she was, how do they say it these days, born on the wrong side of the tracks. Not that Anouk sees it, of course. As far as she is concerned, Joann is the golden boy and Josef is the…' she trailed off.

Hugo bit his lip, desperate for her to finish. 'Josef is the what?' he asked finally.

'There are two sides to the Levy family,' Madeline stated. 'And Anouk thinks she has produced the perfect combination. Two sons to continue both sides of the family line.'

Hugo frowned. 'What do you mean?'

'It was decided before they were born, I'm sure,' Madeline answered. 'Joann will continue with the family retail emporium, and Josef, will follow in his father's footsteps.'

Josef had suggested something similar, but Hugo could not understand why it had to be so black and white. 'Then it's true?' Hugo asked, trailing off, unable to finish his thought.

She nodded. 'Josef will be the next Rabbi.'

Hugo said nothing, instead looking straight ahead.

'Ah, we're here,' Madeline stated, pointing in front of her. Her face wrinkled in apparent distaste. 'I have always hated this house. Just because one has to be seen to be religious, doesn't mean one has to appear to live in poverty and in poor, poor, *poor* taste.'

Hugo closed his eyes and saw only one thing in front of him, and it both terrified him and filled him with an overwhelming sadness. *Rabbi Josef.*

Hugo stepped over the threshold, and his eyes immediately moved to the staircase. That is where you walk, forty-two steps, a turn to the right and the fourth door on the right. Madeline pressed her stick against his left leg, moving him forward. 'I swear to Dieu, Hugo. If you drag this evening out any longer that it needs to be, I'll send you to a boot camp for children who have no interest in looking after their grandparents. And you can be assured there will be no access to maids or,' she paused, 'anything else which may interest you.'

Hugo turned to her, smiling. 'Is there such a place?'

She slapped his forearm. 'I'll open one myself, if I have to, so just behave yourself. Say the right things, nod when you are addressed, and keep your mouth shut until I find the first suitable moment to extract us from what will be the most,' she stopped, shuddering, '*one* of the most *excruciating* evenings I have spent in a very long time.'

Hugo nodded. 'You're really selling it to me,' he laughed. 'Mais, what's in it for me?'

She smiled at him. 'You get to have dinner with Josef,' she said with a shrug of her shoulders. 'I imagine you value that quite highly, non?'

Hugo watched her as she walked past him, his face filled with genuine amazement.

'Come, Hugo,' she gestured, 'let us get this monstrosity of an evening over and done with.' She reached out and touched his hand. 'But just so you understand, whatever the circumstances, do not drag this out, d'accord? Or I will send you to a school you wouldn't appreciate.'

Hugo nodded. 'I know my place, Madeline, as I'm sure does Josef.'

Madeline stared at him. 'You sound exactly like your

grandfather.'

Hugo nodded. 'Bon. At least I don't sound like my father.'

Madeline watched him as he moved towards the door. 'Merci, Dieu,' she said, clasping her hands.

Madeline beamed in the sort of way Hugo was only used to when she was about to fire a maid. 'Rabbi Levy, it has been too long.'

Rabbi Serge Levy laughed. 'Madeline, we've known each other for a long time. I am *always* Serge to you.'

'Bien sûr, you are,' she quipped. She glanced around the large drawing room. 'Your family room is as charming as I remember it,' she said, as if she recalled anything but. 'It's amazing. So many, SO many memories can be crammed into such a tight space. It is as inventive as it is charming.' She shrugged. 'I only wished my own home could be so… so full, but I'm afraid dust in such volumes entirely disagrees with my chest,' she paused, 'and my eyes.'

Hugo looked out from under his fringe, trying to steal a look of the room. An entire wall was lined with bookcases, rows of books after books, not novels it seemed, but rather large obviously old textbooks, most likely religious in content, he supposed. The rest of the room was filled with antiques, but it was not like Madeline's home, where the antiques were pristine, and, so far as Hugo could tell, rarely used. The Levy family room looked lived in. Hugo noticed a pair of trainers sticking out from under a much-maligned sofa. He wondered whether they belonged to Josef and immediately chastised himself for being so ridiculous. His eyes flicked across the mantelpiece, it was filled with ornate framed photographs. He smiled. He instantly recognised an infant naked Josef sitting in a small tub. He frowned at a photograph next to it. It was old and did not match the other frames, and contained two photographs of young boys Hugo did not recognise, but supposed were old Levy family members.

Serge cleared his throat awkwardly. 'Anouk's just checking on things in the kitchen, She'll be with us shortly…'

'Tell her not to hurry on my account,' Madeline muttered under her breath.

'Pardon?'

Madeline smiled sweetly. 'Oh, I was just saying, I hope she's not going to too much trouble on my account. You know, I am a woman of simple tastes.'

Hugo snorted, immediately covering his mouth upon seeing the withering look shot in his direction by Madeline.

Serge smiled, seemingly oblivious to her tone. 'May I offer you a cocktail?' He paused. 'Ah, non, of course. You only drink scotch, oui?'

Madeline bowed her head. 'The Duchamp's only drink scotch.' She pointed at Hugo. 'The boy will have one too.'

Hugo gulped.

'Don't look so horrified, Hugo,' she said. 'It's never too early for a gentleman to begin to learn how to use alcohol correctly.' She smiled sweetly at the Rabbi. 'The older one leaves it, the more difficult it is to drink as a respectable person should - often and little and with decorum and dignity.'

Rabbi Levy handed Madeline a drink. She sipped it demurely. He turned to face Hugo, and for the first time, Hugo had a chance to study him. He could see Josef in him, though his father was shorter, and his hair was cut in a traditional Jewish style. His face was harder, with deep lines under his eyes. The Rabbi stepped forward and handed Hugo a crystal glass. Hugo took it reluctantly and pressed it to his lips, ensuring as little as possible passed them. Even then, he had to fight the urge to spit it out. His throat burned as it went down.

'I've been looking forward to meeting you, Hugo,' the Rabbi said with a sincere smile. 'My son talks of you often, which is unusual as he never spoke of his friends before.'

Hugo nodded, but could think of nothing to say.

'And that is why we thought it best to have this little get together.'

'It has been a long time since I have been in this house,' Madeline said, moving slowly across the room. Her nose wrinkled. 'And I'm pleased to see it hasn't changed a bit.' She stopped in front of an ornate silver photo frame. 'It must have been for the funeral for your father, ten years ago.'

'Fifteen,' the Rabbi corrected.

'Ah, oui, fifteen,' she agreed. 'He was ill for a very long time.'

He nodded. 'He was a martyr to it.'

Hugo watched the interaction between the two of them, and it confused him. They seemed to be saying so much, yet saying nothing at all. He did not know what it meant, but it appeared there was a story connected to Josef's grandfather. Another scandal, perhaps?

They lapsed into silence, interrupted only by the door swinging open, and Anouk Levy swept into the room. She stopped and frowned, confused by the lack of conversation. 'It was so quiet in here, I didn't imagine for a second you had arrived, dear Madeline.'

Madeline sipped her scotch. 'I find it isn't always necessary to speak aloud my every single meaningless thought.'

Anouk touched her shoulder. 'Thank Dieu for that, Madeline, or else you'd turn the air blue!'

Madeline tipped her head. 'You are most probably correct.'

Anouk clapped her hands together. 'Well, the table is set. Shall we go through to the dining room?'

'I can't wait,' Madeline muttered, moving towards the doorway. As usual, Hugo fell into step behind her.

XXVII

'Madeline, you sit there, next to Joann,' Anouk directed with an exaggerated gesture.

Madeline clutched her purse protectively under her arm and moved towards the seat. The Rabbi rushed to her and pulled the chair out for her. She lowered herself gracefully. 'Merci, Serge,' she said, slowly turning her head to the youth next to her. 'Joann. I take it you are well, young man?'

Joann nodded. 'I'm swell, Madeline, swell.'

'Swell,' she mouthed, as if the word bothered her.

As Hugo waited to be seated, he stole a quick glance at Josef's older brother. He was surprised. Josef and Joann were so dissimilar, both from each other and their parents. It was hard to imagine they all came from the same family. He guessed the brothers were roughly the same height, but Joann was much thinner, with a gaunt, pale face and long, thick-veined arms. His hair cut close to his head, almost a skinhead, and his eyes had none of the golden brown warmth of Josef's. His voice was also colder. He was sure they had never met, but he was sure he recognised him from somewhere. He turned his head away. Joann's gaze was as intense as Josef's, but it was different in so many ways. It felt cold and judgemental, as if his eyes spewed the sarcasm his mouth did not.

Hugo lowered his head, blond hair falling from the restraints of the hair mousse he had been forced to apply by his grandmother. He wanted to disappear. He did not want to see Josef again because he knew what sort of feelings it would stir in him, and he did not want that. Not in this room. Not on this night. But then he realised it was too late. Before Hugo lifted his head, he knew Josef was there, standing in the doorway with the same expectant gaze and the eyes which suggested hunger. He stared at him, but found he could not hold the look.

'Hugo?'

Hugo's heard jerked toward Anouk's voice. She was pointing at the seat next to Joann. 'And you can sit there.' She gestured to Josef. 'Josef can sit opposite, next to me.'

Josef shuffled into the room and Hugo could tell that he too was avoiding looking at him. He was dressed in a dark suit which he appeared to be as keen on as Hugo was on his, judging by the way he walked rigidly to his seat. The only person not dressed up was Joann. As Hugo lowered himself into his seat, he could see that as well as a worn white t-shirt, Joann was dressed in a pair of ripped jeans.

'Is this your first Shabbat, Hugo?' Anouk asked.

It's pretty much my first time out of the house, Hugo thought. 'It is, merci for inviting me,' he answered.

Joann turned his head. He pressed his leg against Hugo's and it felt different than when Josef did the same thing. It felt aggressive and domineering. Hugo moved his leg slowly away.

'So, you're the famous Hugo,' Joann said breezily. 'The one my bro…'

'Joann, did I not tell you to change into your suit before Shabbat?' Anouk interjected. Her tone was harsh, but Hugo thought he could detect some reticence, some apparent awkwardness.

He shrugged at his mother. 'I just got in. All my "proper" clothes are in the laundry,' he added as if he could not care less. He winked at Madeline. 'You can't get the damn staff, can you?'

'I laid your suit out on your bed,' Anouk snapped.

He shrugged again. 'I didn't see it,' he shot back. 'Do you want me to go change?'

Anouk glanced at the clock and shook her head. 'Non, it's

too late now.'

'Are you sure?' he retorted. 'I mean, I'd hate to offend your,' he moved his head between Madeline and Hugo, '*special* guests, but if you think they'd be offended, I could always put on something sparkly.'

His mother glared at him. 'You're fine as you are, Joann,' she said with a resigned sigh.

Hugo watched Madeline and saw the unmistakable outline of a smirk on her lips, as if she was undoubtedly taking pleasure seeing Anouk squirm. He turned his head and noticed for the first time Josef was watching him. He was smiling, but not in the way Hugo was used to seeing him smile. His mouth was tight, but the golden brown eyes were still sparkling.

'Ah, here is Serge,' Anouk said with clear relief. 'We can begin.'

Josef stared directly at Hugo. 'We can begin,' he mouthed.

Rabbi Serge Levy moved slowly into the dining room. Anouk rose to her feet, moving quickly as she filled all of their glasses with what appeared to Hugo to be red wine. He watched the Rabbi move to the head of the table.

Serge lowered his head. 'Remember the Sabbath day to sanctify it,' he said. He addressed his guests. 'For those of you unfamiliar with the process of Shabbat, I will now recite Vayechulu.'

Hugo followed him with intense interest, his eyes locked upon him. He had never been raised with any kind of religious influence, but there was something about the way in which Rabbi Levy, Josef's father, spoke which was intoxicating. It was warm, and it was engaging and it reminded Hugo of nothing he had encountered before.

The Rabbi continued. 'I will now wash my hands and we will

begin the process of blessing the bread.' He smiled at Madeline and Hugo. 'As we have two special guests this evening, I will not make this a long, drawn-out process for you to endure.'

Hugo did not need to look at Madeline to know she was mouthing, *merci Dieu*.

'Mais, we will break bread together and spend an evening in each other's company,' Serge added. 'We are connected, after all.'

'In what way, papa?' Joann questioned, his voice filled with faux innocence.

The Rabbi ignored his older son and moved to a table in the corner of the room and began washing his hands. Hugo watched him intently until his attention was drawn to something else. He looked under the table and saw Josef's foot had stretched across the floor and was now resting on Hugo's leg. Hugo shuffled back into his chair, but it only made Josef stretch further, his socked foot pressing itself under Hugo's trousers, touching his skin.

'Stop slouching, Josef,' Anouk snapped, slapping his arm.

Josef pulled himself up, extracting his foot from Hugo's leg. He watched his mother and as soon as she turned away; he slouched again, stretching his leg onto Hugo. To his left, Hugo heard Joann snigger. He turned to him, and the look on his face was clear. *I know what you're doing*. Hugo pushed himself back in his chair, extracting himself from Josef.

The Rabbi returned to the table, spreading his hands in front of him. His jacket lifted and Hugo noticed his shirt was buttoned incorrectly, buttons placed in incorrect slots. Anouk appeared to have seen it too and jumped to her feet, pulling the jacket down again. Serge looked at his wife, his face crumbling in confusion. He placed the bread on the table. 'I'm so grateful for you all being here today of all days,' he said, his voice breaking.

'Today of all days?' Madeline repeated. 'Is there something special about today?' she asked.

Anouk touched her husband's arm. 'Serge is feeling a little

emotional, that's all.'

'Pourquoi?' Madeline countered.

Anouk smiled. 'Because he is grateful to have you both here, that's all.' She turned to Hugo. 'As I said, our families are connected, from the past and to the future.'

Joann covered his mouth and coughed loudly as he tried to disguise the word he spoke. *Faggots.*

Josef turned to his mother. Anouk shrugged her shoulders. 'We should eat,' was all she said. If she had heard what her older son had said, she did not show it.

'We should eat?' Josef countered with clear incredulity.

She turned to him. 'Bien sûr.'

Josef turned back to Hugo. 'Je suis désolé,' he said.

Hugo shook his head and slid down into his seat, kicking off one of his shoes. He reached across the floor until he found Josef's leg, and he touched it with his foot. He smiled. It felt defiant to him. It felt as if he was finally standing up to a bully, but more importantly, it felt right. It felt as if there was nothing unnatural about it.

'Excusez moi, Madame Levy,' an anxious-looking maid said, appearing in the doorway. 'There is someone here.'

Anouk waved her hand dismissively. 'Then tell them to leave,' she scowled. 'You know better than to bother us at Shabbat.'

The maid nodded, her anxiety clear. 'Je sais,' she said, 'mais, it's the police.'

'The police!' Anouk gasped, turning back to Joann.

Joann shrugged innocently. *I don't know.*

'Can't they wait?' Anouk asked.

The maid shook her head. 'Non, they insisted.'

Anouk looked at Madeline. Hugo's grandmother stared stoically back at her.

'Show them in,' Anouk said.

A moment later, Captain Bertram Hervé and Lieutenant

Suzette Carman entered the dining room. Bertram stopped in front of the table, his eyes widening in obvious surprise upon seeing Madeline seated around the table. Suzette watched him, shrugging with confusion.

'What is this about?' Anouk demanded.

Bertram moved across the room. 'I'm sorry to trouble you, but it is necessary that we speak to Rabbi Levy.'

Anouk looked at her husband. Serge dropped his head, his hand shaking as he lifted his wine glass, draining the contents in one gulp. He reached for the decanter and poured another.

Anouk watched Serge, her eyes flecking angrily. 'What is this about?' she demanded again.

Bertram moved closer to the Rabbi. 'We'll discuss it with the Rabbi at Commissariat de Police du 7e arrondissement,' he answered.

'My husband cannot leave the table when he is in the middle of…'

Bertram touched the Rabbi's arm, lifting it gently.

'Is he being arrested?' Anouk cried.

'He just needs to help us with our inquiries, that's all,' Suzette reasoned.

Bertram noticed the smile on Madeline's face and had to hide his own. 'And if he doesn't agree, then we will arrest him. Is that what you want me to say? Is that what you want all of your neighbours to see?'

Rabbi Serge Levy rose to his feet. 'I agree, Captain Hervé. I agree.'

Madeline stood up. She gestured to Hugo. 'Time for us to leave, *finally*, Hugo,' she said. She smiled at Anouk. 'Merci for a lovely meal, Anouk. One of your best, I'm sure, but I find it is always best for guests to leave before a police raid.' She placed her hand on Hugo's bicep, pulling him with a force belying her age. Hugo looked over his shoulder as she dragged him from the room.

He hoped his eyes said enough to Josef.

XXVIII

Suzette stared at Serge Levy. He had removed his coat and hat and was sitting in a plain white shirt and black trousers. He had rolled the sleeves up and his fingers rested on the folds often, gently moving the fold up or down. He did not look up, his head bowed, his lips moving quickly, speaking words she could not catch. Suzette had not been sure about bringing him in, not yet at least. It seemed to her they were showing their hand before they actually understood what the cards meant. However, as usual, Captain Hervé had overruled her. It had seemed almost personal to her. But Bertram was not about to share his thoughts with her, a mere woman, a lesbian of all things. His inferior in all respects.

Suzette knew she was reasonably fortunate to have him as her commanding officer. She had seen first-hand how some captains treated their female detectives, and she knew only one thing for certain. She would not last a day under their command, and most likely would spend a week or two in a cell. Still, "reasonably fortunate" was not enough.

'Can I get you anything, Rabbi Levy?' she repeated, hoping just for something to do while she waited for Bertram to join them in the interview room. 'A café, a thé?'

Serge Levy lifted his head slowly, the peyot's bouncing on his cheeks. He tucked them behind his ears, smiling gently at Suzette's puzzled expression. 'In Vayikra 19:27, the Torah teaches us: "Do not cut off the hair on the sides of your head…"'

Suzette frowned. 'Well, that's an odd thing for it to teach you.'

He slouched his shoulders into a shrug. 'In his commentary on the Torah, Rabbi Hirsh suggests that peyot form a symbolic separation between the front part of the brain and the rear part,' he said. 'Rabbi Hirsh believed the front part of the brain is the intellectual core, the rear part is the more physical, sensual part. Therefore, wearing a peyot suggests the man is aware of both facets of his mind, and intends to keep them to their appointed tasks.'

She nodded. 'And does it work?'

Serge's mouth twisted. 'I have no idea.'

Suzette laughed just as the door swung open, and Bertram entered the room. He snorted. 'Well, I'm sorry if I interrupted a party.'

Suzette's eyes widened with irritation. Bertram flopped heavily onto a plastic chair opposite Serge. He threw a pile of dossiers onto the desk; the thud causing the Rabbi to jump.

Bertram watched as Serge eyed the dossiers. 'You're right to look worried,' he said.

Serge looked at them. 'What are they?'

Bertram tapped the top of the file. 'The past,' he said cryptically, before adding, 'or rather, your past.'

'Let's begin with the night of September 15th 1975,' Bertram began.

Serge sighed. 'Not this again,' he cried wearily.

'I let you get away with this lie once,' Bertram replied. 'And I shouldn't have. I regretted it then, but I thought it had passed. If I had known then what was going to happen now, I would have thrown you in jail that night, to hell with consequences.'

Suzette pulled back her head sharply, fixing him with a shocked look. He turned to her, conveying a simple message. *This isn't the time for explanations.*

The Rabbi threw his hands in the air. 'There is no connection between the two events.'

'How on earth can you say that?' Suzette interrupted.

'Because it's true,' Serge said, his voice cracking. He shook his head. 'Look. It's obvious. Someone wanted to murder poor Raul, and they did, in some kind of warped way, a flashback to what happened to him in 1975. It's gross and evil, but it is what it is.'

'It is what it is,' Bertram repeated. 'It is what it is.'

'Why do you think someone would want to murder Raul Krief?' Suzette asked.

'How am I supposed to know?' Serge hissed. 'Because they're sadistic and they're evil. For some reason they had a problem with him.'

'For some reason they had a problem with him.' Bertram repeated the Rabbi's words again. He reached and opened the first dossier, his eyes scanning the contents. 'Can you think of any reason why someone might have a problem with Raul Krief?' he asked.

Serge clasped his fingers together and began moving his lips again.

'Prayers won't help you now,' Bertram warned.

Serge shook his head. 'I disagree. Prayers always help. Even for non-believers.'

'And what are you praying about?' Suzette countered. 'Asking for forgiveness?'

He smiled. 'Always. As should we all…'

'Ah, we're all born sinners, that sort of thing,' Bertram grumbled. 'I don't buy into that nonsense. It sort of loses its meaning when you see a six-year-old girl who's been gang raped and had her throat cut, all because her crackhead mother sold her for the price of a bag of drugs. Forgiveness is moot then, as far as I'm concerned.'

The Rabbi shook his head. 'Everyone deserves forgiveness.'

'Some people deserve to be strung up and bled to death over a very long, very painful amount of time,' Bertram responded.

'I disagree.'

Bertram snorted. 'We'd soon see how different you'd feel if it was your kid lying there.'

'What were you asking for forgiveness for?' Suzette interjected, eager to move on the interview. 'It can't just be a blanket prayer - *I said a bad thing today, I had a nasty thought about ma femme.*' She leaned forward. 'Dieu's too busy for shit like that, non?'

Bertram smiled. 'The Lieutenant is correct. Dieu has far more to deal with, as do you.'

The Rabbi lifted his head. 'I don't know what you want from me.'

'I want the truth.'

The Rabbi shook his head. 'Non, you don't. You want a version of the truth. You want something to fill the narrative you need to close your case. To move on. To deal with the next case. And then move on to another one. Tell me, what do you think happens to those you leave behind? Those you trample over. Those whose lives you ruin in the name of justice. Do you ever give them a second thought?'

Bertram considered his answer. Finally, he shrugged. 'Not really. I can't. And not just because it's not my job. I have to move on, because if I don't, I can't help the next family. The next devoted wife, husband, child, etc…etc…' he concluded wearily.

'Our jobs are very similar, Captain,' the Rabbi stated.

'Peut être,' Bertram conceded. 'We certainly bow and curtail to those "above" us, I suppose.'

Serge smiled.

Bertram sighed. 'Ecouté. Let's cut to the chase. Twenty years ago you were seen exiting the Faubourg Saint-Germain park around the time of the discovery of the body of Gerard Le Mache and Raul Krief. I was warned off the case then. Is the same going to happen this time?'

Serge stared at him. 'That has nothing to do with me.'

Bertram nodded. 'But it has something to do with your family and their influence, non?'

Serge glanced at his watch. 'We can't do this now. Not on the eve of Shabbat. My father would never have tolerated it.'

Bertram's eyebrows raised. 'What would you have me do?'

'Let me sleep. We can talk tomorrow after I have slept and prayed.'

'And then you'll talk?' Suzette pressed. 'Why would tomorrow be different?'

He shrugged. 'Because I need to pray for guidance. And then I'll talk.'

'I can't let you leave the commissariat,' Bertram said.

The Rabbi rose to his feet. 'That's fine. I'm sure you have a perfectly good cot for me to lay my head on. After all, Jesus made his entrance into this world via the straw in a stable.'

Suzette headed towards the door. 'I'll head over to the pet store and pick up a bag of straw for you, Rabbi. We have to make sure you're perfectly comfortable, don't we?'

Bertram smiled. 'Although we don't have a stable for you, Rabbi, peut être we could find you a bicycle shed to sleep in for the night.'

Serge stared directly at the Captain. 'I don't understand why you are so antagonistic towards me.'

'You don't?' Bertram snapped. 'Well, let me tell you why. It's because I think, non, I KNOW that you have information concerning what happened to Raul Krief twenty years ago which could not only have solved the mystery of why he was left for dead and why Gerard Le Mache died, and why all this time later it has started again.'

Serge smiled. 'We'll talk tomorrow,' he stated simply.

'I don't know why you're smiling!' Suzette shouted. 'Gad Krief and Henri Dukas are still missing. If they end up dead, tied naked to a tree somewhere, then as far as I'm concerned, it's on you.'

'Gad and Henri are not the problem,' the Rabbi stated.

'The hell they're not!' Bertram slammed his fists onto the table. 'The kids are still missing!'

'They are not the problem,' the Rabbi repeated.

Bertram clenched his fists. 'If I have to beat it out of you, Rabbi, I will.'

Suzette reached across the table, placing her hand near Bertram as if she was attempting to calm him.

Serge nodded. 'I'm sure you would, but it won't be necessary.'

'I need answers, and I need them tonight,' Bertram hissed. 'And you're not leaving here until you tell me what I need to know.'

The Rabbi sighed. 'We can do that. But then I will have to ask for an Avocat who is sure to tell me to say nothing. All I am asking is for one night. One more night. And then, when I have prayed, I will answer your questions. Is that agreeable to you?'

Bertram unclenched his fists. 'I don't really have a choice in the matter, do I?'

Serge moved towards the exit. 'My cell is in this direction?'

Suzette stood. 'I'll show you the way.'

The Rabbi smiled. 'À demain.'

XXIX

Hugo's eyes snapped open and for the second time in a matter of days he saw Josef's face, and again it was not in his dreams. This time, Josef was on Hugo's bed, spreadeagled across Hugo, gazing straight down into his face. Hugo struggled in an attempt to extract himself, but Josef's legs held him in place.

'If I was Madeline, I'd have to fire Elise,' Hugo said wearily. 'Get off me, s'il te plaît,' he whispered, hoping no one would walk into the attic and witness the scene. He knew no one would. Still, he wanted space between him and Josef. He pulled his knees together and pushed upward, throwing Josef into the air. He spun around and landed next to Hugo, his head falling on the pillow next to him.

'You just had to ask if you wanted me to get into your bed, Hugo,' Josef laughed, turning his head towards Hugo.

Hugo sat up, throwing his legs over the side of the bed. 'What are you doing here, Josef?'

Josef shrugged. 'I thought we'd spend the day in bed watching old eighties movies. I grew up with Barbra Streisand. I know you probably think she's a bit passé, hell, I did too, but trust me she isn't. You've got What's up Doc, Nuts, The Owl and the Pussycat. She can do drama and comedy; she's like a chameleon. If you're not a fan after that, then you're not… then you're not…'

'Then I'm not what?' Hugo challenged him.

Josef stared at him in surprise. '*Smart*. What did you think I was going to say?'

Hugo turned away again. 'I don't know.' He sighed. 'Why are you here?' he asked again. 'You can't be here. You *shouldn't* be here.'

'Are we still doing this, H?' Josef asked. 'Haven't we moved past this point in our relationship?'

Our relationship. Hugo wanted to cover his ears. He wanted to stop hearing his voice. He wanted it to stop haunting him. He wanted it to never stop. 'How is your father?' Hugo asked.

'Don't spoil things, not today.'

'Did he come home last night?'

Josef shook his head.

'He's still at the police station?' Hugo asked in surprise.

Josef shrugged. 'I guess so. Maman is even more secretive than usual, so I don't know what's going on.' He smiled sweetly at Hugo. 'Can we watch Barbra now and maybe make out a little?'

'I've been thinking…'

Josef threw his hands in the air in an exaggerated way. 'Oui, fine, I will put out on the first date.'

Despite himself, Hugo smiled. He shook his head, his hair covering his eyes. He brushed it away.

'Will you stop doing that!' Josef wailed, throwing himself back onto the bed. 'You have no idea what it does to me.'

'I've been thinking…' Hugo continued. 'The party was supposed to be tonight, wasn't it?'

'The party?'

'Oui, the party Gad and Henri were getting drugs for.'

Josef patted the space next to him on Hugo's bed. 'Why are you asking about that? We've got spooning and Barbra to get to, non?'

'Don't you want to help your father?' Hugo pushed.

Josef stared at him, but did not answer. Hugo studied his face, and he recognised the look. The dilemma was clear on Josef's face. Hugo understood it. When his own father had dropped Hugo off at Madeline's, Hugo had known he should be angry or upset, but the truth was, he was neither. He was relieved. Relieved he would not have to see the disappointment, irritation and anger on his father's face. Hugo surmised that whatever sort of relationship

Josef had with his father, it was most likely not an easy one.

'How could telling you about the party help?' Josef asked finally.

Hugo shrugged. 'I don't know really, but the disappearance of Gad and Henri, and what happened to Gad's father, now and twenty years ago, is all connected. It's obvious the police think so, and I have to say it makes sense.' He paused. 'You know about twenty years ago, don't you?'

Josef stared at him. His eyes flared angrily, but it was momentary. 'Our house might be big, but my mother's voice carries,' he said with a weary smile.

Hugo paused. He did not want to pry, so he was unsure how to proceed. But Josef had come to him in the first place, so it appeared he wanted help. But help with what?

'I still don't get what Gad and Henri have to do with it,' Josef added.

'Maybe nothing,' Hugo continued. 'But it's a start, and it's all we have. About the party. Where was it going to be?'

'One of the kids at school has a summer house just outside of Paris,' Josef replied. 'His parents are out of France most of the time, so the house is never used. It's a pretty cool place. It has an enormous pool and a big horse stable. There are no horses in it though, so it makes a pretty excellent venue for the party once it gets dark.'

Hugo tapped his chin. 'Would you take me?'

'To the party?' Josef asked, a sly smile appearing on his face. 'Or do you mean, "take me" a different way?'

Hugo hid his own smile. 'Not to the party,' he said with obvious distaste. 'To the place where the party happens.'

'Pourquoi? What are you expecting to find?'

'I don't know,' Hugo responded. 'Probably nothing. Is the party still happening tonight?'

Josef shook his head. 'Nope. After everything that's

happened, everyone figured we should lie low for a while.'

Hugo considered. 'So the place is empty?'

'I guess.'

'Hmm,' Hugo mumbled. 'Then it might be a good place to hideout.'

'Hideout?' Josef asked with a frown. 'You think that's all this is? Gad and Henri are playing a game, or something?' He shook his head. 'It doesn't make sense. What would be the reason?'

'I have no idea,' Hugo answered honestly. 'But it wouldn't harm to check it out, would it? Especially if it could help your father in some way.' He looked at the television in the corner of the room. 'I'm sure Barbra can wait.'

Josef's tongue traced across his bottom lip. 'Maybe, but I'm not sure I can.'

'Be serious,' Hugo scolded.

'I am!'

'Josef!' Hugo cried wearily.

'D'accord! D'accord!' Josef sighed. 'But how would we get there?'

Hugo pondered. 'We can take Madeline's car and driver.'

'Is that allowed?'

Hugo shrugged. 'I don't know. I've never tried it before. I've never had anywhere to go. But I don't see why it wouldn't be allowed. Anyway, Madeline has her old cronies from the club over for lunch. They'll be there for at least four hours gossiping and drinking their tiny body weight in gin.'

Josef jumped off the bed. 'Okay. On one condition.'

Before Hugo could answer, Josef was in front of him, grabbing him by the waist and pulling him forward, his fingers in the belt loops of Hugo's jeans. Josef pressed his lips to Hugo's. It seemed to last forever, but Hugo supposed it was only seconds. He watched helplessly as Josef skipped towards the attic stairs. 'What condition?' Hugo asked breathlessly.

'Next time, you kiss me,' Josef called over his shoulder.

XXX

Hugo stuck his nose out of the window, the breeze blowing his hair around him. He squinted, watching the busy streets of Paris whizz past him as the limousine sped out of the city. It felt exciting to him in ways he did not understand, but the pressure of another thigh against his may have a part in his excitement. His mind felt cloudy and foggy, and he did not like it at all. It felt distracting and dangerous. His life was staid, and he had become used to it, because he could control it. In his attic, with his videos and his music, he felt safe and focused. And now he felt as if he was lost in the middle of an ocean in a sinking rowboat without an oar.

He stared at his feet, stabbing his foot against the floor as if he was attempting to stem the flow of water. He did not like feeling this way, and it troubled him that Josef had so easily spotted the secret Hugo had been running from for so long it had become second nature. What troubled him more was that Hugo was sure if Josef had spotted it so easily, there was not a chance Madeline had missed it. She most likely knew Hugo's secret before he had.

The fact remained he was not yet fifteen. He was still a child, but he did not feel like one. He never had. Madeline had once said, *you were born old Hugo, and you have most certainly been here before*. He had not understood what she meant, other than it had struck a chord with him. He did not necessarily believe in such things, but he had always known, always believed, his eyes were different to other people's. He saw things they did not. He saw details most people missed, ignored, or disregarded. Hugo did not know what it meant, but he knew it was not something he could turn off.

He had spent the last few nights trying to understand what had happened to Raul Krief, and how it was connected to the past, and in particular what it could mean for his son and his friend. There was a link. Hugo was not sure what it was. But he was certain of one thing - the past had come back to haunt the future.

'You're off in your own world again, H,' Josef said. He touched Hugo's hand.

Hugo looked at it and did not remove it. 'Why do you keep doing things like that?' he asked.

Josef frowned. 'Why do you think? Because I want to. Because I REALLY want to.'

Hugo nodded. 'So, you keep saying. But why? What are your intentions?'

Josef snorted. 'What are my intentions?' he shouted with incredulity. 'Where are we? The 1890s instead of the 1990s?'

Hugo shook his head angrily. 'That's not what I meant.'

Josef stared at him. 'Hugo, we're kids. This is what kids do. This isn't serious. We're kids,' he repeated.

'I've never been a kid,' Hugo retorted.

'Then it's about time you fucking tried to be one,' Josef hissed.

Hugo turned away from him.

'Désolé,' Josef whispered. 'It's just I don't understand what it is you're trying to say.'

Hugo turned back to him. 'You seem to keep suggesting we're two kids, and messing around is what we should be doing. Do I have that right?'

Josef shrugged. 'Well...'

Hugo nodded. 'Then, by your same theory, you suggest I can "mess around" with you and whoever else I want to, am I correct?'

Josef stared at him. 'Well, I didn't say that. I just meant we're kids.'

'Stop saying that,' Hugo snapped. 'And more importantly, stop sending me mixed messages.'

Josef leaned towards him. 'Mixed messages are all I have.'

Hugo turned his head. 'I think that's the first time you've actually been honest with me, and I appreciate it. I get you are the sort of boy I could never be. The sort of boy who loves everyone and everything. But I'm not that boy. The only thing I know for certain since I met you is I can't be you. I can't be like you.'

'What do you mean, H?'

Hugo stared at him. 'My mother left me. My father hates me. My grandmother thinks of me as one of her buddies from her club. I can't be anything to any of them because it's all different. They all want me to be different. At some point all I can be is me. I can't be anything for anyone because everyone wants me to be something different.'

Josef shook his head. 'I don't get it.'

Hugo nodded. 'Oui, you do. You want me to be different too.' He took a deep breath. 'You want me to be your secret.'

Josef stared at him. 'Secrets aren't such a bad thing.'

Hugo's face tightened. 'I'm a terrible liar, and I suspect that is exactly what you need me to be.'

'Will you always live in Paris?' Josef asked, changing the subject and breaking the silence.

Hugo shrugged. 'I've never really thought about it,' he said honestly.

'You should.'

Hugo frowned. 'Pourquoi?'

'Because you have options, and…' he paused, 'well, not to be rude, but isn't Madeline like a hundred years old?'

Hugo snorted. 'I'll tell her you said that!'

Josef held up his hands. 'Don't! I have a feeling she'd castrate me with her bare hands!' He stared at Hugo. 'But I meant it. You have options. If your father really hates you, he isn't going to care where you are as long as you're not with him. Doesn't your mother like live in New York now or something?'

'I don't really know where she lives, but I think so,' Hugo

answered honestly. 'Not that it matters. I can't imagine living with either her or my father. I guess I'll live on my own.' He pondered. 'I'm almost fifteen. I can be on my own if I have to. But to answer your question. I'm not sure where I'd go, or what I'd do. Without Madeline… or any other reason to stay in Paris, then I might go somewhere else.' He stopped, realising the thought of leaving the safety of his attic terrified him, but he knew he would have to one day, eventually. His life had to begin, whether or not he was ready for it. He stared at Josef. He had always refused to hope that there would be someone who would want to share his life with him.

'What about you?' he asked.

Josef did not answer.

'You'll stay in Paris?' Hugo pressed.

Still, Josef did not answer.

'Josef?'

Josef sighed. 'Haven't you figured it out yet?' He stared at Hugo. 'My life was decided for me from the second I was born. Outlined in fine detail, and there was never going to be any deviating from it.'

'That's crazy,' Hugo. 'Lives can't be planned that way. Things change. People change.'

Josef shook his head. 'Not in the Levy family. We have two sides. Both businesses. My parents produced an heir for both sides and that's that.'

'You can say no,' Hugo reasoned.

'How?' Josef replied. 'Run away? Disown my family, have them disown me? Spend the rest of my life an outcast, cut off?'

Hugo considered his response. 'If that's the way it has to be.'

'Not all of us are brave like you, Hugo,' Josef answered. 'I can't be alone.'

'You don't have to be alone,' Hugo reasoned. 'That's the point. Families can be formed. People do it all the time.'

'And will you?'

He shrugged. 'I hope so. I don't know how, or when, but I hope one day I'll be ready, and when that happens, I hope I have the courage to take it. Rather than living a life I didn't choose for myself.'

Josef sighed. 'I don't want to talk about this right now. I've just turned fifteen. I want to enjoy being fifteen for as long as I can. I don't want to think about, or worry about my future yet. I'll deal with that when I can face it.' He moved closer to Hugo. 'Hold my hand,' he whispered.

Hugo glanced forward. He could see the chauffeur was watching them through the rear-view mirror. Hugo did not move his hand. He knew for certain if he did what Josef wanted, it would surely get back to Madeline.

'Hold my hand,' Josef repeated. 'I know you want to. And I know I desperately want you to.'

Hugo took a deep breath. He lifted his hand, staring at it like it was dead weight. He moved it slowly, as if he had no control over it. Finally, it stopped, and he took Josef's hand in his own, fingers instantly entwining.

'Monsieur Duchamp,' the chauffeur called from the front seat. 'We have arrived at the address.'

Hugo looked to Josef. 'We have arrived, mon ami.'

'Don't call me that,' Josef snapped.

Hugo opened the door. 'Isn't it what we are? Isn't it what we will always be? Because I don't know much, Josef, but I know this - I'm never going to be a secret, not if I can help it,' he said. He raised his hand. 'Anyway, that's not important right now, but finding Gad and Henri is. Shall we go?'

He stepped out of the car, Josef watching helplessly after him.

XXXI

Hugo took in his surroundings, and surprisingly he could imagine a few dozen teenagers partying in the gardens. It felt alien to him, but not too far removed that he could not imagine it. There was a part of him which could imagine himself in it - dancing, laughing, playing. Throwing his head from left to right, his hair flailing, his laugher disappearing into the beat of the music playing from an obnoxiously loud speaker. Music he did not know or understand. A life he did not know or understand. He stole a secret look at Josef. His head was turned away, tilted slightly, so he could enjoy the breeze coming from the window on his side. He looked happy, and he appeared free of constraints. It saddened Hugo, but he felt no jealousy. He wanted Josef to be happy. He wanted everyone to feel so free. He just hoped that one day, he too would be free.

Josef ran happily into the garden, spreading out his arms. 'Damn, if this house could talk about the things it's seen.'

Hugo closed the car door gently. He did not want to acknowledge the images flowing through his mind. Josef dancing, drinking, *fucking*. He reached his head into the driver's window. 'We won't be long, can you wait?'

The chauffeur regarded Hugo with a wry smile. *I know your secret, and soon so will everyone else*, the smile clearly stated. 'Take your time jeune Monsieur Duchamp,' he said, pressing his body back into the seat. 'I'll just have a little nap.'

Hugo nodded and moved away from the car, taking in his surroundings. It certainly was an impressive country retreat, with a large, impressive mansion. The sun bounced off the gently swirling water in the pool. As impressive as it was, the house and its grounds felt vast and empty. It seemed so rarely used that it had no lingering memories. He was glad at least that teenagers had a chance to own it, even for a short period of time.

'Where does the party usually take place?' Hugo asked.

Josef pointed to his left, and then to his right. 'It usually starts out over there, by the pool and when it starts to get dark, over there in the old stables.'

Hugo narrowed his eyes. A row of tall oak trees partially hid the stables. 'Show me,' he said.

Josef nodded, striding purposefully around the trees, Hugo a few steps behind him.

'Do people usually sleep here?' Hugo asked.

Josef laughed. 'Sure, but there's not usually a lot of sleep going on!' He stopped upon hearing the involuntary sharp intake of breath from Hugo. He stared at him. 'Does that make you jealous?'

'Non, it doesn't,' Hugo said defiantly.

'Liar,' Josef shot back. 'If you said that, I'd be crying by now.'

Hugo turned away. It bothered him that Josef knew all the right things to say, because he was not sure if he meant it. It felt like a game to Hugo and the rules were incomprehensible to him.

'This is it,' Josef said, stopping in front of a vast stable. He moved towards the wide doorway and yanked the two levers apart, the doors sliding to the left and right with a loud squeal. Hugo stepped into the wide empty space and for a moment he could hear the loud music, the excited squeals and screams from dozens of drunk, high teenagers. Despite his own age, Hugo realised he had never felt so old as he did at that moment.

'Ah, memories,' Josef said, stepping around Hugo, his fingers trailing across his shoulders. Hugo shrugged them off as if he could not bear his touch. 'Touchy,' Josef laughed.

Hugo ignored him, stepping further into the stables. Without sunlight, he was suddenly plunged into the much cooler and darker centre of the stable. He suddenly felt uneasy and unsteady on his feet. Within seconds, Josef appeared by his side, and as if he was sensing Hugo's reticence, placed his hand once again in his.

'I don't get it,' Josef said. 'Why did you want to come here?'

Hugo shrugged. 'I don't know. Once you said it was empty most of the time, it just seemed like something worth checking out.'

'Checking out for what?'

'I don't know,' Hugo repeated. 'Just that, there's something not right about what's happened, and until we find out what happened to Gad and Henri, then I don't think any of it is going to make sense.'

Even in the darkness, Hugo could see the doubtful look on Josef's face. He inched forward, stopping near an enclosed horse stable. The door was slightly ajar. He pulled it open, his eyes widening in surprise. 'Do you see this?'

Josef peered over Hugo's shoulder. 'Well, that's weird.'

Hugo moved inside the stable, as his eyes tried to focus on what he was seeing. 'Someone has been staying here. And they've been here recently,' he added, noticing the empty boxes and food wrappers scattered around the floor.

Josef pointed. 'Two people have been staying here,' he corrected, pointing at two mattresses lined together against a wall.

Hugo stepped in front of him. The pillows and ruffled blankets did not look old. There was no dirt or dust. It appeared whoever had been staying there had done so up until recently. 'Well, this is odd,' he mused.

'Sure is, don't…'

Hugo froze. It was not just because Josef had suddenly stopped talking; it was because of the loud thud which had permeated the air. Hugo turned around quickly, but it was too late to stop the baseball bat from smashing into his face. He fell backwards, the pain unbearable, the world crashing around his skull. *Josef.*

The chauffeur stared at the two five hundred franc notes.

'The kids just want to be alone. You get that, don't you?'

The chauffeur smiled. 'Sure.'

'Bon. Just don't tell anyone about this, d'accord? I mean, if anyone were to find out you drove two rich kids out of the city so that they could engage in illegal activities, well, that wouldn't go down too well, would it? At best, you'd lose your job, at worst, you'd end up in jail.'

The chauffeur nodded. 'I was never here,' he said.

'You were never here. Au revoir.'

XXXII

'I just checked on the Rabbi,' Suzette called from the doorway to Bertram's office. 'And he's sleeping like a baby. Should I wake him?'

The Captain stared at his watch. A little after eight. 'Leave him.'

'Bon,' she replied, stepping into the office and dropping two bags onto his desk. 'Café and croissants.'

Bertram clasped his hands together, ripping open the croissant bag and immediately snapping off the top of one of them with his teeth. 'Oh, je t'aime, Lieutenant,' he cried. He stopped, biting his lip. 'Ah. I'm not allowed to say those sorts of things, am I?' He moved his fingers into air quotes. '"I've been on THE course."'

Suzette laughed. 'I've got a thick skin, Captain. As long as you don't put your hand on my ass, then you and I will not have a problem.'

He stared at her with utmost seriousness. 'I've seen your ass, Lieutenant, and trust me, I have no intention of doing that.'

Suzette pointed at him. 'And vice versa.'

Bertram stared sadly at the remains of the croissant in his hand. 'Madame Hervé would agree with that assessment. She says my best days are behind me, which in reality only makes me want to eat more of these delightful creations.' He shrugged. 'I suppose she wants the best for me…'

'Or she wants to you reach retirement age before you die, so she can get the maximum death benefits,' Suzette reasoned.

Bertram conceded. 'I suspect it's the only reason we're still married.' He placed the croissant down in front of him. 'My dear wife will just have to wait a little longer,' he stated. 'So, tell me, what do we have?'

Suzette flopped into a chair. 'Not a lot,' she sighed. 'The Rabbi is clean.'

Bertram snorted. 'A religious zealot is never clean. They just know where to hide the skeletons, and they have plenty of people to help them.'

She shrugged. 'Peut être, but he doesn't have so much as a parking or speeding ticket, or any kind of ticket, for that matter. I can find no record of an arrest or even him being questioned in relation to any crime either as a suspect or a witness.'

'What about the rest of the family?'

'Anouk Levy has been cautioned three times for speeding,' Suzette said. 'Always in a hurry to the knitting circle at the synagogue, I suppose,' she added.

'What about the elder boy, Joann?'

Suzette pursed her lips. 'Nothing either,' she replied. 'But I've asked around, and it's pretty clear he hangs around with some really dodgy characters.'

Bertram laughed. 'As do we all.'

'True,' she conceded. 'The younger kid is an excellent student, no alarm bells there.'

'And the rest of the extended Levy family?'

'Nothing in the files, as far as I can see.'

Bertram stood. 'What I don't get is this. If Rabbi Serge Levy had a thing for black hookers back in the day, it can't just have been a one off thing, surely, could it? I mean, you don't have that craving, fulfil it once and think, "hey, I've done that, move on!"'

'Peut être the time he got caught was the first time,' Suzette reasoned, 'and therefore it was a wake-up call in the worst way. He got his kicks, and he learned his lesson.'

'Or else he was driven underground,' Bertram reasoned.

'It's possible, I suppose,' she replied doubtfully.

'What else do you have for me?' Bertram grumbled. 'Because I'm still not seeing a single reason why someone would want to kill Raul Krief after all this time.'

'I also looked into Gerrard Le Mache and his family,' Suzette replied. 'And while it was clear they weren't happy with what they called Raul's "refusal" to assist with the investigation, there are several statements from psychiatrists who examined Raul and not one of them concluded he was deliberately withholding information concerning his abduction and attempted murder. Gerrard Le Mache's parents are dead now. As far as I can tell, he had a younger sister, Anna, but her records show she moved to America in the eighties.' Suzette stared at the Captain. 'Which brings us back to the same point. Why this and why now?'

'If I knew that, I wouldn't still just be a Captain after all of these years.' The telephone on his desk began ringing. 'Oui?' he said, snatching the receiver. 'D'accord, show her into my office.' He put down the phone. 'Anouk Levy is here,' he said to Suzette. 'And she insists on speaking to us before we speak to her husband again.'

'*Insists?*' Suzette questioned.

He nodded. 'And I got the impression she wasn't about to take no for an answer.'

Suzette smiled. 'Then we'd better talk to her, non?'

'She may just tell us what her husband cannot.'

The Lieutenant frowned. 'Why would she do that?'

The Captain laughed. 'Because she's an upper class Parisian housewife. The only thing she is really interested in is her social position. She'll do anything to protect that. She'll walk over anyone she has to, to protect her nice, neat life.' He smiled. 'It used to bother me a lot, but now that I'm old with one foot in the grave, I see it for what it is. An opportunity to bring me closer to retirement.'

'My husband is innocent,' Anouk Levy announced matter-of-factly. She had seated herself on the edge of the battered leather chair opposite Bertram's desk. She pulled tightly on the Hermès headscarf she had tied around her wig. She ran her finger across her chin, the tip of her fingernail leaving a line in the powder. She either did not notice, or did not appear to care.

Bertram nodded. 'Of what?'

Anouk leaned forward, steadying herself on the armrest. Small, painted on eyebrows pinching in confusion. 'What do you mean?'

'Your husband is innocent of what?' he expanded.

She tutted. 'Well, of everything, of course.'

Bertram emitted an impressed whistle. 'Well, isn't that something? He really must be a pious, saintly man.'

She shrugged her shoulder nonchalantly. 'Bien sûr.'

Bertram smiled at Suzette. 'Did you hear that, Lieutenant Carman? Rabbi Serge Levy is innocent of *everything*.'

'That's what the lady said, Captain,' Suzette agreed.

Anouk pivoted her head between the two of them 'I have spoken with our family Avocat. He has informed me he will be instructing my husband to remain silent until you have issued him with an exact list of the questions you intend on asking him, and more importantly, why you have kept him here without a single charge being issued. Our Avocat is at this very moment having a meeting with the Procurer, a close personal friend of the family, and I am told they are both awaiting my news following this meeting.'

'Is that all?' Bertram interjected.

'What do you mean?' she snapped.

Bertram shrugged. 'It's just that I'm wondering who else you're going to pull out of that rather fetching scarf you're wearing. The Prime Minister? The President himself?'

Anouk smiled demurely. 'If I have to, Captain Hervé. If I have to.'

Bertram nodded. 'I don't doubt you could manage it, Madame Levy. I don't doubt it at all.'

'Bon,' Anouk replied. 'Then my husband will be released immediately?'

'I'm afraid not,' Bertram retorted. 'Unless there's something in it for me.'

Her eyes widened. 'I'm not sure I understand what you mean.'

He leaned forward. 'I'm not sure what you're hiding, you and your husband. But I know you're hiding something. And I'll find out what it is, no matter how many people breathe down my neck. Because, as far as I can tell, the Krief's and the Dukas' have just as as many important friends. That's why I'd hate this to become a popularity contest.'

'What do you want from me?' Anouk asked with a resigned sigh.

'Are you familiar with chess, Madame Levy?' Suzette interrupted.

Anouk turned her head, studying Suzette as if she was a creature from another planet. 'What a bizarre question.'

'Not really,' Suzette replied. 'I'm just thinking about sometimes to win, it is necessary to sacrifice a pawn.'

'Et?' Anouk hissed. She turned back to Bertram. 'Je suis désolé, Captain Hervé, but I don't have time to deal with nonsense from your,' she shot Suzette a withering glare, 'assistant. Are you, or are you not, going to release my husband?'

'Not,' Bertram answered.

Anouk balled up her fists and slammed them on the corner of his desk. Although she was small, she did it with such force it appeared as if it should have hurt, but she showed no signs of it. 'This is outrageous!' she screeched.

Bertram pointed at Suzette. 'Lieutenant Carman has a point. I don't play chess myself, a bit above me, but I get the general idea. As far as I can tell, Madame Levy, you want your husband to go free so you can go back to your nice, neat life, where he is the lauded Rabbi, and you the dutiful and respected wife. I get that you're worried about that all coming crashing down, and because of that, I suspect you'd do just about anything to stop it. Non?'

Anouk glared at him. 'I don't know what you want of me.'

'Sacrifice your pawn,' Suzette said.

Anouk ground her teeth together. 'There is no damn pawn, you idiot.'

Bertram held her gaze. 'Then we've reached an impasse, haven't we?'

Anouk rose slowly to her feet. 'Then that is what I will tell my Avocat and the Procurer.'

Bertram watched her as she moved towards the door. 'This will not go away, you know, Madame Levy.'

She stopped, turning back to him slowly. 'It never has.'

XXXIII

Madeline Duchamp awoke with a start, the dregs of a café cup falling from her lap and clattering against the ground. Her eyes widened in confusion as she came to her bearings. She tutted. 'I hope it didn't break,' she cried. 'The damn cups a hundred years old.' She pulled herself upright in her chair, wincing at the pain she felt. 'Getting old is getting old,' she said with a sigh. It took her a moment for the fogginess in her brain to clear. What day was it? Saturday? No, it was Sunday, she realised. She reached over and picked up a large, ornate bell. She shook it with as much vigour as she could. A few moments later, the door opened and Elise, her loyal maid, entered.

'You rang, Madame Duchamp?' Elise asked politely.

Madeline smiled at her. Of all the maids she had ever had, Elise was her favourite, though she most certainly never would tell her that. 'What are my plans for today, Elise?' Madeline asked, before quickly adding. 'I seem to have misplaced my diary.'

'You have a dinner at the symphony this evening. A fundraiser.' Elise answered.

Madeline stifled a yawn. 'Another one? The damn symphony has been fundraising for a new wing since I was a young woman. Perhaps they'll finish it before I become an old one.'

Elise smiled, but did not answer.

'What am I wearing?'

'The purple Chanel suit.'

'The new one?'

Elise nodded. 'The new one.'

Madeline shrugged. 'What a waste.' She sighed. 'Then again, what am I saving it for?' She gestured to Elise. 'Help me to my room. As this evening is likely to go on and on, I should perhaps have a small repose beforehand.'

'Bien sûr,' Elise answered, rushing towards her mistress.

Madeline pulled a cashmere stole tight around her shoulders. 'When was the last time I saw Hugo?' she asked.

Elise frowned. 'I'm not sure. Yesterday, I believe.'

Madeline sighed again. 'Ah, well, I suppose I should see him. Can you ask him to come to my room?'

Elise's eyes flashed warily. Madeline, despite her age and failing health, caught it instantly. 'What is it?'

Elise did not respond.

'What is it?' Madeline pressed, her voice rising sharply.

Elise stared at her. 'I don't believe he's in at the moment.'

Madeline shrugged. 'I know he's not the sort to have much to do with his time,' she reasoned, 'but it's not too much of a stretch to assume he might have plans, is it?'

'Bien sûr, non,' Elise replied. 'Mais, it's just that…' she trailed off.

Madeline tutted. 'Get to the point, fille, or I'll be dead and buried before you do.'

'I do not believe jeune Monsieur Duchamp came home last night,' Elise said quickly.

'You do not believe jeune Monsieur Duchamp came home last night,' Madeline repeated, unable to hide the fact she was impressed in her tone. She stopped, frowning. 'Hugo didn't spend last night in his room?' she said, as if she could not imagine such a scenario. She stared at Elise. 'And what are you basing this on? His clinically re-made bed?' She snorted. 'My grandson could show most of the maids who have ever been in my employ a thing or two on that account!'

Elise shook her head. 'It's not just that,' she said. 'I left his breakfast tray outside of the attic as I do every morning, and an hour later I go to retrieve it. This morning it had not been moved, nor touched.'

Madeline's mouth twisted. 'Perhaps he's dieting. I hear even boys do that these days.' She stared at the maid. 'You look worried. Why are you worried?'

Elise shrugged slowly. 'Because it's not like him. He normally leaves me a note.'

Madeline frowned. 'And have you asked the other members of staff?'

'Who is there to ask?' Elise answered. 'Nobody really sees Hugo.'

Madeline considered. 'Hugo is almost fifteen years old. He's practically a man.' She laughed. 'He's certainly not a boy…' she trailed off. 'He's certainly not a boy…' she repeated.

'What is it, Madame Duchamp?' Elise pressed.

Madeline's mouth twisted into a distasteful grimace. 'Boys become men eventually. And I suppose even Hugo can't escape the hormones that come with that particular minefield.' She stopped, staring at the telephone, wrestling with a thought. 'Non, we need to nip this in the bud before it gets out of hand. Elise, have the driver bring around my car.'

'Oui, immédiatement, Madame Duchamp,' Elise replied. 'Where shall I tell him you are going?'

Madeline rose slowly to her feet. 'To the Levy family home.'

Elise nodded and prepared to leave.

'Attend. Elise,' Madeline interrupted. 'What time is it?'

Elise glanced at her watch. 'It's just turned 11H00,' she answered.

Madeline frowned. 'Well, it's a little early, but if I'm to face Anouk Levy, I can't do it unprepared. Pour me a scotch.'

Elise nodded. 'Oui.'

Madeline pursed her lips. 'Make it a large one. A <u>very</u> large one.'

Madeline glanced around the Levy living room, her face wrinkling. She had always hated this room, and the fact it had never changed in over forty years bothered her more than it should. The room was dark and full of shadows, and though she was not a woman prone to fancy, even she could not deny the presence of ghosts in the room. She had first come as a young girl, accompanying her parents. Then the Levy's were much more of a force to be reckoned with, and their dominance over the Faubourg Saint-Germain area was unparalleled. But something had changed. And it had begun with Serge Levy's father, Ari. A dull, listless man, prone to melancholy. But as Madeline recalled him, there was an essence of arrogance always bubbling beneath the surface. As far as she could tell, the arrogance had carried into one of his grandchildren, Joann. A boy who not only looked like Ari, but had taken the arrogance of his grandfather and amplified it, buoyed no doubt by the accumulating wealth and position of the family. Arrogance was something which irritated Madeline immensely, but the irony was not lost on her that she had not been able to eradicate it from her only child.

'Where are you going this time?'

'None of your damn business, mother.'

Madeline pulled herself up rigidly in the seat, straining her ears towards the door and cursing her failing hearing once again. The raised voices coming from the hallway had caught her attention, and she immediately recognised them as belonging to Anouk Levy and her elder son, Joann. Madeline smiled to herself, realising the maid had seemingly not told Anouk she had a visitor. Madeline shuffled, moving her head as far to the side as she could, hoping there was more to come in the conversation.

'The hell it isn't, you damn brat. Your father's still at the police station.'

'What the fuck has that got to do with me?'

'It has everything to do with you. It has everything to do with us all. If any of this comes out, we're all ruined, don't you get that, you stupid, spoiled child?'

If any of this comes out, we're all ruined. The words struck Madeline, her tongue moving slyly across her bottom lip. She had always known the truth was buried well in the Levy family, but she had never dared hope it would make its way to the surface.

'Then make sure father keeps his stupid mouth shut.'

'Of course, he'll keep his mouth shut. That's not what's worrying me.'

'What is?'

'You, you fool! You're careless and you'll make mistakes. You're so arrogant you think you're untouchable.'

'I AM untouchable!'

Madeline could vaguely make out heavy footsteps retreating along the hallway.

'Where are you going, Joann?'

'Out. I've got things to take care of.'

'I need you here.'

'You don't need anyone, mother. You never have. At least I take after you in that respect. Now quit bugging me!'

The front door slammed and Madeline sank back into her chair, realising Anouk was now likely to come into the living room.

Moments later she did and stopped dead in her tracks. 'Madeline,' she said, her voice rising with clear panic. 'I didn't know you were here.' She glanced over her shoulder, her eyes narrowing into angry pinpricks.

Someone's in trouble, Madeline thought with a little satisfaction. 'Oh, I haven't been here for long,' Anouk, smiling knowingly at her. *Just long enough.*

'Well, this is certainly a pleasant surprise,' Anouk said, moving into the room, her voice levelling as she attempted to regain her composure. 'I barely see you from one year to the next, and then suddenly it's twice in a week. Tell me, what have I done to deserve such a,' she paused, '*unexpected* delight.'

'I wanted to speak with you,' Madeline began, slowly turning her head as if satisfying herself they were still alone, 'and under the circumstances, I didn't want to do it over the telephone. Staff like to lurk where we least expect them.'

There was no hiding the surprise and thinly veiled interest on Anouk's face. 'Dieu knows where my staff are. They appeared to have let you in and then scuttled off somewhere to hide.' She flashed a sickly sweet smile. 'Your reputation for terrifying staff obviously precedes you, dear Madeline. Now, what is so important that you had to come all the way to see me?'

'I'd like to speak to your son,' Madeline said.

'Joann?' Anouk gasped with evident concern. 'Why on earth would you need to speak to Joann?'

Madeline shook her head dismissively. 'Not Joann. I'm talking about Josef. Where is Josef?'

Anouk frowned. 'What is this about, Madeline?'

Madeline sighed. 'It appears Hugo did not sleep in his own bed last night.'

Anouk snorted. 'Listen. I know we both have concerns regarding Josef and Hugo's… ahem, blossoming friendship. It just needs a little guidance, that's all, so that there can be no misinterpretation or misunderstanding. I'm afraid time has gotten away from me just now, but I will speak to Josef when I can, and you should speak to Hugo.'

'I'd like to speak to Josef,' Madeline hissed. 'And I want to speak with him now. I want to know where Hugo is.'

'What makes you think Josef would have any idea?' Anouk snapped. 'Just because your petit fils didn't sleep in his own bed, it has nothing to do with my son.'

Madeline shook her head irritably. 'Hugo was a different boy before he became involved with your son. Now he's smoking, listening to strange music. He's daydreaming, he's…' she trailed off, seemingly unable to finish the sentence. 'This didn't begin with Hugo, it began with Josef. Your son turned his head.'

Anouk lowered herself onto the seat opposite Madeline. 'I don't know what you're suggesting, Madeline Duchamp, mais…'

'Is Hugo sleeping in Josef's room?'

'Bien sûr, non,' Anouk snapped.

'Then show me,' Madeline retorted. 'When was the last time you saw Josef?'

Anouk did not answer.

Madeline sighed. 'I take it by your reticence to answer, you don't have an answer to give, am I correct?'

Anouk glared at her. 'And when was the last time you saw Hugo? Tell me that, Madeline, before you come here all high and mighty with me.'

Madeline rose slowly and painfully to her feet. 'Take me to the child's room and we'll deal with this once and for all.'

Anouk stared at her, weighing up her options, before it appeared she realised she was no match for the Grand Dame. 'Follow me.'

Madeline's face crinkled in disgust. 'Why do boys' rooms always smell so…' she searched for the words, 'as if something is ripening and on the verge of going off.'

Despite herself, Anouk cackled. 'And it doesn't make any difference how many times you send in the maid to clean them. An hour later it smells worse than before. I can't even get a maid to go into Joann's bedroom.'

'Hugo's a clean boy, so I'm told,' Madeleine conceded, 'but even he seems unable to outrun the stench of puberty and testosterone.' She stopped, apprising Anouk warily.

Anouk smiled. 'Well, that felt weird, didn't it?'

Madeline nodded. 'Decidedly so.'

'Shall we go back to formal disdain for one another?'

Madeline nodded again. 'Oh, oui. I'd hate anyone to think I was mellowing.'

Anouk stepped further into Josef's room. She pointed at the neat, made-up bed. 'You see. Nothing sordid going on in my house.'

Madeline stared at Anouk as if she could not believe her less. She took her own tentative step into the room. She did not know why, but she could tell Hugo had been here. His laughter echoed in her ears. The laughter she heard so rarely because she did not know how to instigate it. If Josef made Hugo laugh, was it such a bad thing, she asked herself.

Anouk began busying herself, tidying and moving things around. She pulled open a drawer which was ajar, a pair of pants sticking out. She gasped. Madeline rushed to her side, pushing her aside with her cane in an attempt to see what had caught her attention. It was a picture of Hugo in his school uniform. It was not the photograph itself which had elicited the reaction; it was the way it looked. Someone had taken a pair of scissors and cut around the photograph of an anxious-looking Hugo, not looking at the camera, cut into the shape of a perfect heart. Next to it was a packet of condoms.

Madeline gestured to Anouk. 'We need to talk.'

XXXIV

'Do you think they've run away together?' Anouk asked, panicked.

Madeline considered lowering herself back into the chair in the living room. She did not want to imagine it possible, but she could not ignore the timing. 'If the children were planning on leaving, they may have seized upon the opportunity when there is so much else going on,' she reasoned.

Anouk stared at the drink table in the corner of the room. 'Scotch?' she asked.

Madeline smiled. 'Bring the bottle.'

Anouk trudged across the room, picked up the bottle and two glasses, and moved back across the room. 'So, about our problem. Where do you think they could have gone?'

Madeline shrugged. 'I can't begin to imagine, I'm afraid. We sold the country estate after Hubert died. He was the only one who ever used it. I just can't envisage a single place where Hugo might go, or know to go.'

'Hubert.'

Madeline grabbed a glass and poured herself a healthy serving of scotch. 'Why did you say his name like that?'

Anouk poured her own drink. 'No reason.'

'No reason,' Madeline repeated. She sipped her drink but said nothing. 'No reason,' she repeated.

'Aren't you bored?' Anouk asked finally.

Madeline smiled. 'Well, I'm hardly ready to do cartwheels. I mean, there's not even a string quartet. Your scotch is passable.'

Anouk laughed.

'Isn't that what you meant?' Madeline asked.

'I'm half your age, and I'm already desperately bored with Parisian society,' Anouk said.

Madeline raised her hand. 'Half my age? You disgusting woman, I've had people killed for less.' She sipped her drink. 'Désolé, I didn't mean to touch a raw nerve.'

'And nor did I by mentioning your husband.'

Madeline pulled herself erect in the chair. 'Let's cut to the chase, shall we? I have better things to do with my time, and I'm sure you, have… well, another family member to bail out of jail.'

'You really are the most horrible woman, aren't you?' Anouk hissed. 'You think because you're old and rich and born into a family of position that it makes you so much more important than everyone else, don't you?'

Madeline shrugged. 'Clearly.'

Anouk shook her head. 'Non. I'm sick of this old family bullshit. Just because I wasn't born into the society you all find so acceptable, you somehow deem me less worthy than the rest of you.'

'You said it,' Madeline mouthed.

Anouk smiled. 'But I've spent the last twenty years of my life dealing with it and I'm frankly sick of all of you old, wrinkled matrons looking down your collective noses at me. I've spent decades covering for my family. But I've also spent the same decades covering for all of everyone else's family secrets.' She poured herself another drink, apparently warming to her diatribe. She smiled. 'Some have more than others, non?'

'Your son has seduced my petit fils,' Madeline bristled.

'Or vice versa,' Anouk answered, before adding, 'after all, it runs in the family.'

Madeline opened her mouth to speak, but no words emerged.

Anouk stood. 'And before you look down your nose at me and my family, I'd remember your own situation first. After all, it's public knowledge where you were when your husband was on his deathbed.'

'I counsel you to watch your mouth, Anouk Levy,' Madeline warned.

Anouk smiled. 'Don't you imagine that for every snide comment you make about someone, that someone else is making a similar snide comment about you, behind your back?'

Madeline shrugged nonchalantly. 'I'm bored with this conversation.'

'The fact remains, Madeline, families such as ours keep our secrets. We gossip amongst ourselves, but when it comes down to it, we close ranks. That is why no one talks about the scandal when you were shacked up with that rotund police officer at the exact moment your husband, your *homosexual* husband left this mortal coil.'

Madeline glared at Anouk. 'That was not a scandal, you silly woman. It was merely bad timing. If I had known my husband was about to expire, I would have changed my plans accordingly.' She helped herself to another drink. 'Do you think that somehow gives you the upper hand over me, you foolish woman?'

'We keep each other's secrets,' Anouk responded. 'That's what people of our class do.'

Madeline laughed. 'The Levy family have never been in the same class as the Duchamp family. The fact is, I'll be dead soon, but before I'm gone, I'll make sure no one accepts you in proper Parisian society.' She saw the doubtful look on Anouk's face. 'And if you think I can't do that, then you really are as stupid as you look.' She raised her hand. 'I don't have time for your faux protests. We have more pressing issues to deal with. Hugo and Josef are missing. Your husband is in a police cell and your other son,' she paused, 'well, let's be honest he's either going to end up dead or rotting in a police cell of his own.'

'What do you want from me, Madeline?' Anouk sighed.

'My petit fils is missing,' Madeline said. 'I've never told him how much I love him, because I was never taught how to. Or rather, I was always taught not to. I don't know how the Duchamp family created such an oddity as Hugo, but it has made me happy. He has made me happy. He will outlive us all, and he will do wonderful things. He won't do what I want of him, or else I would insist he does. But he will do something wonderful, and the Duchamp name will mean something, something different from what I envisaged, but it will be powerful and it will all be down to Hugo.'

Anouk shrugged.

'But there is something very wrong,' Madeline continued, 'and I can't bear the thought Hugo has somehow become involved in it all.' She paused. 'So, let's stop all of this nonsense and tell me what I need to know, so that we can go back to smiling and politely ignoring each other and then telling everyone else how much we hate each other. The only way we are going to do that is by doing the one thing the police can't.'

'And that is?' Anouk asked.

'By telling each other the truth,' Madeline replied. 'And we begin by you telling me the truth about what happened to Raul Krief and Gerrard Le Mache twenty years ago.'

'What good will come of that?' Anouk reasoned.

Madeline sighed. 'Because unless I'm very much mistaken, I believe Hugo and Josef's lives could depend on it.'

XXXV

Anouk stared at Madeline, her eyes sweeping over her as if she was trying to read the old woman's face. 'You can't be serious,' Anouk cried. 'Bien sûr, you're not being serious. You're being overly dramatic. You're well known for it, Madeline Duchamp.'

Madeline did not reply, instead moving slowly to the liquor cabinet and pouring herself a scotch. She also refilled Anouk's glass and handed it to her.

Anouk stared at it. 'I shouldn't. The last few have gone to my head.' She pointed at Madeline. 'As has yours, I'm sure.'

Madeline laughed. 'It has barely touched the sides, you silly woman.' She stared at Anouk. 'When was the last time Josef went missing?'

Anouk considered, staring at the glass as if she was wrestling with something. Finally, she raised it to her lips and drained the contents. 'He never has. He has always been a good boy. He has always known his place. It is a mystery to me how I produced two such different sons.'

'Perhaps they have different fathers,' Madeline quipped.

Despite herself, Anouk smiled. 'Ah, if it were only that simple, old woman,' she laughed. 'You may not think much of me, but I can assure you, when I was younger I could have had my pick of men.'

Madeline pointed to Anouk's wig. 'I'm sure. There are an abundance of men who fantasise about running their fingers through nylon.'

Anouk snatched the wig from her head, revealing a short, red-coloured pixie style haircut.

Madeline raised an eyebrow. 'Well, that's certainly *somewhat* of an improvement,' she said.

Anouk balled her wig up in her hands. 'If we were talking about Joann, I wouldn't be so worried. He could always look after himself, mais Josef…' she trailed off.

'Exactement,' Madeline continued. 'And the same goes for Hugo. He would never leave my home without telling me.'

Anouk snorted. 'Everyone knows you keep him locked up in your damn attic. He could be missing most nights and you'd never know the difference.'

'While it's true, I extend Hugo his freedom, I do so because he is more than capable of taking care of himself. He's never needed coddling, and I don't believe he would respond well if I tried,' Madeline answered. 'And there isn't a single reason why he could not come and go as he pleases without my permission.' She narrowed her eyes. 'Mais, despite all that, I know my grandson. He would not simply disappear without telling me, or his maid at the very least.' She paused. 'The fact is, I feel somewhat responsible.'

Anouk's eyes widened. 'You do?'

Madeline sucked in her cheeks. 'I said, *somewhat* responsible,' she snapped. 'As are we all. The simple fact is two boys went missing, and now a further two more have gone missing. This time it is closer to home. And it can only mean one thing - someone is not done with the past.'

Anouk tutted. 'Madeline, you really have to let this obsession of yours go. It's bordering on the pathological.'

'Raul Krief was murdered because of what happened to him in the park twenty years ago, you don't have to be a genius to understand that,' she gazed at Anouk. 'Although I suppose you do need a modicum of intelligence…'

'This has nothing to do with what happened twenty years ago, it can't…'

'Why not?' Madeline interjected quickly. 'Because Ari Levy is dead?'

Anouk's eyes flashed darkly. 'I don't know what you're suggesting, Madeline, mais…'

'This was never about your husband frequenting the park to visit black prostitutes, was it?' Madeline quipped.

'Bien sûr, it wasn't,' Anouk hissed. 'Not that it ever stopped you whispering about it behind his back.'

'I never told the police.'

'You told your lover,' Anouk cried.

Madeline shook her head. 'Non, I never did. I'm sure he knew, but it didn't come from me. Most likely, it came from one of Serge's "friends."'

'You told no one?'

Madeline pursed her lips. 'Bien sûr, non,' she answered. 'You and I agree on very little, Anouk. But we agree on this. Families such as ours must stick together.' Her lips twisted into a cruel smile. 'However, don't think for a moment I kept quiet for any other reason than I never believed Serge had anything to do with it, and yet…' she trailed off. 'I always wondered why none of you ever bothered defending yourselves from the gossip. I always assumed it was because it was true, which it was, but men visit prostitutes all of the time, even black ones. Hell, I know a high-ranking General in the French army who has a fetish for women with missing limbs.' She shuddered. 'I can't imagine what he does with them, but by all accounts it keeps him happy and focused on protecting the Republic.' She took a gulp of scotch. 'As I said. I never quite understood the wall of silence. Somebody lied that night, and it wasn't me, that's all I know.' She stared at Anouk. 'Well?'

'She called the house that night,' Anouk said after a minute had passed, the only sound in the room emitting from the ancient clock on the wall and Madeline's heavy breathing. 'His "woman" friend,' Anouk added with contempt.

'For what reason?' Madeline gasped. 'Women like that know better than to turn up at the marital home. What was on her mind?

Blackmail?' She turned her head, reminded of a similar incident in her own life.

Anouk shook her head. 'Surprisingly not. She wanted to warn Serge about something she'd seen.'

Madeline leaned forward in her chair. 'Ah, so Serge wasn't in the park that night because he felt like a little recreation. It was because he was there to do what, to stop someone?'

'Serge and I had only been married for a few years,' Anouk said after a few moments. 'And believe it or not, back then I was a little naïve. My family had worked hard on the match between our families. The Levy's were and still are a formidable family. I was very lucky to become a part of it. Everyone thought so…' she trailed off.

'Often the reality is quite different to what we imagine,' Madeline added.

Anouk nodded. 'You're right. This was never about prostitutes - black or otherwise. I came to marriage inexperienced, but I knew enough to know the intimacy should have been… *better*. I wasn't what Serge wanted, but I was what he needed.' She stared at Madeline. 'But, of course, you of all people know exactly what I'm talking about, don't you?' Madeline did not respond, her head still turned firmly in the other direction. 'Non, the problem was Serge's father,' Anouk continued.

'Ari Levy.' Madeline whispered the name. 'Always struck me as a quiet, stoic and dignified man,' Madeline stated. 'Which, of course, probably meant he was anything but. Mind you, I heard nothing untoward about him. He appeared to me to be a little too wrapped up in his religion. He was from the old world, and I heard he had seen some terrible things during the Holocaust.'

'He had,' Anouk replied. 'And it changed him. It made him cold. It made him,' she searched for the word, 'judgemental.'

'Judgemental? In what way?'

'He was obsessed with sin,' Anouk replied, before adding

with a sad smile. 'And not in a good way. You're right. He did witness some terrible things during World War Two. It wasn't just about what happened to the Jews. It was everything. Neighbours selling out neighbours in exchange for their own safety, or sometimes not even that. Sometimes it was about getting a loaf of bread to feed their children. Women lay with the Nazis to secure safe passage. And somewhere, somewhere amongst the maelstrom of his mind, it all became confused.'

Madeline frowned. 'I understand how the horrors of war can cause turmoil, believe me. I saw it with my own family. What I don't see is how any of this manifested itself into what happened to Raul Krief and Gerrard Le Mache?'

'Ari's zealousness had always been bad, but in 1974 he was diagnosed with a terminal brain tumour. The entire family was in shock, but Ari seemed to just accept it. I think he saw it a sign from Dieu. Obviously, doctors would say it was the tumour which affected him, cutting off parts of his brain, or whatever, mais he changed. I'd always been frightened of him. He was intense and cold and he had very little time for women or children. But the tumour made him worse, particularly his feelings concerning sin and repentance.'

'But what did that have to do with Raul and Gerrard?' Madeline asked, shaking her head in confusion.

'Ari knew everybody. Not just the local Jewish community. He knew everyone,' Anouk said. 'And a Rabbi, like a priest, is privy to secrets and lies. People want to believe there is a Heaven and that they will get there, and they need a religious person to tell them that.'

Madeline nodded. 'So people confessed their sins to Ari? And he did what with it? Blackmail them?'

'Non, absolutely not,' Anouk snapped. 'This was never about money. We had enough money of our own. I suppose in his addled brain, it was about power for him. Raul and Gerrard both had families who were a prominent part of the community. In fact, Ari had known both Raul's and Gerrard's grandfathers during the War. Both of the families had connections to Spain, as I recall. I don't really understand what it was all about. But the Krief and Le Mache family had worked together to establish their fortunes, and I think it had something to do with collecting and reselling property stolen from the Jews during the War.' She took a drink of scotch. 'Somewhere in his confusion, it all became too much for Ari. And then it was Rosh Hashanah, and I think it tipped him over the edge. I'm not a doctor, nor an expert, but it seems the tumour brought up all the old resentments he had been carrying.'

'Rosh Hashanah?' Madeline questioned. 'Isn't that the Jewish New Year?'

'Oui,' Anouk replied. She placed her wig back on her head. 'But really, it's more than that for believers. It is also the beginning of ten days of penitence, which culminate on Yom Kippur - the day of fasting, prayer and repentance,' she added.

'The Day of Atonement.'

'Exactement! The Day of Atonement,' Anouk repeated. 'The forgiving of sins.'

Madeline shook her head. 'Are you seriously telling me Ari Levy kidnapped Raul Krief and Gerard Le Mache as a way of punishing their families because of their past sins?' she asked with clear disbelief.

'I didn't say it made sense, Madeline,' Anouk conceded, 'but that is what happened. The older generation were gone, but Ari saw the sins on the faces of the children.'

'None of this makes sense,' Madeline reasoned. 'It can't have been Ari's intention to punish those poor boys in such a horrific way.'

Anouk took a deep breath. 'You have to understand, we knew nothing about this, not until later, not until…' she gulped, 'the end.' She took another sip of the scotch. 'Ari told Serge about it later. Both Raul and Gerard were part of a Torah study group. Ari said he had been reading about Rosh Hashanah all day and when the boys came into his study, something snapped. He claimed it was because Raul was the double of his grandfather, and in that moment Ari's muddled brain flashed back to the War, and the things he'd seen the families do. He told Serge that it all became clear to him in that moment. His final act on this earth was to make the sinners repent their sins.'

'And how did he plan to do that? By stringing the children up naked, tied to a tree?' Madeline shook her head irritably. 'Non, I thought about it then, and I still think about it now. This was about sex. It's *always* about sex, in one way or another.'

'He swore it wasn't,' Anouk responded. 'Ari just wanted the Krief's to repent, to pray. He drugged the boys and took them to our country house. It was rarely used. Then he spent the next ten days counselling their parents. Encouraging them to pray and ask Dieu for help. He intended to bring the boys back on Yom Kippur. The nakedness was a symbol - the symbol of being reborn. Coming back into the world washed clean. Ari's intent was always just that - to bring sinners back into the light.'

Madeline poured herself another drink. Her hand shook as she raised it to her lips.

'That night - the night the boys were discovered,' Anouk continued. 'Ari took a turn for the worse. Maybe it was the stress of it all, I don't know, but he was weak, so he finally confessed what he had done. Serge went berserk. He was furious. I'd never seen him like that before, and I haven't again. He wanted to call the police, but in the end…'

'Self-preservation kicked in,' Madeline added matter-of-factly.

Anouk nodded. 'He knew whatever happened, his father's reputation would be ruined forever, as would the entire family name. There was only one thing he could do. Finish the job.'

'He killed the boys?'

Anouk slammed her fists on the table with such force the glass beneath her cracked. 'Non, you silly old woman. He went to the country house and brought the boys back. They were still drugged, in and out of consciousness, it seemed. Ari had been feeding them a cocktail of his cancer medication and some other drugs he had managed to find. Serge said it was relatively easy. He brought them back into the city and prepared the scene just as his father had intended. And then he left them. He made it appear just like a kidnapping which had gone wrong.'

'What did the prostitute have to do with all of this?' Madeline questioned.

'Serge called her after you saw him leave the park,' Anouk replied.

Madeline nodded. 'Because he realised he needed an alibi, and even a sordid one was better than the truth.'

Anouk sighed. 'Oui. She came to the house and agreed to go along with his story.' She laughed. 'Why wouldn't she? She was well compensated for telling a lie she probably didn't even know was a lie. She was as high as a kite when she came here. For all she knew she had been with my husband, fornicating in the damn bushes.'

Madeline stood, moving to the drinks cabinet and extracting another bottle of scotch. 'It might be cheaper than I'm used to, but once you get going with it, it's rather passable,' she stated, cracking open the bottle and refilling both of their glasses.

Anouk stared sadly at the glass. 'I suppose I might as well spend the day in a stupor. It can't get any worse, can it?' She stared at Madeline. 'What are you going to do with this information?' she asked.

Madeline settled herself back in the chair. 'Well, that depends,' she replied. 'On what it is you have left out.'

Anouk frowned. 'What do you mean?'

Madeline raised an eyebrow. 'The scene you just described is not the one which the police discovered later.' She clasped her hands in front of her. 'Alors…'

'What are you saying?'

Madeleine shrugged. 'Only that someone is lying. You claim Serge brought the boys back to Paris with a view to staging a scene which had no connection with his father, but yet both boys were left for dead. One did die.'

'But not at his hand.'

'Then whose?' Madeline demanded, slamming her cane on the ground.

'Serge swears they were alive,' Anouk cried. 'And I believe him. I know what my husband is capable of, and he isn't capable of such a horrific thing. He was so worried they wouldn't be discovered quickly that he tied the bindings loose. He said they were already starting to come around. He wanted to make sure they were able to escape themselves if no one came to rescue them.'

Madeline stared at her. 'You do realise how fanciful this all sounds?'

Anouk nodded. 'I do, and I also hope you know how much I hate having to share it with you. It is our family's greatest shame. I had hoped shame was something you would understand.'

Madeline scoffed. 'I had a homosexual husband, and I probably have a homosexual grandson. My shame is in no way comparable with yours, Anouk Levy. Our shame is comparable only to the marriages our families arranged for us.'

'Serge did what he had to do,' Anouk said softly. 'Just as we all would have done for our families.'

Madeleine did not respond.

'He did not kill those boys,' Anouk cried. 'Not then, not now.'

'And yet here we are,' Madeline replied pensively. 'You have just told me how far Serge was prepared to go to protect his family.'

'Oui, mais, that has nothing to do with what happened

afterwards, or what has happened this week,' Anouk shouted. 'This is different. Just as it was then.'

Madeline gave her a doubtful look.

'Whatever happened to Raul and Gerrard in the park after Serge left them, is nothing to do with us.'

Madeline snorted. 'I doubt the police would see it that way.'

'Je sais,' Anouk agreed. 'And that's why we've had to keep quiet. They would read too much into this. Serge didn't kill Gerrard Le Mache then, and he didn't kill Raul Krief now. I'd swear my life on it.' She stared at Madeline. 'Do you believe me?'

'I suppose I do,' Madeline conceded. 'For all the good it does. Because if it wasn't Serge or his father, then it was someone else, and that means we're no closer to discovering what happened to Gad and Henri, and now Hugo and Josef.'

'I still maintain Josef and Hugo have run off somewhere to be alone.'

Madeline nodded. 'I never thought I'd say this, but I completely agree with you.' She took a breath. 'In the meantime, I'll speak to Bertram.'

'Can you make him understand?'

Madeline shrugged. 'I am not sure my influence extends in such a way.'

Anouk gave her a sad smile. 'I doubt that.' She paused. 'You really slept with him? I mean, I heard all the rumours, but I never really believed them. I mean, he seems so…' she searched or the words. 'Dirty. Fat.'

Madeleine raised her hands. 'You should talk about men and their habits.'

Anouk shook her shoulders in a conceding way.

'I had a very small barometer on which to measure men,' Madeline continued. 'Fortunately, Bertram's barometer was not so small that he did not indoctrinate me in something I had apparently been missing.'

Anouk threw back her head and laughed. 'Then, peut être I underestimated him,' she conceded doubtfully. 'Whatever you do, Madeline, try to make him understand,' she pleaded. 'I need Serge home.'

'I'll try,' Madeline replied. 'But this is beyond us. Serge is going to have to come clean if he wants the police to believe him. This is not just about protecting the past. It is now about protecting the future, and making peace with what has happened. I will not tolerate silence when my Hugo could be in danger.'

'If he talks, he will end up in prison.'

Madeleine laughed. 'That's a chance he's going to have to take. If he doesn't, he will have to deal with me, and after that, I'm sure he will think prison a much safer place for him to be.' She stood, steadying herself on the sideboard. 'And besides, isn't that what this was all about to begin with? Repentance? A new year to atone for past sins. Serge needs to atone and repent, because if he doesn't, there is a very real possibility that four boys could die.'

'I'll get my coat and come with you to the Commissariat,' Anouk exhaled. 'I'll tell Serge he has to talk to Captain Hervé.'

Madeline looked towards a large ornate wall calendar. 'When does Yom Kippur begin?'

Anouk sucked in a breath. 'Tomorrow.'

Madeline nodded. 'Then we have no time to lose.' She strode forcefully towards the door, slamming her cane against the ground.

XXXVI

Captain Bertram Hervé turned his head towards Lieutenant Suzette Carman. His eyebrows arched into an expression he hoped clearly said. Are you buying any of this bullshit?

Madeline smiled at him. 'I can't say I'm completely convinced by the entire story myself, Bertram,' she said. 'Mais it has a certain logic, but more importantly it is also likely very difficult to prove one way or another.'

Bertram looked towards the door, where only moments later he had asked an officer to take Anouk Levy to speak with her husband.

'It all seems very neat,' Suzette chimed in. 'Too damn neat, if you ask me.'

'You're probably quite correct, jeune femme,' Madeline conceded. 'However, as I stated, I can't imagine any of this will unravel easily. Par example, I'm sure they can interview Ari Levy's doctor who will produce a report indicating that Ari was not in his right mind at the time, and therefore cannot be held responsible for what he did.'

'Exactement!' Suzette exclaimed. 'Then you have a bona fide excuse. Why go to all of this trouble to connect a fairy-tale. Ari Levy is dead. His doctor would say he was not acting in his right mind. Therefore, case closed. No punishment.'

'One must always do what one can to protect the family name and reputation,' Madeline interrupted.

'That can't be all this is all about,' Suzette reasoned.

Madeline laughed. 'Then you didn't grow up with money or social position.' Her eyes flicked over her. 'Clearly.'

Suzette glanced down at her coffee-stained sweatshirt and

shrugged. 'Yeah, clearly.'

Bertram cleared his throat. He rose, pacing around his desk. 'Then what are we missing? Why on earth would Serge Levy claim Raul Krief and Gerrard Le Mache were very much alive when he left them?'

'Because they were,' Madeline reasoned. 'It's the only explanation.'

Bertram raised an eyebrow in Suzette's direction. 'Then what does that leave us?' he asked her. 'The actual murderer?'

Suzette shook her head. 'How would anyone else even know the boys were there? It makes no sense.'

'The prostitute did,' Madeleine reasoned.

Bertram shook his head. 'I knew her. She'd kill a John for short changing her, but I am absolutely one hundred percent certain she wouldn't murder a couple of naked teenagers.'

'Absolutely certain, are you?' Madeline repeated, with a hint of playfulness in her tone.

Bertram shrugged, round cheeks flushing.

Suzette tutted. 'It had to have been Serge. Or his father, and Serge is covering up for him.' She pointed to Bertram. 'Either way, we can't let Serge Levy go until he damn well tells us the truth.'

Bertram turned back to face Madeline. 'What do you think?'

'Madame Duchamp is making police decisions now, is she?' Suzette snapped. She pulled herself back in her chair upon seeing the scolding look on Bertram's face.

'Madame Duchamp knows these people. And she knows them in ways we don't. She understands them in ways we never could,' Bertram stated. 'And we all know what will happen next. They will close ranks and protect themselves. We've already seen the amount of power they wield.'

'But they can't get away with murder!' Suzette cried. 'I won't stand for it!'

Bertram appeared surprised. 'I'm very pleased to hear it,

Lieutenant Carman. You might actually do better in this job than I ever managed to do.' He turned back to Madeline. 'So, Madeline. Tell me what you think I should do.'

Madeline bowed her head in mock deference. 'Well, far be it from me to interfere in a police investigation.' She paused for a suitable amount of time. 'We have a more pressing problem,' she stated simply. 'Namely, the disappearance of Gad and Henri and,' she paused, swallowing a breath which seemed to pain her, 'and Hugo and Josef.'

'What are you proposing, Madeline?' Bertram asked with clear concern.

She shrugged. 'Well, it seems to me you have little to go on. You can play the waiting game. Lock the Rabbi in a cell and sweat it out of him. He's likely able to outlast you, so as I see it, the only thing you can do is cut him a deal.'

'Cut him a deal?' Bertram laughed. 'How do you even know such an expression?'

She shrugged again.

'Even if I wanted to, which I don't,' Bertram continued. 'I don't see how it can help us.'

'Because tomorrow is Yom Kippur,' she replied. 'And if this whole sorry affair is connected, then surely we can expect it to come to a head tomorrow.'

'The park is under constant surveillance,' Suzette interrupted, 'so I can't see anyone dumping the bodies in there.'

'The boys aren't dead, Lieutenant!' Bertram shouted.

Suzette nodded. 'Oui, oui, bien sûr. I just meant…' she trailed off, as if she was unsure how to finish the sentence.

'If Anouk told me the truth,' Madeline continued. 'The scene of the crime was not symbolic. Rather, I suppose, Serge Levy just wanted to get the boys out of the family home in the country where his father had been holding them.'

'The family home in the country,' Bertram repeated, tapping

his chin. 'What do we know about it?'

Madeline shrugged. 'Anouk didn't say.' She leaned forward. 'Bertram, écoute, I'm worried about Hugo.'

'Do you really think he's somehow got himself mixed up in this?'

'I don't know what to think,' she responded, 'other than to say I don't believe he is the sort of boy who would run away for whatever reason. He's not that dramatic. Yet.' She smiled. 'And he would hate the fact we'd even think he would. Non. I'm afraid I have to believe he's in trouble.'

'Then where do we begin?'

'We can find out what happened to the Levy country retreat,' Suzette suggested.

'If there is a connection, it could be relevant,' Madeline agreed.

'And there's something else that's been bothering me,' Suzette continued. 'Why did someone call in to report the fights between Rabbi Levy and Raul Krief? I mean, how did they know each other, other than what happened twenty years ago? What could possibly have inspired Raul to be angry with a Rabbi, a pillar of the community?' She paused. 'Fighting with someone shows to me they knew each other, or something had happened between them to cause animosity.' She extended her hands. 'And if that's true, then perhaps all of this time Raul was lying about what he remembered. He knew Serge Levy was involved and for some reason he was lashing out at him.'

Bertram pushed himself to his feet. 'Well, instead of sitting here throwing one theory after another into the air, let's go and put those very questions to the Rabbi himself.' He looked at Madeline. 'You stay here, Madeline.'

Madeline snorted, slamming her cane against the ground. 'Absolutely not,' she said, her tone insistent. 'Mon petit fils is missing. I have no intention of sitting on the sidelines.' She smiled.

'Besides, if Serge Levy refuses to answer your questions, I'll throttle the answers out of him with my own bare hands.'

'I'd have to arrest you,' Bertram said wearily.

She smiled at him. 'I'd like to see you try.' She moved her cane in the direction of the door. 'Now, take me to the cells!'

Rabbi Serge Levy lifted his head slowly. His eyes widened in surprised upon seeing Bertram, Suzette and Madeline standing in the hallway outside his cell. Anouk rose to her feet, offering Madeline her seat. Madeline took it with obvious reluctance. 'Have you made him see sense?' she asked Anouk.

Anouk shrugged. 'You know what men are like,' she answered. 'They always think they know best.'

Madeline slammed her cane against the ground with a force belying her age. 'Serge Levy. You were always a weak, dull child. You grew into a weak, dull man. Now is not the time to grow a backbone.' She pointed at Bertram. 'Now answer Captain Hervé's questions and do them quickly and fully, or,' she paused for dramatic affect. 'I'll join you in that cell, and we'll see who is the only one to emerge from it unharmed.' She smiled sweetly. 'And I guarantee, it won't be you.'

Serge stared blankly at them all. Madeline slammed her cane against the ground again. 'Don't look to them for help, you plebeian. I'm an old woman, but I can still pack a punch when I need to. And more importantly, I'll likely be dead before I even had to stand trial.'

'What do you need to know?' Serge asked with a sigh.

'Everything,' Bertram answered. 'But let's begin with this. Your family had a country estate your father used to hide Raul Krief and Gerrard Le Mache when he kidnapped them. Where is it and what happened to it?'

Serge frowned. 'After... after what happened, we sold it. I

didn't want any part of it.'

'Sold it to who?' Bertram asked.

Serge shrugged. 'I don't know. My avocat dealt with it. You can ask him.'

Bertram turned to Suzette. 'Find out who owns it now.'

Suzette nodded and moved to the doorway.

Bertram turned to Serge. 'Next. Why were you and Raul Krief fighting in recent months?'

Serge turned his head. 'We weren't.'

Madeline slammed her cane against the ground again. The force of it made Serge jump.

Serge lowered his head. 'He came to see me a few times, that's all,' Serge said. 'None of it made any sense. He was usually drunk, or on drugs, I don't know which.'

'What do you mean, it didn't make any sense?' Bertram asked.

'He was just angry. He was *always* angry.'

'And yet he came to see you,' Bertram reasoned. 'Which must have meant he remembered something. What sort of things did he say to you?'

Serge looked at his wife. Anouk nodded slowly.

'He said he knew what I'd done,' Serge said finally.

Bertram exchanged a look with Madeline. 'And what did you say?'

'Rien,' Serge replied. 'What could I say? I could hardly admit to what had happened.'

Bertram tapped his chin. 'And yet he came to you with his accusation, which suggests only thing. He remembered.' He paused. 'Which begs the question. Had he always remembered? And if so, why had he remained silent for twenty years?'

'Peut être he had a flashback or something,' Anouk Levy interjected.

'Or he'd always remembered,' Madeline added pensively.

'Then why keep quiet?'

Madeline shrugged, but did not respond.

'And he said nothing else?' Bertram pressed the Rabbi.

He shook his head. 'Non, I told you, very little of it made sense. Raul was an extremely troubled young man. He said he would not allow me to ruin his life.'

Madeline turned her head to Bertram, raising an eyebrow. She turned back to Serge. 'Forgive me,' she said with a confused expression, 'mais, hadn't you done that already?'

Serge gave her a sad smile. 'The thought occurred to me, mais he said, encore.'

Madeline moved her hand across her chin. 'This is important. I don't know why it is, but is important, I'm sure of that.'

'What do you mean?' Bertram asked.

She shrugged. 'I wish I knew.'

Bertram wrapped his hands around the bars of the cell. 'Is there nothing else you can tell us, Rabbi Levi? People are missing and obviously in very real trouble.'

'I wish I could!' Serge sobbed. 'But he was clear. He said my family would not ruin his life for a second time.'

Madeline cocked her head. 'He said your family?' she blurted. 'A moment ago, you said he would not allow *you* to ruin his life. Did he say that, or did he say "your family?"'

'It is the same thing, non?' Anouk interrupted.

Madeline shook her head. 'Not here, not now,' she retorted.

'I don't understand,' Anouk said.

Serge frowned. 'I think he said my family, but I can't be certain.'

Madeline lifted her hand slowly, eyes narrowing so she could see the watch on her wrist. *19H00.* 'Someone is playing a game with us,' she said. 'And just because we don't understand the rules, doesn't matter at this moment.' She stomped towards the exit. 'I will not allow my Hugo to succumb to something which has nothing to do with him.' She took a deep breath, steadying herself on the wall. *'Keep safe, Hugo, keep safe. We're coming for you,'* she whispered.

YOM KIPPUR

PARIS, FRANCE
OCTOBRE 1995

I

Hugo's head jerked upwards, a trail of vomit spraying from his mouth. Instinctively he went to move his hand to wipe his mouth, but to his surprise he found he could not move it. He turned his head, his eyes widening in horror when two disparate facts exploded in his brain. *You are naked and your hands are tied.* The words kept bouncing around his head. He felt groggy, a feeling he was not used to. It felt strange to him. As if he had suddenly jumped up, stumbling forwards from a dark room into a room filled with sunlight. He felt disorientated and confused. He vomited again, his head lurching forward.

'Dieu, aren't you done being sick yet? I was done being sick about ten minutes ago.'

Hugo gasped. He spat the rest of the vomit from his mouth. 'Josef?' he gasped.

'Ah, at least you remember my name,' Josef replied.

Hugo wriggled uncomfortably. 'What is that behind me?' he asked.

'It's my ass,' Josef said with a hint of playfulness.

'Your *what?*' Hugo gasped. He moved his body as best he could, realising he was restrained. And then he stopped, realising what it was he was feeling behind him was, most probably, Josef's ass.

'Where are we?' Hugo asked. His voice sounded feint and alien to him.

'Beats the shit out of me,' Josef said. 'But we're together, so at least that's something.'

Hugo was about to reply when he felt Josef push against him. 'Why are you doing that?' he asked.

'Doing what?' Josef responded, his tone breezy.

Hugo shook his head again, confused as to what about the situation could possibly make Josef sound so cheerful. 'Why are you pressing your buttocks into mine,' Hugo spluttered.

'Because you have nice buttocks,' Josef responded.

Hugo snorted. 'Stop it!' he cried. 'I don't know what's going on here, but we're in trouble, Josef,' he added. 'I feel so groggy, and my brain doesn't seem to be cooperating with me.'

'As I said, I'm a bit ahead of you,' Josef replied, 'and therefore I've had a chance to evaluate and,' he paused, 'appreciate our current circumstances.'

'We are tied to a tree,' Hugo said, spelling out each word slowly and deliberately.

'We're still at the house. The barn is just in front of me,' Josef added.

'I don't remember getting here, which likely means we've been drugged. None of these scenarios suggest anything good for us.'

Josef shrugged. 'Exactly,' he replied. 'So because of that, and in case we don't make it out of here in one piece, I want to make sure I make the most of it.'

'Make the most of it?' Hugo asked with incredulity.

Josef laughed. 'Sure. So, I've been conducting some research and I can confirm,' he pressed himself against Hugo again, 'that you have a mighty fine ass.'

Hugo hoped the smile would not be evident in his response. 'You can't possibly know that.'

'Oh, I can,' Josef replied, 'because I've been feeling it against mine for the last ten minutes. It's firm, but not in an annoying way. There's a give which I find very, *very* acceptable. It's big enough to feel, but not big enough that it takes up too much space on a seat next to me. All in all, I'd give it a nine out of ten.'

'You've given this a lot of thought,' Hugo said, smiling

despite the situation they had found themselves in.

'Sure. These things are important,' Josef answered.

Before he could stop himself, Hugo said. 'A nine out of ten?'

Josef laughed again. 'Well, yeah. I'd have to actually see it to confirm it's worth a ten.' He sighed. 'Do you know what I want right now?' he asked.

'A telephone? A police officer? A pair of scissors?' Hugo interjected.

'Well, yeah,' Josef replied. 'But I'd settle for you turning around and facing me.' He sighed. 'I want you to face me. I want to *feel* you facing me.'

Hugo said nothing, because he did not know what to say.

After a minute had passed, Josef sighed again. 'Big Joe wants to say bonjour to Big Hugo.'

Hugo laughed. 'Big Joe?'

'Sure. That's his name. Doesn't yours have a name?'

'Lonely Hugo,' Hugo mumbled under his breath.

'Give me a minute, and he won't be so lonely,' Josef retorted.

Hugo closed his eyes. 'Stop doing that.'

'Stop doing what?' Josef replied, his voice light and playful.

'Distracting me,' Hugo said. 'And… the other thing.' He shook his head. 'Stop distracting me. We're in trouble here, Josef.' He felt Josef nod, his head resting against the back of Hugo's.

'I know that, Hugo,' Josef agreed. 'But right now, all I'm thinking about is you and the fact we're tied naked against each other. Not by choice, I grant you, but certainly something I've thought about once or twice…'

'Josef…' Hugo sighed.

'All I'm saying is,' Josef continued. He smiled. 'You've got a nice ass.'

Hugo sighed again.

'Would it kill you to give me a compliment?'

For the third time, Hugo sighed. 'I think we've been

kidnapped, like Gad and Henri. Whatever happened to them could be about to happen to us.'

'Exactement!' Josef cried. He took a breath. 'Don't you get it? If I'm going to die, without the bang, then I'm going to take what I can. You're against me, and if that's all I have, I'm going to take this moment and enjoy it. I'm going to press my ass against yours. I'm going to reach around these ropes tying us together and touch your fingers and imagine we're walking down a boulevard holding hands for real. That's my world. That's the world I imagine every time I close my eyes at night. I always hope it's with you, but I'm a realist. I imagine you'd always find someone better for you than me.'

'I don't think that's true,' Hugo said.

'Oh, there is,' Josef said. 'You'll have to kiss a few frogs, but you'll get your prince one day.' He coughed as if he was fighting back tears. 'I want to be your prince, Hugo, but all I have for you right now is to be a frog.'

Hugo took a breath. 'Green is my favourite colour,' he said.

Josef laughed, throwing back his head and making the sound of a frog.

A moment passed. Hugo finally spoke. 'What is going on, Josef?' he asked. 'And I'm not talking about us, before we go down that particular road again.' He could feel Josef moving around, the binds tightening between them.

'We're in trouble,' Josef said. 'But don't worry, I'm ready to fight to the death to save you.'

'Well, that's comforting,' Hugo retorted. He glanced around. As far as he could tell, they were next to the old horse barn, tied together around a tree. 'There's something very wrong here, Josef.'

Josef looked down. 'I want to agree, but my body seems to be reasonably happy right now.'

'Be serious,' Hugo scowled. 'I want to get out of here. I'm fairly sure you want to get out of here too…'

'The only thing I'm sure of is I want us both to turn around…' Josef countered.

Hugo's eyes rolled. 'Then if you ever want to achieve that, you can only do so by helping me figure out what the hell kind of mess we've found ourselves in.'

Josef tutted. 'You fight a hard bargain, Duchamp.'

Hugo shrugged. 'Mais, I'm worth it. Alors,' he turned his head around him, trying to take in their surroundings. The night had descended and twilight was nearing, but he was reasonably sure they were still in the same country retreat.

'I don't think we've been moved very far,' he said. 'Which makes me wonder - what happened to Madeline's chauffeur?'

Josef looked around. 'Well, I only feel your ass, thank Dieu, so I don't think he's anywhere nearby.'

'Be serious, Josef!' Hugo hissed. 'Or else we're really in trouble. I can't do this alone. I need you.'

Josef gasped. 'Well, that took you a long time to admit. Bon. Now, we can move forward. You need a hero. Therefore, I gratefully accept the position. I will be your hero. The hero you have held out for.' He paused. 'I promise you, Hugo. I am strong and I'm fast, and I'm always fresh for a fight.'

Hugo's head tilted to the side. 'Yeah, and you're my very own Superman, aren't you, Bonnie?'

Josef tutted. 'Oh, you know nothing about culture, garçon,' he cried.

Hugo took a deep breath. 'Let's just figure out why we are here and who did this to us. Once we do that, we can go back to real life and continue this conversation.'

'In my real life, I don't get to stand naked tied to a tree with Hugo Duchamp,' Josef stated. 'So, it's a little swings and roundabouts for me right now. Besides, I feel weird.'

'It's probably shock,' Hugo replied.

'Or like you said, they could have drugged us,' Josef added.

Hugo considered. He did not feel as if he had been drugged, but his head was cloudy and he felt dazed, so he could not be sure.

'Don't be a sourpuss,' Josef said. 'Let me have my tree fantasy.'

Hugo sighed. 'Well, once we're free, I'll ask Madeline if I can have some kind of tree installed in the attic. She'll give me a withering look, but I'm sure she'll arrange it.' He paused. 'In the meantime, let's just solve the problem at hand first, d'accord?'

'A tree in your bedroom?' Josef questioned.

Hugo shrugged. 'Why not?'

'Okay, you tease,' Josef responded. 'I'll go along with your sordid plan to get me into your attic…'

Hugo smiled. 'Now, be serious. We have to get out of here, we just have to.'

'I know, I know.'

'When you were attacked. Did you see anything? Anything at all.'

'Non, it all happened so quickly.'

'Was there nothing? No sound, or smell, a glimpse of something as you went down?'

Josef considered. 'I don't think so. I don't remember anything. What about you?'

'I remember nothing, either,' Hugo conceded. 'There is one piece of good news. We didn't come here alone.'

'Ah, I forgot about the chauffeur,' Josef replied. 'But, wait. Why hasn't he come looking for us?'

Hugo pursed his lips. 'I've been wondering about that myself, and I can only think of two plausible explanations. First, he is responsible for this.'

'Dieu, do you think so?' Josef gasped

'It's certainly possible,' Hugo replied. 'I can't image why he would be involved, but we can't rule it out.'

'What's the other explanation?'

'That whoever attacked us somehow got rid of him too.'

'Rid of him? You mean...?'

Hugo shook his head. 'I don't think he would have been murdered, that would be too risky. It's far more likely he was sent away. If that's the case, it's good news for us, because once people realise we are missing, he can tell them where he took us.'

They lapsed into silence. There was something about the second scenario which bothered Hugo, but he did not want to say it aloud.

'That doesn't make any sense. Why would they let him go and identify themselves,' Josef said finally. 'Unless…'

'Don't, Josef,' Hugo whispered.

'They know it won't matter,' Josef continued, 'because by the time people realise we're missing and he tells them where he took us, it will be too late. The only thing they'll find is us tied to this damn tree with our throats cut. Dammit!' He began wriggling, thrashing against the ropes. 'HELP! HELP!' he screamed.

'Stop, Josef!' Hugo cried. 'The more you move, the tighter the ropes become.' He struggled to try to relieve the pressure the ropes were inflicting on him.

'Désolé,' Josef said, his body falling limp in defeat.

They lapsed into a much longer silence. Five minutes passed, then ten. Finally, Josef lifted his head. 'How long do you think we've been here?'

Hugo glanced toward the barn. 'It must be Monday,' he said. 'We'll be missed at school.'

'Maybe,' Josef spoke softly, 'but by the time anyone figures out where we are, we'll already be dead.'

'Don't be so defeatist, Josef,' Hugo snapped. 'Where there's life, there's hope.'

'I guess,' Josef answered reluctantly. 'I wonder if my father has been released yet? It's Yom Kippur this week. If he misses that there'll be a huge brouhaha because he'll have to explain to the

Jewish authorities exactly why he was missing, and he's not going to want to do that.'

'Yom Kippur?' Hugo asked, eager to change the subject.

'Oui. Jewish New Year,' he replied. 'Follows on from Rosh Hashanah, which is basically ten days of penitence, repenting our sins. You know the usual good stuff. On Yom Kippur we're supposed to fast and say lots of prayers and hope we're forgiven for all the terrible things we do. It's a pretty big deal for our people.' He stopped. 'Good job at changing the subject.' He pressed his buttocks into Hugo's again. 'For that, I get an extra-long squeeze.'

This time Hugo did not stop him. 'Did you say ten days of penitence?'

Josef continued squeezing. 'You pick your moments. Yeah, Rosh Hashanah.'

'And it began ten days ago?'

'More or less. It's Yom Kippur eve tomorrow.'

Hugo began counting backwards.

'What are you doing?'

'I'm just trying to work out when Gad and Henri went missing.'

'Last weekend, I think. Pourquoi?'

Hugo considered. 'No reason, really,' he answered. 'Just with you talking about penitence and asking for forgiveness - well, there's been a lot of talk about there being a symbolic element to it all.'

'That's just because of the similarity to what happened to Gad's father,' Josef reasoned.

'Twenty years ago.'

'Twenty years ago. And as everyone keeps saying, his death was almost to the day of what happened to him before.'

Hugo turned his head. 'What do you mean by that?'

'Rien. It's just the whole kidnapping slash murder was big

news, still is big news. My father always says prayers for them on the anniversary every year,' Josef replied. 'Can't be sure, but I think it's right around Yom Kippur.'

'Well, that's interesting,' Hugo said. 'Or not.' He shook his head. 'Oh, I don't know. I guess I'm just clutching at straws. Not that it matters now, anyway.'

Josef pressed against him. 'Hey, now don't you start getting maudlin on me,' he scowled. 'You're the one supposed to be cheering me up.'

'Désolé,' Hugo said.

'Hugo,' Josef whispered.

'Yeah?'

Josef cleared his throat. 'I think I love you.'

Hugo could not stop the gasp from escaping his mouth.

Josef laughed. 'Not quite the reaction I was expecting, but at least it was a reaction.' He paused. 'That's all you've got to say, big fella?'

Hugo smiled. 'I don't think anybody's ever said that to me… *about* me. It just feels… weird,' he said.

'Good weird?'

He shrugged. 'Yeah, I guess.'

'It's just if we're not going to make it out of this, I wanted the chance to say it.'

'We are going to make it out of this,' Hugo said. 'Because I refuse for this to be the end of my story.' He took a deep breath. 'And for what it's worth, I think I love you too.'

II

Hugo's head jerked upwards, his eyes widening in fear. He sighed. 'I fell asleep again, didn't I?'

Josef squeezed against him. 'You snore.'

'Non, I do not!' Hugo exclaimed.

'It's cute. Don't worry about it.'

Hugo looked around. 'I can't believe I fell asleep again. How long was I gone?'

'About an hour, I think.'

'An hour.' Hugo winced as he strained against the ropes. He could feel the blood trickling down his arm. 'It's getting painful,' he winced.

'It sure is,' Josef agreed. 'Let's just keep talking, take our minds off it, d'accord?'

Hugo nodded. 'I had a dream.'

Josef laughed. 'How dirty was it?'

Hugo suppressed a smile. 'Not one of those sorts of dreams, you sick boy. The dream was about your father.'

'Quoi?' Josef spat. 'Low blow, Duchamp!' he cried.

'I can't help thinking your father's arrest is the key to all of this.'

'Then you're wrong. You're dead wrong,' Josef snapped.

Hugo sighed. 'I don't need to see your face to know you're lying to me, Josef. So, why the secret? If you care about me the way you say you do, then surely you can be honest with me. Especially because of the circumstances we're in right now.'

'I don't know what you want me to say,' Josef said finally.

'Why was your father arrested?' Hugo repeated.

'Because everybody is crazy.'

'What do you mean?'

'I really don't want to talk about this, Hugo,' Josef replied. 'Not to you, of all people. We should be in the showing off in front of each other stage of our relationship, not the "I'm going to tell you all about my bat-shit crazy family" stage.'

Hugo snorted. 'Bonjour! You know ALL about my bat-shit crazy family. *Everyone* knows about it. My dirty secrets walk in front of me wherever I go, like some goddamn annoying neon sign. I don't judge; I *can't* judge.'

Josef sighed. 'My grandfather was a little weird.'

'I just found out my grandfather was a closet homosexual,' Hugo retorted. 'I win.'

Josef shook his head. 'Non, you don't, not even close. He was dead before I was even born, but for as long as I can remember, he intrigued me for one reason and one reason only. Nobody ever talked about him.'

Hugo nodded. He understood completely about guilty secrets within families. 'And that made him all the more interesting to you, non?'

'Bien sûr!' Josef shouted excitedly. 'Because no one talked about him, or mentioned him, he became even more interesting to me. I remember growing up I'd hear things, my parents arguing behind closed doors. Shouting, but then whispering his name as if was too difficult to speak. Obviously, as a kid, it intrigued me. They wouldn't speak to me about it, but then one day Joann came to me and he said, *Grand Père was a serial killer*. He said it so simply, like it was a perfectly normal, natural thing to say. *Grand Père was a serial killer*'

'A serial killer?' Hugo questioned. 'Your brother said that?'

'He did,' Josef replied. 'Although as usual, Joann was exaggerating.'

Hugo sighed with relief. 'Phew.'

'That doesn't mean he wasn't a crazy man,' Josef continued.

'A crazy man who did some crazy things.'

Hugo nodded. 'He was responsible for what happened to Raul Krief and Gerrard Le Mache in 1975, wasn't he?'

'How do you know that?'

'It's the only thing that makes sense,' Hugo responded. 'Your father was there, and I imagine it was because he was trying to protect his father, or save Raul and Gerrard, or both. I don't know and I can't say, it's not my place to guess.'

'I don't know the whole story, Hugo,' Josef stated. 'You have to believe me.'

'I do, of course I do,' Hugo replied. 'Tell me.'

'My grandfather was involved in what happened to Raul and Gerrard,' Josef continued. 'I don't know all the details, because I've only ever overheard conversations behind closed doors about him. All I know is that he was really sick. He was dying and somehow it messed up his mind and he got really confused. It was all tied to some nonsense about atoning for sins. He may have done some crazy things but from what I heard, he had nothing to do with actually murdering Gerrard and almost killing Raul.'

'You're sure?' Hugo asked doubtfully.

Josef shrugged. 'That's what my parents said, and I don't see why they would lie about it when they were talking about it behind their own closed doors.'

Hugo considered. 'Then it was your father?' he countered.

Josef shook his head. 'Non. My father was just trying to clean up the mess my grandfather made. My grandfather may have kidnapped Raul and Gerrard, but he didn't try to kill them. It was just symbolic for my grandfather.'

'And they were alive when your father left them?' Hugo asked.

'Oui, he swears they were,' Josef responded. 'He left them loosely tied to the tree so that they could escape when they came too.'

'Then I don't understand,' Hugo countered. 'Because somebody did murder Gerrard and almost Raul. Could your grandfather have gone back?'

'Not according to what my parents said,' Josef replied. 'The old man was rambling, so they called his doctor, who gave him a sedative. He never left the house again that night and my parents were together with him the whole time. They sounded as if they were genuinely shocked to hear what happened the next day.'

Hugo frowned. 'Then I really don't understand. Could it have been a prostitute, or a pimp, or one of their clients, or a drug dealer or…' he trailed off.

'Sure, it could have been anyone in the park that night.'

'But why?' Hugo interjected. 'Why would someone see two kids tied to a tree and rather than help them, decide to murder them instead? It really makes no sense.'

Josef laughed sadly. 'I've seen how wasted and crazy my brother gets when he's high. Half the time, I don't even think he knows what he's doing. He could murder someone and he'd probably not even be aware he's doing it.'

Hugo took in a sharp breath. Somewhere in his brain it felt as if a light had been switched on. He could see it, but it made no sense to him.

'Are you okay, H?' Josef asked.

'I don't know,' Hugo replied. 'It's something you just said. Something I don't understand.' He paused. 'Did you say, your father left Raul and Gerrard tied loosely to the tree?'

'Yeah. He didn't want to risk them being outside all night.'

'And you truly believe he left them alive?'

'Of course I do!' Josef shouted. 'Papa is many things, but he's not a murderer. He was just protecting his family, that's all. I mean, why would he do such a terrible thing?'

'As you said, he was protecting his family,' Hugo reasoned. 'And if Raul and Gerrard were alive to tell what happened to them, then they would tell the police your grandfather kidnapped them.'

'I don't think so,' Josef retorted. 'They were drugged, and according to Papa, they never saw my grandfather. And as my mother reasoned, even if they did, who would believe them over a well-respected, and more importantly a dying Rabbi?' He shook his head. 'And it would have been their word against my parents, and they would have maintained my grandfather had been ill in bed all the time. Hell, it wouldn't surprise me if they could get a doctor to lie and agree with them. I know it sounds suspicious, and if it was anyone else, I'd probably agree with you. But I know my father. He wouldn't murder anyone in such a horrible way.'

'But somebody did,' Hugo continued. 'And I just don't see…' he trailed off.

'What is it, H? What are you thinking?'

'Well, something occurred to me when you were talking about how people on drugs don't always know what they're doing.' He shook his head 'Mais, it wouldn't make sense,' Hugo said distantly. 'Or maybe it would explain it all…'

'You're the one not making sense, Hugo,' Josef stated.

Hugo jumped, startled by a sudden noise behind them. He frowned. It sounded like someone was clapping. He turned his head, but he could not move it far enough to see behind him.

'What's going on, Josef?' he asked, realising the noise was coming from behind him, which most likely suggested it was in front of Josef.

Josef exhaled. 'They're here.'

'Who's here?' Hugo asked quickly. 'Our kidnapper?'

'This isn't good, Hugo,' Josef whispered. 'We're in a lot of trouble.'

III

Madeline was unsure how long she had been staring at the ornate telephone on the side table. Her hand had reached to it several times, but she had withdrawn it as quickly. She knew she should call her son, but for reasons she could not quite fathom, she could not bring herself to do it. Her relationship with Pierre had always been a difficult one, traceable as far back as his conception. She had been unused to men, and her first time with Hubert had left her underwhelmed of a process she had no burning desire to replicate. The pregnancy itself had been traumatic. It had almost felt as if her body was being taken over by an alien being. She was totally unprepared and recognised nothing of herself as her body stretched and morphed away from her. And then, almost nine months later Pierre had appeared, ripped from her in a pain so excruciating she knew right then and there nothing like it would be produced from her again. She vividly recalled the long, gangly, screaming purple creature attached to her by a tube and she was convinced she had indeed been carrying an alien child.

Matters had not much improved as Pierre grew and she realised she should be grateful for the man he had grown into - a successful, prominent lawyer with his own hugely successful firm. But the fact remained. She did not like him, because ultimately he was unlikable. Her own involvement was not lost on her. She had raised him the only way she knew how - a barrage of disparate nannies, teachers and maids. Each one seemingly more inadequate and incapable than their predecessor. It still amazed Madeline he had managed to produce someone like Hugo. *Hugo.* She had insisted on the name, believing it to be a proud and distinguished French name. She suddenly found it difficult to breathe. Her chest felt tight, and she was light-headed. She reached over and rang the bell. It took only a matter of a few seconds before the door opened and Elise ran into the room.

'You rang, Madame Duchamp?'

Madeline pointed to the antique bureau in the corner of the room. 'My tablets,' she croaked.

Elise ran to the bureau and pulled open a drawer. Moments later she ran to her mistress, pouring a glass of water and handing it to her along with the pills. Madeleine took them. 'Merci, Elise,' she said, swallowing the pills. 'I'm not sure what came over me.' She slumped back into the chair, emitting a tired, weary sigh. She turned back to her maid. 'You were very quick getting here. I'm impressed.'

Elise bowed her head. 'Merci, mais I was on my way to see you already.'

Madeline pulled herself erect. 'Is it Hugo? Has he returned?' she asked desperately.

'Non, désolé,' Elise replied with clear sadness. 'Mais, it was concerning the young garçon.'

Madeline leaned forward. 'What about him?'

Elise looked at the door. 'Anders came to see me a short while ago.'

'Anders?' Madeline reacted, her forehead creasing. 'My chauffeur?'

Elise nodded.

Madeline's nostrils flared. 'What does my chauffeur have to do with Hugo's disappearance? Tell me now, fille, and tell me quickly.'

The maid took a deep breath. 'Anders has just told me that yesterday he took young Hugo and his friend, the Rabbi's son, to a house outside of Paris.'

Madeline's eyes widened. 'For what purpose?'

She shrugged. 'I don't think he knew. Monsieur Duchamp

requested it, and Anders saw no reason to refuse the request. Indeed, he states he felt unable to refuse the request.'

Madeline shrugged her shoulders with reluctant agreement. 'And where is he now?'

'It seems Anders was told to leave and that the boys would make their own way home,' Elise replied.

'And he didn't think to mention it before now?' Madeline hissed shrilly.

'He didn't know until now,' Elise answered. 'He's been out most of the day at the garage with the car, and he only discovered the jeune Monsieur did not return home when he heard the other staff talking about it.'

'And this place where he dropped my petit-fils off. Where was it?' Madeline commanded.

Elise handed her a piece of paper. 'I had him write it down.'

Madeline reached into her pocket and pulled out her pince-nez. 'Where is this place?'

Elise shrugged. 'He just said it's about a forty-minute drive from Paris.'

Madeline yanked the telephone closer to her, fingers stabbing angrily at the buttons.

'Allô, Hervé,' a gruff voice called down the line.

'Bertram, this is Madeline.'

'Ah, Madeline. I was going to call you,' Bertram said, the tone in his voice lifting. 'We've found the country estate that used to belong to the Krief family. Lieutenant Carman and I are just about to leave.'

'Bon,' she replied. 'It seems as if my chauffeur, or *rather* my former chauffeur, drove Hugo and Josef there.'

Bertram chuckled. 'Your poor chauffeur. Try not to hurt him too much, will you?'

Madeline smiled. 'I'll be waiting by the door for you.'

'Non, cheri. Lieutenant Carman and I will take care of this

and we will bring Hugo home to you before you know it.'

She snorted. 'If you think I am the sort of woman who is capable of sitting cooling her heels, then you have very much underestimated me, Bertram Hervé.'

'We don't know what we're walking into, that's all,' Bertram retorted. 'I'd be much happier if you were safely tucked up at home.'

'Safely tucked up at home?' Madeline spat back. 'Who do you think I am? A twelve-year-old ballerina? I haven't made it to my age by listening to men who think they know me better than I know myself, and I don't intend on starting now.'

'Je suis désolé,' Bertram replied more firmly. 'I can't take the risk. Now you sit tight and try not to worry your pretty little head, and I'll be back soon with Hugo. You have my word. Au revoir.'

Before she could respond, Bertram disconnected the call. She stared dumfounded at the receiver. 'Well, of all the things… the audacity of the man…'

Elise inched forward. 'Is there a problem, Madame?'

Madeline tapped her chin. 'Where is Anders now?'

'I told him to pack his belongings and leave,' Elise answered. 'He agreed, realising it was most likely the safest option.'

Madeline laughed. 'Very wise.' She paused. 'But that leaves me with a little bit of a problem.' She clapped her hands together. 'Tell him he's unfired,' she said, 'for now. He's loyal and discreet, I'll give him that, and that's hard to come by in staff.' She considered. 'At least he came clean.' She nodded. 'Tell him he can have a second chance and have him bring the car to the front. I want him to take me directly to where he left Hugo.'

Elise nodded. 'Right away, Madame Duchamp.'

'Mais, Elise,' Madeline called after her maid. 'Tell him that I may forgive, but I don't forget. And I don't do third chances. In fact, tell him that if he crosses me again, I'll kill him myself with my own bare hands. And make sure he knows I'd get away with it, and that,' she laughed, 'they'd never find his body.'

The maid smiled. 'I'll make sure he understands, Madame Duchamp.'

IV

Hugo shook his head, unable to process what he was seeing. He had only seen him in passing, but he knew who he was looking at and it bothered him because he could not understand what it meant.

'You've really messed up our plans.'

Josef stared at Gad Krief. 'Gad, what are you doing?' he asked, his tone indicating his confusion. 'But it's great, get over here and untie me.'

Henri Dukas stepped out of the shadows of the horse stable. 'Yeah, Gad, why don't you go untie Josef and his,' he coughed, '"buddy?"'

Behind him, Hugo could feel Josef straining against the ropes.

'Henri. Is that you?' Josef cried.

'Sure is, old buddy,' Henri said cheerfully.

'Thank Dieu, you're okay!' Josef cried. 'Well, what the hell are you doing? Get us out of here.'

Neither Gad nor Henri moved.

'C'mon,' Josef repeated. 'Get us out of here.'

Hugo sighed. 'I don't think that's the plan, Josef,' he whispered.

'Henri,' Josef wailed. 'We've known each other since kindergarten. We've been to each other's Bar Mitzvah's. What's going on?'

'It's about money,' Hugo sighed. 'It's always about money.'

Gad Krief stabbed his finger into Hugo's stomach with such force it caused him to cry out. 'It's never just about money. Sometimes, it's about what's right. What's due to someone and, more importantly, revenge. Money is the reward for the need to exact revenge.'

Hugo frowned. 'Non, it isn't,' he countered. 'That's an excuse.'

'I wish someone would tell me what the hell is going on here!' Josef yelled.

Gad poked Hugo again. 'Ask your boyfriend,' he hissed, 'because he seems to have all the answers.'

Hugo shook his head. 'I don't have any of the answers. I wish I did, but I am trying to understand.'

'Then you weren't kidnapped, after all?' Josef called out.

'I don't think they were,' Hugo answered. 'I think this was all set up for reasons we can't begin to understand.'

Gad began pacing. 'You've really disrupted our plans, you two,' he grumbled, 'but in the end, I think it'll all make sense.'

'What does that even mean?' Josef interrupted.

Gad looked to Henri. 'We just have to come up with an alternative plan.'

'And we think we have,' Henri concluded. 'We think it'll all make perfect sense and people won't look too closely at it. You see, you two heroes came looking for us, you found us and being the swell young men you are, you rescued us.'

Gad took over. 'But then, as we made our escape, our captor came back and caught the pair of you. A fair swap. We run for our lives, run into traffic, the police are called. We're confused, a little dazed. Hugo and Josef rescued us, we'll say, but then they got caught. By the time the police find you, you'll be dead. We'll all be sad, but we'll move on.'

'That's all very neat,' Hugo stated. 'But who is really calling the shots here?'

'That would be me,' a woman's voice called from behind them.

Josef pulled at the ropes. 'Who is that?' he called out.

'It's Anna Moire,' Hugo stated.

'Directeur Adnet's assistant?' Josef interrupted. 'What the hell are you doing here? And more importantly, why the fuck is no one actually rescuing us.'

Hugo sighed. 'I saw the photograph.'

'The photograph?' Josef questioned.

Anna Moire moved out of the stable and stepped in front of Hugo. He tried to hold her gaze. He remembered her being tall and painfully thin, with alabaster skin and bright ginger hair, but in the light her skin and eyes now seemed to shine with a confidence he did not remember seeing when he had spoken to her before. Her lips twisted. 'The photograph?' she questioned.

Hugo nodded. 'When you spoke to me at school, you handed me your card,' he stopped for a moment. 'You were very sweet to me, by the way. Was it real? Or was it all part of some elaborate charade I don't understand.'

'Bien sûr, it was real,' she snapped, as if she was evidently offended.

Hugo's eyes widened. 'Then you can maybe understand why I'm a little confused, particularly bearing in mind our current circumstances?'

Anna clenched her fists. 'Two similar and yet disparate factors can operate at the same time, Hugo. You do see that, non?'

'This isn't a class,' Hugo snapped. He turned his head, looking at Anna, Gad, and Henri. 'And I'm fairly sure the four of you aren't here to grade us on our damn asses.'

She smiled. 'You see, you have spirit when it suits you.'

Hugo snorted. 'I have spirit when I'm tied naked next to…' he pressed himself against Josef, 'my *friend* and when it is quite clear we have been abducted by people who are seriously and ridiculously insane, dragging us into a mess which has nothing to do with us.'

'You walked into this "mess,"' Anna snapped.

Hugo shook his head angrily. 'Non, we did not. This is about the three of you. Josef and I have wandered into something that has nothing to do with us.' He took a breath. 'Mais, you have to understand, whatever you are thinking, whatever you are planning, you haven't crossed a line yet, at least, not in a way which can't be undone.'

'I'm curious, Hugo,' Anna interrupted. 'Why did you mention a photograph?'

Hugo's lips extended into an angry smile. 'That bothers you, huh? Not being in charge.'

Anna coughed. 'Hugo, I haven't been in charge for a long time.'

He nodded. 'Not since your brother died.'

'Her brother?' Josef interrupted.

'Oui,' Hugo replied. 'Gerrard Le Mache.'

'The kid who was tied to a tree with Gad's papa?' Josef asked.

'*The kid who was tied to a tree with Gad's papa*,' Anna repeated. 'How nicely put. It sounds so simple when you put it that way. But it wasn't simple. Nothing about it was simple.'

Hugo shook his head. 'I didn't mean it disrespectfully. When you handed me your card, I looked down and saw the photograph in your wallet. I didn't give it much thought. A photograph of you when you were younger with a boy. I guess I thought it was your boyfriend, or your husband, or something. But then it came to me. I'd seen the boy in the photograph before. It was in a frame. A remembrance of your brother Gerrard by a family who didn't want to forget him.'

Anna's jaw flexed. 'The Levy family has a lot to answer for.'

'Oui, we do,' Josef stated. 'And I'm very sorry for that.'

Anna looked at Hugo. 'They have a photograph of my brother?'

Hugo nodded, relieved he could not see Josef's face. 'On the mantelpiece in their living room. Of course, I didn't recognise who the photograph was of, nor did I place where I had seen one of the boys before. Not until just now.'

Anna stepped away from him and moved towards Josef. 'Is this true? You have a photograph of my brother and Raul in your house?'

Hugo could feel Josef's body tensing and the fact he was slowly moving his head into a nod.

'Why?' Anna cried. 'Why would you have a photograph like that in your house?' she hissed. 'Guilt?'

'I've seen that photograph every day of my life,' Josef said softly. 'And up until recently, I had no idea who it was. I suppose I just assumed it was some old relatives or something. But then when Raul died last week, I heard my parents talking about it. I swear I never knew.'

Anna tutted. 'And what did they say about it?'

'Only that my father wanted the photographs there as a reminder.'

'A reminder?' she snapped. 'A reminder of the terrible crime he committed.'

Josef did not answer immediately. 'A reminder of the terrible crime he did not prevent. Ecouté, I'm not defending what my father or grandfather did to Raul, to Gerrard, and their families. I can't defend it because I would be lying if I said I understood. All I can tell you is this - my whole life, my father has devoted himself to being a good man. A good Rabbi and a decent member of the community. I have to think part of that came as some sort of desire to repent, which is how this all began, it seems.'

'I can't believe the bastard had Gerrard's photograph all of this time,' Anna hissed.

'This was a long time ago. I can't pretend to understand what's going on here and now, but it seems there's a lot of anger and ill feeling,' Josef added desperately. 'And you have every right to be angry. But you gotta know this has nothing to do with Hugo.

If this is about punishing the Levy family, then so be it. Take it out on me, but dammit, let Hugo go.'

'It's too late for that,' Gad Krief spoke up. 'This all has to be neat.'

'Neat is ridiculous,' Hugo snapped. 'Let's talk about what is really happening here.'

'And what exactly do you think is happening here?' Anna asked.

'How and when did you discover that twenty years ago, in 1975, Raul Krief and Gerrard Le Mache were abducted by Rabbi Ari Levy?' Hugo asked.

'What do you mean?' Anna asked, stepping back in front of him.

Hugo inhaled. 'I mean. If you'd known all along, why wait until now to get your revenge?' He shook his head. 'Non. I think you only discovered what happened very recently and for the last twenty years you've been living an awful, traumatic existence.'

'What do you know of my life?' Anna cried. 'And how it affected my entire family? It wasn't just Gerrard who died that night. It killed my parents too; it just took them a little longer to die. We left Paris for a new start, but before I knew what happened, I was alone in a foreign country with nothing but terrible memories to plague me.'

Hugo turned his head to her, his hands straining against the too-tight ropes that bound him to Josef. 'And then you returned to Paris,' he stated. 'What was your intention?'

'There was never any intention other than to be close to the place where I had once been happy,' she answered.

Hugo nodded. 'When did you discover the truth?'

She shrugged. 'It doesn't matter when. The fact is, I discovered that the Levy family had been covering up the truth all these years, living their best lives without a care in the world.'

'That's not true,' Josef wailed. 'My father has been suffering for what he did, I'm sure of it. And the fact is, as much as you want to blame him and my grandfather, your brother was alive when they left him.'

Anna scoffed. 'Your family murdered him, in one way or another. They are certainly responsible for what happened to him.'

Josef nodded. 'I understand that, and I agree, but still…'

Hugo lifted his head. He had walked into the dimly illuminated room in his mind, and for the first time he saw clearly. 'Raul Krief killed his friend, didn't he?' he whispered into the air.

Nobody spoke, but Hugo imagined he could hear them all holding their breath. 'Didn't he?' he repeated.

Gad Krief moved across the grass. He dropped, flopping heavily onto a tree stump. 'What makes you say that?' he asked Hugo.

'It's the only thing which makes sense,' Hugo replied. 'If Josef's father is correct that he left both Raul and Gerrard alive, then what does that leave us? Some random person who was already in the park?' He shook his head. 'That makes no sense. I've been trying to get my head around how someone, a stranger, would murder two naked, vulnerable, defenceless boys. It really makes no sense, and therefore it made me think of something else. Something else, which makes little sense either, but could just be an explanation.'

He trailed off. 'We already know Serge Levy left the ropes loose, so that when Raul and Gerrard came around, they could escape. I can't pretend I understand, but here's what I think happened. Raul Krief woke up as someone in the park appeared and was most likely trying to cut him and Gerrard free. We already know Raul and Gerrard had been given some pretty heavy drugs to keep them docile. They were most likely out of it. So when Raul woke up and found someone was rescuing them, he misinterpreted it, most likely assuming it was his kidnapper. Again, I'm only guessing this, but peut être Gerrard had already been freed. Raul panicked, and a struggle ensued, a struggle which resulted in Gerrard dying.'

'That's rather a lot of guesswork, Hugo,' Josef interjected, uncertainly clear in his voice.

Hugo nodded. 'Je sais, mais…'

'And what about the person who freed them? What happened to him or her?' Josef furthered.

Hugo shrugged. 'Again, I don't know. But if they were in the park that night, with a knife, there's every chance they weren't there for a casual walk. No doubt they panicked, especially after the struggle resulted in Gerrard Le Mache dying.'

'And Raul? What happened to him?'

'He most likely realised what he had done, and he also panicked,' Hugo reasoned. 'He tied Gerrard back up, and then he made it appear as if he was also attacked. Peut être he wanted to kill himself or he just wanted it to appear as if he had been attacked and left for dead. He told their rescuer to run, or else he would say it was him. The rescuer ran, leaving Raul and Gerrard as he had found them, with one obvious difference.' He stopped and looked at Gad. 'Am I right?'

Gad Krief lowered his head. 'My father used to have nightmares. For as long as I can remember, he'd wake up screaming, jabbering. He made no sense, but then one day, he did,' Gad said. 'I heard what he said, and it all made sense finally.'

'What do you mean?'

'Nobody bought the whole, "I don't remember anything," shit he'd been spouting for decades. But what could they do? They couldn't call him a liar,' Gad continued. 'The fact was, my father remembered it all.'

'Then why not confess?' Josef asked. 'Or name my grandfather as their kidnapper?'

'He couldn't,' Gad said, 'because he'd risk them telling what actually happened. As it stood. Only my father and his rescuer knew what really happened. My father left town as soon as he could, but he never really managed to put it behind him. He came back to Paris, had me, tried to make sense of his life, but in the end he became a junkie.'

Hugo nodded. 'And that's when this all began again.'

'I'm really confused,' Josef exhaled.

'I think once Gad heard what his father had to say, he saw an opportunity.'

'An opportunity?'

'Oui,' Hugo replied. 'To make some money.'

'What do you mean?' Josef frowned. 'The Krief's have lots of money already.'

Gad laughed. 'Yeah, but it hasn't trickled its way down to me yet, and the truth is, as self destructive as my father was, I was fed up with waiting for him to implode, so I decided to do something about it.'

'But you needed help,' Hugo said.

Gad nodded. 'I told Henri about what Raul said about the kidnapping.'

Henri Dukas moved in front of Josef. 'And what the pervert priest had done to him and Gerrard.'

Josef's nostrils flared. 'First off, he was a Rabbi, and he wasn't a pervert. He was dying of a brain tumour, and he was really fucked up. He shouldn't have done what he did, but I can't let you accuse him of something so horrible.'

Henri shrugged. 'Whatever you say, but as far as I can see, perverts run in the family…'

Hugo cleared his throat. 'What happened next? You saw an opportunity to make some money, didn't you?'

Gad nodded. 'Papa needed drugs, and I wanted rid of him once and for all.'

'What's that expression, something about "poetic justice?"' Henri continued. 'Imagine our surprise when we found out our dealer was related to the pervert who kidnapped Raul in the first place.'

'My brother, Joann?' Josef gasped.

'You knew he was dealing,' Gad stated.

Josef remained silent.

'Imagine his surprise when we told him what we knew,' Henri continued. He laughed. 'We told him we wanted our drugs for free from now on.'

'What does this have to do with Mademoiselle Moire?' Josef asked. 'How does she fit into this?'

Hugo turned towards her. 'You overheard them, didn't you? You heard Gad and Henri talking to Joann Levy about what his grandfather had done twenty years ago, and more importantly, what Raul had done to your brother?'

Anna nodded. 'I wasn't angry at Raul, not really. I mean, it wasn't his fault to begin with,' she stated. 'But what happened later was.' Her voice cracked. 'My parents died without ever knowing what really happened and all because Raul and the Levy family kept their mouths shut. They worried more about their damn fortunes and reputations rather than honouring my brother. I hated them all.'

'And you wanted to make them pay,' Hugo whispered.

'Oui,' she replied. 'They all had to pay for what they did to Gerrard.' She began pacing. 'When I heard Gad and Henri talking to Joann, I realised they were all as bad as each other. They didn't want anyone to pay for what they had done, rather they were just going to keep peddling the same lies forever.' She shook her head. 'But not me. I wanted to make them pay.'

'So you went to Joann,' Hugo interrupted, 'and told him you wanted his help.'

'What are you saying, Hugo?' Josef interrupted. 'That Joann murdered Raul?'

'I don't know who actually murdered, Raul,' Hugo replied.

'But Joann certainly was involved.' He paused, talking a deep breath. 'But why don't we ask him ourselves? Joann? Are you there?' Hugo called out.

A moment later, the door to the stable swung open, and Joann Levy stepped out. He rushed towards them, stopping in front of Josef. He smiled at him. 'Your fag friend certainly has all the answers, doesn't he?'

'Joann!' Josef cried. 'What have you done!'

V

As they sped away from Paris into the countryside, Captain Bertram Hervé and Lieutenant Suzette Carman had remained silent, each locked in their own thoughts. As usual, Bertram was preoccupied with his forthcoming retirement, imagining his new life ahead of him. A life he had no concept of. He could not imagine growing old, nor could he imagine not having anything to do with his days, under the feet of a woman who had long since stopped caring about him.

'You're very quiet,' Suzette spoke, finally breaking the silence.

'As are you, my dear,' he stated.

'Are you worried?'

Bertram shrugged. 'Always.'

'I'm sure the boys will be fine,' Suzette said reassuringly.

Bertram's eyes widened, staring at the road in front of them. He felt guilty his only current thoughts were about his own predicament. He said nothing, instead tightening his grip on the steering wheel.

Suzette cleared her throat. 'Would you think I'm a terrible person if I told you all I've been thinking about is my own career?'

Bertram laughed. 'We're not so different after all, you and I, Lieutenant.'

She blew her lips. 'Don't tell me that,' she cried. 'I'm depressed enough already!'

Bertram momentarily turned his attention away from the road. 'What is it that's worrying you? My imminent retirement is making you blue, is that it?'

Suzette laughed. 'Oui, that's obviously it.' She glared out of the window. 'Mais, you are right, though. Your retirement is something I've been thinking about.'

'Counting the days?' he asked.

'Something like that,' she responded.

Bertram frowned. 'What is it?'

Suzette shrugged. 'I've always imagined you'd pop off into some home for the bewildered and leave me to run Commissariat de Police du 7e arrondissement. And yeah, I've been counting the days, but lately…'

He smiled. 'You realised you'll miss me?'

She laughed. 'Now, steady on, old man. That's not what I'm suggesting.' She took a deep breath. 'But this entire investigation has told me something I suppose I always knew. Something I thought didn't bother me, and that I could rise above, but right now, I'm thinking I can't. Too much of this job is about politics. Especially in this part of Paris where social position and wealth is more important than truth and honesty.' She sighed. 'I just don't think I can play the game.'

Bertram smiled at her. 'Ah, is that all?' He pointed at himself. 'Do you think I can play the game?'

'Haven't you been all these years in one way or another?'

His lips twisted. 'I suppose I have,' he answered. 'If I can offer you one piece of advice, it would be this - play the game because it will allow you to choose your arguments.'

'What does that mean?' Suzette asked.

'When it comes to wealth and power, when you have none, you will always feel like a bastard at a family reunion,' Bertram said. 'You will feel like an outsider, unwanted and under-appreciated, but they need you as much as they hate you. They're only as good as the people who play the game.'

Suzette frowned. 'And we play the game?'

Bertram nodded. 'We are the game. They need us. They hate us, but they need us. They know they have no choice but to protect themselves most of the time, but all the same, they know we have to go along with it.'

'And that's your advice?' Suzette questioned. 'We have to go along with it, no matter what they do?'

He shook his head. 'Not at all.' He sighed. 'Listen, I know you want me to impart some really wise words to you before I leave you the keys to my door, but I can't. What I can tell you is this. Look into their faces and promise to help them so long as they tell you the truth.'

'And that works?' she asked, disbelievingly.

'Not a bit. But you'll learn to see the lies in their eyes, and more importantly you'll learn to see the truth. Rich people think they can get away with anything, and mostly they can. But the truth is, the worse the crime, the bigger the adversary telling you to ignore the crime.'

'I don't get it.'

'Choose your battles, Suzette,' he said. 'And know your opponent.'

'And that's what you've done all these years?' she asked. 'That's what you did with the Levy family?'

'They made a mistake,' Bertram replied. 'A terrible mistake. But they didn't murder the boys. If they had, I would have chosen a different response, just as you're going to have to do with the next case. These people go on with their lives without a care about people below their station. We're just a collection of nameless faces to them. But they cannot completely ignore us, not when we know their secrets.'

Suzette nodded. 'And what do we do with those secrets?' she asked.

'We figure out how to live with them.'

She shook her head. 'I don't think I can.' She stared at him. 'Is that what you did with the Levy family secret? You learned to live with it?'

Bertram shrugged. 'I made peace with this a long time ago. And when a similar circumstance presents itself to you, so will you, and do you know why?'

'Why?'

'Because it will enable you to go on and solve the next crime, and the crime after, and so on and so forth.'

'I'm not sure I can.'

Bertram pointed ahead of him. 'You can. And here we are. Now we are going to rescue the missing boys. Tonight we will go home and be happy with what we did. Tomorrow is another battle and another day.' He drew the car to a halt and pushed open his door. 'Some days we get to be heroes.'

Suzette looked around the vast manicured gardens. 'There's nobody here,' she whispered.

Bertram stamped his foot on the ground. 'You made a mistake.'

She shook her head with determination. 'I checked and double checked. This is the country estate once owned by the Levy family. It is now owned by an Arab family who are rarely in Paris.'

Bertram stepped forward. 'Nobody has lived here for a very long time,' he said. 'And certainly there are no missing boys.'

Suzette moved to his side. 'Then what are we missing?' she asked. 'You told me Madeline Duchamp told you her chauffeur brought Hugo Duchamp and Josef Levy here. So, where are they? Is the chauffeur lying?'

Bertram turned away, hurrying back toward his car.

'Where are you going, Captain?' Suzette called after him.

'We're in the wrong fucking place,' he hissed.

Suzette broke into a trot to keep up with him. 'Where should we be?'

'I don't fucking know,' Bertram hissed. 'But I can guess one thing for certain. Madeline Duchamp is probably already on her way there. Despite what I told her.'

'I don't understand,' Suzette wailed.

'We're not meant to,' Bertram called into the air. 'All we can do is try to get there before the shit really hits the fan. Move, fille, and move quickly!'

VI

Madeline Duchamp continued glaring at her chauffeur. Since leaving her home, she had envisaged several ways in which she would extract her revenge upon him. It had also puzzled her that within her fury, she had discovered something else, something she supposed she had always known but had refused to acknowledge or discuss. She loved her grandson, Hugo, and for the first time since his birth, she had a chance to think about it, and she realised with utmost certainty that he did not know she loved him. Why would he? She had certainly never told him. There were days, weeks even, when she barely bothered to acknowledge his presence. She insisted that he remained in his room, far removed from the rest of her household. She had always taken some kind of perverse comfort in his relative proximity and yet safe distance away from her. Madeline liked Hugo being close to her, but not enough to reach out and touch.

Things will change when you get home, darling boy, she cried out to herself, not really believing it to be true. It was enough that she imagined she could try, because it was all that really mattered. To try. You are incapable of love, a man had once informed Madeline, and the accusation had incensed her, despite the fact she knew it to be true. That fact remained, she had never been shown how to love - the offspring of a Victorian couple, bathed in the pomp and ceremony of a Republic which had once been much greater. They had birthed her, but their involvement had ended there. And she had done the same herself, first with her only child and finally with Hugo. The child she wished she had birthed herself because she felt sure if she had, both of their lives would have been different.

'Madame Duchamp,' the chauffeur called from the front seat,

his voice piqued with deference. 'We are here.'

Madeline nodded, tired eyes flicking around her. It appeared to her to be like every other country estate she had seen in her life. It pained her in ways she did not understand that Hugo might be nearby and in danger, or worse.

'Stop the damn car,' she hissed.

The driver slammed on the brakes, and before it had stopped, Madeline had kicked open her door and was pushing herself out, using her cane to steady herself. Once on the ground, she pulled herself erect.

'In which direction did Hugo go?' she commanded.

The chauffeur moved from the driver's seat, his head dropping as if he could not look in her direction. 'Je suis désolé, Madame Duchamp,' he said helplessly, 'mais, I didn't pay attention.'

Madeline slammed her cane on the ground. She pointed in the direction of the house and the swimming pool. 'That way?'

The chauffeur shrugged helplessly.

Madeline's eyes wrinkled in confusion. 'A comfortable place to hide,' she muttered. 'Mais…'

'Mais?' the chauffeur asked.

She turned to him, fixing him with cold eyes. 'My grandson was not here to hide,' she stated coolly. 'He was here to be hidden.'

The chauffeur nodded, turning his attention elsewhere. He pointed to the right. 'There appears to be some kind of barn over there.'

Madeline nodded. 'A place entirely suitable for being hidden.' She pointed her cane towards it. 'Come along, Anders,'

'Bien sûr, Madame Duchamp,' he answered quickly.

Madeline stopped and studied her chauffeur. 'You disappointed me, Anders. You disappointed me very much.'

Anders lowered his head. 'I beg your forgiveness, Madame.'

She sucked her teeth. 'Begging serves no purpose, you foolish man, but actions do.'

'Actions?'

Madeline nodded. She pointed her cane towards the barn. 'We don't know what we might find over there.'

'Then we should wait for the police, non?'

She snorted. 'I have no time for people who are late,' she quipped. 'And patience is for young people.' She stared at him. 'I don't care what happens here today, Anders, other than one thing.'

'Oui, Madame?' he asked.

'Hugo will walk away today and live. As for the rest, I could not care less. Do you understand what I am saying?'

Anders nodded. 'I will make sure Hugo is safe.'

'Bon,' she replied, moving quickly away from him. 'And if you do a good job, then you might just make it back into my good books again.'

Anders smiled. 'I would like that very much, Madame,' he replied.

VII

The relief was obvious on Josef's face when he saw his brother Joann enter the stables. He gasped, spittle dribbling down his chin. 'Oh, thank Dieu,' he cried. He strained against the ropes which still bound him to Hugo. 'C'mon, get us out of here. These people are crazy and they're gonna hurt us…' He trailed off, his face crinkling with confusion. 'Why aren't you moving?'

'Because he's not here to help us,' Hugo whispered.

'What are you talking about?' Josef yelled. 'Of course he's here to help us. He's my damn broth…' Josef trailed off again, fixing his eyes on Joann. 'Oh, Jesus fucking Christ, Joann. What have you done?'

'Only what everyone in our family always does,' Joann retorted. 'Look after number one.'

'I don't understand,' Josef wailed.

Hugo closed his eyes for a moment, wishing he and Josef could be far away, anywhere, rather than where they were now. He opened his eyes again. He knew time was not on their side. If they were to survive, he had to think quickly. Joann stepped in front of Hugo, cold eyes fixing on him. Hugo still had trouble reconciling the fact Josef and Joann were brothers, such was the disparity between them. Joann's voice was as cold as Josef's was light.

'So, gay boy, you think you have all the answers?' Joann snapped.

Hugo shook his head. 'I don't think that at all.'

Henri Dukas appeared by Joann's side. 'We don't have time for this,' he said desperately. 'Anna paid off the chauffeur, but it's only a matter of time before he fesses up and the police will come.' He shook his head. 'This was just meant to make us rich and stick it to our parents. I won't go to jail for anyone.'

Joann brushed him aside, moving closer to Hugo. 'In a minute, first I want to know what the smug fag knows, and then we'll deal with him.'

'Call him a fag, or gay boy once more, and you'll be the one being dealt with!' Josef screamed.

Joann threw back his head and roared with laughter. 'Is that right, petit garçon? Nice try. You were always a snotty-nosed kid I could use for target practice, nothing has changed.' He turned back to Hugo. 'Okay, smartass. Tell me what you "think" you know.'

Hugo took a deep breath. He was having trouble keeping eye contact with Joann, but he knew he had to try. He had to be strong, for Josef's sake, if nothing else. 'I think after Gad heard his father's confession, he went to Henri and between them, they came up with a plan to get their hands on the Krief fortune. Then they came to you.'

Joann snorted, stabbing a finger towards Henri. 'Do you know that little punk actually had the audacity to threaten me? Me?' He added with incredulity, his voice rising.

'Threaten you?' Josef questioned.

Joann nodded. 'Yeah. Little punk threatened to tell everyone about our grandfather. Like I give a fuck?' He laughed. 'He imagined it meant they could get free drugs from me for life in exchange for their silence.'

Hugo nodded. 'Instead. They gave you an idea.'

Joann shrugged his shoulders. 'I figured there was enough money to go around.'

'And you overheard them, didn't you?' Hugo asked Anna at school. 'I overheard you talking to someone I didn't recognise at the time, but I now know was Joann.'

'Oui,' she replied. 'For them it was all about money, but for me it was all about answers. I finally knew what happened to my brother, not just for the ten days he was missing, but when he was murdered and by who, and those who had covered it all up to protect their damn reputations. This was never about money for me.'

'I believe you,' Hugo responded. 'But why did Raul have to die? Was it you?'

'It doesn't matter,' Anna answered. 'All that mattered was the truth finally coming out. Both the Krief family and the Levy family would be shamed. It's not much, but it's all I have left that I can do for Gerrard.'

'It was an elaborate plan,' Hugo said. 'If this was really about money, why not just kill Raul Krief and be done with it?'

'Because the truth needed to come out,' Anna replied. She sank onto a stool opposite Hugo. 'I can imagine none of this makes sense to you, but for me, it was really just very simple. Payback.'

'Joann. What was in this for you?' Josef called from behind Hugo.

Joann moved in front of his brother. 'Don't you get it? Once our parents know you're gay, they're never going to allow you to be a Rabbi. It's all they've wanted for you.'

'Listen, I don't know what the future is going to hold,' Josef reasoned. 'I don't know what I'll do. I'm fifteen. There's time for me to figure this shit out.'

Joann shook his head. 'Non, there isn't. What's the alternative? You live a lie for the rest of your life? Get married to some wig-wearing shrew and raise a gaggle of nice polite Jew kids? All the time you secretly resent your wife, and your kids, because you didn't get to the live your life with who you wanted.' He stabbed his finger towards Hugo.

'It doesn't have to be that way,' Josef reasoned. 'And I certainly wouldn't blame my kids for something which was never their fault.'

Joann laughed. 'You wouldn't be able to hide it. And the kids would see it in your face every time you looked at them. They'd see the same look I've always seen when our parents look at me. Disappointment and despair.'

'I will hide my feelings,' Josef said with force.

'Nah, you won't,' Joann stated. 'Not really. I've seen the way you look at Hugo. Hey, you might do a decent enough job at hiding, but we both know it will keep coming back. And is that what you want? Hooking up with one random dude after another because you can't bury your feelings deep enough. Just like Papa and his desires? You'll think you're smart, and you'll think you're discreet, but then one day you'll get caught by your wife, or worse, the police. And you'll either end up dead or in jail. Either way, the whole sordid secret will come out. The Levy family has been running from scandal for too long, we can't get ahead of it. It's in our genes. And it has to stop.'

Josef frowned. 'Maybe you're right. I don't know. I don't have the answers. I don't have any answers yet, but I will when I'm older. So, what is your plan? What are YOU going to do?'

'I'm going to finish this,' Joann said, scratching his chin as he stared at his brother. The veins on his arm seemed to pulsate as he did as if adrenaline was beginning to course through him.

'Always so damn dramatic,' Josef complained. 'Even when we were kids. You always had to shout loudest, throw the biggest temper tantrums. You'll always be the same, Joann. If you're not the centre of attention, you always do whatever you have to so people pay attention to you.'

Joann snorted. 'Easy for someone who is ALWAYS the centre of attention to say,' he snapped back. 'Don't you get it, little bro? You're the golden child, and I'm not just talking about your curls and your eyes. You were literally born to run the family business. Both of the family businesses, actually.'

'I don't understand, Joann,' Josef sighed. 'What are you talking about?'

'Bro. You're the dutiful son. Born to grow your hair and wear a nice hat and bounce your head up and down for little old Jewish women…'

'Stop!'

'But the fact is,' Joann continued. 'Being the perfect son makes you perfect for everything. Even if you're the gay one, they'll find a way to move on, to "rehabilitate" you, so you'll end up running the other family company.'

'And?' Josef cried.

'Gay son runs the company. What does that leave me?'

'In jail?' Josef shot back. 'What is it you're getting at, Joann? You're saying if I'm gay our parents will swap our roles. I'll be the CEO and you'll be the Rabbi?' He shook his head. 'None of this has to happen. I get that our parents are steeped in a tradition that has nothing to do with us, but everything to do with the past. They'll move on and that'll be that.'

'You know that's not true,' Joann whispered. 'All my life I've been told I'm not good enough, but by default, I'd at least get to run the family business. And then little old perfect you came along and nobody looked at me twice.'

'And your solution to that is letting me die?'

Joann shrugged. 'Well, it was never my plan, but in the grand scheme of things, it's not such a bad solution. You might say, it's a win-win. The great Levy family get taken down once and for all, and with you out of the picture I get it all - the company and the money. Our parents won't even try to stop me. They'll probably disappear somewhere because of the shame of it all.'

Josef gawped. 'And you think me dying is the only solution?'

Joann shrugged again. 'What are the alternatives? You "come out" and you'll end up CEO and you'll be bossing me around. I can't let that happen.'

'So, you'd rather see me dead?'

Joann extended his hands. 'And your life would be better? Living a life you don't want? Is that really better? At least this way, you'll be going with the person you love.'

'Before we've actually had a chance to love one another!' Josef cried. 'It's not enough.'

'And therefore, avoiding our parents having to be embarrassed by having a fag in the family.'

Josef shook his head. 'When this all comes out, my sexuality is going to be the least of their problems. Their psychotic other son will be more of a pressing concern, I would imagine! I really don't understand you, Joann. What is really in this for you?'

'Money,' Hugo answered. 'Just like Raul and Henri. With you out of the way and your family humiliated, he gets to run the family business, or rather, he gets someone else to run the family business for him. Nobody to bother him, nobody to question him.'

Joann nodded. 'Yeah, I'll pay someone to look after the supermarkets and kick back, put my feet on the table. It'll be a good life. I'll get high a lot, I'll get laid a lot. It'll be a fantastic life!'

Hugo turned to face Gad and Henri. 'And Gad and Henri get rescued and they get rich, too. Everyone wins.'

'But how?' Josef interrupted. 'I get the plan, but it just doesn't make sense. We're missing something.'

Hugo nodded. 'We certainly are. The scapegoat.' He turned to Anna. 'And that's you.'

VIII

'I'm the scapegoat?' Anna asked, her eyebrows knotted in confusion.

Hugo nodded. 'I'm afraid so.' He stared at Gad Krief. 'When did you first know that Mademoiselle Moire was Gerrard Le Mache's sister?'

Gad looked to his left, exchanging an anxious look with Henri Dukas. Neither of them spoke.

'I'm guessing it was from your father,' Hugo continued.

Gad sighed. The sigh indicative he was resigned to the situation he had found himself in. 'Do you know how often my father showed an interest in me, or what I did?' he asked.

'About as often as mine,' Hugo answered.

'Then you get it,' Gad replied. 'They're all the same. My mother is fucking Henri's father. She hates him, and he probably hates her, but they've concocted some kind of weird way to make sure that she funnels money from my father's business, and Henri's father steals money from his father. It's fucked up, but it's what these rich families do. They lie and they spread their hatefulness and then they get surprised when us kids join in.'

'When did you discover who Anna was?'

'During one of Raul's lucid moments, he decided yet again to reboot the whole father thing,' Gad replied. 'So for some weird reason he decided he just had to come to parents' evening.' He pointed at Anna. 'And he recognised her instantly.'

Anna sucked in some air as if her life depended on it.

Hugo stared at her. 'What happened twenty years ago to your brother, but also to Raul Krief, was very cruel. Neither of them deserved what happened to them - you understand that, don't you?'

Anna turned away from him and did not respond to his question.

Hugo turned his attention between Gad, Henri, and Joann. 'And yet the three of you came up with a really awful scenario, setting up a chain of events based on nothing more than money. Money you didn't earn but feel as if you're entitled to.' He turned back to Anna. 'It seemed like an odd coincidence that you overheard them talking, but it wasn't, really. They already knew who you were. Raul had most likely told Gad, and he told the others, and between them they imagined a scenario that would involve getting everything they wanted, but keeping their hands clean. It was like winding a clock. They set you up and watched you and I'm sorry for that, it was cruel and it was unnecessary.'

Anna shrugged. 'I did what I did. Raul murdered my brother, and he told me he didn't want to live. I listened to him.'

Hugo breathed outwards, pushing as much air from his body as he could. 'I am sorry, Mademoiselle Moire. You have been dealt horrible cards in life. Mais, you have to understand, Josef and I have nothing to do with this.'

Her eyes widened. 'I know that.'

Hugo nodded. 'Then you have to know that Joann, Henri, and Gad are not thinking straight. I don't know whether it's because of drugs, or just plain greed.' He pulled against the ropes which bound him to Josef. 'But as you can see. Josef and I are being held hostage, just like your brother was…'

'Don't talk about Gerrard!' Anna screamed, covering her ears.

'Je suis désolé,' Hugo cried, 'mais, I have to. This is serious. They're going to blame you for everything that happened.'

'I am to blame,' she replied. 'I killed Raul.'

Hugo sighed. 'Je sais, but this isn't all your fault. You can talk to a Juge and tell him your story. You'll be in trouble, you'll probably go to jail, but people will sort of understand what you did.' He stopped, lifting his hand as far as he could until the ropes stopped him. 'But if anything else happens, anything which you could have prevented, then people won't understand that.'

Joann tutted loudly. 'I'm bored with this.' He looked at Henri and Gad. 'Let's finish this and get out of here.'

'Are you sure?' Gad asked.

Joann glared at him. 'Bien sûr. I'm not going down for any of this. We stick to the plan, we all get rich, and we all get rid of the people we hate. It's as simple now as it was then. No deviating from the plan.'

Hugo narrowed his eyes. There was something over Joann's right shoulder which had caught his attention. It frustrated him because he could not see what it was. He held his breath and then a moment later he saw something he recognised. The door to the stable was being pulled open by a long, ornate cane. A long, ornate cane he was very familiar with. He turned his head back quickly towards Joann. 'If I'm going to die, can I at least have a cigarette before you finish me off?'

'Really, H?' Josef cried. 'That's all you're thinking about, right now?'

Hugo pressed himself against Josef. 'Trust me,' he whispered, so only Josef could hear.

Joann laughed, pulling a cigarette out of his pocket. He moved towards Hugo, placing a cigarette into his mouth. 'You know it's nothing personal, don't ya, kid?'

Hugo muttered, pulling the cigarette between his lips. 'It's entirely personal, you idiot,' he mumbled. His emerald green eyes watched intently as Joann lifted his hand towards Hugo's mouth and, with the flick of a lighter, illuminated Hugo's face. Hugo sucked hungrily on the cigarette, the smoke quickly filling his lungs. He looked again over Joann's shoulders and his lips moved into a smile and he spat the cigarette out, wrapping his mouth around Joann's hand and biting it with as much force as he could muster.

Joann jumped back, shaking his hand and crying in pain. 'What the fuck you doing, you pervert?'

Behind him, Madeline Duchamp strode into the barn, slamming her cane against the ground as if it was a weapon. Her chauffeur a step behind her, a brick in his hand. Despite her age, Madeline made it to Hugo within seconds. She stabbed her cane at Joann, pushing him to the ground. 'Stay there, Joann Levy, or believe me, I'll crush your throat with my cane.' She pointed it towards Henri, Gad, and Anna. 'The same goes for you all.'

'The police will be here soon,' Anders added.

Madeline snorted. 'And that's the best thing you've got going for you. You'd better hope they get here soon, or,' she stabbed her cane against the ground four times. 'My cane has a lot of power in it.' She looked at Hugo, a smile appearing on her face. He smiled back at her. She shook her head. 'Did you really have to bite him?'

Hugo tried to shrug. 'I didn't know what else to do. I was just trying to buy time.'

She tutted. 'Boys really are disgusting, dirty creatures. Remind me when we get home to call your doctor,' she groaned. 'We need to make sure your tetanus injections are up to date.' She turned away from him, facing her chauffeur. 'Anders, tell me, do you have any blankets in the car?'

The chauffeur flashed her a confused look. 'Well, I think so.'

Madeline flicked her eyes quickly over Hugo and Josef. 'Bon. Then perhaps you'd bring them here. I find it to be slightly inappropriate for one to see their grandson naked when he is fully grown.'

Hugo smiled, pressing himself against Josef. 'We're going to be okay,' he whispered.

Josef dropped his head, but did not reply.

IX

Hugo dropped onto the antique chaise longue in Madeline's living room with such a thud, a plume of old dust shot from beneath him. He knew he should not be sitting on it. It was not the sort of seat made for use. He stole a look at Madeline, expecting there to be a look of reproach on her face. There was none, and that only made it worse somehow. He looked down. He was now wearing an ill-fitting faded grey tracksuit, but it still felt as if he was naked. *The first time I'm naked in front of someone, I'm tied to a tree with four people standing in front of me, threatening to kill m*e, he thought to himself. *That just about sums up my life.*

The preceding few hours had passed in a blur, and Hugo found he recalled little of it. All he really remembered was that in the back of the police car, Josef placed his hand in Hugo's under the blankets which had been wrapped around them. And then they had arrived at Commissariat de Police du 7e arrondissement and that had been that. Josef had been whisked away and after several cups of sweet tea Madeline had insisted her own private physician attend to Hugo, and despite Hugo's protests that he was fine, the elderly doctor arrived and checked him over. Madeline had also refused to allow Hugo to be interviewed at the police station, insisting that if Bertram and Suzette wished to speak to him, they could do so only at her home. She had then taken Hugo's arm and led him towards her limousine, informing Bertram he could follow in his own vehicle. As Hugo watched her, he realised it was because she wanted to speak privately with him to get their stories straight.

'The doctor said you were fine,' Madeline spoke in a soft tone, one which Hugo was not used to hearing.

Hugo nodded. 'They didn't hurt me, not really.' He stared

numbly at the red binding marks on his wrists. They seemed to throb in front of him.

'He suggested,' Madeline replied before shaking her head distastefully, 'that you speak to a psychiatrist.'

Hugo smiled. 'Don't worry, I'll be fine.'

She nodded. 'Not that there's anything wrong with… *therapy*, I mean, for some people who like to talk I would imagine it can be very beneficial.' She narrowed her eyes in his direction. 'Mais, I want you to know, I would understand if you needed to speak to someone in a professional capacity.'

'Merci, Madeline, but non,' he replied. He adjusted himself on the seat. 'Captain Hervé and Lieutenant Carman will be here soon,' he stated.

'Oui,' she replied. 'And they're going to want answers.'

'Oui, they are,' Hugo agreed.

'And you're going to give them what they want.'

Hugo raised an eyebrow. 'I am?'

Madeline nodded. 'There can be no secrets, not anymore.'

'Mais…'

She tapped her cane against the ground. 'Mais, rien. Mais, rien!' she shouted. 'They would have killed you.'

'We don't know that for certain,' Hugo reasoned. 'Anna Moire wanted revenge, mais not on me, I don't even think she intended Josef harm.'

'The others did. And they would have murdered you both. Greed and drugs are all they are interested in, and I don't care about that,' Madeline continued. 'What I do care about is what they were prepared to do to get what they wanted. And for that reason, they will pay.' She pointed at her cane. 'And you will tell Bertram what you know, so that the whole damn lot of them pay for what they were about to do.' She tapped her cane again. 'Do I make myself clear to you, petit fils?'

Hugo nodded. 'What about what you saw twenty years ago?'

She shrugged. 'That as well.'

'Won't you get in trouble?'

Madeline laughed. 'Peut être. I mean he could try, but in the end I saw nothing of value, and I am an old woman after all.' She laughed again. 'Don't look so surprised, I can admit to being old when it suits me.' The smile disappeared from her face. 'The real reason I wanted to speak to you in private first, was because we need to discuss what to do about the Levy family.'

'What to do about them?'

'Oui,' she replied. 'They've been lying for a very long time. They're not about to start telling the truth now.'

'But what about what Joann has done?' Hugo reasoned. 'There are witnesses. I'm no expert, but now they've all been arrested, it's only a matter of time before they all start turning on one another.'

'I agree,' Madeline conceded. 'And you are happy about that? Your friend's family is going to be in a lot of trouble.'

'Mais, pas Josef.'

'It's still his family.'

'I can't help that,' Hugo retorted. 'And nor can he. If I know Josef at all, he will not want this covered up either.'

Madeline moved her shoulders slowly. 'I hope you are right.'

The doorbell rang.

'Let's put this whole sorry business behind us, once and for all,' she said.

'I want to thank you for speaking with us, Hugo, after what was a terrible ordeal,' Bertram said. 'Can I get you anything, a drink?'

Madeline sighed. 'You can get on with it, that's what you can do, Bertram Hervé. Hugo should not have to live through this ordeal again, and especially not so soon.'

'I agree,' the Captain conceded. 'Mais, I find in circumstances such as these, it is best to deal with the matter as soon as possible when the recollection is fresher.'

'I'm fine!' Hugo exclaimed, louder than he meant. 'Let's just get this over with.'

Suzette leaned forward, the chair groaning underneath her.

'Careful, Lieutenant,' Madeline warned. 'That chair is over two hundred years old. I would hate it to lose a battle with your derrière.'

Suzette's mouth opened in horror.

Hugo smiled. 'Grand Mère, behave,' he whispered. 'Ask your questions, Lieutenant,' he said.

'We're trying to get an idea of what happened,' Suzette began. 'Mais, we're not really getting any sort of consistent answers from the accused.'

Bertram turned his head towards Madeline. 'Want to take a guess who the Levy's got to represent Joann?' He paused.

Madeline's face remained stoic. 'Well, they're not stupid, I'll give them that.'

Hugo frowned. Was the Captain suggesting that Pierre Duchamp was representing Joann? If so, Hugo was not sure how he felt about it. All he really knew of his father's career was what he had heard from Madeline, and as far as he could tell, Pierre was a ruthless and vicious avocat.

'So, of course Joann is saying nothing,' Bertram continued. 'And neither are Henri Dukas or Gad Krief, whose own families have found them similar Rottweilers to protect them.'

'The only one who is singing, and singing like a bird, is Anna Moire,' Suzette added.

Hugo sighed. 'That doesn't surprise me,' he said. 'She's probably the only one of the four of them with any conscience, and ironically the one with any real motive in the first place.'

Madeline cocked her head. 'Speak up, child.'

Hugo shook his head. 'Désolé,' he blurted. 'This really isn't any of my business.'

'Au contraire, jeune Hugo,' Bertram reassured. 'I have a feeling this is going to be your business for a very long time.'

Hugo frowned at the Captain, unsure what he meant.

Madeline sighed. 'I have a feeling you are correct, Bertram.'

Bertram smiled at her. 'It could be worse. He could become an avocat like his father.'

Madeline shuddered. 'Or an actor like his mother!'

'What did you mean about Anna, Hugo?' Suzette asked.

He shrugged. 'I can't be certain. I mean, I only spoke to her for a brief time, but I believe she is a very sad, troubled lady.'

'Then you don't believe she came back to Paris for revenge?' Suzette asked.

'Only she can answer that question,' Hugo reasoned. 'It seems to me she came back because she had nowhere else to go. Her parents were dead, her brother was dead. Paris was the only place she had really known, a place where they had been all together. From what she said in the stable, I don't even think she recognised Raul. I mean, it had been more or less two decades since she'd since him.' He paused. 'But he recognised her. The sister of the boy he'd murdered. And that's how Gad Krief found out about her. He told the others, and it seems as if they manipulated her, played on her emotions.'

'But she murdered Raul?' Suzette pressed. 'She admitted it?'

Hugo took a deep breath. 'It's not a very clear picture, but oui, I think she did. Mais, she didn't do it alone. The others were right there with her. She couldn't have done it alone. Joann provided the drugs to keep Raul docile and the three of them helped stage the murder.' He clenched his fists. 'This was about getting to the truth for Anna and exposing the lies of the Levy and Krief families. Even if Gad had offered her a cut of his fortune, I don't imagine she would have taken it.'

Suzette stared at Bertram. 'This is going to be very hard to prove. There's going to be a lot of finger pointing.'

'And she can't be the only one without a hotshot avocat,' Hugo interrupted. He looked at Madeline. 'If my father is representing the Levy family, he's going to make sure someone else takes the blame.'

'If what you're saying is correct, Hugo,' Madeline replied. 'Then she IS to blame.'

He shook his head. 'Only partly to blame,' he reasoned. 'I'm not trying to justify what she did, or her part in it. Mais, I believe she didn't act alone. She needs to be punished, but so does everyone else involved.'

'Josef will stand by his brother,' Bertram said.

'I don't believe he will,' Hugo answered. He noticed the doubtful look on all of their faces. 'In any event, it doesn't matter.'

'It doesn't?' Bertram asked.

'Non, it doesn't,' Hugo replied. 'Because I was there. I heard all of their confessions. Joann included.'

'And you'll give evidence to a Juge and to a court?' Suzette asked.

Hugo looked at Madeline before nodding at the Lieutenant. 'Oui. I've decided this generation will not keep secrets. At least I'm not. Josef is going to have to do whatever it is he feels he has to do, just as I do.'

Bertram turned his attention to Madeline. She shrugged her shoulders. 'Don't look at me. He'll do whatever he thinks best. I have no control over my grandson, and no interest in starting now.'

Bertram raised an eyebrow. 'You're a constant surprise, Madeline Duchamp.'

She lowered her head. 'And I hope I always will be.'

The maid Elise appeared in the doorway. 'Excusez moi. Monsieur Josef Levy is here, he said he must speak with Hugo.'

Hugo gasped. He looked at Madeline. She nodded.

Hugo jumped to his feet, unable to hide the smile which had appeared on his face.

'We're not finished here, jeune homme,' Bertram interrupted. 'We still have to take a statement from you.'

'The statement can wait,' Madeline interrupted. 'After what the boys have been through, I think they deserve a little time to unwind, non?'

Bertram studied her, as if assessing whether it was worth arguing with her. He shrugged his shoulders, seeming to have come to a decision.

'One thing, Hugo,' Madeline called after him. 'I shall have Anders follow you.'

Hugo looked aghast. 'We're just going to talk, maybe go for a walk. What do you think we're going to get up to?'

She shrugged. 'I could not care less what the two of you get up to,' she stated. 'What I do care about is what other people get up to, and under the circumstances I would prefer not to have to rescue my naked grandson twice in a matter of days.' She smiled. 'Don't worry, I'll tell Anders to keep a safe distance. Now, go.'

X

'Shall we walk?' Josef said softly, stepping out of the doorway.

Before Hugo could respond, Josef was already striding away from Madeline's house, causing Hugo to break into a trot to catch up with him. 'Are you okay?' Hugo asked breathlessly.

Josef said nothing, instead continuing his purposeful walk.

'Where are we going?' Hugo cried. He grabbed Josef's arm, dragging him to a halt. 'Talk to me, Josef.'

Josef stared at Hugo, but only for a few seconds. It was as if it was more than he could bear. 'Just walk, dammit,' Josef hissed.

Hugo opened his mouth to protest but stopped himself, realising it was probably useless to protest. Whatever was going on with Josef, it appeared he needed time to find the words he needed to say. Whatever it was, Hugo suspected it would not be good. They carried on in silence for five minutes until Josef finally stopped. Hugo looked up and realised where they were going. Faubourg Saint-Germain park. The scene of the crime. The scene of so many crimes.

'What are we doing here, Josef?' Hugo asked.

Josef did not turn around, instead he was staring directly into the dense park. 'Let's go inside,' he said.

'I don't want to,' Hugo whispered.

'Let's go inside,' Josef repeated, hurrying ahead.

Hugo bit his lip, wondering what he should do. The last thing he wanted to do was to go inside the park after what had happened there, but at the same time he did not want Josef to go in alone. Hugo looked around him, narrowing his eyes into the distance. He exhaled with relief when he saw Anders, Madeline's chauffeur, walking slowly along the boulevard. At least we are not alone, Hugo reasoned. He took a breath and walked into the park. Although it was still daylight, he was immediately enveloped by the darkness of the trees, making it clearly as simple as walking from day to night. He could still hear Josef's footsteps moving forward. Hugo knew they were going to the tree where Raul Krief and Gerrard Le Mache had died.

Josef stopped, reached into his jacket and pulled out a packet of cigarettes. He extracted two and lit them, passing one to Hugo. Hugo looked at it and for a moment thought to refuse, but then he noticed the red glow of the tip and the smell of the tobacco as it drifted towards him. He snatched the cigarette and drew on it as if his life depended on it. This time he did not feel faint or queasy. He felt comforted in a way he had rarely ever done before.

'Are you going to tell me what this is about?' he asked.

Josef shrugged. 'The past. The future. A shitty life.'

Hugo frowned. He reached out and touched Josef's arm and he immediately noticed him tensing as if it made him uncomfortable. Hugo pulled back his hand and stuffed it in the tracksuit pocket. 'I don't understand,' he whispered.

Josef turned his head. 'I saw the flics were at your house.'

Hugo nodded.

'What did you tell them?'

'The truth,' Hugo replied, confused.

Josef shook his head.

'Haven't you?' Hugo asked.

'I haven't spoken to the police. I WON'T be speaking to the police,' Josef responded before adding. 'Our avocat insisted on it.'

My father. Hugo was not sure what to say. 'Why did you want to speak to me?'

Josef faced him. 'What do you mean? I *always* want to speak to you.'

Hugo shook his head. 'It doesn't feel like it, not now, at least.

What's going on?'

Josef turned away again. 'We just have to get our stories straight.'

'Our stories straight?' Hugo asked, his voice shrill. 'There is only one story. The truth.'

Josef cackled. 'The truth? Kid, I know you're naive, but c'mon.'

'Stop calling me a kid,' Hugo snapped. 'I told you that already. I'm not a kid. My point is, I can only tell the police what happened.'

'From your perspective?'

Hugo shrugged. 'Well, yeah, sure. What's your point?'

'We were beaten up, tied up, naked,' Josef shot back. 'It's obvious we'd be confused. Our minds playing tricks on us. We were lucky to make it out alive… We were victims of the actions of others. We can't be expected…'

Hugo sighed. 'That's my father talking, Josef. I can hear his voice when you speak. It's Pierre doing his best to get someone off for committing a crime.'

'That's what he does best, I'm told,' Josef stated. 'The point is, Hugo, families such as ours have to stick together.'

'Tell me what it is my father wants, Josef.'

'He just believes we should stick together, for all our sakes. After all,' he continued, 'we can't be certain what happened exactly, other than…'

'Other than what?' Hugo snapped.

Josef took a deep breath. 'Other than Anna Moire, a woman filled with hate and anger, did something very wrong because she wasn't right in the head and we all got caught up in it.'

Hugo shook his head and moved into the clearing. He stopped by the row of trees. His fingers slowly tracing around the remaining police tape.

'What are you doing?' Josef called after him.

Hugo finished the remainder of his cigarette and stubbed it out. 'Twenty years ago, your father and your grandfather did something horrible…'

'Hugo, s'il te plaît,' Josef cried.

Hugo ignored him. 'And Gerrard Le Mache died,' he continued. 'And whatever happened, it wasn't really Raul's fault. But either way, it ruined the rest of his life. And then, twenty years later he ended up back here, and all because he'd never found a way to live with a guilt that was never his to begin with.' He turned back to Josef. 'But that guilt was seized upon by three kids who cared nothing about the past, or what he had been through. Three kids who could have done the one thing he needed more than anything else.' He stopped. His eyes were watering, but he did not want to cry. 'And that was helping him. All Raul needed was for someone to listen. Someone he could tell the truth to. And his own son and his friend, and your brother just saw it as an opportunity to make money. And then they found the perfect person to blame it all on.'

'Hugo, I know all this…' Josef cried.

'Then why don't you say it!' Hugo wailed. 'Why don't you speak the truth for Raul?'

'Because he's dead. What good would it do?' Josef reasoned. 'And do you really think Raul would want his own son to go to prison?'

'Oui, if he deserved it,' Hugo replied. 'Mais, my views aren't important. But if you're asking me to believe Raul Krief would want Gerrard Le Mache's sister to take the blame for everything, then I will not say I do, because I don't.'

'All we have to do is keep quiet,' Josef begged. 'For our families sake.'

Hugo shook his head. 'Not for my family, Josef, certainly not for my family.'

'If you cared about me…'

Hugo clenched his fists. 'Don't do that. Don't you dare do

that! I think you've been playing games with me all along, and it stops now.'

'Non! I haven't been playing games! I love you!'

'Then prove it,' Hugo said. 'Don't ask me to lie. And don't you lie.'

'I can't, Hugo,' Josef cried desperately. 'My parents are devastated. They can't lose both sons. I know everyone thinks Anouk is this strong, bitchy woman, but she's not. Not really. And she's just about holding on. And as for Papa…' he trailed off. 'He sees his whole family, our history, our legacy disappearing, and it's too much for him. I'm worried that he's gonna…' his voice cracked, 'that's he going to do something stupid.'

Hugo fought the urge to run to Josef and take him in his arms. 'And what does that mean for you?'

Josef shrugged. 'Family,' was all he said.

Hugo nodded. 'Family,' he repeated. 'I'd better get back. Au revoir, Josef.'

'Don't go, Hugo. Je t'aime,' he cried. 'Can't you see how fucked up this all is? I don't know what to do!' he cried. 'I'm out of choices.'

Hugo's mouth pulled into a sad smile. 'We're never out of choices, not really. Not if we're honest. And certainly if we promise ourselves not to be afraid. I'm sure of nothing, and I know I have a lot to face in my future. But, mon Dieu. I will never be a liar. Not for anyone.' He moved across the clearing.

'Hugo! Hugo!' Josef wailed.

Hugo did not look back, instead focused on Anders, the chauffeur standing at the entrance to the clearing.

XI

'I don't want to go,' Hugo snapped.

Madeline smiled. 'Stop pouting, enfant. Petulance is acceptable in a baby, but in an adult it is tiresome, and in a Duchamp it is embarrassing.'

'I'm fifteen years old. I'm allowed to be a child.'

Madeline slammed her cane against the ground. Hugo watched her and then lifted his foot, slamming it against the ground as well. Madeline smiled. 'I hope that hurt.'

Hugo's mouth twisted. 'It did.'

'Bon,' she retorted. 'Petulance should come with a price.'

'It's been two weeks,' Madeline added.

'Et?'

'Failed love affairs have a shelf life,' she retorted.

'I would hope it would be longer than two weeks,' Hugo sighed.

'Your grandfather took to his bed after his.'

Hugo lifted his head towards the attic, realising he had pretty much being doing the same himself. He had not been back to school, and he did not imagine he would again. His future was going to have to look different.

Madeline rose unsteadily to her feet. Hugo watched her, and it was as if he had noticed it for the first time. *It's all an act. She's old and she is getting ready to die. I'll be alone. Really alone.*

'It's a service at the synagogue for Raul and Gerrard,' Madeline continued. 'And the very least we can do is attend.' She paused. '*Whatever* our feelings.'

'I can't face…' Hugo began, realising he could not utter the name, '*any* of them.'

'Nonsense,' Madeline snorted. 'They are the ones who should

worry about facing us. Now come, Hugo, and for goodness sake, tell your face to catch up with mine. There will be no pouting today!'

Rabbi Serge Levy stood in front of the auditorium, turning his head slowly. The synagogue was overflowing with people, each seat taken and still filled with people lining the walls and the back. His chest extended as if he was proud, proud of his synagogue bursting at the seams.

In their seats, Madeline nudged Hugo as he fidgeted with the yarmulke he was wearing on the back of his head.

Rabbi Levy took a deep breath. 'I am so grateful for you all coming here today to honour and show our respect to those we have lost. We have all been through so much, but we have survived it because we have come together as a community…'

As Hugo was listening to the Rabbi speak, something happened, and it was suddenly as if everything moved in slow motion. He did not see it happen, but it seemed as if it had, before he had a chance to take a breath and blink his eyes. The space next to him was occupied and his hand had been grabbed from his lap and pulled away. He turned his head and saw his hand was now being held by Josef. Josef's head was straight, pale and serious, pointing directly towards the Rabbi, his father. He did not look at Hugo, but he squeezed his hand. Hugo tried to move his hand away, but Josef would not let it go. Hugo watched his face. His lips were twisting as if they were wrestling with something.

Finally, Josef turned his head to Hugo. 'Let me have this moment.'

Hugo grimaced. Not sure what he meant, but he was surprised when, to his left, Madeline gently touched his leg.

'Let him have his moment,' she whispered.

Hugo was not sure how long the moment lasted. It could

have been a minute. It could have been ten. All he knew was that at some point, it was over. He did not even know why until his attention was drawn to the loud applause in the auditorium, and then he realised everyone was looking in his direction. He snapped back his hand away from Josef, sucking in as much air as he could, his face swelling with blood as he realised everyone was looking at him. But then Josef rose to his feet and Hugo understood what it meant. Rabbi Levy was extending his arms in Josef's direction.

'And I ask you to please welcome my son, Josef,' Rabbi Levy clapped. 'The next generation, et…' he paused as if for dramatic effect, 'your next Rabbi.'

Hugo felt the overwhelming urge to vomit, but he was caught up in the rapture and the applause which heralded Josef moving quickly along the aisle, his head bowing and moving, his hands touching those hands extended in the aisles and for the first time Hugo realised what was happening. It was the end. Or it was the beginning. He did not understand what was happening when he felt his left hand being pulled away from his leg. Madeline was pulling it into hers.

'This moment will pass,' she mouthed without looking at him.

Hugo nodded. He watched as Josef took his place next to his father on the stage. More than anything, he wanted to leave, but he knew he could not. And more than anything, he wanted to cry. Anouk Levy joined her husband and son on the stage. Her face beheld a smile, but Hugo could see beneath it. The smile was painted on. And then, a step behind her, Anouk's eldest child joined his family on the stage as Joann Levy stood, his lanky, slender frame in an ill-fitted suit. He moved his head around the auditorium, finally settling on Hugo and Madeline. He smiled, lifted his hands, and blew Hugo a kiss.

Madeline squeezed his hand. 'It's impolite to leave early, Hugo,' she said. 'But in this case, I find it wise, don't you agree?'

Hugo took his grandmother's arm, and they moved towards the aisle. He turned to her. 'In case I never get the chance to say it, Madeline, I want you to know that I love you.'

Madeline looked at him in surprise. 'I'm glad if I have in any small way taught you to say those words,' she said. 'And if it matters to you, then you should know I feel the same way.'

Hugo smiled. 'Should we hug?'

Madeline snorted. 'Only if you want me to slap your face. Now move on, enfant. I have dinner plans.'

FIN

trois mois plus tard

Hugo heard the steps approaching the attic, and he knew it was not Elise. Her steps were light and careful, as if she was worried about being heard, or offending someone. These steps were determined. These steps belonged to Josef.

The door burst open. 'Can we go for a walk?' Josef asked cheerfully, in a way which both angered and confused Hugo. It had been three months since they had seen each other, and Hugo suddenly felt as if he was being torn apart by two conflicting emotions. The first to run to Josef and embrace him, the second to run to him and beat his clenched fists against his chest.

'Madeline's out,' Josef said, 'if that's what you're worried about.'

'I know she's out,' Hugo snapped. 'And it's not me who should be worried about where Madeline is.'

Josef shrugged. 'You've got a point,' he conceded. 'My mother is terrified of her, she won't admit it, but she is.' He mused. 'Still, a walk? You owe me that at least.'

'I OWE YOU THAT, AT LEAST,' Hugo spelled out the words with incredulity.

Josef beamed at him. Beamed at him in a way, Hugo knew he had already lost the battle.

'It's been three months, Josef,' Hugo sighed.

Josef nodded. 'Je sais. Things have been… complicated.'

Hugo stood. 'Let's walk.'

Josef smiled and reached over and touched Hugo's arm. 'I thought this was going to be easier,' he breathed.

'You thought what was going to be easier?' Hugo asked. 'Saying goodbye?'

'Seeing you and not wanting to be with you.'

Hugo did not answer, because he did not trust his voice or what his brain would make him say.

'Can we just hold each other?' Josef whispered.

Hugo stared at him. 'It's not that simple, Josef.'

Josef shook his head. 'We're kids, Hugo. Let's be kids for a little while longer.'

'I… I….' Hugo stammered.

Josef began walking towards the bed.

The afternoon sun bore onto the back of Hugo's neck, and it felt unlike anything he had experienced before. There was a gentle wind blowing, and he watched it as it moved through the overgrown grass in the park. Of course they had returned to the park. It had begun there, and it was there it would end. Josef was holding his hand and for the first time Hugo did not care that people would see them and what their reaction might be. He had opened a door and walked through it, and he knew his life would never be the same again.

Josef lit a cigarette and handed it to Hugo. He took it from him and noticed his hand was shaking. He reached up and touched it, pulling it to his lips and pressing them against it. Josef watched him, his eyes bulging as he fought away tears.

'Don't make this any harder,' Josef cried.

'It's not like we're breaking up,' Hugo responded. 'We've never actually been going out.'

'That's not fair!'

'But it's true,' Hugo reasoned. 'Where have you been for the last three months?'

'Our family had a lot to deal with,' Josef said.

Hugo knew little about it. He had not been back to school since they had been kidnapped, and nor had Josef. Hugo had enrolled in a different school, on the opposite side of Paris. He had settled in reasonably well, or as well as could be expected. The school was smaller, and he had found as long as he kept his head down, there was no bullying as he had endured at the other school. There was also no Josef, or anyone like him, which he had reasoned was not such a bad thing. As for the Levy family, it appeared as if Hugo's father had done a good job representing them.

'Joann's in a military school in Germany,' Josef stated. 'It was part of the deal your father got for us. Mandatory drug testing and he has to stay there for four years.' He smiled. 'He hates it, but even he's not so stupid as not to realise how fucking lucky he got.'

Hugo nodded. Joann was lucky. Four years was nothing for his part in what had happened. But in the end, it had been as Hugo suspected it would be. Anna Moire was the only one of the four people to receive any kind of punishment. Hugo had seen it on the news. She had been sent to an asylum for the criminally insane for an undetermined period of time. She had not spoken of the events which lead up to her arrest, nor had she implicated anyone else.

'What happened to Gad Krief and Henri Dukas?' Hugo asked.

'Nothing,' Josef answered. 'Your father spoke to the police and laid out a pretty good case for them being completely innocent. In the end, I suppose it came down to your word against theirs.'

'It should have been OUR word, Josef, not just mine,' Hugo snapped. He sat down on the stump of a felled tree. The exact tree where Gerrard Le Mache and Raul Krief had died twenty years apart.

'I told you I had to stand by my family,' Josef whispered.

Hugo nodded. He did not have the energy or strength to

argue with him. What was done was done. A chain of events which had begun with the decaying mind of Josef's grandfather had ended tragically. Hugo had heard Madeline arguing on the telephone with Bertram about it, but he could see it on her face and hear it in her voice that she thought it had all turned out for the best.

'I'll be sixteen next month,' Josef said. 'And I'm leaving for a Kibbutz in Israel next week. I'll be gone for two years and when I return…'

Hugo held up his hands. 'I don't want to know,' he cried.

'I want you to know this afternoon, the time we spent in your bedroom will be the happiest memory I think I will ever have. I will hold it close to my heart for as long as I live.' Josef said, fighting back tears. He snorted, snot dripping from his nose. 'For the last three months the only thing which has got me through is the memory of being tied naked to you on a tree!'

Hugo laughed, his voice cracking as he did.

'I never imagined I would have something else to get me through.'

'You don't have to live your life for other people,' Hugo said. 'I'm not saying you have to be with me, but you should be able to choose.'

Josef shook his head. 'It's not that easy, Hugo. I don't have the freedom you do. I don't have the choices you do. My parents are devastated. Whatever happens with Joann, they know they can't expect anything from him. My father said he is lost to them because I think we all know that when he leaves Germany, even if he comes back here, he'll never be the sort of man they need him to be, which leaves…'

'You. The Rabbi.'

Josef nodded.

'With a wife and children,' Hugo continued.

'It's not true what Joann said,' Josef interjected. 'I won't resent anyone. I will be a good man. I will be a good…' he stopped as if he could not say the word, *husband*. 'I will be a good man to them all, and I won't risk any more scandal in the Levy family. Not even if that means I have to bury my own secret.'

Hugo nodded. He knew he should argue, but he was aware enough to know the argument was already lost. Josef was already lost.

Josef wiped tears away from his eyes. 'But I want you to know that today, this time we spent together, will sustain me. I will always have it in here,' he pointed to his head, 'and here,' he pointed to his heart. 'And in another life, a parallel life, I will always imagine I'm living my best life with you. And we're so SO happy.' His mouth spread into a huge grin. 'We have a nice house and a dog, maybe even kids of our own. Who knows? But mon Dieu, we are *so* happy.'

'I like the sound of that life,' Hugo whispered.

'But in this life - in this life I have to be strong and I can only do that if I'm not around you.'

Hugo nodded. 'I'd better go.' He moved past him, leaping over the edge of the clearing. He needed to put as much space as he could between them. 'Au revoir, Josef,' he whispered into the air.

Josef watched him leave, tears falling down his cheeks. 'You will always be the love of my life, Hugo Duchamp. Au revoir.'